After spending three years as a die-hard New Yorker, **Kate Hewitt** now lives in a small village in the English Lake District with her husband, their five children and a golden retriever. In addition to writing intensely emotional stories, she loves reading, baking and playing chess with her son—she has yet to win against him, but she continues to try. Learn more about Kate at kate-hewitt.com.

*USA TODAY* bestselling and RITA® Award–nominated author **Caitlin Crews** loves writing romance. She teaches her favourite romance novels in creative writing classes at places like UCLA Extension's prestigious Writers' Programme, where she finally gets to utilise the MA and PhD in English Literature she received from the University of York in England. She currently lives in the Pacific Northwest, with her very own hero and too many pets. Visit her at caitlincrews.com.

D1464340

**Also by Kate Hewitt**

*Desert Prince's Stolen Bride*
*Princess's Nine-Month Secret*
*The Secret Kept from the Italian*
*Greek's Baby of Redemption*
*Claiming My Bride of Convenience*

**Also by Caitlin Crews**

*My Bought Virgin Wife*
*Unwrapping the Innocent's Secret*

**The Combe Family Scandals miniseries**

*The Italian's Twin Consequences*
*Untamed Billionaire's Innocent Bride*
*His Two Royal Secrets*

Discover more at millsandboon.co.uk.

# THE ITALIAN'S UNEXPECTED BABY

## KATE HEWITT

# SECRETS OF HIS FORBIDDEN CINDERELLA

## CAITLIN CREWS

**MILLS & BOON**

All rights reserved including the right of reproduction
in whole or in part in any form. This edition is published
by arrangement with Harlequin Books S.A.

This is a work of fiction. Names, characters, places, locations
and incidents are purely fictional and bear no relationship to
any real life individuals, living or dead, or to any actual places,
business establishments, locations, events or incidents.
Any resemblance is entirely coincidental.

This book is sold subject to the condition that it shall not,
by way of trade or otherwise, be lent, resold, hired out
or otherwise circulated without the prior consent of the publisher
in any form of binding or cover other than that in which it is published
and without a similar condition including this condition
being imposed on the subsequent purchaser.

® and TM are trademarks owned and used by the trademark owner
and/or its licensee. Trademarks marked with ® are registered with the
United Kingdom Patent Office and/or the Office for Harmonisation
in the Internal Market and in other countries.

First Published in Great Britain 2019
by Mills & Boon, an imprint of HarperCollins*Publishers*
1 London Bridge Street, London, SE1 9GF

The Italian's Unexpected Baby © 2019 by Kate Hewitt

Secrets of His Forbidden Cinderella © 2019 by Caitlin Crews

ISBN: 978-0-263-27797-5

MIX
Paper from
responsible sources
FSC
www.fsc.org    FSC® C007454

This book is produced from independently certified FSC™ paper
to ensure responsible forest management.
For more information visit www.harpercollins.co.uk/green.

Printed and bound in Spain
by CPI, Barcelona

# THE ITALIAN'S UNEXPECTED BABY

## KATE HEWITT

# CHAPTER ONE

'HE'S COMING!'

Mia James's stomach clenched unpleasantly as she hurried to stand behind her desk, shoulders back, chin up, heart pounding.

'He's in the lift now...'

The numbers above the silver doors glowed, one after another. *Two...three...*

Mia watched out of the corner of her eye as her fellow colleagues at Dillard Investments did the same as she had, scurrying to desks, standing up straight. They were like schoolchildren awaiting an inspection by the head teacher. A particularly strict and perhaps even cruel head teacher... the notoriously ruthless Alessandro Costa, self-made billionaire and, as of yesterday, the new CEO of Dillard Investments.

Yesterday the company had been taken over by Alessandro Costa in a calculated and clever manoeuvre that had shocked everyone involved in the company right down to their toes, including Mia's boss and the CEO, Henry Dillard. Poor Henry had looked terribly shaken, aging ten years in a matter of minutes as he realised there was nothing he could do to stop Costa International from gaining controlling shares; it had all happened before he'd even had a chance to realise, Costa stalking the company the way a ruthless predator would a prey.

*Four...five...* The lift doors pinged open and Mia drew her breath sharply as the new CEO of Dillard Investments stepped through them. She'd seen photos of him online, having done an exhaustive internet search last night when the news had been confirmed that Dillard's had been taken over. What she'd learned had far from reassured her.

Alessandro Costa specialised in hostile takeovers and then stripping the companies of their assets and employees, to be absorbed into his behemoth of a corporation, Costa International.

A few months ago, he'd taken over a company similar to Dillard's—small, family-owned, a bit antiquated. Now it was virtually gone, swallowed up by the man who was striding onto the top floor of the building Dillard's owned in Mayfair.

Mia tried not to make eye contact with Alessandro Costa, but she found she couldn't stop looking at him. The photos on the internet didn't do him justice, she realised with an uneasy pang of physical awareness. They didn't communicate his intense energy, as if a force field surrounded him, as if he *crackled*.

Cropped dark hair, as black as midnight, framed a face that was all angles and hard lines, from his jaw to his nose to the dark slashes of brows over cold, steel-grey eyes. His body, tall and lethally powerful, was encased in a hand-tailored suit of dark grey silk, the silver tie at his throat matching the colour of his eyes. He made Mia think of a laser, or a sword...something powerful and lethal. *A weapon.*

He came onto the floor with its open-plan desks with quick, purposeful strides, his narrowed, hawk-like gaze moving in quick yet thorough assessment around the room, pinning people in place. It felt as if the very air trembled. Mia was afraid she did. Alessandro Costa was incredibly intimidating.

She knew everyone's job was up for grabs, and most likely down the drain as well. In his last takeover, it had been rumoured that Costa had kept three employees out of forty. As personal assistant to the CEO, Mia knew her position would almost certainly be cut. Costa undoubtedly had his own executive assistant already in place, and as he didn't seem likely to keep Dillard's going as a separate entity, her job had most likely become obsolete last night, with the takeover.

Still, she was determined to try to do *something* to keep it. She'd been working for Dillard Investments since she was nineteen, fresh from a B Tech business course, bright-eyed and determined to make something of herself and, most importantly, to finally be independent.

All her childhood she'd been under the controlling thumb of her unbearably autocratic father, having to do as he said and dance to his tune, however discordant its notes. Her mother had been the same, cringing and hopeful in dispiriting turns, and Mia had vowed to gain her freedom as soon as she could—and never make the same kind of mistake her mother had, by marrying a charming yet controlling man…or any man at all.

So now, while Mia knew she could find another job, she resisted the prospect of being fired from this one for no good reason. She'd been here a long time, had worked hard, and had made a few friends along the way.

She might be likely to lose her job anyway, but she'd go down fighting. She had to, as points of both pride and principle.

Alessandro Costa had stopped in the centre of the room, his feet spread wide, his hands on his hips. He looked like the king of an empire, surveying his domain. Like something out of a fairy tale, except in a three-piece suit.

'Who is Mia James?' he asked, his voice slightly ac-

cented, the words crisp and precise as they echoed through
the open space.

Mia felt every eye on the floor turn instinctively towards her. Like a child in school being called on by a
teacher, she raised her hand, hoping her voice would come
out strong.

'I am.' She might have overshot it, she realised; she
sounded strident. Aggressive, even, to hide her nervousness.

Alessandro Costa's eyes narrowed even further in appraisal, and his lips flattened into a hard line.

'Come with me,' he said, and walked into Henry Dillard's office, the only private space on the floor, an elegant
room with wood panelled walls and leather club chairs,
tasteful oil paintings and heavy curtains. It felt like a gentleman's club, or the study of an elegant townhouse, which
it very well might once have been. Dillard's offices were
in a former home, although much of it had been gutted
for desk space.

Costa strode towards the big, mahogany desk, inlaid
with leather, that Henry had always sat behind while Mia
had taken notes or dictation. Henry had been eccentrically
old school; he'd only bought a laptop a few years ago, and
he'd still depended on Mia to manage emails and spread-
sheets, finding both quite beyond him, and not seeming
to mind.

It gave her a pang now to think that was all over; Henry
had retreated to his estate in Surrey, and Mia half wondered if she'd ever see him again. Last night, as he'd shuf-
fled out of the office, his business in ruins around him,
he'd seemed like an old, broken man, and it had wrung her
heart right out. And it was this man's fault.

Alessandro Costa stood behind Henry's old desk, his
hands placed flat on its surface, fingers spread wide, as he
stared at her, his eyes magnetic, his body radiating barely

suppressed energy. Although his expression was focused, it wasn't unfriendly. He looked like a man intent on action, and it made Mia tense, something in her kicking up a notch, ready to respond.

'I need you.' Costa spoke the words matter-of-factly, but stupidly they made Mia's heart skip a silly beat. He didn't mean in *that* way, of course he didn't. But perhaps he meant she might keep her job…

'You…do?'

'Yes, for the moment, at least.' Costa straightened, his gaze surveying her with cool appraisal. 'You've been Dillard's PA for how long?'

'Seven years.'

He nodded slowly. 'And, as far as I can see, you were the plug on his life support.'

Mia blinked, absorbing the cruel bluntness of that statement. 'I wouldn't go that far,' she said quietly, although admittedly there was some truth in it. In reality, Henry Dillard would have been happy playing golf and letting the company his father had founded dwindle away to nothing. The company had been ripe for a takeover, even if he hadn't seen it himself, and Mia had never let herself consider such a possibility.

'Perhaps that's a bit harsh,' Costa allowed, 'but Dillard himself admitted he was behind the times. Of course, many of his clients are, as well.'

'Which begs the question why you took it over,' Mia returned. Costa's eyebrows rose as he kept her gaze, and something sparked to life in Mia, something she most certainly wasn't going to acknowledge.

'Yes, it does, doesn't it?' he remarked. 'Fortunately that is not something you need to concern yourself with.'

And that was her, put firmly in her place. 'Very well.' She met his narrowed, steely gaze unflinchingly, although it cost her. Every time she looked at him she felt something in her spark and tingle in a way she definitely didn't like. The man was intense and a little scary, but there was something that drew her to him as well—something in his fierce energy, his incredible focus. 'So why do you need me?' she asked, deciding that keeping things on track was her best bet.

'I need you because I require your knowledge of Henry's clients so I can deal with them appropriately. So as long as you prove useful…'

Which sounded like a barely veiled threat, or perhaps just a statement of fact. Mia couldn't imagine Alessandro Costa putting up with anyone who wasn't useful.

'And when I don't prove useful?' she asked, although she had a feeling she didn't want to know the answer.

'Then you'll be let go,' Costa said bluntly. 'I don't keep useless employees. It's bad business practice.'

'What about the rest of the staff?'

'Again, none of your concern.'

Wow. The man had no hesitation in being blunt, yet Mia didn't sense any cruel relish in his words, just simple bare statements of fact, which she could appreciate, even if she didn't like them.

In any case, needlessly sparring with Alessandro Costa was a fast track to being fired, and she wanted to keep her job. She *needed* to keep her job. It felt like the only thing she had.

'All right.' She straightened, tipping her chin up, determined to stay professional and match his focus. 'What would you like me to do?'

Something silver flashed in Alessandro's grey eyes; it almost looked like approval, and it made a ripple of pleased awareness race through her, treacherous and molten, racing through her fingers and down to her toes. 'I want files on all of Dillard's major clients, with notes about any potential quirks, habits, tendencies, or any other pertinent information within the hour. We'll talk through it all then.'

'All right.' Mia thought she could manage that, if only just.

'Good.' Without another word, Alessandro Costa strode out of the office, closing the door firmly behind him.

Mia let out a gusty breath and then, on watery legs, she sank into a chair in front of the desk. Now that he was gone, she realised afresh how much energy Costa drew from her, how much adrenalin he stirred up so her heart still pounded and her head felt light. Talking with him had felt like a full mental and physical workout. Ten minutes of it and she was, strangely, both exhausted and energised.

She was also...affected. The man's forceful personality was only part of his intense charisma; she'd felt as if she couldn't look away from him—the eyes that almost glowed, the barely leashed energy that radiated from him, the power that was evident in every taut line of his body. Even now she breathed in the faint scent of his aftershave, something with sandalwood in it, and she felt the urge to tremble. Thankfully, she didn't.

On still shaky legs Mia rose from her chair. She needed to show Alessandro Costa she was oh-so-useful, and more than that, she was necessary. Essential, even. Because she wasn't ready to contemplate the alternative.

Quickly Mia left Henry's old office and went to her desk immediately outside of it. The crowds that had been waiting for Alessandro Costa's arrival had dispersed, and people were back at their desks, attempting to at least seem as if they were working.

Alessandro was nowhere to be seen, and Mia wondered what he was doing. Inspecting the ranks? *Firing someone?* If the rumours were true, he'd fire most of Dillard's staff, just as he had countless other times, something she couldn't bear to think about. She had to focus. She had a job to do.

\* \* \*

Dillard Investments was even more of a sorry mess than he'd realised. After a morning of meeting employees and assessing the company's condition, Alessandro Costa felt nothing but a scathing derision for Henry Dillard, a man whose affable exterior hid a terrible weakness—a weakness that had caused the inevitable loss of his company, his clients' assets, and the well-being of his employees. The man had the appearance of a lovable teddy bear, but Alessandro was glad he'd put an end to his benevolent ineptitude.

By refusing to keep up with the times and seek out new opportunities and investments, Henry Dillard had been slowly, or not so slowly, running his company as well as his clients' portfolios into the red, content to live off his dwindling profits and focus on his golf game. If Alessandro hadn't taken over the company, someone else surely would have.

Better, though, that it was him. This was his field of expertise, after all, and what he'd made his life's mission: taking over failing or corrupt companies and turning them into something useful, or else dismantling them completely.

As Alessandro knew and had seen, over and over again, the opportunity of defeating the enemy lay within the enemy himself…discovering his weaknesses and finding his vulnerabilities. It was a concept from Sun Tzu's *The Art of War*, and what Alessandro had learned long ago was that not only was business war, but *life* was war, a battle fought every day, and he had the scars to prove it. Yes, life was war… And he was in it to win.

At least a third of the employees he'd met with today would have to be fired. It seemed as if Dillard had never let anyone go, whether out of sentimentality, stupidity, or just sheer laziness Alessandro didn't know or particularly care.

He always tried to keep redundancies to a minimum, preferring to transfer people to other positions within his portfolio of companies, but many of the staff he'd met here clearly didn't deserve such an opportunity. Dillard's PA, Mia James, being a notable exception...

Surprisingly, reluctantly, Alessandro had been intrigued by her. She was beautiful in a very boring, very English way—straight blonde hair, cornflower blue eyes, a clear, healthy complexion, a tall and athletic figure, without any noticeable curves. *Competent*...in every way, and not the kind of woman that usually sparked his sensual interest.

She was the kind of woman, Alessandro reflected, who had probably been captain of her hockey team at school, who hiked on weekends and had had crushes on horses rather than boys growing up. Who would marry a suitable man and have the requisite two children, a boy and a girl. No one, clearly, whom he would let himself be interested in, much less pursue.

Yet she'd intrigued him. And he didn't like to be intrigued, especially not by a PA whom he would most likely transfer as soon as possible, because he worked best alone. Always had, always would, in every way possible. That was the only way he knew how to conduct his life, learned in childhood and honed to a highly polished skill in adulthood, and he didn't see it changing. Ever.

Mia James was waiting for him in Dillard's office when he walked in an hour after he'd last seen her, to the minute. Alessandro always kept to time, kept his word. Stayed in control, even in such seemingly small, incidental matters, as a point of principle, a matter of pride.

'Well?' he asked. 'Do you have the files?'

She'd risen from her chair as he'd entered, making him notice, rather unwillingly, her long, slender legs encased in sheer black tights, her feet in low black heels. She wore a black pencil skirt and blazer, a crisp white blouse, a simple gold pendant at her throat. Her long, wheat-coloured hair was caught cleanly behind in a clip. He could not fault anything about her, and yet he still felt discomfited. Irritated, even, by his own interest as much as her presence.

He didn't let people affect him. He didn't *do* emotions, and he most definitely didn't act on them. His own unsettled childhood was testament to the power of emotions, as well as the danger, which was why he behaved in a tightly controlled way that made *sense.* Because Alessandro Costa needed to be in control. Always.

'I have everything right here,' Mia said, her voice calm and cool. Unflappable, unlike how he was feeling, which annoyed him further. 'Personal files and relevant information on Dillard's ten most important clients.'

'And how did you determine they were the most important?' Alessandro asked, his voice something close to a snap.

Her clear blue gaze met his; she seemed untroubled by his tone. 'They are the largest investors, and they've been with Dillard's the longest amount of time.'

'Everyone's been with Dillard's since the time of dinosaurs,' Alessandro returned, his irritation making him more callous than he normally would have let himself be. 'That's the nature of the place.'

'Dillard's longevity is one of its points of pride,' Mia agreed, her voice—and what a low, pleasant voice it was—carefully equable. She would not rise to his irritable bait. Another point in her favour, yet unreasonably this just annoyed him further.

He sprawled in the chair behind the desk, beckoning her forward with one hand. 'So show me.'

Mia hesitated for the barest of seconds—hardly noticeable except Alessandro felt so weirdly attuned to her—and then she scooped up the pile of folders and walked around to his side of the desk, placing them in front of him and then flipping the first one open.

'James Davis, a millionaire who set up his own company to manage his financial interests. Inherited money. Generous to a fault. Affable and easy-going but very little common sense. Happy to follow a lead, generally speaking.'

Alessandro was silent, reluctantly impressed by how quickly and clearly she'd summed up the client. Given him all the relevant information, without anything unnecessary, exactly as he would have wanted. So few people impressed him, but Mia James had. *In more ways than one.*

He glanced down at the top sheet detailing the man's investments but the figures blurred in front of him as he inhaled Mia James's scent—something understated and citrusy. She was standing quite close to him, her breasts on a level with his gaze. Not that he was looking, but he did notice how the crisp white cotton with discreet pin tucks highlighted her trim figure. Perhaps curves were overrated.

*What was he thinking?*

Now seriously annoyed with himself and his unruly thoughts, Alessandro flipped through the pages, skimming all the relevant details with more focus than usual. 'He's operating at a loss,' he observed after a moment.

'Yes.' Another tiny hesitation. 'Many of Dillard's clients are, in the current financial climate. Henry—Mr Dillard—was confident things would bounce back, or at least even out, in the next eighteen months.'

When he would have been retired, with no need to worry about the financial markets or how they were affecting his clients. Alessandro had spoken to Henry Dillard on the phone yesterday, when the takeover had been complete. He always tried to treat his adversaries with dignity, especially when he'd won, which he always did.

Dillard had been furious to be bested by someone he

considered his social inferior—and had made that quite clear. Alessandro had taken it in his stride; it was hardly unusual when he chose to target companies run by men like Henry Dillard—entitled, wealthy, and weak. He almost felt sorry for the man; he hadn't been corrupt, like some of the CEOs Alessandro had taken down, just inept. He'd frittered away his family's company, indifferent to his clients' needs, and now he was angry that someone he didn't think deserved his company had won it fairly. Alessandro had no respect for such people. He'd dealt with too many in his life—first as a child, when he'd had no power, and then as a man, when he'd made sure that he did.

'Eighteen months is a lifetime in the stock market,' he told Mia. 'Henry Dillard should have known that.'

Mia drew a quick breath. 'As I said, longevity—'

'Was one of Dillard's assets. It isn't any more.' He swivelled to face her, tilting his head up to meet her blue, blue eyes. As their gazes met and tangled something clanged inside him, like an almighty bell. He felt it reverberate through his whole body, and he thought Mia did as well, judging from the way her pupils dilated, and she moistened her lips with her tongue.

'Sit down,' he ordered, and surprise flared briefly in her eyes before she complied silently, taking the seat across from him, so the desk was between them.

That was better. Now he wouldn't be distracted. He wouldn't let himself.

'Next, please,' he ordered, and calmly Mia took him through the rest of the clients—all of them old money, with an outdated view of investment, wealth, risk, everything. Dillard Investments was an institution that had lazily rested on its well-worn laurels for far too long…which was exactly why Alessandro had bought it.

Finished with the files, he glanced at Mia, who was sitting perfectly straight in her seat, legs to the side, ankles neatly crossed, her expression deliberately serene. She looked like a duchess. It annoyed Alessandro, as everything about her seemed to, which was a reaction he knew didn't make sense, and yet it *was*. It was, because he'd much rather be annoyed by her than affected. Which he also was. Unfortunately.

'Thank you for this,' he finally said, his voice clipped.

'Will there be anything else?'

'How well do you know Dillard's clients?'

Surprise rippled across the placid expression on her face, like wind on water, and then she gave a tiny shrug. 'Fairly well, I suppose.'

'Do you interact with them often?'

'When they visit the office, yes. I chat with them, give them coffee, that sort of thing.' She paused, her gaze scanning his face, looking for clues as to what he wanted from her. 'I've also organised the annual summer party for clients and their families, held at Mr Dillard's estate in Surrey, every year.'

'You have?' He would have expected Dillard to hire an event planner for such a high-profile event, but perhaps he was too indifferent even for that. 'That must have been quite time consuming.'

'Yes, but rewarding. I enjoy meeting and seeing the families. I've become friends with some of them, in a professional capacity only, of course. But after seven years, I believe I can say that I know many of them quite well.'

Alessandro could picture it—Mia circulating quietly through the crowds, always at the ready to help, providing whatever was needed—a tissue, a glass of champagne, a shoulder to cry on. Learning the secrets and weaknesses of Dillard's clients and their families, as well as their strengths.

Which made Mia James invaluable...for now. She could

help him to get to know Dillard's clients, so he could make a more informed decision about which to pursue or keep.

'So,' Mia asked as he continued to stare at her, his mind clicking over, 'was there anything else you needed?'

'Yes,' Alessandro stated as realisation unfurled and then crystallised inside him. 'Your attendance at a charity gala with me tonight.'

CHAPTER TWO

MIA STARED AT Alessandro's determined, unyielding expression, registering the iron in his eyes, the laser-like focus of his gaze, and tried to make sense of his request.

'Pardon?' she finally said, wishing she didn't feel wrong-footed by his invitation. She'd been doing her best to be the perfect, unflappable PA since he'd stormed into the office, practically vibrating with energy. At moments like this it felt like no more than a flimsy façade.

'A charity gala at the Ritz,' Alessandro clarified, his voice now very slightly edged with impatience, as if she wasn't catching on quickly enough. 'Many of Dillard's clients will be there. I'm attending to reassure them of their assets' safety. You will attend with me.'

A command, then, and one she couldn't afford to disobey. Still, Mia's mind whirled. She'd never attended such a highbrow function, and in what capacity? As his PA? *As his date?*

No, of course not. She was mad to think that way even for a second, and yet somehow the way he'd said *'with me'* had felt...

Possessive. As if he were staking his claim on her, branding her with his words.

But of course that wasn't what he meant. The prospect horrified her, and would undoubtedly horrify him even more. Alessandro Costa most certainly didn't think of her like *that*. And she most certainly didn't want him to.

But why did he need her at such an event? When she'd been Henry Dillard's PA, she'd always had a quiet, unnoticeable presence. Invisible on purpose, gliding through the shadows. She'd attended the summer party, yes, but only as the organiser, slipping quietly behind the scenes, doing her best to be both indispensable and out of the way.

She'd never gone to any other of Henry's many social functions—the balls and cocktail parties, fundraisers and expensive, boozy dinners in Michelin-starred restaurants. Of course she hadn't.

'I'm not sure...' she began, and then stopped, because she wasn't sure what she was trying to say. That she wasn't the kind of person he should ask? That she didn't normally go to these events? That she'd be out of her depth? All three, but the last thing she wanted to do was admit her weakness or unsuitability. Alessandro Costa seemed as if he was simply waiting for her to give him one good reason to fire her, and she was determined not to humour him in that regard.

'You're not sure...?' he prompted, an edge to his voice, as if he was daring her.

Mia lifted her chin. 'When is the gala?'

The tiniest smile quirked the corner of his mouth, electrifying her. The man was devastating already, but heaven help her if he *smiled*. His eyes turned to silver and Mia's insides turned molten. She swallowed audibly and kept her chin up.

'Seven o'clock.'

Mia's mind raced. It was undoubtedly a black-tie event, formal wear absolutely necessary, and her only appropriate outfit was a basic and rather boring black cocktail dress, back at her flat in Wimbledon. It would take nearly an hour to get there, and then back again...

'What is it?' Alessandro demanded, now definitely starting to sound annoyed. 'Why are you looking like this won't be possible, when I can assure you it is?'

'No reason,' Mia said quickly. She'd manage. Somehow she'd manage. 'I'll be ready at seven.'

'Six forty-five,' Alessandro returned. 'On the dot. I like to be punctual.'

Back at her desk Mia couldn't concentrate on anything, not that there was very much for her to do. Like everyone else she was in limbo, waiting to find out how Alessandro Costa decided to handle his new acquisition, and whether they would have jobs come morning.

A few minutes after she'd left the office, Alessandro strode out of it, without sparing her a single glance. As he stepped into the lift, she tried not to notice how the expensive material of his suit stretched across his shoulders, or his dark hair gleamed blue-black in the light. She certainly wasn't going to remember that twang of energy that she'd felt reverberate between them when she'd been standing close enough to inhale the heady scent of his aftershave. No, definitely not noticing any of those things. In fact, she decided, now was as good a time as any to go back to her flat and fetch her dress.

Her heart tumbled in her chest as she grabbed her handbag and headed out, half afraid of running into Alessandro and having to bear the brunt of his ire. It was lunchtime, so she had a reason to be leaving the office, but she still felt nervous about crossing or irritating him in any way. Her job, she acknowledged grimly, was in a very precarious place, no matter how *useful* she seemed to him at the moment.

An hour and a half later, Mia was breathlessly hurrying back into the office, her dress and shoes clutched in a bag to her chest. As the lift doors slid open, she stepped inside—and smack into Alessandro Costa.

The breath left her chest with a startling whoosh, and she would have stumbled had Alessandro not clamped his hands on her shoulders to steady her. For a heart-stopping second his nearness overwhelmed her, the heat and power rolling off him in intoxicating waves. Her mind blurred and then blanked, her palms flat on his very well-muscled chest, fingers stretching instinctively as if to feel more of him. She could not think of a single thing to say. She couldn't even move, conscious only of his powerful, hard body so very near to hers. If she so much as swayed their hips would actually *brush*...

Then Alessandro released her, stepping back, his mouth compressed in a hard line as he raked her with a single, scathing glance. 'Where have you been?'

'I'm sorry, were you looking for me?'

'I wanted the files on Dillard's less impressive clients. Did you think I'd be satisfied with only the top ten?' Even for him, he sounded on edge, his body taut with barely suppressed tension.

'I'm sorry, I was at lunch.'

'For an hour and a half?'

Mia shook her head, a flush fighting its way up her throat and across her face. She'd been afraid of this exact scenario, and now that it was a reality she couldn't handle it. He was still standing so close, and every time she took a breath she inhaled the aroma of his aftershave, felt his heat. 'No, of course not.' She drew herself up, holding onto the last threads of her composure. She could do this. She needed to do this. 'If you must know, I went back to my flat to find a dress to wear this evening. But I will have the other files to you shortly, I promise.'

Alessandro stared at her for another agonising moment before he gave a brief, terse nod. 'Very well. I expect files on all the other clients within the hour. Exactly.'

Mia had no doubt he'd been timing her to the second.

The man was a stickler for detail…among other things. Back at her desk she hung her dress up on the back of a door and hurried to amass the files Alessandro had demanded. She'd be hard-pressed to do it in an hour, but she was determined to show Alessandro she could.

Fingers flying, mind racing, she managed to assemble everything and jot down relevant notes, stepping into Henry's—now Alessandro's—office with one minute to spare. Alessandro glanced at his watch as she stepped through the doors, and then one of his faint smiles quirked his mouth for no more than a second, making her catch her breath.

*Heaven help her.*

'Impressive,' he said after a moment, sounding both amused and reluctantly admiring. 'I didn't think you could do it in an hour.'

'You underestimate me, Mr Costa.'

His gaze lingered on her, and Mia felt her body start to tingle and hum. 'Maybe I do,' he murmured, and held out his hand for the files.

Mia handed them to him, and then took him through each one, making sure to sit on the other side of the desk as he'd requested before.

It was surely better for her to have a little distance between them; being near him had the troubling side-effect of short-circuiting her brain. She didn't know whether it was his intimidating presence, his undeniable charisma, or the unavoidable fact of his outrageously good looks that turned her mind to slush, but something about him did, and that was definitely not a good reaction to have to her boss, or even to anyone. Mia never wanted another person to have any power over her—not physical, not emotional, and certainly not sensual. Just thinking about it made goose-pimples rise on her flesh. Alessandro certainly had the last one…if she let him.

'Is there anything else you need?' she asked once they'd

gone through all the files, her body tense from holding herself apart and doing her utmost not to notice the powerful muscles of his forearms when he'd rolled up his shirt-sleeves, or the stubble now glinting on the hard line of his jaw. No, she was definitely not noticing anything like that.

'Yes,' Alessandro told her shortly. 'Show me your dress.'

Her mouth dropped open before she snapped it shut. 'My…dress?'

'Yes, your dress. I want to make sure it is suitable. As my companion, how you look is important.'

'Your companion…' Her mind spun emptily again. *Surely he wasn't suggesting…?*

'We are attending together,' Alessandro clarified pointedly, as if to highlight the utter impossibility of whatever she might have been thinking. 'You must be suitably attired. Now show me the dress.'

Wordlessly Mia rose from her seat. She had no idea what Alessandro Costa considered *suitably attired*, but she had a feeling her plain black cocktail dress, bought from the bargain rack, wasn't going to be it. Unless he wanted her to be discreet, even invisible, as Henry Dillard had? As she was used to being from childhood, slipping in and out of the shadows, trying not to draw attention to herself, in case she provoked her father's anger? Because in all truth she wasn't sure she knew how to be anything else.

She grabbed the dress and returned to the office, holding it in front of her. 'Will this do?' she asked, unable to keep the faintest tremble from her voice. She'd never had her boss vet her clothing choices before, and she didn't like it. She certainly didn't like feeling controlled, even in as small a matter as this. She'd had enough of that in her life, and she didn't want or need any more, not even by the boss whose good side she was trying to stay on.

'You intended to wear *that*?' Alessandro sounded both

scandalised and completely derisive. 'Did you want to be mistaken for one of the serving staff?'

Mia's chin went up. 'It's perfectly appropriate.'

'It's perfectly dreadful, like something a junior secretary would wear to the office Christmas party.'

She *had* worn it to such a party, and so Mia did not deign to reply to his remark. Alessandro might be offensively blunt, but there was more perception and truth to his remarks than she wanted to acknowledge.

'You can't wear it,' he stated. 'You won't.'

'I don't have anything else,' Mia returned. 'So if you wish for me to attend...'

'Then I will make sure you do have something.' He slid his phone out of his pocket. 'I will not have you on my arm looking like Cinderella still in her rags.'

'So you'll be my fairy godmother?' Mia quipped before she could attempt a more measured reply. What was it about this man that made her hackles rise, everything in her resist? Henry Dillard had certainly never made her respond like this, but then Henry Dillard had never spoken to her in such an arrogant, autocratic way. He'd been affably incompetent, content to let her organise everything.

Alessandro's eyes gleamed like molten silver as his mouth quirked the tiniest bit, making her respond to him. *Again.* A very inconvenient response, when her stomach fizzed and her heart leapt. Mia was determined to ignore it. 'Now, that is the first time anyone has called me that,' he said, his mouth curving deeper, and Mia forced herself to look away.

Alessandro angled his body away from Mia as he spoke into the phone, asking for a personal stylist to be brought to the office immediately. His right-hand man, Luca, took the rather unexpected request in his stride.

Ending the call, Alessandro turned back to face Mia,

trying not to notice the rise and fall of her chest with every agitated breath she took; clearly she didn't like him deciding what she should wear, although she should be thankful he'd vetted her selection. That black bag of a dress looked cheap and boring and was hardly what he needed his companion for the evening to turn up in.

'As your PA, I don't see why I need to wear some fancy dress,' Mia said, clearly striving to moderate her tone. 'Or, in fact, why I need to attend this gala at all. It's highly unusual…'

'You need to attend because many of the guests there will be Dillard's clients,' Alessandro answered. 'And you will know them better than I do. I require your knowledge in this matter.'

'Still…'

'And you need to wear a gown worthy of the occasion,' Alessandro cut across her. He didn't like her protestations; he was used to being obeyed instantly, and Mia James seemed not to have realised that.

'The clients will know I'm Henry's PA,' she protested. 'If I dress up like a proper guest, they'll think I'm putting on airs—'

'You are my PA now, and you are my guest,' Alessandro returned. 'You will wear an appropriate gown. I am sure there will be something you fancy from the selection provided.' He gave her a quelling look. 'Most women I know would be thrilled to have such an opportunity of choice.'

'Somehow I don't think I'm like most women you know,' Mia returned tartly, making him smile.

'That is very true. Even so, I would like you to pick a dress that is suitable.'

Mia nodded, setting her jaw, her eyes sparking like bits of blue ice. 'Very well,' she said, sounding far from pleased about the matter. Despite the difficulties of the situation,

Alessandro would have thought she'd enjoy the opportunity to select a new gown.

'The stylist will be here shortly,' he told her. 'Until then you may return to your work.'

With a brief, brisk nod Mia swivelled on her heel and walked out of the office, closing the door behind her with a firm click that was halfway to becoming a slam. It annoyed and amused Alessandro in equal measure. Normally he didn't like people to oppose him; in fact, he hated any sign of disobedience or disrespect.

As he was a man of both drive and focus, work was a well-oiled machine and rebelliousness was inefficient as well as time-consuming. And, while Mia's rebelliousness did annoy him, that contrary spark of defiance somehow... *enflamed* him.

The knowledge rested uncomfortably with him. He was attracted to her, he acknowledged starkly, and that was something he most certainly could and would control. There was no place for attraction within the workplace, and self-control had always been his personal creed, the way he lived his life. The way he stayed on top.

He would never, ever be like his mother, whose sorry life had been tossed on the waves of other people's whims, her poverty and powerlessness making her constantly vulnerable, searching for love and meaning in shabby, shallow relationships.

Alessandro would never be like that...never at another person's mercy...not even for the sake of a very inconvenient desire.

Still, he was uncomfortably aware of the simple *fact* of his attraction, as well as the realisation that his desire to see Mia attired in an appropriate gown was not quite as professional and expedient as he'd made it seem.

As she'd pointed out herself, she was known as Dillard's PA and a simple, serviceable dress would certainly have been adequate. Yet he hadn't wanted to see his date in something resembling a bin bag. He hadn't wanted to see *Mia* in it.

Still, he told himself, he needed to make the right impression tonight. The last thing he wanted was for people to look at him and think that an impostor had shown up along with his secretary. Because Alessandro had earned the right to be at the party, just as he'd earned the right to be sitting in the office. Just as he'd earned everything he had, fighting for it and winning it, time and time again, a man with a mission. A man who won.

A few minutes later Luca texted him that the stylist had arrived, and Alessandro rose to find Mia. She was at her desk, and as he came to stand behind her, glancing at the screen of her laptop, a cold wave of displeasure and shock rippled through him.

'You're working on your CV?'

She swivelled sharply in her chair, her eyes widening with alarm at the sight of him looking at the screen, but when she spoke her voice was cool. 'For when I'm no longer *useful*.'

'And that is not now.' With one brisk movement Alessandro clicked the mouse to close the document, without saving any changes. Mia's mouth compressed but she did not protest against his action. 'The stylist is here. You may use my office.'

Mia's eyes flashed and he wondered what she objected to—his dismissal of her dress, or his order for a new one? Or simply his manner, which was even more autocratic than usual, because it felt like the best defence against this irritating and inconvenient attraction that simmered beneath the surface, threatening to bubble up?

Even now he found himself sneaking looks at the tantalising vee of ivory skin visible at the all too modest neck of her blouse, and noting the soft curve of her jaw, and the way a wisp of golden hair had fallen against her cheek. He itched to tuck it behind her ear, let his fingers skim to her lobe, a prospect which was too bizarre to be entertained even for a second.

He didn't want to do things like that. *Ever.* Relationships were not on his radar, and sex was nothing more than a physical urge to be sated like any other. He'd always been able to find women who were agreeable to his terms. More than agreeable, so why was he feeling this strange way about Mia James?

He wasn't. Or at least he wouldn't. He wouldn't let himself. Work was too important to risk for a moment's satisfaction, even with someone as annoyingly beguiling as the woman in front of him.

'Are you coming?' he asked tersely, and she nodded, rising from her seat with unconscious elegance, following him with a graceful, long-legged stride. Alessandro found himself watching the gentle sway of her hips before he resolutely turned his gaze away.

A few minutes later the stylist arrived with a flurry of plastic-swathed hangers, an assistant behind her carrying several boxes and bags. Alessandro supervised their setting up before he decided to leave Mia to it.

'Let me see your final choice,' he instructed, and she arched one golden eyebrow.

'To approve it?'

'Of course.' That was the point of this whole exercise, was it not? Still, he decided to temper his reply, for her benefit. 'Thank you for attending to this matter.'

She pressed her lips together. 'It's not as if I had much choice.'

Alessandro frowned. 'I'm offering you a *dress*. Is that so objectionable?'

'It's not the dress and you know it,' she snapped, and surprisingly, he let out a laugh.

'No, I suppose not.'

'It's your entire manner,' she emphasised, and he nodded.

'Yes, I realise,' he said dryly. 'So at least we're in agreement about something.'

For the next few hours he found he could not concentrate on the business at hand, a fact which annoyed him as much as everything else about Mia James had done. What was it about the woman that got under his skin, burrowed deep inside? Was it simply her attractiveness, which was undeniable, or something else? The hint of defiance in the set of her shoulders, the surprising vulnerability he sensed beneath the surface? Why on earth did he *care*?

It was annoying. It was alarming. And it had to stop.

'Mr Costa?' The stylist's fluttering voice interrupted his unruly thoughts; he'd been staring at his laptop screen for who knew how long? 'Miss James has selected her dress and is ready for you to see it.'

'Thank you.' He rose and walked quickly to the office, steeling himself for whatever he was to see. Despite his best intention to remain utterly unmoved, he was still shocked by the sight of her, her slender body swathed in an ice-blue gown of ruched silk that hugged her figure before flaring out around her ankles in a decadent display of iridescent, shimmering material. Instead of back in a sedate clip, her hair was twisted into an elegant chignon. Diamonds sparkled at her ears and throat. She looked like a Norse goddess, an ice queen, everything about her coolly beautiful, icily intoxicating.

Desire crashed over him in an overwhelming wave, unexpected even now in its intensity and force. He wanted to pluck the diamond-tipped pins from her hair. He wanted to tug on the discreet zip in the back of her dress, and count the sharp knobs of her vertebrae, taste the smooth silkiness of her skin.

He *wanted*. And he never let himself want.

'Well?' Mia asked, her voice taut. 'Will I pass?'

'Yes,' he answered after another beat of tense silence, barely managing to get the word out. 'You'll pass.'

She let out a huff of sound, turning away from him, and the stylist's face fell a little bit at his damningly faint praise. Alessandro didn't care. Already he was regretting his command to have Mia accompany him tonight. Already he was looking forward to it far more than he should.

'I'll go and change myself,' he said when a few seconds had ticked by without anyone saying a word. 'Be ready to leave in ten minutes.'

Mia nodded, not quite looking at him, and again Alessandro was captivated by the curve of her jaw, the hollow of her throat, the dip of her waist, each one begging to be explored and savoured. He turned away quickly, striding out of the office without another word.

The sooner this evening was over, the better. This desire he felt was inconvenient and overwhelming and very much unwanted. But, like everything else in his life, he would control it. It would just take a little more effort than he'd anticipated.

# CHAPTER THREE

MIA FELT AS if she'd fallen down a rabbit hole into some strange, charmed alternative reality...a reality where she rode in limousines, and drank champagne, and walked into a glittering ballroom on the arm of the most handsome man there.

Of course, as PA to Henry Dillard she'd ridden in plenty of limousines. She'd drunk more than enough champagne. But it had always been as an employee, someone to serve and be invisible while she was at it. Someone to make sure the champagne was flowing, and that the limousine arrived on time. Someone who didn't stride into parties, but sidled along the sidelines, checking that everything was going according to plan and keeping out of the way.

Tonight was entirely different. Tonight, much to her own amazement, she felt like the belle of the ball. It was beyond bizarre. It was also intoxicating, far more than any champagne she might quaff.

It had started with the stylist bringing out several exquisite dresses for Mia to choose from, and then doing her hair and make-up as well, before finishing off her incredible ensemble with the most beautiful diamond earrings and necklace Mia had ever seen.

As someone who had prided herself on always being smart and sensible, no-nonsense and pragmatic, it had felt to her as decadent as an endless dark chocolate sundae to be so pampered and primped. She hadn't expected to enjoy it; she'd been fully intent on chafing at every opportunity, resenting Alessandro's needless autocratic intervention, but then...she hadn't.

She'd submitted to the stylist's every instruction, and then she'd started to enjoy it. To *relish* it. Part of her was horrified by her own acquiescence, and what it might mean. And yet...it was one night. One magical night after a lifetime of having her head down, working hard. Why shouldn't she enjoy it?

At some point she'd let her mind slide into a comforting sort of blurry nothingness, floating on a sea of ease and comfort. As she usually tried to anticipate every possibility, consider every choice, it felt wonderfully relaxing not to overthink this. She wasn't going to wonder what Alessandro Costa wanted with her, or with Dillard Investments, or whether her job, not to mention any of her friends', was secure. She was just going to enjoy a night like no other, because she doubted she'd see another one like it, and that was fine.

And then the moment when Alessandro had come into the room and looked her over...that moment had felt as if the world was tilting on its axis, as if everything was sliding away from the comforting security of its anchor even as it came into glittering focus.

For that one second Mia had seen a flash of masculine approval blaze in his eyes like golden fire and it had ignited her right through, as her blood heated and fizzed and her mind spun out possibilities she'd never dared to dream of.

Then he'd told her she'd pass, his voice as laconic as ever, and she'd wondered if she'd imagined it. She must have. This was *Alessandro Costa*, after all. The ruthless, arrogant CEO she was a little bit scared of. Not a man interested in her. Not her *date*.

It just felt as if he were. And, more alarmingly, she

*liked* that feeling. She, who had steered clear of love and romance and even anything close to a flirtation, because she did not want someone to have that kind of power over her. Because her mother had fallen in love with her father all those years ago, and look how that had gone.

*'He loves me, Mia. Really. He just has trouble showing it.'*

Mia had listened to far too many of her mother's excuses before she'd died of cancer when Mia was fourteen, too broken and despairing to hold on any longer. Mia had had to wait four more years before she was finally free of her father's sneering control. And since then she'd made it her life's mission to stay strong, independent and alone. *Safe.*

But tonight she let her rules bend and even break. Tonight she let herself forget they existed. It was just a night, after all. Just one wonderful night where she could pretend, for a few hours, that she was a young woman with a gorgeous man, Cinderella with her prince before the clock inevitably struck midnight.

They'd ridden in a limousine to the Ritz, and Alessandro, devastating in black tie, his hair midnight-dark and his hard jaw freshly shaven, had barely said a word, which was fine by Mia because she could barely think. Dressed to the nines and even the tens in a gorgeous gown, on the arm of a beautiful man…going to the kind of party where she'd normally be holding doors or serving champagne… together, all of it, was utterly overwhelming. Intoxicating. *Wonderful.*

A valet had opened the door of the limousine as they'd pulled up to the front entrance of the hotel, and flashbulbs had popped and sparked as Mia had stepped out, blinking in the glare. She wasn't used to the spotlight; she always stood to one side, watched it from afar. It felt very different to be the one basking in the bright light, especially when

Alessandro had slid his arm through hers and smiled for the cameras, their heads nearly touching.

*What was he doing? And why?*

She still didn't really understand the need for her presence at the ball. Yes, she knew Dillard's clients, but she'd already given Alessandro all the relevant information in the files. And this was a charity event, not a business meeting. Surely he had someone else, a dozen 'someone elses', to accompany him to such a glittering occasion, a supermodel or socialite who would fit in more easily with all this well-heeled crowd? Mia didn't know how to rub shoulders with these people; she was used to fetching them coffee. She was out of her depth, and she never felt it more so than when Alessandro approached a group of people, some of whom she knew, and introduced her as his 'companion'.

Mia clocked the raised eyebrows, the curious smiles, the speculative looks, and like everyone else in the group she wondered what Alessandro Costa was playing at.

'Why don't you just tell people I'm your PA?' she asked when they had a moment alone. She'd drunk two glasses of champagne in quick succession, more to have something to do than because of any desire to be drunk, but now her head was spinning, her tongue loosened.

'Because tonight you are a beautiful woman who is accompanying me to a gala.'

'But…' She shook her head slowly, trying to discern the emotion behind his cool, mask-like exterior, his eyes like blank mirrors. The man gave absolutely nothing away. 'Why?'

He shrugged his powerful shoulders, muscles rippling under the expensive material of his tuxedo. 'Why not?'

'You seem like a man who has a very clear reason for everything he does,' Mia said slowly. 'So your "why not?" doesn't actually hold water with me.'

'Oh?' One dark slash of an eyebrow arched in cool

amusement. 'You surprise me with your perception, Miss James.'

'If I'm your companion, perhaps you should call me Mia.'

Something flickered in his eyes, and Mia felt a shiver through her belly in response. She hadn't meant to sound flirtatious, but she realised she might have…and she didn't actually mind. 'Very well,' Alessandro said after a moment. 'Mia.' His voice, with his slight accent, seemed to caress the two syllables.

'Where are you from?' Mia asked. 'It didn't say when I looked online.'

His eyebrow arched higher. 'You did a search on me?'

She shrugged. 'After I heard you'd taken over the company, yes, of course. Information is power.'

'True.' His gaze held hers, his expression considering. 'And is that what you want? Power?'

'I want to keep my job,' Mia said after a second's pause. 'And knowing my employer helps with that.'

'Mia!' A woman approached them in a flurry of cloying scent, kissing Mia on both cheeks while Alessandro stepped back discreetly. 'Darling, how are you? I heard about poor Henry…'

Mia shot an alarmed look at Alessandro; his expression seemed dangerously neutral. 'Diane,' she said, after she'd returned the woman's tight hug. 'This is Alessandro Costa, the new CEO of Dillard Investments.'

'New…oh.' Diane Holley's mouth dropped into a comical 'o' as she swivelled to face Alessandro, her eyes widening in shocked speculation.

'Pleased to meet you…?'

'Diane. Diane Holley.' She took Alessandro's outstretched hand, looking a bit dazed. As Diane shook his hand, Mia saw her expression change from surprise to admiration, her lowered gaze sweeping speculatively, and almost avariciously, over Alessandro Costa's admittedly impressive form. 'Very pleased to meet you too, of course...' she murmured.

Mia felt a sharp tug of jealousy, a reaction which surprised and appalled her in equal measure. *What on earth...?* She had absolutely no reason to feel remotely jealous in any way. She didn't *care* about Alessandro Costa. She didn't even like the man. And jealousy was not an emotion she'd ever let herself entertain. It was so weak and needy. It was also dangerous.

And yet...she was wearing a beautiful dress, and he'd looked at her, for a brief second, with desire in his eyes, and for a single evening she'd felt like someone else entirely, someone transported into a fairy tale, from the shadows to the spotlight.

Perhaps one evening was too much, after all. The last thing she needed to do was lose her head, even for an evening, over Alessandro Costa. The man was too dangerous, and too much was at risk. Not just her job, but her very self. She couldn't let Alessandro Costa affect her. Make her want. Make her weak. Not even for a moment.

Then he put another flute of champagne into her hand, and her fingers closed around the fragile crystal stem automatically. 'You looked as if you were a million miles away,' he murmured, his voice low and honeyed. 'Don't you like hearing about Diane Holley's corgis?'

'Corgis?' Blinking, Mia realised Diane must have been chatting to Alessandro for a few minutes at least and she hadn't taken in a word. The older woman, the wife of one of Dillard's most important clients, had already moved on. 'She told you about her corgis?'

'I asked about them. You mentioned them this afternoon.'

'Did I?'

Alessandro arched an eyebrow, looking more amused

than annoyed—for once. 'You really haven't been paying attention, have you?'

'Of course I have. I always do.' She took a defiant sip of champagne. 'Diane has four corgis, and one of them has digestive issues.'

'She didn't mention those tonight, thankfully.'

'You were lucky, then.' Mia's breath came out in a surprised hiss as Alessandro took her elbow, his hand warm and dry and so very sure as he steered her towards another cluster of people. 'Where…where are we going?'

'To mingle, of course. That's why we're here. You're going to introduce me to all these people, and then tell me their secrets.'

'I thought I'd already done that this afternoon. Besides, I don't know any secrets.'

'I still need to put names to faces. And I think you know more secrets than you realise…always working behind the scenes, listening in the shadows.'

'You make me sound like a snoop.'

'No, someone who is smart.' His gaze lingered on hers for a tantalising second as his hand had moved from her elbow to her waist, his fingers splayed across her hip. Heat flooded Mia's body, and once again she was in danger of drifting along this lovely tide of feeling. 'Mr Costa…'

'You must call me Alessandro.'

'*You* must stop acting like I'm your date.' She knew she never would have said the words if she hadn't had two glasses of champagne, and just chugged half of her third. If she wasn't so afraid of how much he affected her.

'Why? You are my date.' He sounded utterly unruffled, like someone making a simple statement of fact.

'No…' Her breath came out in a rush. Her head spun. People were *looking* at them. Wondering. 'I'm not. Not really…'

'Yes, you are.' They'd reached the group of people, and

Alessandro kept his hand on her waist as he stretched out his other one. 'Alessandro Costa, CEO of Dillard Investments.' In turn, everyone shook his hand, with varying expressions of pleasure, speculation, or snobbery. It made Mia wonder yet again about Alessandro. What was he doing here, exactly? Why did he want her with him? Who *was* this man at her side? And how much did she want to know?

The chit-chat washed over her as she took in Alessandro's easy, urbane manner. The man could be charming when he chose, a fact that alarmed her. If Alessandro Costa affected her when he was blunt and brusque, heaven help her when he was easy and affable.

She knew a few people in the group through Dillard's, and somehow, her mind still spinning, she made chit-chat, introduced Alessandro to a few others, and stumbled through the evening, feeling as if she were acting a part in a play, desperate now to get to the end of the evening without embarrassing herself or losing her head entirely over the man at her side.

When they were alone again, and she was finishing her third glass of champagne, she rather recklessly asked him about it all.

'I can make conversation, if that's what you mean,' he answered as he sipped his own champagne.

'What do you want from these people?' Mia asked, her tongue well and truly loosened by now. 'Why did you buy Dillard Investments, really?'

A guarded look came over his face before he shrugged, the movement clearly meant to be dismissive. 'Why do I buy any company?'

'You tell me.'

The tiniest of pauses. 'For financial gain.'

'But you said yourself Dillard's was operating at a loss.'

'That doesn't mean it always has to.'

'Still…' She shook her head slowly. 'A man like you…'

'A man like me?' Alessandro's voice sharpened. 'What does that mean, exactly?'

'Only that you must always have your eye on the bottom line.'

'True.' He eyed her thoughtfully. 'So what did you learn about me, during that online cyberstalking session?'

Mia let out a choked laugh. 'I was hardly *stalking*.'

'Weren't you?'

'Gathering information. Big difference.'

'Hmm.' She felt dizzy with the turn in their conversation. It almost felt as if…as if they were flirting. But of course they couldn't be. 'So,' Alessandro asked, stepping closer, 'what did you learn about me, Mia?'

Alessandro hadn't meant to ask the question. He surely didn't mean to bother with the answer. He was curious despite his determination never to be curious about anyone. Curiosity implied caring, and he didn't care. And yet… 'Anything interesting?' The words sounded provocative.

Mia licked her lips, her tongue looking very pink as she touched it to her full, lush lips, the instinctive movement causing a dart of desire to arrow through him, unsettling in its intensity. 'Not really.' Her gaze skittered away from his. 'Not much.'

'Tell me.' His voice was low, the words a command, but with a thread of something dark and rich running through it, a promise he hadn't meant to make. Mia turned to look at him, her eyes widening, looking very blue and clear. Eyes he could drown in if he let himself. He stepped closer. 'Tell me,' he said again.

'Well…' Again her tongue touched her lips. 'You have a reputation for being ruthless. You take over companies, strip them of their assets, and fire about ninety percent of the staff before absorbing the company into Costa International.'

That was the gist without being entirely true, but Alessandro wasn't about to defend his actions. They spoke for themselves.

'Are you going to do that with Dillard's?' Her chin lifted a little. 'Fire everyone? Get rid of it all?'

He eyed her for a moment, considering what to tell her. For some contrary reason he didn't like the thought of her thinking badly of him, which was ridiculous, because he'd been thought of far worse by the furious CEOs he'd displaced.

'I'm not going to fire everyone,' he said at last. 'I never do.'

'Ninety percent, then.'

'Your percentages are a bit off.'

'Do you enjoy it?' she asked, her voice choking. 'Ruining people's lives?'

He stared at her for a moment, fighting the urge to explain the truth of his mission. But, no. He was not going to justify himself to her. He was certainly not going to care about her opinion. 'Does it seem as if I do?' he asked, meaning to sound dismissive.

Slowly she shook her head. 'You don't actually seem *cruel*.'

'No?' He tried to keep his voice disinterested.

'The media portrayed you as a bit of a cowboy... someone who came from nowhere and had a meteoric rise. Not entirely respectable, but not cruel.'

'Well, they were wrong,' Alessandro said lightly, even though her words were like razors on his skin. 'I'm not at all respectable.'

'Is that why you took Dillard's over? To seem respectable?'

The question grated. As if he wanted to don Dillard's

shabby suit and call himself a gentleman. 'Not at all. I don't care one iota if I seem respectable or not.'

'Then why bother with them? Where is the profit?'

'In the clients I keep.' Although Alessandro suspected there would be little profit indeed. Profit was not why he did what he did, at least not in regard to companies such as Dillard's.

'And what about all the employees? Innocent people… don't you care about them?'

*More than she would ever know.* 'You're sounding like a crusader, Mia,' he warned her. He did not wish to discuss this any longer. 'It's quite dull.'

Her eyes flashed. 'So sorry I'm boring you, but people's lives are at stake. Besides… I would have thought you might understand how they felt.'

He tensed, the perception in her eyes like a needle burrowing into his skin. 'Oh?'

'The media said you came from a poor background… the slums of Naples.' He angled his head away from her, not trusting the expression on his face. 'Is that true?'

'Slums is such a pejorative word, but I suppose, in essence, yes.' He did his best to sound bored. He *was* bored.

The last thing he wanted to talk about was his pathetic past…the endless chaos of moving from grotty flat to grotty flat, the stints in foster care when his mother had lost custody of him, the endless jobs she'd taken cleaning office buildings, the countless boyfriends she'd had in a desperate bid to assuage the despairing sadness of her life. A childhood he'd done his best always to remember, to remind him of how he would be different, even as he pretended to forget.

'Then if you know what it's like to be poor, to live from pay check to pay check, how can you fire people like that?'

'Because I know what it's like to work hard,' he said in a steely voice, 'and to earn what I have. And anyone who does those things will have a position with Costa International, that much I guarantee.'

Her eyes widened. 'They will?'

She sounded so hopeful it made him cringe. 'Dillard Investments was dying on the vine. I just plucked it before it fell, withered, to the ground. If anything, I've *saved* people's jobs in the long run.'

'Do you really mean that?'

Impatient now, he shrugged. 'Henry Dillard was charming, I'll grant you that, but he was a terrible businessman. I did his employees a favour.' *Why* had he stooped to justifying himself? 'I'm not the monster you seem to think I am,' he finished levelly. 'Regardless of what you read online.'

She stared at him for a moment, and he felt as if she were seeing right inside him, that blue, blue gaze burrowing deep down inside his soul, reaching places he'd closed off for good. He looked away, shrugging as he took a sip of champagne, struggling to master his wayward emotions.

'No,' she said softly. 'I don't think you are.'

'You've changed your mind?' He'd meant to sound offhand and failed.

'I think you like to present yourself as someone hardened and ruthless,' she said slowly. 'It's the right image for someone who specialises in corporate takeovers, isn't it?'

'I suppose.' What else could he say? She saw too much already.

'I wonder who you really are,' she murmured. 'I wonder what you're hiding.' Alessandro stared at her, unable to look away. He felt a tug low in his belly, pulling him towards her. She wanted to *know* him. It was beguiling, alarming. Nobody knew him, not like that.

'Let's dance,' he said, his voice roughened with emotion. When they danced, they wouldn't talk. She wouldn't say things or see inside him. He would make sure of it.

Wordlessly Mia nodded, and after depositing their

empty champagne flutes on a nearby table, Alessandro took her by the hand and led her to the ballroom's parquet dance floor. The music was a slow, sensuous piece, the sonorous wail of a saxophone wrapping its lonely notes around them as Alessandro took her into his arms.

Her hips bumped his gently and heat flared white-hot, making his hands tense on hers before he deliberately relaxed his grip and began to move her around the floor.

She was elegant in his arms, matching the rhythm of his movements, her hips swaying, her body lithe. Lithe and eager. He felt her tremble and knew, like him, she felt this most inconvenient and heady desire, growing stronger with every second they swayed together. The realisation only stoked his own.

Sex, for him, had always been a matter of expediency, a physical need to be met like any other—food, water, sleep, sex. That was how he'd viewed it. Something to be ticked off, the same as he would with a physical workout or a medical examination.

This felt different. *More.* This desire, twining through him like some dangerous vine, felt capable of overwhelming him. Overtaking the rational thought, common sense and, far worse, the self-control that were the touchstones of his life, the anchors of his soul. And the most alarming part was, in this moment he didn't even think he cared.

The pressures of overseeing the takeover, the twenty-hour work days and the ceaseless striving, for years now, decades…in this moment he sloughed it all off like an old skin, let it slither about him in dead, dried peels, as desire birthed him anew.

The song ended and another started, and still they kept dancing. He pulled her closer, so her body nestled into his. She came willingly, twining her arms around his neck, her breasts brushing his chest. Her head was slightly bowed, so he could see the delicate, vulnerable curve of her neck and he had the nearly irresistible urge to press his lips there, against the skin he knew would be warm and soft and silky.

They twirled around again, and she shifted in his arms, the material of her dress rustling and sliding, pulling taut across her breasts, revealing the pure line of her collarbone. He could press his lips there too.

He could do it, and in the haze of his desire, as well as his exhaustion and the champagne he had drunk, he couldn't remember a single reason not to.

The music swelled and the world around him fell away. There was nothing but this. *Her.* They turned again, her dress flaring out from her ankles, brushing his legs.

Some last, desperate part of him tried to claw back his sanity, his sense. This was a bad idea. A terrible, terrible idea. Mia James worked for him, and he never mixed business with pleasure. Ever. It was far too dangerous. The last thing he needed was a woman at work laying claim to any part of him, or, heaven forbid, accusing him of something.

But there was nothing accusatory in the way Mia was melting into him, her body pliant and willing in his arms. Then she lifted her head, tilting her face upwards, her gaze clashing and then tangling with his.

It felt as if they shared an entire conversation in that silent gaze, a shared yearning and a deeper need, a question and an answer, all encapsulated in a single, burning glance.

Neither of them said a word, but Alessandro felt a shudder run through her as he held her in his arms. The last part of his sanity trickled away. He didn't care.

*He didn't care.*

'Let's go,' he said, his voice rough with need.

'Where?' Even with her in his arms, he strained to hear her breathy whisper.

'Anywhere.'

Her eyes widened, her lips parting. She swallowed, and he waited for her answer, the one she'd already given in the silent yearning of her gaze. The song ended, and their bodies stilled. Still Alessandro waited, his breath held, his body taut.

Then wordlessly, her eyes wide, Mia nodded.

Alessandro didn't wait for more. Taking her by the hand, he led her from the dance floor and out of the ballroom, out of the hotel, into the warm spring night.

# CHAPTER FOUR

THE COOL NIGHT air felt like a slap on her face as Mia left the hotel, Alessandro clasping her hand tightly. It felt like an urgent and much-needed wake-up call.

*What on earth was she doing?*

What madness had possessed her up there in the ball-room, with the music and the champagne and the slow sway of Alessandro's body in rhythm with hers?

A limousine pulled up to the kerb; Alessandro must have texted his driver while she'd been in this heady daze of desire, a fog that had wrapped her up in its sensuous, blinding warmth, making her immune to everything, including her own common sense. Wordlessly he opened the door and ushered her into the sumptuous leather interior.

Mia slid to the far side of the limo, shivering slightly in the still cool air, despite the sudden blast of warmth from the heater. Now that she was no longer in Alessandro's arms, in that strange, suspended, otherworldly reality... she realised there was no way she could go anywhere or do anything with Alessandro Costa. No matter how she felt. No matter what she'd wanted.

Already she cursed herself for having danced with him at all, swaying in his arms, moving closer, falling under his sensual spell.

What had she been thinking? He was her *boss*, and not a particularly pleasant boss at that, even if she now questioned whether he was as ruthless as he'd been rumoured to be.

Even so, getting involved with him in any capacity would be a serious, serious mistake, and one she had never intended on making with *anyone*. She sneaked a glance at his harsh profile, wondering what he was thinking, now that they were away from the ball, the music and champagne. Was he having second thoughts as she was? Regrets?

'Where…?' Her voice came out scratchy and she licked her lips. 'Where are we going?'

'Back to the office.' Alessandro spoke tersely, and when he turned to her there was something hard and resolute in his face, and his eyes looked dark and flat. Looking at him, taking in that unyielding expression, Mia felt chilled. Clearly he was having second thoughts as well, a thought that should bring sweet, sweet relief, but instead she felt disappointed.

*Stupid, stupid.*

They rode in silence to the Dillard building in Mayfair, the night a blur of dark sky and city lights all around them. The air in the back of the limo felt taut with tension, and Mia let out a quiet sigh of relief when the limo finally pulled up in front of the office.

'I need to get my things,' she murmured. She'd left her work clothes, coat, and handbag at the office, an oversight she hadn't even considered when she'd been dazzled by being the belle of the ball. The party was well and truly over now, the clock striking midnight, everything turning back to the way it was. There seemed to be no question of their going anywhere together, as Alessandro had hinted at the ball. All Mia wanted to do was go home.

'I need to get my things as well,' Alessandro replied. 'I'll let you go up, and the limo can drive you home.'

'There's no need…' Mia began half-heartedly, feeling

she should take the tube as a matter of principle, and after giving her a hard look, Alessandro shrugged, supremely indifferent.

'As you like.'

He swiped his key card and ushered her inside the building, everything now cloaked in darkness and quiet. Mia had been in the office late at night before, when she'd had to work longer hours for one reason or another, but it felt different now, with Alessandro walking right behind her, and gooseflesh rippling over her skin at the knowledge of him being so close.

The lift had never felt so small or suffocating as they rode up in a silence taut not with expectation but the sudden, unsettling lack of it. Then the doors swished open and they stepped onto the top floor of the building, where Henry's office was located. Mia walked through the dim open-plan space, lit only by the streetlights outside, thankful that this ordeal was almost over.

She'd come so close to losing her mind and heaven knew what else over this man. She could consider herself lucky, she told herself, even if she didn't feel all that lucky right then.

'I left my things in Henry's—I mean your—office,' she said, and Alessandro merely nodded as he opened the door and ushered her through. He flicked on a table lamp, bathing the room in warm light, while Mia hurriedly hunted for her bag and discarded clothes. She hesitated, knowing she didn't want to brave the tube home at ten o'clock at night in a floor-length evening gown.

'Do you mind if I change…?'

Another hard, fathomless look, another shrug. 'As you like.' He left the office, and Mia let out another sigh of relief and pent-up tension as the door closed behind him. Her head still felt fuzzy from the champagne, even though the main part of her was stone-cold sober, longing only to be curled up in her bed with a comforting mug of hot chocolate, this whole evening behind her.

Her fingers fumbled as she unclasped the diamond necklace that now felt heavy and cold around her neck. Carefully she replaced it in the black velvet box the stylist had brandished so proudly just a few short hours ago. It felt like another lifetime. Had she really danced with Alessandro? Flirted with him? Felt she had a connection with him, that something important and intimate had pulsed between them when she'd told him she didn't know who he was? And then she'd twined her arms around his neck and told him she'd go anywhere with him. She'd even believed it.

Her breath came out in a shuddery rush as she acknowledged the folly of her actions. She had done all those things and more, and all she could do now was thank heaven that it hadn't gone any further, and that Alessandro at least seemed to have had the same second thoughts she had.

The best-case scenario now was that they would both pretend to forget everything that had—and hadn't—happened. And really, she told herself, it wasn't as if they'd actually *done* anything. They hadn't even kissed.

But she'd wanted to…

Forcing those pointless, treacherous thoughts away, Mia took off the diamond earrings and put them back as well. Then her heels, silver diamanté-decorated stilettos, and her sheer tights, bundling up the tights and putting the shoes back in the box. Now the dress.

She reached behind her to unzip the dress, her fingertips brushing the top of the zipper but unable to pull it down. Mia groaned under her breath, nearly wrenching her arm out of its socket as she tried again, desperately, to unzip her gown. No luck. She couldn't do it on her own. And she couldn't go on the tube in this. She was going to have to ask Alessandro to help her, a prospect that filled her with dread as well as a tiny, treacherous flicker of excitement she chose to ignore.

Alessandro rapped sharply on the door. 'Are you nearly ready?'

'Yes.' Her voice wavered and she took a deep breath before going to the door and opening it. Alessandro stood there, frowning at the sight of her.

'You haven't changed.' He sounded disapproving.

'I know. I can't manage the zip of the dress.' She met his gaze even though it took effort. 'Do you mind helping me?'

'With the zip?'

Why did he sound so surprised, so scandalised? 'Yes,' Mia answered, and then, pointlessly, 'I'm sorry.'

Wordlessly Alessandro nodded and stepped into the room. Mia took another deep breath as she silently turned around, showing him the zip that ran from the nape of her neck to the small of her back.

Moonlight poured through the windows, bathing everything in silver, as for a hushed moment neither of them moved. A tendril of hair had fallen from her chignon and Alessandro moved it from her neck, making her shudder.

She hadn't meant to, heaven knew, she *hadn't*, but the response rippled through her all the same, visceral and consuming, and more importantly audible.

What was it about this man that made her respond this way? She never had before, not even close. Her romantic and sexual experience was basically nil, and that by her choice. Perhaps that was why she was reacting the way she was now, because she had nothing to compare it to.

And yet Mia knew it wasn't that. It was the man. The man whose sandalwood aftershave she breathed in, making her senses reel. The man who was now tugging the zipper down her back, slowly, so achingly slowly, inch by tempting, traitorous, *lovely* inch. Tug. Tug. Mia held her breath as Alessandro's breath fanned her neck, and then her bare back as the dress began to fall away, leaving her skin exposed.

The air was cool on her bared back, but Alessandro's breath was warm. Mia tensed, trying to keep herself from shuddering again, but she failed, a ripple of longing trembling over her skin and right through her. She knew Alessandro saw and heard it, felt it even.

And she felt his response in the sudden stilling of his fingers on the small of her back, the zip almost all the way undone. Still he didn't move, and Mia didn't either.

The world felt stilled, suspended; everything a hushed, held breath as they both remained where they were, *waiting*. Mia knew she should step away, just as she knew she wouldn't. Couldn't. In fact, she did the opposite, her body betraying her as she swayed slightly towards him.

Slowly, so slowly, Alessandro leaned forward. His breath fanned Mia's already heated skin as his lips brushed against the knob of her spine and he pressed a lingering kiss to the nape of her neck.

He hadn't meant to do it. Of course he hadn't. Alessandro didn't know what madness had claimed him as he leaned forward and kissed the back of Mia's neck. Everything about the moment felt exquisitely sensual, as if a honeyed drug was stealing through his veins, obliterating all rational thought, everything but this. Her.

*And he didn't even care.*

He felt Mia's instant and overwhelming response, her body shuddering again under his touch, and he moved his lips lower, kissing each knob of her spine in turn, letting his lips linger on her silky skin.

The moonlight turned her ivory skin to lambent silver; she was pale, a perfect goddess, like an ancient marble statue, the paragon of classical beauty. He continued to kiss his way down her spine, feeling Mia tremble beneath his feather-light touch. Then he reached the base of her spine and he fell to his knees, anchoring her hips with his hands, as he kissed the small of her back, a place he hadn't even considered sensual or enflaming until this moment, when it was, utterly.

'*Alessandro...*' The name was drawn from her lips in a desperate plea as the unzipped gown slid from her hips and pooled around her feet, leaving her completely bare. She started to turn and Alessandro rose, pulling her into his arms as his mouth came down hard and hungry and demanding on hers. She responded to the kiss with a frenzied passion of her own as they stumbled backward together, lips locked, hands roving greedily, until they hit Henry Dillard's desk.

Alessandro hoisted her on top of it, stepping between her thighs, as he deepened the kiss. He couldn't get enough of her. He didn't want to. All he wanted was more—more of this, and more of her.

He broke the kiss only to kiss her elsewhere, wanting to claim all her body for his own—her small, high breasts, her tiny waist, her endless legs. Mia's head fell back, her breath coming in desperate pants, as Alessandro explored every inch of her and still felt as if he hadn't had enough, a thirst and craving welling up inside him that could never be slaked.

He ran his hand from the delicate bones of her ankle up her calf, along her inner thigh, before his fingers found the heart of her and she tensed under his touch, her breath hitching as he deftly stroked her.

'Alessandro...' Another plea, and one he answered with his sure caress.

But even that wasn't enough; it wasn't enough when she surrendered entirely to his touch, her voice a broken, shuddering cry. He needed to possess her fully, to make her his own.

Still, one last shred of sanity made him hesitate. 'Mia, are you sure…?' His voice was low, ragged, but certain. He had to know that she wanted this as much as he did.

Her eyes fluttered open, the look in them both dazed and sated as she nodded, her pulse hammering in her throat. 'Yes,' she whispered. *'Yes.'*

Alessandro needed no further encouragement. He spread her thighs wider as he fumbled with his own clothes. Then seconds, but what felt like an eternity, later he thrust inside her, groaning with the pleasure of it.

Mia let out a startled gasp and Alessandro stilled, shock drenching him in icy waves. 'Mia…' He could barely believe what had just happened. 'Mia, are you…' he could barely manage to say the words '…a *virgin*?'

She let out a choked laugh, her fingernails digging into his shoulders as she anchored him in place. 'I *was*.'

Alessandro swore. 'You…' He bit off what he'd been going to say.

*You should have told me. I should have known. I never would have…*

He'd *asked*, after all. He'd asked her if she was sure. Now, his body aching and still thundering with need, he started to withdraw.

'No. *Don't.*' Mia clutched his shoulders as she wriggled into position underneath him. 'I'm all right.' She shifted again, her body opening beneath him, inviting him in further, and as Alessandro felt her welcoming warmth he knew he was a lost man. He started to move, and Mia gave a breathy sigh of pleasure as she started to match his rhythm.

The regret and uncertainty he'd felt fell away like a mist as they moved together, climbing higher and higher, until they both reached that dazzling apex, and Alessandro let out a shudder of sated pleasure as he pulled her even closer to him, her body wrapping around and enfolding his. He could feel her heart thudding against his own, and he knew he'd never been as close to another person as this.

Seconds ticked by and neither of them spoke or moved. Alessandro had the strange and unsettling feeling that he didn't *want* to move; he didn't want this to end. He had never, ever felt that way before after being with a woman.

Yet of course he had to, and so did Mia, and after another few soul-shaking seconds she started to pull away. Alessandro let her go, tidying himself up as Mia eased off the desk. Her head was bent, her face averted as she walked quickly to her clothes and pulled them on. Alessandro saw that her fingers trembled as she buttoned the now crumpled white blouse he'd admired earlier that day, in what felt like a lifetime ago.

Alessandro knew he should say something, but he had no idea what. Now that the haze of incredible pleasure was no longer clouding his mind, he was realising what an enormous, idiotic mistake he'd just made. Mia James was his PA, and he'd had her on his desk like a…like a…

*No.* He could barely believe this had happened. This *never* happened to him, because he never let it. He was too self-controlled, too contained, too certain of what he wanted, to let something as stupid as *desire* cloud his mind and guide his actions, even for a few seconds.

And yet that was precisely what had just happened. He could scarcely credit it, and yet it had. It *had*.

Mia had finished dressing and she stood there, her handbag clutched to her chest, her hair in tangles about her pale face, her eyes wide and dazed.

'I should go.' Her voice was a whisper, and guilty regret lashed him like a whip, which made him, unreasonably he knew, feel angry.

'You should have told me you were a virgin.'

Her already wide eyes widened even further, looking huge in her face. 'Would it have mattered?'

'Yes. I'm not accustomed to...' Alessandro gestured to the desk, unwilling to put it into words, furious with himself as well as with Mia. What had she been thinking? *What had he?*

'Well, obviously neither am I.' Her voice was grim, humourless. 'Let's just say the moment got the better of us, and move past it, shall we?'

He stared at her, surprised and a little discomfited that she was offering so pragmatic an approach, and the one he would have suggested but now oddly resented. Minutes before they'd been twined around each other like...but, no. He wasn't going to think about that. Mia was right. They needed to move past this—immediately.

'Yes.' His voice was tight. 'Yes, that is exactly what we shall do.'

Mia nodded, still looking grim, and Alessandro felt the need to gain control of the situation; somehow it had slipped entirely out of his hands, and he needed to come to grips with it. He needed to remind himself what kind of man he was, and it most certainly wasn't one who unzipped a woman's dress and then ended up having her over a desk in a darkened office.

Those were the actions of a man who had no self-control, no common sense, no sense of containment. They were the actions of a man who allowed lust or any other unruly emotion to control him, and that was not who he was. It couldn't be.

'Are you all right?' he asked stiffly. 'You're not...?' The question nearly brought a blush to his face. He'd never slept with a virgin before. 'You're not hurt?'

'I'm fine,' Mia said flatly. She reached for her coat and shoved her arms in. 'I just need to go home.' She made to leave and Alessandro stayed her with one hand; she flinched under his touch, which both shamed and hurt him.

'Mia, please. Don't leave like this.'

Her eyebrows rose. 'How am I supposed to leave?'

Alessandro didn't know how to answer, couldn't even determine what he wanted. For this never to have happened, he supposed, but there was nothing he could do about that. 'Take the limo,' he said at last. 'It will be safer and quicker.' She stared at him for a moment, her face like a mask, and Alessandro realised how little he was offering. *A lift.* But he didn't know what else he could give her.

'Fine,' she said, and then she shook off his arm and walked out through the door.

# CHAPTER FIVE

MIA WOKE UP to bright, wintry sunlight streaming through the window of her bedroom, her head fuzzy and full of cotton wool from the three glasses of champagne she'd had the night before, her body aching in all sorts of unexpected places.

For a single second she simply lay there, enjoying the sunshine, and then memory slammed into her, again and again, as the events of the last evening played in her mind in an unwelcome and humiliating reel.

What had she been *thinking*? During the half-hour ride in Alessandro's limo the night before, she'd been too dazed to truly consider what had happened or its potential consequences, and so she'd simply blanked her mind, stripping off her clothes and falling into bed as soon as she'd returned home, surrendering to the welcome numbness of sleep, except it hadn't claimed her.

She'd tucked her knees up to her chest and scrunched her eyes shut tight, trying to block out the memories that insisted on coming anyway, relentless and so awful. So embarrassing, so full of shame and regret, as well as pleasure and wonder.

She could hardly believe that she'd been so heedless, welcoming Alessandro's kiss, begging him to touch her... and losing her virginity on Henry Dillard's desk. How could she have let that happen? How could she have let herself be so shameless, so *weak*? What if this ruined everything?

Now, in the cold light of morning, she let out a choked sound, something between a sob and a horrified laugh, as she considered what she'd done.

Of course, it had been amazing. There was no denying or hiding from that stark truth. She'd been transported to a world of pleasure she'd never even known existed, and yet, despite that, she hated how in thrall she'd been to her own body, as well as to Alessandro's touch.

He had a hold over her that she both resented and feared, and the result was she'd lost something precious, something that had been hers, in the blazing heat of a single moment…and to a man who most likely didn't like her and intended to fire her in the foreseeable future.

Stupid, stupid, stupid. Stupid and shameful and wrong.

Slowly, still aching, Mia rolled out of bed and headed for the shower, more than ready to wash away the scent of Alessandro from her skin. She turned the water up to as hot as she could stand and let it beat down on her until her skin turned pink and then red.

She knew she needed to get out, get dressed for work, get *going*. She needed to face Alessandro, even if she dreaded it with every cell of her being. Judging from his reaction last night, he regretted their encounter as much as she did, something which was both a relief and an insult. Still, it was better for them to do their best to move past it, and pretend it had never happened…if they could.

Mia felt as if the memory of Alessandro, the strength of his body, the sureness of his touch, was emblazoned on her brain, branded into her skin. It was going to take a huge act of will even to pretend to forget it. *Him.* And yet she had to. The alternative was inconceivable.

Quickly Mia stepped out of the shower and dressed in a crisp skirt suit of navy blue with a pale grey blouse. She put her hair in a tight bun, determined to look every inch the efficient PA and not the kind of woman who had sex late at night in an empty office. Because she wasn't that person. At all.

Since she was eighteen, Mia had been focused on one thing—finding her freedom and forging a career that would give her independence and security. She'd seen how her mother had been miserably beholden to her father throughout their entire marriage, before the release of her death; she'd lived through the awful ups and downs, her father's sudden, inexplicable rages, his emotional blackmail and silent disapproval, his moods and tempers dictating the unhappy tone of their fractured home, and all the while her mother too scared and unsupported to leave.

Diana James had insisted she loved her husband, even when he'd never shown a reason to deserve that love. Mia had been desperate to escape it herself, as soon as she could. And she had vowed she would never lose her control because of a man—any man—the way her mother had. Yet last night, if just for a few moments, she had lost control, willingly, *joyfully*…and she was horrified by it.

Resolutely Mia gazed at her pale reflection in the mirror, determined to put last night behind her completely. Hopefully Alessandro would do the same, and she would return to being the useful PA he required…and nothing more.

The office seemed quiet as Mia headed up in the lift, everyone working quietly with their heads down, seeming apprehensive. Alessandro hadn't started firing people yet, and perhaps if what he'd implied last night was true, he wouldn't.

But who was the real man? The lover who had shown her a hint of vulnerability in his eyes, or the ruthless tycoon everyone said he was? Who did she want to believe in—and did it matter anyway?

At her desk, Mia let out a little sigh of relief as she looked around and didn't see Alessandro anywhere. In an ideal world, she wouldn't see him all day. She could organise the files he'd requested yesterday, and update her CV, just in case. After that, she'd just have to pretend to look busy until Alessandro issued some directives.

As it happened, Mia had barely sat down and clicked on her computer mouse before the lift doors opened and Alessandro strode onto the floor, emanating power and authority in a navy blue suit, looking freshly showered and shaven, reminding Mia of how he'd smelled. Felt.

She tensed where she sat, memories assaulting her senses, and then his steel-grey gaze clashed with hers before he nodded towards the office doors.

'Miss James...?'

Wordlessly Mia rose on rubbery legs and followed him into the office. Her heart was thudding unpleasantly as she closed the door behind her, trying to avoid looking at the desk. Last night when he'd hoisted her up on it, she remembered papers falling, the phone skittering across the polished surface with a clatter. Now, at least, everything had been neatly replaced and there was no way to tell or even guess what had happened there last night.

But Mia remembered. As much as she was trying to forget, she remembered... Alessandro's hands on her hips, her mouth pressed against his shoulder. The way she'd cried out...

Resolutely she looked away from the desk and fixed her gaze on an innocuous spot on the wall. She wasn't ready to look at Alessandro's face and see what expression resided there, derision, desire, or just remembrance. She couldn't handle any of it.

Alessandro cleared his throat. 'Last night...' he began, and then stopped.

Mia reluctantly forced herself to look at him, even

though everything in her resisted. His face was bland and closed. She couldn't tell what he was thinking, but she shivered just from the coolness in his eyes.

*Last night.* The two words did not bode well.

Somehow she forced herself to speak, even though her lips were dry, her voice a papery thread. 'Last night didn't happen.'

'While I'd like to agree with you, I can't.' Alessandro met her gaze unflinchingly. 'We didn't use birth control.'

Shock jolted through Mia at the stark realisation but she kept her gaze and voice steady as she answered. 'I'm on the pill.'

Alessandro raised his eyebrows, seeming sceptical. 'You are? Even though you were a—?'

'Yes.' She cut him off. 'It was to regulate my periods, if you must know.' Except she had, in the welter of her own emotions, forgotten to taken it that morning. And now that she thought about it, with the news of the take-over, she hadn't taken one yesterday either. It had hardly seemed important, considering her lack of a sex life, and yet now...

Mia swallowed hard. Surely skipping just two didn't matter so much? She'd take one later today, in any case. The amount of risk wasn't worth telling Alessandro about. She could not possibly handle his reaction to a potential pregnancy right now. She couldn't get her head around it herself.

'Fine,' Alessandro said. 'It's good to know a pregnancy will not be a concern.'

*A pregnancy.*

No, she really could not handle thinking about that now. And it was surely so very unlikely. 'No, it is not a concern,' she managed.

'And you do not need to worry about any possible disease,' Alessandro continued steadily, starkly. Something else Mia hadn't even considered, not remotely, although if she'd been thinking straight, she surely would have.

'That's good to know. Thank you.'

They stared at each other, the tension in the room ratcheting up with every second until it felt unbearable. 'Then there's nothing more to say,' Mia said finally, desperate to have this over, to move beyond this moment, and more importantly, beyond last night's moment. 'So, as far as both of us are concerned, last night didn't happen. We can move on as if it didn't. We need to, for the sake of…everything.' She drew herself up, determined to do just that. 'Is there anything you need from me today?'

Alessandro stared at her for a long, hard moment, a muscle ticking in his jaw. 'I'm going to write a letter to all of Dillard's clients,' he said at last. 'You can take it down and then show me a draft copy.'

Mia's heart tumbled in her chest as she felt a weird mix of relief and disappointment that she didn't want to understand. Alessandro was doing what she wanted…trying to act normal. 'Very good,' she said, and turned from the room to get her laptop.

A few minutes later Alessandro was sitting behind his desk and Mia was in front of it, the laptop opened on her knees, her fingers poised on the keyboard, as professional a look as she could manage on her face. This was going to work. She was going to make this work.

She was not going to think about how Alessandro had felt or smelled or tasted, how she'd come apart in his arms and was still desperately trying to put herself together. She wasn't. She absolutely wasn't.

And yet the memories still bombarded her as Alessandro began dictating the letter. It took all her mental power, all her energy and willpower, to focus on the words forming on the screen in front of her instead of what had happened between them last night.

*It will get better,* Mia told herself. *The memory will fade.* This was going to work.

This wasn't working.

Alessandro couldn't keep from the glaringly obvious fact as he dictated his letter to Mia. Twice he had to start over, correcting himself, because he was hopelessly distracted by the sight of her, looking as prim and proper as you please, yet still, amazingly, seeming sexy to him.

That tight topknot made him long to pluck the pins from it and run his fingers through the spill of straight, wheat-gold hair. The crisp grey blouse with the mother-of-pearl buttons seemed to be begging to be undone, button by tiny button. The crisp navy suit would look far better crumpled on the floor.

'Mr Costa?' Her voice, crisp and precise, broke into his scattered thoughts. 'You were saying…?'

'I think, considering the circumstances, you should call me Alessandro.'

Something sparked in her eyes. 'I do not wish to consider the circumstances, and I didn't think you did, either.'

'I meant,' Alessandro clarified, 'as your employer.' But he hadn't been thinking of her as his employee. Not at all.

A faint pink touched Mia's cheeks, making her look all the more delectable. Making him want her all the more. 'Of course,' she murmured, and turned towards back to her laptop, her gaze focused determinedly on the screen.

Alessandro went back to dictating the letter, but again he lost his train of thought, which infuriated him. This was *not* who he was. This was not who he could be.

'Mr… Alessandro?' Mia prompted. Again. Her eyebrows were raised, her eyes so very blue.

'Type up what you have,' Alessandro said abruptly. 'And I'll look at it then. Thank you.'

Wordlessly Mia nodded, rising from her seat in one elegantly fluid movement. Alessandro couldn't keep from watching her as she left the room, noting her long, slim legs in sheer tights, the low navy pumps. As far as he was concerned, she could have been wearing a negligee and stiletto heels. Her staid, puritanical outfit still enflamed him, and that was most definitely a problem.

The door clicked shut softly behind her, and Alessandro swivelled in his chair, too restless to get back to his work, although he certainly had plenty to do. He needed to weed through Dillard's clients and decided which ones were worth keeping. He needed to woo the clients he wanted to stay on and make sure that they did. And he needed to find positions for the employees he intended on keeping, and offer redundancy packages to the ones he didn't.

Which made him think of Mia. He'd intended on keeping her in the office for at least another week, to help smooth the transition period, but that thought felt like torture now. He could at least check on the details for her eventual transfer, to make sure it happened as easily and quickly as possible.

He was always generous with his offers, and so he would be with Mia. It made the most sense. It filled him with relief, that he could be proactive about arranging her inevitable transfer. All it would take were a few phone calls.

Alessandro felt his shoulders loosen at the thought of being free of this alarming obsession he'd developed— and over someone so unprepossessing. He'd been with women, *many* women, who were far more attractive and alluring than Mia James, with her straight hair and English schoolgirl looks. What was it about her that affected him so much, drove him to such irritating distraction?

It didn't matter. His involvement with Mia James was thankfully going to come to an end. He was just reaching for the phone to make the first call when a knock sounded on the door.

'Yes?' he barked.

'It's Miss… Mia. May I speak to you?'

After a second's hesitation he put the phone down. 'Come in.'

She slipped into the office, her blue eyes looking crystal-bright as she met his gaze, a hint of determined challenge to the tilt of her chin.

'I wanted to speak to you.'

'About?'

She angled her chin a bit higher. 'I'd like to request a transfer.'

Shock rooted him to the spot, the phone dangling from his hand. 'A what?'

'A transfer. I don't think it is prudent for us to work together. You mentioned that you found positions for your employees when possible, so I'm asking for you to find me one.' Her eyes blazed as they met his. 'Somewhere preferably not in London.'

She wanted to be shot of him, Alessandro realised dazedly. Just as he wanted to be shot of her…so why did the thought rankle so much?

'Where is this coming from?' he asked, even though he knew. Of course he knew.

'Where do you think?' she returned sharply. 'You mentioned my usefulness as your PA would only be for so long.'

'But it's not finished yet,' he returned, surprised and a bit alarmed by his own annoyance. He'd been planning this very thing, and yet absurdly he resented her suggesting it first.

'I think it is finished,' Mia answered levelly, her tone brooking no disagreement. And, despite the instinctive, gut-level reaction that he had to argue with her, even to insist that she stay, Alessandro held his tongue. Mia wanted what he wanted. Surely he wasn't so pig-headed as to re-sist simply because it was now her idea rather than his?

'There are two possibilities, actually,' he said after a moment. 'I was looking into them myself, for this very eventuality.'

'I'm sure you were,' Mia returned dryly and Alessandro had the uncomfortable feeling she'd known what he'd been thinking, and had simply pre-empted him. 'The first is as personal assistant to the CEO of the Arras Hotel Group, based in Los Angeles,' he said. 'It's a property company I acquired two years ago, running luxury hotels on Amer-ica's west coast.'

'Los Angeles…' She nodded slowly. 'And the other?'

'Personal assistant to the CEO of a tech company in Sweden. Or, if you prefer, you can take the standard re-dundancy package. You'll find I'm very generous.'

'I'm sure.'

'I'll get you the details of both positions.' He leaned down to his laptop, and a few clicks later he'd printed it all out and handed Mia the pages.

She took them calmly, scanning them with a cool com-posure that somehow rattled him.

'Both positions come with accommodation provided, and the salary is fifty percent higher than yours was here,' he felt compelled to point out.

'And I can start immediately?'

She couldn't wait to leave, could she? 'If you like. Of course, you can have some time to pack up and arrange your travel. All paid for, naturally.'

'Naturally.' She glanced at the paper again. 'I choose Los Angeles,' she said firmly, although underneath that conviction he heard a tremble to her voice that unnerved him. He almost told her that she didn't need to do this, but of course she did. If not now, then next week, or the week after that. Better for her to feel it was on her terms.

'I'm sure you'll be very happy there,' he said as equably as he could manage. 'Good luck with your move.'

She stared at him for a moment, her lips twisting and then tightening. 'I'll clear my desk, then,' she said, which made it sound as if she'd been fired.

'You don't have to do—' Alessandro began, and she gave him a piercing look.

'I think it's better this way, don't you?'

Yes, he did. Of course he did. Even if he didn't feel like it just then. 'Enjoy LA,' he said stiffly, and she gave him one last accusing look before she nodded and walked out of the room.

# CHAPTER SIX

THREE WEEKS AFTER she'd left Alessandro Costa, Dillard Investments, and her home country, Mia came home from work, unlocking the door to her sumptuous apartment in Santa Monica, one of Los Angeles' best neighbourhoods, with a tired sigh as she kicked off her heels.

Choosing to transfer workplaces had been the only way she'd known how to salvage what was left of her pride as well as her working life. She hadn't been able to stand working with Alessandro, and in any case she'd sensed that he would have her transferred or even fired if she'd waited long enough; she was no longer *useful* in the way he required. In fact, she'd become rather inconvenient. Choosing it herself first had felt like the best way to take control.

Since she'd left she'd heard through the grapevine that at least half of Dillard's employees had been made redundant with packages as generous as hers; the other half had been offered positions within Alessandro's portfolio of companies. He wasn't the ruthless tycoon she'd thought he was, at least not in that regard.

It was just in his personal relationships where he was truly ruthless. Because no matter how elegant her apartment, how cushy her job, Mia couldn't escape the feeling that Alessandro had wanted her gone, more even than she'd wanted to go. She hadn't seen him since the day she'd walked out of her office, which was how she'd wanted it—and how Alessandro had seemed to want it, as well.

Sighing, she changed out of her work clothes into more comfy ones, anticipating another evening in front of the TV. She'd been invited out for drinks with some of her colleagues, but for the last few days Mia had been feeling a bit off, tired and nauseous. She hoped she wasn't coming down with the stomach flu, and decided that a good night's sleep, not to mention a healthy dose of Netflix, would knock whatever she was fighting off on its head.

The next morning she woke up with her stomach roiling, and she barely made it to the toilet in time before it emptied its contents. She called in sick, although by the afternoon she was feeling better again. When the same thing happened the next day, and then the next day after that, realisation sliced through her, as sharp as a knife, and just as shockingly painful, even though she'd known all along it had been an admittedly small risk.

She hadn't had a period since she'd come to Los Angeles. Sick in the mornings, better in the afternoons, and so, so tired. She might have been a virgin, but she wasn't completely naïve.

She'd missed two birth control pills, and even though she'd taken one later that day, Mia had read online that she'd opened herself up to a small risk of becoming pregnant. And a small risk was still a risk.

Yet even so, she had trouble believing it.

*One night. Two pills. Surely not...*

Her heart turned over, an unpleasant sensation, as realisation trickled icily through her.

*She couldn't be...*

After work that day she went to the nearest pharmacy to buy a pregnancy test, flushing in embarrassment as she paid for it, even though the pimply-faced teenaged boy ringing up her purchase looked completely bored and indifferent.

She took it home, unwrapping it with shaking fingers, staring at the slim white stick in disbelief that she was holding such a thing, needing it.

*She couldn't be...*

She read the directions twice through, still in a haze of incredulity, and then she took the test, all the while telling herself this was crazy, impossible, nothing more than a needless precaution. The chances of falling pregnant after one time, and just two missed pills...

But she wasn't stupid. She knew it could happen. She just couldn't believe it could happen to her.

And then she turned the test over and stared down at the two blazing pink lines in disbelief.

She couldn't be, but she was.

She spent an hour simply sitting on her sofa, staring into space, having no idea what to think, much less to do. Her mind felt fogged with incredulity, unable to think beyond the reality of those two lines. She couldn't yet consider what they meant or would mean, or how she would respond to them.

Then, at some point, she roused herself from her stupor and made herself a cup of tea. Pregnant. She was pregnant. By Alessandro Costa, a man she barely knew and definitely didn't like, a man known to be ruthless in both personal relationships and the business world. And he was going to be the father of her child.

Realisation slammed into her with that thought; this was her *child*. The family she'd never truly had. And she knew, no matter how inconvenient or unexpected, she was going to keep this baby, this child of her flesh and blood.

And Alessandro's.

Armed with a cup of milky tea, Mia flipped open her laptop and did another internet search on Alessandro. She had deliberately not searched anything personal about him before. She hadn't wanted to know, or to wonder.

Now she blinked as image after image came up on the screen of her laptop of Alessandro. The sight of his commanding profile, those steely eyes, that impressive form… it all battered her senses, made her remember far too many things. The lingering way he'd undone her zip. The press of his lips to the base of her spine…the sudden frenzy of passion they'd both felt, obliterating all thought and reason for those few crucial moments.

As she clicked through the photos, she noticed a common feature, and her expression hardened. In nearly every image, Alessandro was with a woman. A different woman. Over the last month he'd attended a variety of glittering events, in London, in Paris, in Rome, always with a sexy, pouting woman, and usually one who was poured into a dress, on his arm. Clearly he'd completely forgotten about her.

She pushed the laptop away and took a sip of her tea, feeling sick in a way that had nothing to do with the tiny being she nurtured in her womb. That man—that ruthless, arrogant, philandering man—was her baby's father. And she knew she would have to tell him so.

She shuddered with dread at the thought of Alessandro's reaction. Disbelief? Displeasure? He was not going to be pleased, of that Mia was completely certain. And, judging by the way he handled hostile takeovers, he was going to expect Mia to fall in with his plans, whatever they would be.

And what *would* they be? Would he want to, heaven forbid, get rid of their child, considering him or her an inconvenience he couldn't abide? Or would he throw money at her, to make her go away? She knew he would want to do something, but she had no idea what it would be.

And what did *she* want? Never to see Alessandro Costa

again, preferably. Perhaps he wanted the same thing. Hopefully they could come to an agreement, even if this wasn't a scenario either of them had envisioned or wanted.

Of course, she had to get in touch with him first, and Mia didn't really know how to do that. She'd never had his personal information and she certainly wasn't going to find it online. The best she could hope for was to call the headquarters of Costa International and hope the message was passed on. After that…it was surely up to him. The thought comforted her. All she could do was try, surely.

The next morning, Mia made the call to Costa International in Rome, and got the switchboard.

'I'd like to speak to Alessandro Costa, please.' She tried to make her voice sound confident and firm, and had a feeling she failed.

'I'm afraid he's not available.'

'This is important and personal. Is there another number on which I could reach him?'

'I'm afraid not.'

Mia bit her lip, fighting both frustration and a treacherous relief. *She'd tried…* 'Then may I leave a message?' she asked, and the receptionist's voice was toneless as she answered.

'Of course.'

'And can I be sure it will get to him?' Mia pressed, determined to make a good effort. 'It's important.'

'Of course.'

She left her name and number. 'Please do give him the message,' she said, knowing she was probably annoying the receptionist but needing, as a matter of principle, to communicate the urgency of the matter. 'It's important.'

'He'll get the message,' the receptionist assured her in a bored voice, and then disconnected the call.

Mia sat back, feeling the tiniest bit relieved. She'd made

the effort. She'd tried to be in touch. If Alessandro didn't get the message…

Guilt needled her at the thought. She knew she could ask her boss for his personal details, although whether he'd be willing to give them out, she didn't know. Still, she supposed she could try harder.

But the grim truth was, she didn't want to. She knew what it was like to be controlled by a man, someone who dictated what she wore and ate and did. Her father had done all of the above, simply because he could. Mia had lost track of the times he'd insisted she change her clothes, or told her she couldn't go out, or insisted the dinner her mother had made was inedible when it had been fine. Her entire childhood had been one of barely endured oppression, and she could not bear the thought of opening herself up to that again.

Alessandro might not be as odiously domineering as her father, but already in their short relationship he'd told her what to do, what to wear, where to go. It was obvious to Mia that he was someone who liked being in control, not just of his employees, but everyone in his life. And she could not let him be in control of her, or her child. Not like that.

She'd *tried*. She'd left a message, she'd said it was important. And that, Mia told herself, pushing away the guilt that still pricked her, was all she could do.

*A year later*

He hadn't meant to look her up. He'd excised her from his mind and memory, or done his very best to, even if some nights he still woke up with dreams of her lingering in his mind like an enticing mist, making him remember. Making him want.

In his waking hours, he thought of her not at all, an act

of sheer, determined will, and yet, a year later, as he returned to the office of Dillard Investments that he'd done his best to avoid for the last twelve months, he realised some part of him had been thinking of her all along.

Alessandro had worked hard this last year to incorporate Dillard's clients and assets into his ever-increasing portfolio. He hadn't been back to London in all that time, but now, with another recent British acquisition under his belt, he had needed to return to the former office of Dillard Investments, now part of Costa International.

As he strode through Henry Dillard's old office he tried not to look at *that* desk. Yet even when he was determinedly not looking at it, he was remembering. Remembering Mia's innocent and yet overwhelming response, the way her body had clasped his in complete embrace and surrender. The dazed look in her eyes afterwards, the way her fingers had fumbled as she'd buttoned her blouse. And the next day, when she'd asked for a transfer before he'd been able to order it himself.

A year on, Alessandro could reluctantly acknowledge that perhaps he should have taken a bit more care with Mia's rather abrupt transfer. And now she was on the other side of the world, admittedly by her own choice, but he hadn't even checked whether she'd settled in or was enjoying her job.

It would be the right thing, Alessandro mused, to check on her, just to see how she was doing, that she was enjoying Los Angles and her position with the Arras Hotel Group.

He wouldn't have to talk to her; she wouldn't even have to know. He could ask Eric Foster, the CEO of the Arras Group, a man he'd put in place to run the half-dozen exclusive hotels located on the west coast of America that he'd taken over five years ago. This was nothing more than a courtesy call, a way to clear his conscience…if it needed clearing in the first place.

And yet, as he dialled the number, he felt his heart rate quicken. What if he was put through to Mia herself? What if she was happy to hear from him?

As if, on both counts. He was a fool for thinking it, for wanting it even a little.

'Mia James?' Foster sounded surprised when Alessandro mentioned her. 'She was working out wonderfully, of course. I knew she would, if you'd recommended her.'

'Was?' Alessandro frowned, a sense of unease clenching his gut. 'Isn't she still working for you?'

'Not at the moment.' Taylor let out a little laugh that Alessandro didn't understand. 'She stopped about three months ago, but she's expecting to be back this summer, no pun intended.' He let out another laugh, and Alessandro's frown deepened, his body tensing.

*No pun...?* What was that supposed to mean? 'Has something happened to make her take such a leave of absence?'

'Has something happened?' Taylor repeated, sounding surprised. 'I guess you don't know...no reason why you would, although I thought she was a personal friend of yours...'

'Know what?' Alessandro demanded, brushing the man's other words aside. He was not about to explain his relationship, or lack of it, to Mia James in any detail whatsoever.

'Sorry, sorry. She's on maternity leave. She had a baby three months ago. A little girl.'

For a second Alessandro couldn't speak. Couldn't think. He felt as if his brain were short-circuiting, misfiring. *A baby.* A baby three months ago...nine months after their night together.

It was impossible. *Impossible.* She'd been on the pill. She would have told him. Surely, no matter what had or hadn't happened between them, she would have told him. *It couldn't be...*

'Right, I must have forgotten that.' His voice, attempting joviality, sounded forced. 'Of course.'

'I hope she comes back,' Taylor said. 'She's a good PA. The best I've ever had.'

'Yes.' Alessandro's mind felt as if it was buzzing, full of static and white noise. He could not form a single coherent thought. 'Yes,' he said again, and then he disconnected the call. He flung the phone across his desk, glad when it clattered noisily across the surface. He half wished it would break, that something would, because he realised he was furious.

*Furious*, because Mia James might have had his baby and not even told him. Not *ever* told him. His fists clenched as his blood pumped through his body in hectic, vengeful thuds. How dared she? *How dared she?* To not tell him something so critical, so utterly important... To deprive him of knowing his own child...

Unless it wasn't his child?

*A little girl.* His mind raced as he paced the confines of the room like something caged. Could it be another man's? Yet she'd been a virgin, no other men in the picture as far as he knew, but of course he *didn't* know...anything. And yet he couldn't believe Mia would have gone with another man so soon after. Surely it was his. Surely...

There was only one way to find out.

He took his private jet to Los Angeles that night, cancelling half a dozen meetings without a word of explanation. The flight felt endless, his mind going in pointless circles as he considered what he would say to Mia.

If it was his child, his daughter, then he knew what he wanted, and he knew he'd do anything, *anything*, to see it happen. He'd grown up without a father, and it had tormented him for all his childhood. He would never, ever allow a child of his to experience that same sense of loss, confusion, and grief. He'd never walk away from his own flesh and blood the way his father had, without a single thought or care.

But perhaps the baby wasn't his. A thought that, irrationally, gave him a little lurch of disappointment, even as he recognised that his treatment of Mia had been less than admirable. Could he really blame her if she'd met someone else and forgotten him?

A limo picked him up at the airport and drove him to the address of Mia's apartment that he'd had on file. It was a beautiful, balmy evening, the sun setting over the ocean, its placid surface shimmering with crimson and gold, palm trees silhouetted against a darkening sky.

The apartment building where Mia lived was a two-storey stucco house with an apartment on each floor and a pool in the back. Hers was on the second floor, and he mounted the steps with grim determination. Rapped once, short and hard. Waited.

A few seconds later he heard light footsteps, and then the slip of a chain before the door opened. Mia stood there, the questioning smile on her face morphing into an expression of complete and utter shock.

'Alessandro…' His name came out in a whisper.

'You should have told me.' The words came out before he could stop them.

Her face paled and one hand fluttered to her throat. 'How did you…?'

'So it is mine?' he interjected grimly, and her eyes sparked.

'It is a she, which you probably already know, considering you're here.'

'Yes, I do.' He'd forgotten her fire, and how it annoyed and impressed him in equal measure. 'Are you going to let me in?'

Wordlessly she stepped aside, closing the door behind him. Alessandro looked around the room, noting its bland corporate furnishings softened by familial touches—a co-lourful mat and baby's activity gym on the floor, a pink bouncy seat in one corner, a wicker basket of bright toys by the coffee table.

He turned to Mia, taking in how she had changed. Her hair was pulled back loosely, golden tendrils framing a rounder, softer face. Her figure was rounder and softer too, more womanly. She was dressed in a tunic top and capris, casual clothes he realised he'd never seen her in. Of course, he'd barely seen her at all. He'd known her for two days. Two short, incredible, life-changing days.

Neither of them spoke; she regarded him nervously, wiping her palms down the sides of her flowing top.

'Where is she?' he demanded.

'Sleeping in her nursery. Alessandro…'

'You should have told me.' He couldn't get past that. 'No matter what did or didn't happen between us, you should have told me.' He shook his head. 'I can't forgive that, Mia.'

'You can't *forgive*?' Her nervousness fell away as she stared at him incredulously. 'You have some cheek, Alessandro Costa.'

Now he was glaring as well, both of them with daggers drawn, only moments into their meeting. 'What is that supposed to mean?'

'What makes you think I didn't try to tell you?' She planted her hands on her hips, her eyes furious slits of bright, bright blue. 'Why do you *assume*?'

He shook his head slowly. He wasn't buying that. 'If you'd tried, I would have known.'

'Oh, really? You, the head of a huge, sprawling multi-billion-dollar organisation? You think a message from a nobody PA would have been passed on?'

He frowned. 'So how did you try to reach me?'

'The only way I knew how,' she snapped. 'Through the switchboard of Costa International.'

His frown deepened, but he still couldn't concede the point. 'There must have been a better way…'

'And what way would that have been?' Mia challenged. Now she was the one who sounded angry and aggrieved, the one who was in the right, and yet Alessandro felt she couldn't be. *She couldn't be.* 'You didn't exactly want to keep in touch, did you? I didn't have any of your contact details, and I was under the distinct impression you never wanted to lay eyes on me again. Which was fine by me, because I didn't want to lay eyes on you.'

Which, absurdly, stung, even though he knew it shouldn't have. It wasn't as if they'd had a relationship, or even been friends. 'A baby changes things, obviously,' he snapped. 'A baby changes everything.'

# CHAPTER SEVEN

MIA STARED AT ALESSANDRO, a feeling of dread surging along with the anger that had been her instinctive response, even though she knew he had a point. For the last year she'd been fighting a sense of guilt over the fact that she hadn't tried harder to tell him, but she'd always justified it to herself, telling herself at least she had tried to give him a message, and in any case he wouldn't have cared anyway. Presumptions, she realised now, that were utterly wrong, because Alessandro looked as if he cared very much indeed.

Now he was standing there in front of her, she felt overwhelmed by the sheer presence of him, too dazed to hold on to a single coherent thought. When she'd seen him at her door, she'd felt the blood rush from her head, and she'd had to clutch the doorframe to keep herself upright.

She'd never thought she'd see Alessandro again. She'd convinced herself that he would never find out, that he'd never look for her, that he'd never care. Clearly she'd been wrong.

Several times she'd wondered about making more of an effort to let him know he was going to be a father, but she'd never felt brave enough, and as the months had gone on and on it had felt harder and harder to do.

Once Ella had been born, she'd been too tired and overwhelmed to think about Alessandro at all, much less worry about him.

But now he was here, looking furious and wronged, and she had no idea what to do about it. After everything she'd been through—terrible morning sickness, a difficult labour and delivery, and Ella's colicky start to life—she didn't think she could handle Alessandro's outrage on top of it.

'I'm sorry,' she said as she did her best to stand her ground and meet his stony gaze. 'But I did try to reach you.'

'So what are you saying?' Alessandro demanded. 'You left a message with the switchboard saying you were having my baby?' He sounded scathing.

'No, of course not,' Mia answered with dignity. 'I would never be so indiscreet, especially concerning a matter so personal to both of us. I simply said it was urgent and very important that you receive my message, and I asked you to return my call. Which you never did.'

'Because I never got the message!' Alessandro exploded. 'As you very well should have been able to guess.'

Mia drew a steadying breath. 'That is not my fault, Alessandro.'

'No?' Alessandro shook his head slowly. 'Surely there were other ways, Mia. You could have told your boss, Eric Foster. He has my details. You could have got them from him, and contacted me directly.'

Mia looked away, knowing she could have done exactly that. Guilt needled her again, sharp, painful pricks. 'To be honest, Alessandro, I didn't think you'd care.'

The silence that met this statement was thunderous. Alessandro stared at her, his mouth open, his eyes flinty, before he folded his arms across his impressive chest and raked her with a single, scathing glare. 'You didn't *think*? Or you didn't want to know? You hid my own child from me—'

'Yes, I did,' Mia cried. 'I felt I had to.'

'Why?'

'Because…because I was scared.' She hated admitting it, but she didn't know what else to do.

'What were you scared of?'

'You. Sweeping into my life, making demands.'

'Like seeing my own child? Is that such an outrageous demand?'

'I was afraid you might ask for something else,' Mia admitted in a low voice. Alessandro's eyes narrowed to deadly slits.

'Ask for something else…?'

'A termination,' she admitted, unable to look at him as she said it. 'You didn't seem thrilled about a potential pregnancy when you mentioned it to me…' She trailed off, because the absolutely outraged look on Alessandro's face kept her from any speech or thought. She shrank beneath his anger, hating that she was doing so.

She'd promised herself never to cower or cringe, and yet here she was, doing both.

'A termination,' Alessandro said, and then swore. 'How dare you make such decisions for me?'

It seemed a strange twist of irony that in trying not to be controlled, she had come across as controlling. Mia sank onto the sofa, overwhelmed by Alessandro's anger, by the way everything had been turned upside down.

'I'm sorry,' she said in a low voice. 'I see now that I shouldn't have. You just seemed so alarmed by the possibility of a pregnancy…'

'And you assured me you couldn't be pregnant! You were on the pill.'

'I was, but I missed two, because of…well, because of everything.'

'And you didn't think to tell me that? To alert me to the possibility?'

'It seemed such a tiny risk…'

'Obviously not.' He wheeled away from her, his anger making him need to move. 'You made decisions you had no right to make.'

'I thought I was doing what was best. And it isn't as if you were checking up or even thinking of me all year, were you?' she flung at him, tired of being on the defensive. 'I did an internet search on you, you know. And I have to tell you, Alessandro, what I saw made me less inclined to search you out.'

Alessandro turned back to her, his powerful body taut and still. 'What you *saw*?'

'It looked like you were with a different woman every night.' Mia lifted her chin. 'Supermodels and socialites, by the look of them. Your bedroom must have a revolving door.'

'You almost sound jealous,' Alessandro remarked in a low, dangerous tone.

'Hardly,' Mia scoffed. 'But from what I saw, you didn't seem like father material.' As soon as she said the words, she knew she'd gone too far. Something dark and deadly thrummed through Alessandro, tautening his body, flaring in his eyes.

'You are not in a position to judge my parenting skills,' he said in a voice that was all the more frightening in its quiet intensity. 'That was not your right, just as it was not your right to keep this information—and my own child—from me.' Mia opened her mouth, trying to frame a response that was not quite an apology, but Alessandro cut across her before she'd barely drawn a breath. 'In any case, whatever you saw online…those were nothing more than social engagements.'

'Are you saying it never went further?' she scoffed. 'I have trouble believing—'

'I'm not saying one thing or the other,' Alessandro replied, his voice rising, edged with ire. 'It has no relevance. We weren't a couple. *I didn't know.*' He took a step towards her, menacing in his stature, his pure physical presence. Mia held her ground, but only just. 'No matter what photos you saw of me online, you should have told me I was going to be a father. *End of.*'

'Fine.' Her voice quavered as her hands once more bunched into helpless fists at her sides. 'Fine, I should have. I admit that. But…can't you admit your part in this? Getting rid of me the day after…' Her voice trembled and broke. 'The very next day, Alessandro. Can't you realise how that made me feel?'

Colour slashed his cheekbones as he jerked his head in a brief nod. 'It would have happened eventually, but I admit, our…liaison precipitated it. I thought working together would be a distraction. Perhaps I shouldn't have been quite so…abrupt.'

'So that was you making a unilateral decision,' Mia returned, her voice shaking, 'while calling me to account for doing the same.'

'They're entirely different situations, Mia. A job versus a baby. You cannot compare,' Alessandro fired back, taking another step towards her so they were nearly standing toe to toe. Mia felt exhausted by his anger; her daughter was three months old, she'd been going it alone the entire time, and she was hormonal and sleep deprived and very near tears. Still, she took a steadying breath and met his furious, narrowed gaze with a challenging one of her own.

'I'm not comparing, I'm only asking you to understand where I was coming from.'

'I can't understand at all where you're coming from,' he snapped. 'What you did was inexcusable—'

'Did you come here to blame me, Alessandro, for everything? Because I get it. This is all my fault. Message received. Now you can go home.' Her voice trembled and tears she was desperate for him not to see stung her eyes. She turned away from him, too tired to keep battling.

She flopped onto the sofa, tucking her knees up to her chest. She'd just put Ella down for a nap and she'd been hoping for a little sleep herself. Clearly that was now an impossibility, which alone was enough to make her cry.

'I'm not going home.' Alessandro came to sit on the sofa opposite her, his hands resting on his knees. He gave her a level look that Mia could barely summon the energy to return.

'What do you want, then?' she asked tiredly, only to realise how open and dangerous that question was.

Now that she could think about it all properly, the shock of seeing him finally starting to fade, she realised he'd flown a long way for nothing more than a confrontation. He couldn't have come simply for that. He had to want more. A lot more. But what?

'I want my daughter,' Alessandro stated simply, the words icing the blood in her veins and freezing her soul. She stared at him, as trapped as an animal in a snare, as his iron-hard gaze slammed into hers. 'And I'm not leaving without her.'

Alessandro hadn't meant the words as a threat, but he recognised that they sounded like one. He saw it in the flare of Mia's eyes, the pulse that beat in her throat, as her hand crept up to press against her chest as if to still her fast-thudding heart. No, it wasn't a threat. It was a promise.

'Alessandro, be reasonable...'

'Reasonable? What is reasonable about having my child hidden from me for three months—?'

'I didn't *hide*.' Her voice trembled but he still heard a note of quiet dignity in it that struck an emotional chord within him. 'Please, Alessandro, for...for our daughter's sake, can we not play the blame game? Surely we can reach some kind of…of arrangement…'

An *arrangement*?

Was she hoping to fob him off with some half-baked idea of shared custody, parental visitations? 'The only arrangement I'm interested in,' Alessandro told her curtly, 'is to take my daughter back to where she belongs.'

Mia's eyes looked huge and dark in her face. 'Which is where?'

'Home. My villa in Tuscany. It is the perfect place to raise a child.' As he said the words, he knew how much he meant them. His daughter would not have the kind of chaotic, unstable childhood he'd had, filled with strangers and strange places. She would have every need provided for, emotional *and* physical. And that required a home, with two parents fully involved in her life. He would not negotiate on any of those points, as a matter of principle and honour.

Mia pressed her lips together; Alessandro saw the sheen of tears in her eyes, giving them a luminous quality. 'And what are you expecting me to do? Just…just hand her over?'

It took Alessandro a moment to realise what she thought, what she'd assumed—that he would take their daughter, and leave her here. Did she really think him such a monster? Had she thought he'd been threatening *that*? He felt both hurt and shamed by the idea.

'No, of course not. I would never ask or expect such a thing. A child belongs with her mother as well as her father, especially one as young as ours.' *Ours.* A ripple of shock went through him at the thought; he had a *child*. They did. He still couldn't grasp it fully, the implications crashing over him in endless waves.

'Then…' Mia's worried gaze scanned his face. 'You

want me to go with you?' She sounded as if she could scarcely credit such a possibility.

'Yes, of course I do.' It had been obvious to Alessandro from the beginning, considering his own unfortunate background, and one he would never, ever wish on a child of his own. A child belonged with his or her parents. Always.

He could see now from Mia's stunned expression that she had not considered that. No wonder she'd been so hostile; she thought he'd been going to *steal* their child, as if he'd ever do such a despicable thing.

Mia shook her head slowly. 'Go with you…to Tuscany?' she clarified, as if she still couldn't believe it.

'Yes.'

'But…' Mia continued to shake her head, as if she could not imagine such a thing coming to pass.

'There is surely nothing keeping you here,' Alessandro observed. 'You've only lived here a year.'

'As you know so well,' she returned.

'So I fail to see any problem.'

'You just expect me to—to *uproot* myself yet again…'

'For our child.' As if on cue, a faint cry sounded through the flat, making them both still and stare at each other. The moment spun on, both of them frozen, and then she cried again. *His daughter.* 'Where…where is she…?' Alessandro began, barely able to form the words.

Wordlessly Mia rose from the sofa and went down the hallway to the flat's bedrooms. Alessandro followed, his heart starting to thud. *His daughter.*

'Hello, darling.' Mia's voice had softened into an unfamiliar coo as she opened the door to a small bedroom decked out in pale grey and mint green. Alessandro stood in the doorway, transfixed, as Mia went to the cot and bent over it, then scooped up the tiny form that had been inside.

She turned to Alessandro, the baby pressed to her shoulder, one hand cradling her head possessively. She was *tiny*, a mere scrap of humanity, and so very precious, bundled in a white velveteen sleepsuit.

'This is Ella.' Mia's voice trembled. 'Do you…do you want to hold her?'

*Hold her?*

Alarm warred with a deep longing. Alessandro stared at her for a moment, speechless and uncertain for what felt like the first time in his life.

Did he want to hold her? *Yes.*

Was he terrified? *Yes.*

He nodded, not trusting himself to speak, not sure what to do. How did one hold a baby? He had no idea. He had never held one before.

Mia walked towards him, still cradling their daughter. *Ella.* She came to stand in front of him, close enough that Alessandro was able to breathe in her achingly familiar scent of understated citrus. It assaulted his senses and made him remember far too many things.

'Hold your arms out,' Mia instructed, and Alessandro thrust both arms out stiffly in front of him. 'Not like that,' she said with a small smile, a surprising and strangely gratifying trace of laughter in her voice.

'How?' Alessandro demanded. 'I don't know what to do.' This was a vulnerability he couldn't hide. Knowledge he had never possessed.

'Like this.' Gently, holding Ella with one arm, she guided Alessandro's own, manipulating his limbs as if he were a mannequin, until one arm was bent as if to cradle a football, the other arm to support it. 'Now we just add the baby,' she said softly, and before he knew what she was doing, she put Ella into his arms.

He cradled her to him instinctively, pressing her tiny body gently against his chest as she snuffled into his neck. He breathed in the sweet, milky warmth of her as his heart contracted, expanded, and contracted again. He *felt*. It hurt.

'That's the way,' Mia encouraged him. 'You've got the hang of it now.'

He felt like a complete novice, inexperienced, incapable, and if he were holding the most fragile and yet explosive thing possible—a cross between a stick of dynamite and a Ming vase.

'I don't want to hurt her,' he confessed, undone by this child in his arms, this fragile, precious, *impossible* human being.

'You aren't hurting her,' Mia assured him. Tears sparkled in her eyes and she blinked them back rapidly. 'Trust me, she would let you know if you were.'

'Does she cry? Is she…is she a good baby?' He realised how much he wanted to know—all the details, all he'd missed. It didn't matter now that he'd missed them or why he had, he just wanted to *know*.

'She's a wonderful baby, but she's had her moments.' The smile Mia gave him was weary, and he suddenly noticed how tired she looked. Realised how hard it must have been, to parent alone all these months…which was all the more reason for her to come to Tuscany with him, where she could have help, and comfort, and space.

'You'll come to Tuscany,' he said, and it sounded like an order. Mia's gentle, tired smile faltered as a familiar fire sparked in her eyes.

'Alessandro, you can't order me about…'

'You'll come,' he insisted. 'And Ella, too. You must.' His voice was too strident, his manner too abrupt and autocratic. He knew that, and yet he couldn't keep himself from it, because it was so very important. It was everything.

He saw the remoteness enter Mia's eyes, felt her coolness as she took Ella out of his arms, pressing her against her shoulder as she half turned away from him.

'She needs a feed,' she murmured, but it felt like an

excuse. She slipped past him and went back to the main living area, leaving Alessandro no choice but to follow.

When he came into the room, Mia was sitting back on the sofa, Ella brought to her breast, one tiny fist clutching a tendril of golden hair. Shock jolted through him at the sight of her feeding their daughter, the simple, pure *rightness* of it, followed by a rush of primal possessiveness that nearly felled him with its intensity, its sureness.

This was his *family*. The family he'd never had himself, the family he hadn't even realised he wanted. And he was never letting them go.

# CHAPTER EIGHT

MIA WATCHED THE streets of Los Angeles stream by in a colourful blur as the limousine Alessandro had called for her sped towards his luxury hotel in the downtown area of the city. After leaving abruptly the day before, when Mia had begun feeding Ella, he'd commanded she come to where he was staying to discuss their future arrangements...whatever those might be.

Mia had spent a sleepless night, wide-eyed and worried, trying to decide how she was going to respond to Alessandro's suggestion that she move to Tuscany with Ella. Everything in her resisted that notion, and particularly the high-handed manner in which he'd delivered it, as if he expected her to fall in with his plans without so much as a whisper of dissent.

She did not want to be controlled by him, and yet she feared she had no choice. Just like with her father, Alessandro was calling the shots. Just like her father, he had all the power, all the money, all the cards. It had taken years from Mia to break free from her father. She desperately wanted to have the strength to break free from Alessandro now, even as she recognised that Alessandro was a different man from her father, and she'd sensed a kindness beneath his hard exterior that made her want to trust him.

Still, it wasn't enough to move continents for, surely.

And yet... Ella. She couldn't deny Alessandro the right

to see his daughter. After witnessing him holding Ella, the obvious love in his eyes, surprising and powerful, she didn't even want to. So where did that leave her? *Them?*

In the car seat next to her, Ella stirred, blinking wide blue-grey eyes at the world, her thumb finding its way to her mouth, a new discovery. Mia gazed down at her infant daughter, her heart squeezing painfully with love. She hadn't realised just how strong that mother instinct would be, how that natural love would rush in, from the moment she'd felt Ella's first kick. The need to provide, protect, and nurture felt like an unstoppable force. It would make her strong enough to fight this battle with Alessandro…and win. She couldn't contemplate the alternative.

The limo pulled up to a tall, elegant skyscraper, and a white-gloved valet came to open her door. Mia unbuckled Ella's car seat and heaved it out, straightening her tunic top that she'd paired with loose trousers. Three months postpartum, she was still working off the baby weight, something that made her feel self-conscious when she was in Alessandro's hard, honed presence.

Inside the hotel's large and opulent lobby, all marble and crystal, a staff member met her at the door, clearly watching and waiting for her.

'Mr Costa is waiting for you in the penthouse suite,' she informed her crisply, and Mia followed her into a glassed-in lift that soared upwards, her hands slippery on the car seat handle. She wished he hadn't asked—or, rather, commanded—that she come here, to this glamorous place, clearly his turf. It put her at a disadvantage for the battle she knew was coming, and she suspected Alessandro had arranged it for exactly that reason. Still, she would do her best to stand her ground and make her case.

The lift doors opened directly into the penthouse suite, a soaring, open space with floor-to-ceiling windows on every side. As Mia stepped out onto the white marble floor, she felt as if she were flying—or falling. The sight of the city far below all around her made her feel dizzy.

'Mia.' Alessandro's voice was a low, steady thrum as he stepped forward and took the car seat from her, smiling down at a now sleeping Ella. Mia relinquished it unthinkingly as she took a few steadying breaths to combat the sudden feeling of vertigo.

Alessandro looked devastatingly handsome, as usual, in a crisp grey suit with a cobalt-blue button-down shirt and a silver-grey tie. He smelled amazing, too, the same sandalwood aftershave that Mia remembered all too well assaulting her senses and reawakening her memories.

'Would you like a drink?' he asked politely. 'Coffee? Tea? Juice?'

'Just water, please.' On shaky legs she walked to one of the white leather sofas scattered around and sat down. 'This place is amazing.' She glanced around the huge space, noting the king-sized bed, the sunken marble tub, the glittering kitchen with top-notch appliances, all of it open plan, the different areas separated by elegant shelving and tall potted plants.

'The view sold me on it,' Alessandro said as he fetched her a glass of water. 'I wasn't sure about the open plan, but the architect insisted it was the way to go.' He handed her a glass, which Mia took with murmured thanks before sitting opposite her, one leg crossed neatly over the other as he sipped his coffee. Ella sat between them in her car seat, fast asleep.

'So,' Alessandro said, his opening gambit. 'I've arranged a flight to Rome for this evening.'

'What?' Mia nearly dropped her glass, and her surprised squawk made Ella stir in her seat before she settled back to sleep.

'Is that so surprising? I told you what I intended last

night. Why should either of us linger? There's nothing for you here, Mia.'

'How would you even know that?' she demanded. She'd known Alessandro would have a plan, and even that he would insist on it, but she hadn't realised he would enact it so quickly, and without even telling her. It made her furious—and it also made her scared. He had so much more power and money than she did. His will felt like a force of nature. How could she fight it?

'You more or less admitted it yesterday,' he answered evenly. 'You've only been here for a year, and you weren't sure about coming here in the first place. Why stay?'

She'd stayed because it had been worth it financially, and she had no job waiting for her back in London or anywhere else. What friends she'd made in London she'd lost touch with over the last year, and none of them were in a position to help her as a single mother anyway.

She'd been stuck, and Alessandro was right when he said there was nothing keeping her in California, but... that didn't mean she wanted to go to Tuscany with him.

'I'm not committed to LA, it's true,' she said carefully. 'Although I've enjoyed my job here, and I was—*am*—intending to return to it in a few months. But that doesn't mean I want to live in Italy. I don't even know the language, Alessandro.'

He shrugged, dismissive. 'You'll learn. And there's no reason for you to return to work when I will be providing for you.'

'I like working—'

'Then perhaps you can return to it when Ella is a bit older.'

Although she greatly disliked his high-handed manner, Mia wasn't willing to fight that particular battle along with all the others. The truth was, she'd rather stay with Ella when she was so little. But she still didn't want to go to Italy.

'I think we both need to compromise,' Mia said, trying not to sound desperate. 'What if I returned to London? You go there fairly often for business. You could see Ella regularly…' She trailed off at the dark look developing on Alessandro's face, like a storm front coming in, of towering black clouds.

'*That's* your compromise? I see my daughter once a month, if that?'

'Surely you come to London more often than that,' Mia protested. 'To check on Dillard's…'

'Dillard's has been assimilated into Costa International, as I told you it would be. I come to London once or twice a year at most.'

And for that he'd needed to put her on the other side of the world? It was not a point Mia could afford to make now. 'But it's not that far,' she insisted, trying her best to hold on to the plan she'd come up with last night—her in London, living in familiar surroundings with some friends around, and Alessandro safely in Italy or wherever else he travelled, coming by once in a while. She could live with that. Just about.

'Not *far*?' Alessandro's eyebrows rose in incredulity before drawing together in what could only be anger. Mia tried not to shrink back in her seat. 'It's a four-hour plane ride, Mia. How often do you think I want to see my daughter? How much do you think I wanted to be involved in her life?'

She shook her head slowly, afraid to hear his answer. 'I… I don't know.'

'Then I'll tell you. Completely. I want to see her every *day*. Morning and night and even afternoon. I will not have my child growing up without a father in her life. I know what that's like and I will not allow it for Ella, especially when her father wants to be involved.'

*He knew what that was like?*

The terse statement made Mia realise there were depths

of feeling and conviction to Alessandro's stance that she hadn't anticipated. Hadn't remotely begun to guess. 'So what exactly are you suggesting?' she asked faintly.

'You and Ella live at my villa in Tuscany. It is comfortable, in the country, the perfect place to raise a child. I will live there as well, and commute to Rome or wherever else as needed.'

'So…we'd live together?' She hadn't expected that, somehow. She'd anticipated him tucking her away, controlling her as her father had her mother. But now it almost sounded as if he expected them to play at happy families, something she really could not envision, and she doubted Alessandro had thought it through entirely.

Alessandro's frown deepened. 'Of course we'd live together.' He made it sound as if she'd asked something so obvious as to be absurd.

Mia shook her head slowly. 'That's not a given, Alessandro. I mean…we don't even know each other.'

'We have a baby together.'

'Yes, but…we're strangers.' It hurt to say it, because she'd never, ever have wanted to bring a child into the world the way she had with Ella, and yet she didn't regret her daughter for a single second.

'Then we'll get to know each other.' Again he made it all sound glaringly obvious. 'All the more reason for you to come to Tuscany, Mia.'

'So you expect me to follow you to Italy, to live in your house, without even knowing you?'

'You know enough, surely.'

'What I know I don't even like! You're ruthless, Alessandro, completely ruthless when it comes to the companies you take over—'

'That's business, and in any case, I'm not as ruthless as you think.' He almost sounded hurt. 'I thought you realised that.'

Memories of that night flitted through her brain, the man she'd started to dream he was, as well as what she'd learned about Dillard's former employees. No, he wasn't as ruthless as all that. And yet…

'Still, you've been incredibly overbearing since you blasted back into my life,' she persisted, 'demanding everything and making no compromises—'

'Because I'm right.'

She rolled her eyes. 'Of course you are.'

'And because this is important to me.' He lowered his voice, his hands clenched together, as he struggled with a depth of emotion Mia had never seen before. 'I grew up without a father, Mia. He chose to walk away before I was born. All my life I've wondered…' He paused, cleared his throat. 'I cannot abide the thought of my daughter thinking I would do the same thing, even for a moment. I cannot countenance for a *second* that she might wonder why I don't see her more often, or why I don't live in the same country as she does. I cannot stand the prospect that she might think I don't care.'

Tears, unexpected, unwanted, crowded Mia's eyes. 'I'm sorry,' she whispered. 'I didn't realise.'

He nodded jerkily. 'Now you know.'

'But surely you can still see how much you are asking of me.'

'I am asking just as much of myself. Together we will be parents for Ella. We will put aside our own desires and needs for her sake. It is what any good parent would do.'

And how on earth could she argue with that? Mia felt cornered, and yet she could hardly blame Alessandro for it. She agreed with him…she just wished she didn't. That there was another way, and yet there so clearly wasn't.

'So you want us to live together?' she surmised hesitantly. 'In the same house? What about…what about all your women?'

Alessandro looked at her as if she had sprouted horns. 'I would not have *women*.'

'At least a woman, then,' Mia clarified impatiently. 'I've seen the photos, Alessandro—'

'The only woman I will have on my arm is you,' Alessandro returned, his silver gaze snaring hers and pinning her in place. 'As my wife.'

For a second Alessandro thought Mia might faint. Her face drained of colour and she swayed where she sat, her lips bloodless as she parted them and tried to speak.

'What...?' The word was a scratchy whisper. She shook her head, looking as dazed as if she'd been hit on the head. 'What...are you talking about?'

'I thought it would be obvious.' Although he realised now what had been set in stone in his own mind had not even crossed Mia's. He'd been so sure of the way forward he might have skipped a few rather crucial steps in their conversation. Well, he would cover them now. 'I thought I'd made it clear. For Ella's sake, we will marry. You would live in Tuscany as my wife.'

'Was that a *proposal*?'

Her scathing tone caught him on the raw. He'd just offered to *marry* her, and she was acting offended. 'It was a fact,' he stated rather shortly. 'I accept that neither of us expected or even wished this, Mia, but surely we can put aside our personal preferences for Ella's sake. It's the right thing to do.'

'But you're talking about my whole life.'

'And my whole life.' He met her gaze steadily, refusing to be moved. Mia still looked as if she didn't know what had hit her.

'Alessandro, I can't marry you.'

'I'm not asking you to marry me this very minute.' He tried to ignore the sharp needling of hurt he felt at her blunt refusal. 'I understand we'll want to get to know another before we say any vows, although the sooner we make this official, the better, as far as I am concerned. Again, for Ella's sake.'

'I… I can't.' She looked agonised, strangely torn. 'Alessandro, I can't.'

'Why not?' His voice sharpened. 'Are you already married?'

'No, of course not.' She rose from the sofa, rubbing her arms as if she were cold. 'I just can't. I can't be married. I can't be married to a man like you.'

'A man like me?' His tone had turned icy. 'What is that supposed to mean?' A man of low birth? A bastard? He'd heard it all before, of course, but it still hurt coming from her.

'Just…' Mia shrugged helplessly. 'Someone so…rigid and in control. You've done nothing but order me around since I met you, Alessandro, and I can't live like that. I can't let myself live like that.'

Alessandro absorbed her words, as well as the despairing conviction behind them. 'I understand your concern,' he said finally. 'I don't want you to feel as if you've been railroaded into anything. We can leave the discussion about marriage for now. I'm not about to force you to the altar.' The very thought was distasteful. 'But I hope you can see the rightness of coming to Italy with me.'

'For ever?' Mia flung at him.

Startled, Alessandro shrugged. 'At least for an…interim period.'

'How about three months?' she challenged. 'I can just about live with that.'

'Three months,' he repeated. It wasn't so long, but hopefully long enough. 'So we can get to know one another and make sure a relationship between us will work.'

'A relationship?' She frowned. 'Are you saying that we're...*dating*?' She sounded disbelieving.

'If you are asking if there will be a physical relationship between us,' Alessandro said after a moment, feeling his way through the words, 'then I shall leave that up to you.' He could certainly give her that choice.

'You will?'

'I won't force you to the altar, and neither will I force you to my bed. You will come to it when it's your choice, not my decree.'

Colour touched her cheeks. 'So the offer's open whenever...?' she queried a bit sardonically.

'I won't deny that I still find you attractive,' Alessandro said, meeting her gaze boldly. Perhaps if she remembered just how explosive their chemistry had been, she would be less reluctant to go along with his ideas. 'What we shared was brief, I admit, but it was good, Mia. It was very good.' He held her gaze, felt his own heat, and saw that she remembered just how good it had been... just as he did.

'And what happens after three months?' Mia asked after a long, heated moment. 'If I decide it isn't working?'

Everything in him resisted such a notion, but he still made himself say the words. 'Then we will have to consider alternatives. But I hope, for Ella's sake, such a drastic step will not be necessary.'

'You call *that* a drastic step?' Mia let out a huff of humourless laughter.

'I do,' Alessandro returned evenly. 'Because it would be drastic for Ella, unable to have two loving parents in her life.' His voice rose with the strength of his emotions. He'd only held Ella once, had barely spent any time with her, but she was his and he wanted to raise her right, give her the stability and security and yes, even the love that he'd never had growing up. 'Why should I be content with seeing my daughter only on occasion, a deadbeat dad, not by my own choosing? Why don't you want Ella to have two parents fully involved in her life, loving and taking care of her? Who doesn't want that for their child?'

'Is that…is that what it would be like?' She sounded so surprised that Alessandro felt stung.

'You don't think I would love my own child?'

'I'm not saying that, it's just…you're so focused on work, Alessandro. As far as I can tell from the tabloids, you've never had a serious relationship.'

'This is different.'

'How?'

'Because of Ella. I admit, I've never been interested in serious relationships before now.'

'And I'm still not,' Mia interjected, surprising him. 'I've never wanted to get married, be tied down—'

'Too bad you had my baby, then.'

They stared at each other, an emotional standoff, and then Mia let out a ragged sigh and sank back onto the sofa. 'I can't keep arguing about this.'

'Then be reasonable. Three months. That's all I'm asking. You wouldn't be going back to work before then anyway.'

She stared into the distance, her expression remote and a bit weary. Then, to his immense satisfaction, she slowly nodded. 'All right. Three months. I can give you that.'

'Good. We can make this work,' he said, with conviction. Mia did not reply. She stared out of the window, her expression so distant and despairing that Alessandro felt something in him shift, turn over. It was as if an emotion long kept buried was stirring to life, and he didn't He realised he wanted to comfort her. He didn't her sad, but he had no idea how to make her alisations were disturbing. She'd given in and seen the sense in his plan. He should nt, and instead he felt…unsettled.

'You look tired,' he said abruptly. 'Why don't you have a sleep?'

She turned to him, blinking slowly. 'A sleep…?'

'Yes, have a nap. Ella is sleeping, and I can keep an eye on her.' He gestured to the huge bed on the other side of the suite, made into its own cosy enclave with bookshelves and potted palms to give the area privacy without compromising the stunning view. 'Have a rest. You look exhausted, Mia.'

*And we fly to Rome tonight.*

He didn't say the words, but he had a feeling she heard them anyway.

'All right,' Mia said after a moment. 'I am very tired.'

'Good. Rest.'

He watched as she rose stiffly from the sofa, exhaustion apparent in the slump of her shoulders, the lines on her face. Compassion stirred inside him. She needed help; she needed him. He just needed to make her realise it.

Mia bent over Ella's car seat, tenderly touching her daughter's cheek before she straightened and looked straight at Alessandro.

'I don't like any of this, Alessandro, even if I recognise that our being together is best for Ella. But no matter how you spin it, I still don't feel as if I have any choice.'

'I've given you a choice,' Alessandro protested, and she nodded.

'Exactly,' she said. 'You've *given* me.' Without waiting for his reply, she turned and walked towards the bed, everything about her seeming both proud and defeated. The unsettling combination made Alessandro ache. It also made him feel guilty, as if he were doing something wrong, but he wasn't. He couldn't be.

For Ella's sake, this was how it had to be. Mia would come to accept that in time. He would make sure of it.

# CHAPTER NINE

MIA STARED OUT of the window of the private jet as it lifted into the sunset sky. Her stomach clenched with nerves, her insides swooping as the plane rose and then levelled out. She was doing this. She was really doing this.

Because she had to. For Ella's sake, for Alessandro's sake. She'd recognised that this morning, when Alessandro had spoken oh-so-reasonably, but she still resisted. Still hated the thought that she was being backed into a corner.

Three months. She could manage for three months. She could get to know Alessandro. She could try to get along. After that…

Mia had no idea what happened after that.

She glanced across the teakwood table that separated her from Alessandro in the jet's sumptuous living area. Since waking up in Alessandro's penthouse that afternoon, she'd felt as if she'd fallen into a fairy tale, unsure if she was with the prince or the big bad wolf. A little bit of both, perhaps. Alessandro was certainly solicitous of her every need; she couldn't fault him even if she was still on edge.

While she'd been sleeping, something she hadn't even thought she'd be able to do, he'd arranged for all her things to be packed up from her apartment and put onto his private plane. He'd had bags packed for her and Ella with everything they could possibly need for the flight. They'd gone directly from the hotel to the airport, which meant Mia hadn't been able to say goodbye to anyone.

She hadn't made many friends in LA yet, but she still resented his high-handed manner. She didn't think he was even aware of it, which made it worse. Somehow, against everything she believed and hoped for her life, she was ending up with a man like her father. Maybe not in the needless cruelty or sneering manner—Alessandro was certainly better than that. Yet the result was the same— being controlled by a man.

Alessandro, at least, was showing himself to be an attentive father. When she'd stumbled from the sumptuous bed back in the suite, she'd found him on the sofa, cradling Ella in his lap as he cooed down at her, his face softened and suffused with love. Seeing him in that unguarded moment had given Mia the hope that maybe, just maybe, she really was doing the right thing by going to Italy. That maybe it could even be a good thing.

She glanced again at Alessandro, his profile both handsome and hard as he gazed down at his tablet, a faint frown bisecting his patrician brow. He'd shed his suit jacket and rolled up his shirtsleeves, revealing powerful forearms, muscles flexed.

Looking at him now, Mia remembered how irresistible she'd once found him. How Alessandro had informed her it was her choice whether or not she shared his bed. Her choice…and yet she was afraid to make it, afraid of feeling even more under his control, because she knew when he touched her she'd lose her sense of reason completely. And yet she couldn't get the images, the memories, out of her mind.

As if sensing her looking at him, Alessandro glanced up, his frown deepening as their gazes met. 'Is everything all right? Do you need something?'

She shook her head. She'd just fed Ella, and her daughter was asleep in her car seat. 'No, I'm all right.'

'Why don't we have champagne?' Alessandro suggested. 'To toast our future.'

'The next three months, you mean,' Mia couldn't help but correct. She needed to remind herself of that safeguard as much as him. 'I don't know. I shouldn't drink too much whilst I'm breastfeeding...'

'Surely a sip won't hurt.' Alessandro motioned to an aide, and then barked out a command in Italian. Mia watched him silently; he wasn't even aware of how once again he'd exerted his will. It was a small matter, seemingly insignificant, and yet she felt it.

She also felt how, after just one day, she was too weary and defeated to challenge him. What would she be like after a month, a year, a decade? Would she become as worn out and ghost-like as her mother had been, drifting through life, half-heartedly defending her choices, or lack of them?

The staff member came back with a bottle of champagne and two crystal flutes. Alessandro dismissed the man and then expertly opened the champagne, the cork giving a stifled pop before he poured them both glasses.

'To Ella,' he said as he handed her a glass. 'And to us.'

Dutifully Mia clinked her glass against his before taking a tiny sip. The bubbles fizzed through her, pleasantly surprising; it had been over a year since she'd had any alcohol. In fact...

'Do you remember the last time we had champagne?' Alessandro murmured, and Mia stiffened.

'I'm sure you've had champagne last week, if not sooner.'

'I haven't, but I meant when we had it together.'

*Together.* The word held memory as well as promise. Intent. Mia took another sip of champagne, just to steady her nerves. 'I didn't expect you to talk about that,' she said after a moment.

'Why not?'

'The last time we were *together*, you wanted to forget it, just like I did.' Her voice was unsteady, as was her hand as she put her flute of champagne on the table in front of her.

'Things have changed,' Alessandro answered with a nod towards a still sleeping Ella. 'Obviously.'

'They haven't changed that much,' Mia protested. 'You said I had three months to get to know you…to decide.' Something flickered in his face and she leaned forward. 'Did you mean that?'

'Of course.'

She scanned his taut expression, dark brows drawn together, gaze slightly averted. 'Alessandro,' she said slowly, 'what will happen after three months?'

'My hope is we'll get married.'

'Married…' Was she a fool to think he might have relinquished that notion? 'And if I refuse?'

His eyes gleamed as he leaned forward. 'I will make it my life's mission for the next three months to make sure you don't *want* to refuse.'

His voice was a sensuous caress, yet to Mia the words felt like a threat…and one she suspected he could carry out all too well.

'And how will you do that?' she asked, her voice wobbling. She hadn't meant to direct a challenge, but she realised she had as Alessandro smiled knowingly, his lingering gaze as tangible as if he'd touched her.

'I think you know how.'

'By seducing me?'

'Do I need to remind you how explosive our chemistry was?'

'No, but perhaps I need to remind you there is more to

a relationship—to a *marriage*—than what happens between the sheets.'

'Or on a desk,' Alessandro murmured, his eyes glinting.

Mia's cheeks heated and she looked away. 'Indeed.'

Alessandro settled back in his seat. 'Like I said, we have chemistry, Mia. Let's build on that.'

'That's hardly the foundation for a good marriage.' In fact she feared it could be a disastrous one. What about shared values, aspirations, ideals? And besides, she had never wanted to get married, anyway. She'd never wanted to be so in thrall to another person, so under their control…and yet here she was. It filled her with a feeling of fearful hopelessness.

'Chemistry and a shared love of a child is plenty,' Alessandro returned. 'More than many, or even most, have, and something we can build on.'

'Did your parents love each other?' she asked bluntly, and he stilled, clearly surprised by the question, before he gave a terse shake of his head.

'My mother loved my father, but he did not love her in return.'

'So would our marriage be one of love, eventually? Is that what you would hope for?'

Alessandro stilled, a guarded look coming over his face. 'Our love of Ella…'

'You know that's not what I mean.'

'What do you mean, Mia? Yesterday you told me you had never intended on marrying. Are you now telling me you want something different out of your marriage?'

She deflated, wondering why she'd pursued the point. 'No, I'm not saying that. I've never wanted to fall in love.'

'And neither have I, so I think we're a good match.'

Yet why did that make her feel so despairing, so hopeless? She'd never wanted to marry, yet now that she might, she didn't think she wanted a marriage devoid of affection.

She felt trapped, choiceless, and she hated that. At least it was only for three months. It felt like the only silver lining to an otherwise towering, dark cloud.

'My parents' relationship was stormy and difficult,' Alessandro said after a moment. She had the sense he was telling her something he didn't relate often. 'They never married, and, as I told you once before, my father walked out before I was born. My mother spent the next fifteen years beaten down by life, working dead-end jobs, moving from grotty flat to grotty flat, all in pursuit of some man or other…toxic relationships with wastrels or drunks or men who only wanted one thing.' He sighed heavily, his gaze turning distant, as if he was lost or even trapped in a memory. 'And she gave her heart every time, or so it seemed to me. It was no way to live.' Mia heard a raw note of sadness in his voice that she'd never heard before, and it touched her, made her see him in a new and surprising light.

'That must have been difficult for you,' she said quietly, the aggression gone from her voice.

'It wasn't easy,' Alessandro agreed, a dark note in his voice that made Mia's heart ache. She had an image in her head of a little black-haired boy watching with wide, grey eyes as his mother invited another man into their lives, as they were forced to move, as life upended for him again and again. His childhood had been as challenging as hers, if not more so, just in a different way.

'And so this is the alternative?' she asked after a moment.

'It's *an* alternative.' Alessandro met her gaze directly, his expression now one of firm purpose. 'Give us a chance, Mia. I'm willing to. We can have a marriage of companionship and compatibility. It doesn't have to be some terrible truce, or a sorry stalemate.'

'A loveless marriage?'

'Love is overrated. You must think that yourself, with your own background. Why fall head first into something that spins out of control when you can have something so much better?'

He made it sound so reasonable. So possible. Still Mia hesitated. 'We still don't even know each other, Alessandro.'

'Which is why we're giving it three months.' He smiled and downed the rest of his champagne.

Three months, Mia thought, and then he'd expect her to marry him. And at that point, she had a terrible feeling she'd be the subject of another hostile takeover...impossible to refuse or resist. Alessandro would make sure of it.

Ella stirred in her seat, and Mia rose from where she'd been sitting. 'She needs a top-up,' she said. 'And I'm really tired. I'll feed her in bed and then go to sleep, if you don't mind.'

'All right.' Alessandro had a thoughtful look on his face as he tracked her movements. She unbuckled Ella from her seat and scooped her up, breathing in her sweet baby scent, savouring the innocence of it. All this was for Ella's sake, she told herself. Fighting Alessandro at every turn would only end up hurting Ella. For her daughter's sake, she had to get along with this man. She had to give this—them—a try, even if everything in her still railed against it.

'Please let me or a member of staff know if you need anything,' Alessandro said solicitously. 'Anything at all.'

She nodded, knowing she needed to make an effort even though part of her resisted. 'Thank you, Alessandro,' she said stiffly.

Surprise flashed across his features, followed by a ripple of pleasure, and then he nodded. Mia turned and walked towards the back of the plane with Ella in her arms.

He should have thanked her back, Alessandro realised belatedly as Mia closed the door of the plane's bedroom behind her. She'd thanked him; he should have thanked her, for going along with his plans, for agreeing to so much. But he hadn't thought of it, and the realisation shamed him, an unexpected, unwelcome feeling.

What he was doing was reasonable and generous. He was offering Mia far more than she could ever have on her own—a lifestyle of which she would have never been able even to dream. And yet…in some way he was taking her freedom. He recognised that, just as he recognised she was taking his. Still, it had been his idea, his will. He recognised that too.

Restless, Alessandro rose from his seat to prowl the living area of the plane, knowing he wouldn't be able to work or settle to anything. He should be feeling satisfied, having arranged everything as he'd wanted it. Within twenty-four hours of arriving in California, he had Mia and his daughter back on a plane to Tuscany.

All was going according to his plan. So why did he feel so…restless? So dissatisfied and *hungry*, in a way he didn't expect or understand?

He sat down again, pulling his laptop towards him, determined to work. But after only an hour he realised he hadn't got anything done; he'd been staring at a spreadsheet of profit margins for at least twenty minutes.

With a near growl, he pushed his laptop away and strode towards the back of the plane. He could check on Mia and Ella, at least, and make sure they were okay.

He opened the door as quietly as he could; the bedroom was swathed in darkness, the shades drawn down against the night sky, the only light coming from the adjoining bathroom, the door ajar.

Mia lay on her side, her hair spread across the pillow in a golden sheet, Ella in the middle of the bed, cradled gently in her arm, both of them fast asleep. As Alessandro came closer he saw that Ella had finished feeding; a milk bubble frothed at her lips, one fist flung upwards by her round cheek. His gaze moved to Mia, and something in him jolted as he saw she'd changed into a white cotton nightgown, its buttons undone so she could feed Ella, one creamy breast on display.

All of it together—mother, child—was beautiful to him, and made him ache and yearn even more than he had before. More than he'd ever let himself.

He *wanted* this. Not just Mia, not just Ella. All of it together. *Them.* A family, the family he'd always ached for but never known. Finally, it could be his. He hadn't even realised how much he'd been missing it until it was here, offered up in front of him, tantalising and beautiful.

Resolution crystallised inside him, sharpening into focus. Whatever it took, whatever it meant, he was going to knit them into a family. He would make Mia leave her regrets and fears behind; he would work hard to make her want this as much as he did. He'd worked hard for everything in his life, he could work hard at this too, the most important thing. The most important business deal he'd ever make. Not a hostile takeover as Mia had once suggested, but a true and purposeful merger. A marriage.

Carefully, as quietly as he could, he took off his shoes and belt, leaving his clothes on for form's sake as he stretched out on the bed next to Mia, gently putting his arm around her. She stirred, and he waited, his breath held, wondering what she would do. Then she let out a breathy sigh and relaxed into him, her body softening against his.

Desire and something far, far deeper roared through him, elemental and overwhelming. Yes, he wanted this. He wanted it with every fibre of his being. And he would have it. Eventually he would have it.

Alessandro didn't know how long he slept, but he woke when Mia shifted next to him, gasping as she sat up, her hair tumbled about her shoulders, her face flushed.

'I didn't mean to fall asleep…'

Alessandro blinked the sleep from his eyes as he took in the magnificent sight of her, her body rosy and soft with sleep, her eyes bright, her nightgown still unbuttoned.

'I thought that was your intention when you lay down in bed,' he said, keeping his voice light.

'I was feeding Ella, and then I was going to put her in the Moses basket.' She nodded towards the sleeping basket that had been in her apartment, and had been brought to the plane. It was next to the bed, made up with a fleece-lined blanket.

'She can go in there now.'

'I shouldn't have fallen asleep with her on the bed,' Mia said. She sounded upset. 'It can be dangerous…'

'She's fine, Mia. Look.' With one hand on her shoulder, he turned her so they could both look at their tiny, sleeping daughter. 'She's fine. No harm done.' He rubbed her shoulder, a touch meant for comfort but which made him decidedly less so. Her skin was warm and soft, her nightgown slipping off her shoulder. He fought the urge to slip his hand inside and cup the breast he'd already seen and that was quite, quite perfect.

'Still…' Mia muttered. She sounded half-asleep.

'I'll put her in the basket now.' Awkwardly but tenderly Alessandro scooped Ella up, conscious of her fragility, her utter smallness. He still wasn't used to holding her.

The baby barely stirred as he laid her in the Moses basket, drawing the blanket over her. Then he returned to the bed, where Mia had already fallen back to sleep.

Gently he brushed a tendril of hair away from her cheek, letting his fingers skim along her silky skin. Her breath came out in a soft sigh and she relaxed against him, her body warm and pliant.

Alessandro shifted so he was lying behind her, one arm around her waist. Awareness prickled painfully through him. Sleep, he knew, would be elusive. Then Mia sighed again and wriggled closer to him, so her bottom was nestled against his groin, her head tucked under his chin. Yes, sleep would be very elusive indeed.

Alessandro kept his body relaxed so Mia would stay asleep, savouring her closeness even as it remained an exquisite form of torture. He breathed in her citrusy scent, revelling in her soft warmth, the nearness of her.

He never slept with the women he bedded. He'd always operated alone, on every level. He'd been happy with that. Yet now he found her closeness comforting, a balm as well as an undoubted enticement. He desired her, but he was also content to have her simply lie in his arms. For now, it was enough. It was more than he'd ever had before.

For a few moments he let his mind drift back over the years of his childhood, the loneliness, the uncertainty, the endless turmoil of being moved from one grotty flat to another, the parade of boyfriends who had raged or sneered or used their fists. And his mother...

But that hurt most of all. He tried never to think of his mother, to remember the look of weary defeat on her face, the words she'd said to him, too exhausted by life to be spiteful. They'd been simple truth.

*'I wish I'd never had you.'*

No, he didn't want to think of that. And he didn't want his daughter to wonder, even for a day, a minute, if he felt that way about her. He would love Ella the way his mother and father had never loved him. And he would build a marriage with Mia that would be better than the candyfloss froth of fairy tales, a solid relationship of affection and companionship without losing control or being vulnerable the way his mother had been. The way he'd so often felt, as a child.

And yet he recognised, as Mia slept in his arms, that he'd already lost control, in some small but elemental way.

Already he'd been more open and vulnerable, more emotional, with her than he ever had with anyone before...not that she would recognise that.

He still did, and it unsettled him. He'd never told anyone about his parents, or how he'd felt as a child. Already she knew more about him than anyone else, ever.

Somehow he was going to have to find a way to have the family he wanted without losing himself in the process. He could not relinquish the solitary independence he'd cultivated since he could remember. He didn't know who he would be without it. And yet he wanted Mia and Ella in his life. He wanted the three of them to be a family.

He must have slept, because bright sunlight was visible underneath the rim of the shades as he stirred in bed, Mia wrapped even more tightly in his arms. In her sleep she'd rolled over to him, and now she was squashed up next to him so he could feel every delectable line and curve of her warm, warm body.

Her eyes fluttered open and she stared straight into his, her body stiffening as she realised how close they were.

'Good morning,' he said softly. 'Ella is still asleep.'

Mia glanced down at their nearly entwined bodies, her breasts spilling out of her nightgown, pressed up against him. Colour flooded her face as she tensed even more.

'What...?'

'You were asleep,' Alessandro said. 'So was I.'

Her cheeks were stained crimson as she scrambled out of his embrace, buttoning up her nightgown with fumbling fingers.

'I didn't...' she muttered, unable to look him in the eye.

'Nothing happened, if that's your concern,' Alessandro said equably. 'I would never take advantage of you, Mia. I promise you that.'

She opened her mouth, and Alessandro braced himself

for what he was sure she would say. *You already have.* But then she closed her mouth and shook her head.

'I'm going to have a shower and get dressed before we land,' she said. 'Can you watch Ella?'

'Of course.'

She looked as if she wanted to say something more, but then she just shook her head again, slipping out of bed and hurrying to the en suite bathroom. The door closed behind her and Alessandro winced as he heard the lock turn with a decisive click.

# CHAPTER TEN

MIA HELD ELLA to her as she stepped out of the limo into the warm spring morning. Sunlight glinted off the terra-cotta tiles of Alessandro's villa, the Tuscan hills now covered in verdant green and bright blossom.

The place was huge and sprawling, made of white stucco, with terraced gardens on the hillside, bursting with colourful blooms. She could hardly credit that she was going to live in such a magnificent place, if just for three months.

*Or maybe for ever.*

Alessandro gently placed his hand on the small of her back as he guided her towards the imposing entrance. Mia's eyes felt gritty, her body aching with fatigue and jet lag despite the few hours' sleep she'd snatched on the plane, waking up so unsettlingly in Alessandro's arms. For a second, before she'd woken up completely, she'd lain there, warm and comfortable, snuggled and safe.

*Happy.*

She'd been completely wrong-footed when she'd re-alised just how much she'd cosied up to Alessandro, and meanwhile forgotten Ella entirely. He still had that devastating effect on her, she realised. Perhaps he always would—the ability to melt her insides like butter, even as he fanned her to flame. It scared her, the power he could have over her if she let him.

After they'd landed, Mia had done her best to find a cordial but formal middle ground, although he suddenly seemed intent on being close to her whenever he had the opportunity, such as now, when he gently pressed his palm to the small of her back, sending shivers of awareness rippling through her, before he took Ella from her.

'I'll hold her for a bit. You look shattered.'

She *was* shattered, but Ella felt like her safety shield. Without her, Mia was exposed, unsure what to do with her arms, how to look or feel. Everything about this was so incredibly strange. Whether for three months or for ever, she couldn't believe she and Ella were going to *live* here, with Alessandro, as a family.

She glanced around the soaring marble foyer in amazed disbelief. Several doors led off to various impressive reception rooms, and a sweeping double staircase led to the second floor.

'This feels like a castle,' she couldn't help but say.

'And you're the princess,' Alessandro told her as he hefted Ella against his shoulder. Already he was starting to handle Ella with more confidence, although he still carried her as if she was so fragile she'd break…or explode.

The flashes of uncertainty Mia saw on his face as he held their daughter made her melt in an entirely different way—he could affect her heart as well as her body. Both were dangerous.

'You may do whatever you like to the place,' Alessandro continued, a look of nervousness crossing his face as Ella began to fuss. 'Redecorate however you want…it is your home, Mia. Yours and Ella's and mine. Ours.' He jiggled Ella uncertainly, and as their baby started to settle down he looked up at Mia with a small smile.

'Do you think she knows me yet?'

'She's starting to.' Ella gave Alessandro a gummy smile that made him grin back in delight.

'She smiled. She actually smiled.'

Mia couldn't help but laugh. 'So she did.' Watching Alessandro and Ella bond over something as simple as a smile made her heart ache. How could she ever contemplate ending this? Walking away from a family life that neither she nor Alessandro had ever had before?

It was just a smile, she told herself, and in any case, she didn't yet know what kind of family life they would have. How it would work. No matter what assurances Alessandro made, she wasn't yet convinced.

'Thank you,' she said. 'Where…where is my room?'

'Our room is at the top of the stairs, to the right.'

She turned to him, appalled even as a treacherous excitement made her stomach flip. '*Our* room?'

'It will be our room,' he amended somewhat reluctantly. 'For now you may have it. But I look forward to the day when we might share it.'

'If,' Mia couldn't help but say and Alessandro gave her a knowing look.

'When,' he repeated firmly. 'Definitely when. Now, why don't you go upstairs and have a bath, relax for a bit? I'll watch Ella, especially since she seems to like me now.' He smiled down at their daughter.

'She needs a feed…' Mia began, torn between wanting to rest and needing her daughter.

'I'll come and get you if she fusses.'

'You mean when,' Mia returned wryly, and Alessandro laughed.

'True enough. When.' He smiled at her, and Mia found herself smiling back. Maybe she needed to relax…not just in a bath, but with everything. With Alessandro. It was going to be a long, tense three months if she didn't.

Upstairs Mia wandered into the first room at the right, gaping at the sheer opulence of what was clearly the master bedroom. As Henry Dillard's PA, and then, briefly, Eric

Foster's, she'd seen more than her fair share of luxury, even if she hadn't partaken in it directly. But this room exceeded all her expectations.

It was enormous, for a start, its tiled floor supplied with underfloor heating so Mia's feet remained toasty warm as she slipped off her shoes with a sigh of relief. A king-sized bed stood on its own dais, piled high with silk and satin pillows. A separate seating area with deep leather sofas had a stunning view of the garden below, with an infinity pool and hot tub large enough to seat twenty. Thick-pile rugs were scattered across the floor, so Mia's toes sank into their exquisite softness as she walked towards the bed.

It looked amazing, inviting, and huge. And one day—if or when—she was meant to share it with Alessandro. Why did that thought not alarm her as it should? She couldn't deny the lick of excitement low in her belly, even as she tensed at the thought. She knew that giving herself to Alessandro again would come at an emotional cost. He might just see it as sex, but she knew she wouldn't. Already she felt herself softening to him, and it scared her. She had too many memories, too many fears, to let herself relax and trust Alessandro…even if he proved trustworthy.

She pushed such thoughts out of her mind as she turned to the bathroom, taking in the sunken marble bathtub, the shower big enough for two, the double sinks. She turned on the taps to fill the tub, and added nearly half a bottle of high-end bubble bath. She was going to have a good, long soak, and try not to think for a while, because if she did, her head might explode.

Twenty minutes later, having submerged herself in hot, soapy bubbles and nearly fallen asleep, Mia sat up suddenly as her breasts prickled and her body tensed. Faintly, so faintly, she heard Ella cry.

With a sigh she pulled the plug on the bath and swathed herself in the thick, velvet-soft terrycloth dressing gown she'd found hanging on the back of the bathroom door. She finger-combed her hair as she walked through the bedroom and then downstairs, following the sound of Ella's now shrill cries.

She wandered through several empty, elegant rooms before she spied Alessandro rocking Ella in the kitchen, a cheerful and comfortable room at the back of the house, with French windows leading out to a wide terrace with steps down to the garden.

Mia paused in the doorway, spellbound by the simple yet heart-warming scene. Ella was crying with determination, while Alessandro danced around the kitchen, jiggling her rather desperately against his shoulder.

'Now, *bambina*, you need to settle down or you'll wake your *mamma*. Why are you upset, eh? What is there to be so sad about?' He pressed a kiss to Ella's cheek. 'Are you hungry, *cara*? Is that the problem? Am I going to have to wake your *mamma*, after all?'

'I'm already awake.'

Mia's voice came out scratchy as she absorbed the scene in front of her, let it squeeze her heart. She'd never seen Alessandro look so gentle, or approachable, or...*loving*. He'd been loving. And it gave her a glimpse of a future that didn't look as unfathomable or impossible as she'd assumed it would be. In a strange and surprising way, for a few seconds it had looked...wonderful. And that scared her too, because it was not what she'd expected, and it made her want things she was afraid to try for or even to dream about.

What if Alessandro was right, and they could have a relationship, a marriage, that was strong and true and good? Based on companionship and affection? What if that was possible?

Why did that thought both terrify and thrill her in equal measure?

Alessandro gave her an endearingly self-conscious smile. 'I guess she is hungry, as you said she would be. I've been trying to calm her, but no luck.'

'You can't provide the goods in this case,' Mia answered as she held her arms out, and Alessandro danced his way over to her, making her smile.

'Here she is.'

'Has she had a change?'

'Her nappy? Yes.'

'You changed it?' Mia couldn't keep the surprise from her voice.

'It took a few tries, I admit. Thankfully there were enough nappies. Those tapes…' He shook his head. 'They were not designed for durability. I might have to take over the company that makes them, to ensure a stronger design.'

Mia laughed at such an outrageous suggestion. 'Is that how you decide what companies to take over?'

'Actually, no.' He looked serious for a moment before he deliberately lightened his expression. 'But perhaps it will be, as far as nappies are concerned.'

'So how do you choose the companies?' she asked as she settled in a sofa in the cosy nook off the kitchen. Alessandro joined her, sitting on the sofa opposite. Conscious of his gaze on her, Mia bent her head, her damp hair falling forward as she brought Ella to her breast. When she was sure she was presentable and Ella feeding discreetly, she looked up, everything in her jolting at the sudden, blazing look in Alessandro's eyes…a look of pride and possession that made her feel a welter of unsettling sensations.

As he caught her gaze, it faded, leaving scorch marks on her soul. He gave her a small smile. 'I choose companies that have corrupt and weak leadership.'

Startled, she shook her head. 'But Henry wasn't…'

'Corrupt? No, perhaps not. But he was weak and lazy, and he was running Dillard's into the red. I estimated that in another eighteen months, none of you would have had jobs.'

'Surely not...'

He shrugged. 'Two years, at the maximum.'

'I always knew he was a bit old-fashioned,' Mia said slowly. 'And he did like his golf game...' But she'd considered those qualities endearing, rather than damaging. Now she wondered.

'As affable as he could be, he was a weak leader,' Alessandro responded firmly. 'And he would have proved disastrous for the company and its employees.'

'And you care about the employees.' Once she would have said as much incredulously, but now there was the lilt of a question in her tone. 'Because I don't understand that—your reputation is so ruthless, firing most of the employees of the companies you take over. And yet...'

Alessandro smiled wryly as he raised his eyebrows. 'And yet?'

'And yet that didn't seem to be the case with Dillard's. Most of the staff were given jobs elsewhere, better jobs by the sounds of it, and the people who were let go had very generous redundancy packages, which has to cut into your profit. But none of that seems to make it into the press.'

'No,' he agreed, sounding unbothered by that fact.

'Why? Don't you mind being portrayed as some ruthless monster?'

'No, because I can hardly be a teddy bear if I'm going to take over a company. Having a reputation helps.'

'But why do you do it?' Mia pressed. 'What are you trying to achieve?' He hesitated for a long moment, and Mia had the sense they were on the cusp of some great and terrible revelation.

'I do it,' he finally said, 'because I cannot abide having weak or corrupt people in leadership, and I will not stand by and allow them to ruin people's lives.' He paused. 'Like my father did.'

Alessandro gazed at Mia, noticing the way her hair, like a golden slide of silk, hid her face, so he couldn't gauge her expression. He hadn't meant to make that admission, but now that he had he was glad he had. He could hardly expect Mia to come to trust him if he didn't share something of his life and past with her…even if doing so made him feel uncomfortably exposed.

'Your father?' she repeated softly. 'How…?'

'He was the CEO of a company in Rome. My mother was a cleaner in his office.' He could not keep the old bitterness from twisting his words. 'It was, as I'm sure you can imagine, a short-lived affair. He made my mother promises he never intended on keeping. And when he found out she was pregnant, he fired her.'

'Oh, Alessandro.' His name was a soft cry of distress. 'I'm so sorry.'

He shrugged one shoulder, half regretting having told her that much. It made him feel scraped raw inside, to have these old wounds on display.

'What did she do?' Mia asked softly.

'She had me, and then worked one dead-end job after another trying to make ends meet, which they rarely did. She told me about my father when I was quite small, and I followed his career, saw how he abused his power and privilege, not just with women like my mother, who had nothing, but in all sorts of ways.' He shifted where he sat, that old determination coursing through him again. 'I determined then that I would never allow people like that to abuse their power. And I've made it part of the mission of my work to take over companies that are showing such signs.'

Mia shook her head slowly. 'I had no idea...'

'You're not meant to. I can't exactly publicise what I'm doing. Hostile takeovers are just that. Hostile.'

'Still, to do something noble and never be known for it...'

The warmth in her eyes both discomfited and awed him. He realised he liked having her look at him like that, feel like that. And that was alarming.

'It's not as much as you think, Mia. Some people are still out of jobs. I have a reputation for a reason.' Why he was trying to dissuade her from thinking well of him, he had no idea. Perhaps simply because he wasn't used to it.

'Still.' She pursed her lips as she gazed down at their daughter. 'I wish I'd known earlier.'

'Well, now you know.'

Alessandro paused, watching as she cradled Ella in her arms, their daughter feeding happily, one fist reaching absently for Mia's hair.

'It occurs to me,' he said conversationally, 'that you know more about me than I know about you.'

Mia looked up, eyebrows raised in surprise. 'What do you want to know about me?'

'Everything. Anything.' He realised he was truly curious. 'But we can start with the basics. Where are you from?'

'The Lake District.'

'A beautiful area.'

'You've been?'

He smiled. 'I've heard.'

'It is beautiful.' She looked away, seeming almost as if she was suppressing a shiver. 'Beautiful and isolated and very cold.'

'That sounds like a rather mixed description.'

She shrugged. 'I didn't like it growing up. I couldn't wait to get away.'

'Why? Just because it was cold?'

She hesitated, and he waited, sensing she had something more important to reveal. 'No, because my father was… well, suffice to say, we didn't get along.' She kept her gaze on Ella, catching their daughter's chubby hand in her own and gently removing it from her hair.

'And your mother?' Alessandro asked quietly.

'She died when I was fourteen. I'd say of a broken heart, but I know how melodramatic that sounds.'

'No.' His mother had wasted away, worn to the bone by work and poverty. It was possible, Alessandro knew, to die of things that ate at you the same way a physical disease did. 'Is your father still alive?'

'I don't actually know.' Mia looked up at him then, her blue eyes icy with a hard anger he'd never seen before, not even in their stormiest moments. 'I haven't seen him in eight years, and that is fine by me.'

'I see.' Although he didn't see the whole picture, he was starting to get a glimpse. Whatever had happened with her father, Mia clearly had emotional scars from it. He didn't know what they were exactly, but at least he knew they were there.

'Anyway.' Mia shrugged, her gaze back on Ella. 'With the background you just told me about, how did you get to be a billionaire by age—what? Thirty-something?'

'Thirty-seven. I worked my way up.'

'From slums to a billionaire lifestyle?' She shook her head slowly, seeming impressed. 'That's quite a steep climb.'

'Yes.'

'How did it happen?'

Alessandro shrugged. 'I was lucky and I worked hard. I started in property, buying rundown buildings and flipping them. It grew from there.'

'It has to have been more than luck.'

'Like I said, I worked hard.'

'Very hard, I imagine. You've always seemed…driven to me.'

'Yes, I suppose I am.' Although, coming from her, he didn't know whether it was a compliment or not.

'What about your mother?' Mia asked. 'Is she still alive?'

'Sadly, no. She died when I was nineteen, just when I was starting, but we'd lost touch a few years before.'

'That's sad.' Mia hesitated. 'It seems as if we have something in common.'

'Yes.' It saddened him, to think that both he and Mia had come from such fractured, damaged families—and it made him more determined to make sure their own little family wasn't. 'Our family doesn't have to be like that, Mia,' he said, a new note of urgency entering his voice. 'This can be a fresh start for the three of us.'

'I'd like to believe that,' she said after a moment, but her tone sounded wistful, even dubious, and that stung.

'Why can't you?'

'It's just… I don't know enough about you, Alessandro. And sometimes the past isn't so easy to overcome.'

'We're getting to know each other,' he persisted. 'And we'll keep doing that. What's your favourite colour?'

'My favourite colour?'

'We've got to start somewhere.'

She let out a little laugh. 'Green.'

'Favourite food?'

'Raspberries.'

'Favourite season?'

'Spring.' She laughed again and shook her head. 'I suppose I have to ask you all the same questions.'

'Only if you want to.'

Her mouth curved, her eyes lightening. Alessandro liked her that way. 'I do.'

'Then it's blue, steak, and autumn.'

'We're practically opposites.'

He raised his eyebrows. 'Is blue the opposite of green?'

'Maybe not. But the others...' Her laugh turned into a sigh as she glanced down at Ella, stroking her downy head. 'I don't know. Do such preferences matter, really? Shouldn't we be asking each other more important things?'

Alessandro caught his breath as he stared at her intently, trying to decipher her mood. He liked what she'd said, but she'd sounded sad. 'Such as?' he asked after a moment.

'I don't even know. Such as what you want out of life. What you value. What you believe.'

'What do you want out of life, Mia?' He spoke quietly, knowing the question was important, the answer even more so.

She looked up, her expression serious, her eyes bright. 'First, I want to keep Ella safe and healthy and happy.'

'Of course. I want that, as well. Utterly.'

'After that, I want to be independent. With my own money, my own choices. That's...very important to me.' Alessandro sensed a wealth of memory and meaning behind her words, and he nodded.

'Understandable.' He'd seen that all along, how she chafed against any autocratic commands...which, he acknowledged wryly, he had a tendency to give. But they could work on all that.

'What do you want out of life, Alessandro?' She glanced around the spacious kitchen, the sunny garden visible through the French windows. 'It seems like you have everything already.'

'I am thankful for what I have,' Alessandro allowed. 'But what I've wanted...what has driven me, as you've said...' He hesitated, feeling his way through the words. 'First, I want to protect and care for my family.'

'Yes.' The word was a soft assent.

'And second…it is similar to what you want, in a way, I suppose. I want to be in control. I don't want to have my life dictated by other people's whims or poor choices, as it was for all my childhood.'

'I can understand that.'

'Yes, it seems you can. So once again we are in accord, Mia. I think you will find we are far more compatible than you once feared.'

'Perhaps.' She didn't sound convinced, but Alessandro knew he could convince her. He had to.

'I mean it, Mia. I want this to work.'

'That's something, then,' Mia said with a small smile, and as their gazes met and tangled Alessandro found himself remembering a whole host of pleasurable things. The feel of Mia in his arms. The taste of her lips. How sleepy and warm she'd been that morning, snuggled up against him. And he thought how much he wanted to experience all of those things again, over and over.

Yet as his own blood heated, Mia's seemed to cool, for she looked away, her hair sliding in front of her face. Alessandro felt her emotional withdrawal like a physical thing.

'I should unpack,' she said as she brought Ella to her shoulder, pulling her robe closed with her other hand. 'And get dressed…'

'Your things will have been brought up to your room by the staff by now, I am sure. Alyssa and Paulo are the couple who run this place. They're very kind.'

'I look forward to meeting them.' She rose, clutching Ella to her a bit like a shield. 'Will you be…returning to Rome? For work?'

'In a few days.' Alessandro couldn't help but be stung by the question. Did she want him gone already? Resolve hardened inside him. He would break down her defences. He would get to know her…in every possible way. 'Shall we have dinner together tonight? Alyssa is happy to sit with Ella.'

Her eyes widened and then slowly, seemingly reluctantly, she nodded. 'Very well.'

It was a grudging acceptance, and one that irked him just a little. Why was Mia so guarded? Why couldn't she enter into the spirit of what he was trying to do?

But what *was* he trying to do? Alessandro asked himself after Mia had gone upstairs and he headed to his study to check his work emails. Mia had asked him a host of serious questions that he had answered honestly, if not fully. What did he want from life? What did he want from this marriage? And how was he going to get it?

Already being with Mia was drawing emotion from him like poison from a wound. He felt it stir inside him, and it alarmed him. He did not want to be ruled by his emotions the way his mother had been, tossed on the turbulent waves of relationships that never delivered what they'd seemed to promise, and left destruction in their wake.

He'd always vowed he would never expose himself to that kind of horrible, humiliating risk. He would never need someone that way, let that need rule and ruin him. He would always stay in control—of himself, and of his emotions.

And he *could* be in control, Alessandro reminded himself. He wasn't that lost little boy, hiding in the cupboard while his mother screamed and fought with one of her many boyfriends, or curled up on a narrow bed, wondering when she'd finally come home after a night out.

He was a man in control of his destiny and his family. His relationship with—and eventual marriage to—Mia would be on his terms. And they would be favourable terms for her, undoubtedly. He would be generous, thoughtful, kind. But they would still be his.

# CHAPTER ELEVEN

'AREN'T YOU HAPPY?'

Laughing, Mia tickled Ella's tummy as her daughter grinned and giggled back at her. They were sitting on a blanket in the villa's garden, enjoying the warm spring sunshine. It had been two weeks since Mia had come to Italy, and she was finally starting to relax into this strange and amazing new life of hers. She just wasn't sure whether she could trust it...or Alessandro.

He'd been a model of kindness and consideration since she'd arrived; she couldn't fault him for that. The first night he'd arranged for Alyssa to watch Ella while they'd had a candlelit supper out on the terrace, eating delicious food, drinking fine wine, and enjoying each other's company.

And Mia *had* enjoyed his company... Alessandro had kept the conversation light and sparkling, without any of the heavy issues that seemed poised to drag them down.

She'd even enjoyed the heat she'd seen in his eyes when she'd appeared, having changed into one of her few dresses that fitted her post-pregnancy figure, and when he'd taken her hand, butterflies had risen in a swarm from her stomach to flutter through her whole body and send her senses spinning.

It would be so easy, she'd reflected, to let herself fall. To forget her worries, her fears, her choices. She could just gently bob along on the overwhelming sea that was Alessandro...

*And then what?*

Fear had knotted in her stomach at the thought. She'd pictured her mother, looking so worn out and defeated, the wedding album open on her lap.

*'He was so charming, Mia. So forceful and yet so caring. I fell for him hard... I loved him...'*

No matter how many times she told herself Alessandro was not like her father, Mia knew, from both his behaviour and his admission, that he was man who liked to be in control. And that would always be a cause for alarm and even fear.

At the end of that candlelit dinner, Alessandro had brushed a gentle kiss across her lips, like a whisper of a promise.

'For now,' he'd said, and there had been so much intent in his voice that Mia had shivered. It had taken all her strength not to sway into that kiss, not to ask for more. Plead, even, and that scared her along with everything else. She wasn't ready...and she didn't know how long Alessandro would wait.

A fortnight on, Mia still slept alone and Alessandro did no more than kiss her goodnight. The kisses had become a bit more lingering, and last night Mia had found herself clutching his lapels, on her tiptoes, straining for more before she'd finally had the strength of will to wrench herself away.

Alessandro had smiled wryly as he'd cupped her cheek. 'Why are you fighting me so hard, *cara*?' he'd asked gently.

Because I don't know what else to do. How to be. I'm afraid of giving you everything and you taking it. What will happen to me then?

Mia hadn't had the courage to say any of it, and so she'd

just shaken her head and backed away, her body trembling from Alessandro's touch. And he'd let her go, but they'd both known, if he'd wanted to, he could have made her stay.

'Hello to my two gorgeous girls.' Smiling, Alessandro strolled across the lawn to meet them, dropping a kiss on Mia's head before sitting down next to her and tickling Ella's tummy just as she had done. 'She seems happy.'

'Yes, she's very smiley this afternoon.' Mia glanced at him, feeling shy and overwhelmed as she so often did when in his magnetic, compelling presence. He was dressed casually in dark trousers and a grey polo shirt that brought out the silver in his eyes, his hair gleaming blue-black and ruffled by the warm breeze. The sandalwood scent of him still made her senses reel. 'Have you finished your work already?'

'Yes, but I need to go to Rome tomorrow morning, for a few business meetings, as well as a charity ball in the evening.' Alessandro had been working remotely from the villa, with just a few trips to various cities across Europe. Mia wondered how long he could keep such a pattern; he was a very busy, powerful man, with many demands on his time. Surely this idyll couldn't last…and part of her craved a relief from the tension of being with him, even as another part knew she would miss him.

'I think we'll manage to keep ourselves busy,' she said. Over the last few weeks she'd had a few forays into the market town for trips to the shops, and also a baby group that met in a community hall. She was also hoping to start learning Italian, although Mia was wary of putting down too many roots. This still felt temporary rather than like real life, although perhaps that would change the more effort she made.

'Actually,' Alessandro said after a moment, 'I was hoping you would come with me.'

'With you?' Mia was startled. 'But won't Ella and I just be in your way?'

'Not Ella, just you.' His gaze was warm as it met hers and lingered there with intent. 'Just for the evening, so we can spend some time together. Alyssa can watch Ella.'

'You want me to go to a *ball*?'

'Why do you sound sceptical? We've been to one before.'

'I know, but…' Mia felt her cheeks flush as she remembered the last ball they'd been to…and what had happened afterwards. 'I don't have anything to wear.'

'That's easily remedied. I can have a stylist come with a selection of gowns.'

'As you did before?'

He shrugged. 'It's not a problem.'

But it felt like a problem, because Mia wasn't sure she was ready for a night out with Alessandro. Her already wavering defences might crumble completely…and then what?

It was the question that always rose to the front of her mind, popping like a bubble before she could answer it. If she stopped trying to protect herself, keep a safe distance, what would happen?

'What are you scared of, Mia?' Alessandro asked. 'It's just a ball.'

'I know, but…'

'We'll be home before midnight, I promise. And Alyssa will enjoy taking care of Ella.'

'It's not that.'

'Then what?'

He sounded so patient, even tender. How could she doubt him? How could she be so afraid? Mia knew she wasn't being fair, holding back the way she was. Alessandro had been more than generous, more than patient with her. She needed to give something back.

'All right,' she said at last. 'I'll come.'

'Good.' He leaned forward to brush her lips with his, making her whole body tingle. 'I look forward to it. I'll arrange for the stylist now.'

As he left to make the call, Mia realised that, despite her reservations, she wanted to go. She wanted to dress up and walk into a ballroom on Alessandro's arm, just as she had once before. She wanted to spend the evening—and maybe even the whole night—with him. Saying yes had freed her to admit to herself just how much she wanted him, despite her fear. It felt dizzyingly wonderful...as well as incredibly terrifying.

'Here we are.'

Alessandro followed the bellboy into the penthouse suite of the luxury hotel by Rome's Spanish Steps, Mia walking slowly behind them. Since leaving the villa—and Ella—she'd been quiet, even subdued, perhaps wary. Alessandro knew she didn't trust him yet, but at least she'd agreed to come tonight. He hoped to prise her even more out of her shell tonight.

He'd spent the last two weeks trying to gain her trust, win her confidence, and slowly, ever so slowly, he'd felt Mia soften towards him, and he wanted to see—and feel—that even more tonight.

'Wow.' Mia stood in the centre of the large, luxurious living room, with French windows leading out to a wide terrace that overlooked the Spanish Steps. A platter of fresh fruit had been placed on a coffee table, along with bottles of champagne and sparkling apple juice. 'But we're not even staying the night...'

'I own this hotel, and the penthouse is reserved for my exclusive use. I like to have a base while in Rome.' He checked his phone. 'The stylist will be here with a selection of gowns shortly.'

'Will you need final approval, like you did before?' she said, her voice teasing. Alessandro smiled, glad for the bit of banter.

'I think I can leave that to you this time. I look forward to being surprised.'

'All right.' Mia glanced around the living room again, taking in the silk-striped sofas, the original artwork, the marble-topped tables. 'This place really is amazing.'

'I just want you to enjoy everything, Mia,' Alessandro said. 'This evening away is meant to be a break for you, although I know you're worried about leaving Ella.'

'I know it is.' Mia rubbed her arms as if she were cold and then walked to the French windows, before opening them and stepping out onto the terrace. After a second's pause Alessandro followed her, breathing in the balmy air as he joined her at the railing overlooking the city far below.

'What's wrong?' he asked quietly. 'This isn't just about leaving Ella for a few hours.'

'No.' She shook her head. 'It's about…about us.' She glanced at him, her face troubled. 'You've been wonderful these last few weeks, I know. I can admit that.'

'Admit it?' Alessandro tried to keep his voice light, even though he was a bit stung by her words, the reluctance of them. 'You almost sound as if you don't want to.'

'I don't,' Mia admitted. 'It's just… I'm scared, Alessandro. I told you I never wanted to marry or give my life over to another person. A man. And yet here I am.'

'Yes, but…' Alessandro had to feel his way through the words. 'It doesn't have to be something to resist, Mia. We were both in agreement, I thought, about what our relationship could look like. Companionship, trust, affection.'

'And not love.' She spoke flatly, making him hesitate. 'Have you changed your mind on that?'

'No.' She sounded disconcertingly firm. 'It's just difficult to trust you.'

'Have I ever done anything to make you distrust me?' he asked, stung again by her honest admission. What had he done to make her so wary?

'Not recently.'

'What is that supposed to mean?'

'You spend your life taking over other people's businesses,' she said after a moment. 'And sometimes that feels like what you're doing with me.'

Disconcerted, Alessandro did not reply for a moment. Yes, in his own mind he had compared his relationship to Mia in terms of a takeover, although perhaps a merger was a better way of putting it, but it wasn't *hostile*. At least, it didn't have to be.

'I thought you'd agreed this was best for Ella. And I thought you'd enjoyed the last few weeks.' He couldn't keep an edge of affront from entering his voice. It was hardly as if he'd kept her in prison. 'Please believe me, Mia, I am not trying to force you into anything.'

'There are more ways to force someone than strong-arm them.'

'What are you trying to say?'

'I don't *know*,' Mia said helplessly. 'Like I said, I'm scared, Alessandro. You can be ruthless. I know you like to be in control. I understand why you do, but those things scare me.'

'I am hardly going to be ruthless with my family.'

'How do you even know that? You've kept yourself from relationships for so long. Do you even know how to be in a family relationship, one that isn't driven by anger or revenge?'

Hurt flashed through him at her words. 'I can try,' he said quietly, and her face crumpled a little bit.

'Do you really want to?'

'Of course I do,' he snapped, but he heard the anger in his voice and he knew it was wrong. He just didn't know how to show her how he felt. How much he felt. 'I know I like to be in control. But I'm not dictating things to you, Mia. I'm trying to have a real relationship with you, even if I don't understand yet all that it means.' He felt far too vulnerable having admitted that much, and so he pressed his lips together and stayed silent.

'I'm sorry.' She smiled sadly. 'And I need to try, too. I'm sorry I'm so reluctant. It's just…' She paused, and he waited, sensing she was going to say something more. But then she sighed and shook her head. 'I'd better go and choose my dress.' Her lips twisted wryly. 'That's at least one choice I can make.'

The stylist arrived a short while later, and Alessandro busied himself with work while the stylist and her assistants commandeered the bedroom for their beautifying purposes.

As he half listened to the sound of the women chatting in the next room, he found he could not focus on the work in front of him. He kept going over his conversation with Mia in his mind, as if testing it for weaknesses. Why was Mia so wary with him still? What more could he do to gain her trust? He felt as if she questioned his every motive, which made him question them, as well. Was he doing the right thing?

Of course he was. For Ella's sake as well as theirs. He just needed to be more patient. Perhaps Mia just needed more time.

Still, he couldn't keep from feeling a flicker of irritation along with hurt. He'd been trying so hard for the last few weeks, and he'd given Mia everything. What possible cause could she really have to complain? So he liked to be in control. That was hardly the worst thing, was it? It wasn't as if he was abusing his position of power, or forc-ing her to do something against her will.

Her reluctance annoyed him, but it also made him even more determined. He would win her yet. Whatever aspect of their inevitable relationship Mia was resisting, Alessan-dro would discover it and deal with it.

Which, he realised uncomfortably, *did* make this all seem a bit like the takeover she'd suggested. But it wasn't, not like that. It was just…strategy. Common sense.

He slid his hand into the pocket of his jacket, his fin-gers curling around the small black velvet box. Nothing, he told himself. Mia would find fault with nothing. He'd make sure of it.

An hour later, Alessandro had changed into a tuxedo and was waiting for Mia in the living room of the suite, try-ing to curb his impatience. It felt as if she'd been in the bed-room for ages, and he'd heard the chatter and giggles drift out as he'd wondered just how long it took to find a dress.

'She's ready,' the stylist, Elena, sang out as she came into the living room, followed by her bevy of assistants. 'And she's perfect.' She simpered at Alessandro before she thankfully excused herself, her assistants following, so Alessandro and Mia would be alone. He would be sent the undoubtedly outrageous bill later.

'Mia…?' Alessandro called when she still hadn't come out after Elena had left. 'Are you coming?'

'Yes. Sorry.' With a nervous little laugh, she stepped out of the bedroom. Alessandro sucked in his breath. He'd al-ready seen her in an evening gown, a year ago, when he'd lost his head over the slender woman dancing in his arms.

Tonight he felt himself lose everything else. His mind emptied and his heart tumbled in his chest as Mia smiled uncertainly. 'Do you…do you like it?'

'I love it,' he assured her huskily. The gown was a pale, creamy ivory, with a delicate overlay of gold lace. Strapless, with a full skirt, it reminded him of a wedding dress, and that seemed appropriate indeed. 'Your hair…' he murmured, coming forward to loop one golden curl around his finger.

'She curled it,' Mia said nervously. 'I've never had curly hair before.'

'It's gorgeous.' Half being pinned up, the other half tumbled over her shoulders in glossy, golden waves and curls. Gently, his finger still twined in her hair, Alessandro tugged her towards him. Mia came, a smile trembling on her lips.

'Alessandro…'

'You're so beautiful, Mia. Even more beautiful now that you're a mother.'

'No…' She let out an uncertain laugh. 'I haven't lost all of my baby weight…'

'I don't want you to. You're perfect just as you are.' He knew it sounded like well-worn flattery, but the truth was he meant every word. He wasn't saying it to please her or to get what he wanted, as she so often seemed to suspect, but because he *needed* to. Because it was right, and it was the truth.

Which was why he had to kiss her, as well.

'Mia…' Her name was a question and as she moved closer, her silence was his answer. He placed one hand on her bare shoulder, her skin cool and soft beneath his palm. Then he brushed his lips across hers, softly first, another question.

And she answered again with silence, her mouth opening under his, a thousand times yes. Here was another truth, in the simple purity of their kiss, their lips joining together in a brief moment that spun on and on as Alessandro deepened the kiss, unable to keep himself from it, losing himself in her soft and willing response.

Mia clutched his shoulders as she anchored herself to

him, to their kiss, and the world seemed to spin around them. It was just a kiss, and yet so much more. It felt like a promise as well as a seal.

Finally Alessandro lifted his head, breathing raggedly, dazed by the intensity of the moment. Mia blinked back at him, her fingers at her lips. Neither of them spoke.

Alessandro felt the weight of the black velvet box in his pocket, and he almost reached for it. Now was the perfect moment—and yet perhaps too perfect. The last thing he wanted was for Mia to think he was orchestrating the moment when in truth he'd been felled by it...as she seemed to have been.

So instead he left it where it was, and smiled at her instead. And, needing no words, he took her by the hand and led her from the room, out into the warm, spring night and the promise it surely held.

# CHAPTER TWELVE

MIA'S HEAD WAS SPINNING. Her lips were buzzing. And as she and Alessandro moved through the party, meeting and chatting to people, she wondered if she was falling yet again for the fairy tale. Just as before, she was Cinderella for a night, and yet so much more was at stake. Her whole life. Ella's life. Their future together. It all felt as if it hung in the balance now; all she needed to do was say yes.

And for once, with the memory of Alessandro's kiss on her lips, she didn't want to wonder or doubt. She wanted to enjoy the fairy tale; she wanted, at least for tonight, to trust Alessandro's tempting promises. To believe in them and let them sweep her along.

For once she wanted to resist not only Alessandro, but also her own negative history, her persistent belief and fear that keeping herself apart from Alessandro was the only way to stay strong. To feel independent. What if staying strong could mean something else? It could mean choosing him, rather than fighting him. Was it possible?

She pressed her fingers to her lips as she recalled yet again that heart-stopping, breath-stealing kiss. Alessandro had seemed as affected as she'd been. For a few moments, they'd shared something wonderful.

*But was it—could it be—real?*

Dared she let it be real in her own mind, never mind Alessandro's?

Her thoughts tumbled and shifted in her mind in an ever-changing kaleidoscope that she struggled to make sense of. She felt as if she were teetering on a precipice, but she had no idea what lay ahead—or below.

Then Alessandro took her hand as he drew her towards him, his eyes the colour of smoke, his voice husky as he devoured her in a single glance.

'Dance?'

Mia thought of their dance a year ago, when everything had heightened and changed between them. It had been magical…but it had also been dangerous. Where was the danger now? Was it real—or was she imagining it, because she was so afraid of losing herself the way her mother had? Could she let go of it for a night?

Could she let go of it for ever?

She nodded, her palm sliding across his, fingers twining and tightening as they moved onto the dance floor and began to sway to the sensuous music.

'Are you enjoying tonight?' Alessandro asked as he moved her slowly and languorously around the floor, their hips bumping, heat flaring.

'Yes…'

'You don't sound entirely convinced.' He spoke lightly but Mia saw the flash of concern and even hurt in his eyes, quickly masked.

'I don't know what to think, Alessandro,' she confessed quietly. 'So I'm trying not to think at all. I just want to… feel.'

'Feeling is good,' Alessandro murmured huskily. 'Feeling is very good.' His forehead crinkled in a frown. 'But you don't need to be so wary, Mia. So scared.'

'I'm trying not to be.'

'What exactly is it you are afraid of, *cara*?' The endearment slipped easily from his tongue, caressing her with its intimacy, making her want even more to trust this and believe in it. In him.'

She hesitated, unsure what to say. How much to confess. Yet surely Alessandro deserved to know why she was the way she was, what experiences had formed and shaped her, and that she was becoming desperate to shed now? 'I'm scared of losing myself,' she admitted quietly.

Alessandro's frown deepened, a deep line bisecting his brow. 'Losing yourself?'

'Yes. Losing my…my sense of self, I suppose. My ability to make decisions, to be my own person…' She trailed off, realising how vague and really rather ridiculous she sounded. What did it even mean, to lose yourself? Could she even put what she was so frightened of into concrete ideas and absolutes? Or was it just this vague sense of dread, that life was spinning out of control, that she needed to leave behind her, finally and for ever?

'I don't understand,' Alessandro said as he moved her around the dance floor, one hand warm and sure on her waist. 'Please, will you explain it to me?'

She shook her head. 'I don't know if I can. I know it sounds silly and vague, formless, but…it's what I grew up with. My mother and father…' She faltered, her throat growing tight with memories.

'Your mother and father?' Alessandro prompted gently. 'You mentioned you didn't get along with your father…'

'No, I didn't. He was…very controlling. Mostly of my mother but, after she died, also of me.' She shook her head, unwilling to explain just how cruel her father could be, how domineering. She didn't want to explain about the memories that still tormented her—when he'd locked her in her room, or thrown the meal her mother had made in the bin, claiming it was inedible.

*'He's just got high standards, Mia. That's all it is.'*

She couldn't explain the choking frustration she'd felt

with her mother, and then later the awful fear she'd felt for herself, knowing she had to get away before her father controlled her completely.

'Controlling,' Alessandro repeated in a neutral voice. 'This is why you have this issue with control? Why you feel I am too controlling?'

'Yes,' she whispered. 'I suppose so. My father was… awful. He told me what I had to do, or say, or even wear. He enjoyed exerting that power, simply because he could.'

'And so you think I am like this man?' Alessandro asked. His voice was even, but Mia felt the hurt emanating from him, and a wave of sorrow and regret rushed through her.

Alessandro was *nothing* like her father. The realisation washed through her in a cleansing flood. Yes, he could be brutal in business, ruthless in his ambition, but he was never cruel. He'd already shown her how his hostile take-overs were, in essence, mercy missions. Although he could be autocratic, he never sneered or insulted or mocked simply to show his power, because he could. His kindness was genuine.

'No,' Mia said quietly. 'I don't think you're like him, Alessandro.' Another realisation was jolting through her, more powerful than the first. No, she didn't think Alessandro was like her father, not really. Not at all.

*But maybe she was like her mother.*

That, Mia realised, had been her real fear all along. Not that she'd be beholden to a man like her father, but that she would act like her mother. She wouldn't be able to help herself. She'd fall in love with Alessandro, just as her mother had with her father, and give up everything for him—willingly. *That* was what she was afraid of.

Yet how could she admit so much to him now? The last thing she wanted Alessandro to know was the hold he had over her, or that even now she was halfway to falling in love with him, and fighting it all the way.

'I understand why you would be wary, Mia,' Alessandro said. 'Of course I do. But if you know I am not like that…'

Mia shook her head helplessly. The problem was her—her weakness, and her fear. Yet did loving someone have to mean losing yourself? If Alessandro wasn't like her father, was there really any danger? Did she want to be so in thrall to her past and her own fears that she missed out on life, on love?

Yet Alessandro had never said anything about love.

'Mia?' Alessandro prompted gently. 'What is going on inside that beautiful head of yours? Tell me, so I can help.'

'I don't know,' she confessed. 'A million things. I've always believed I would never get married. I'd never…' She hesitated, for she'd been about to say love, and she wasn't ready for that. She was quite sure Alessandro wasn't, either. 'I'd never have that kind of relationship,' she amended. 'And I never wanted it. But now…'

'Now?'

'Now we have to have some kind of relationship, and yes, it scares me. But part of me…wants it, and that scares me, too.'

'All this fear.' The music had ended, and Alessandro stopped their swaying, raising her hand to his lips. He brushed a kiss across her knuckles as his gentle yet determined gaze met hers. 'I will do my best to allay your fears, *cara*. The last thing I want is for you to be afraid—of me, of anyone or anything. I promise never to hurt you, never to take advantage of you, never to make you regret joining your life with mine.'

'Those are big promises, Alessandro,' she whispered shakily. Yet she knew he meant them.

'Yes, they are.' Her hand was still at his lips as he kept

his gaze on her, now fierce and glittering. 'Do you believe me, Mia? Will you trust me?'

*Could she?*

'I want to,' she whispered.

'Then let yourself. See what can be between us, Mia. Discover how good—how wonderful—it could be, if you let yourself trust. *Fall.* I'll catch you. I promise I will.'

His words were a siren song that she ached to listen to, and believe. If only it could be so easy. If only she could leave her fears behind and step into this bright, glittering future Alessandro promised. *Why not?* Why not at least try, for Ella's sake, for her sake, for *theirs*?

'All right,' she whispered, and Alessandro smiled, victory lighting his eyes as he drew her towards him and kissed her right there on the dance floor, in front of the crowd, his lips on hers like a seal, branding her with his mouth just as he had with his words.

As they broke apart, Mia's lips buzzed and her face flamed. She felt as if she'd just jumped off a cliff, and she couldn't yet tell whether she was flying—or falling.

'Shall we go?' Alessandro murmured, and she knew what he was asking. They'd been on a dance floor before, in thrall to their shared desire, and he'd asked her the same question. And once again, she could agree, she could let herself be caught up in what was spinning out between them, let it sweep her along so she didn't have to think or wonder—or fear.

'Yes, let's,' she whispered, and Alessandro laced his fingers through hers once more as he led her through the crowd, the faceless blur barely registering as they left the ballroom and, just as they had once before, stepped out into the warm spring night.

They were both quiet during the limo ride to the private airport where they took a helicopter back to the villa.

Mia's heart thudded in her chest as she thought about what was ahead of them, what she'd agreed to.

*No regrets...*

The short helicopter ride seemed over in a moment, and then they were walking up towards the darkened villa, Mia achingly aware of Alessandro's powerful body next to hers. With murmured thanks, he dismissed Alyssa, who assured Mia that Ella had gone to sleep with no problems, and was still sleeping soundly.

At the bottom of the sweeping staircase, Mia paused as Alessandro stood there, his eyes blazing silver as he looked at her, the villa dark and silent all around them.

*What was he waiting for?*

Why wasn't he taking her in his arms, kissing away the last of her fears and objections? She was ready to be swept up in something bigger than herself, ready to let herself go. At least she hoped she was.

'What now?' she finally asked, when she could bear the silence no longer.

Alessandro met her gaze directly, his hands spread wide. 'You tell me.'

She eyed him uncertainly. 'What do you mean?'

'This moment is yours, Mia. You choose it. You decide what you want now, how far you want this to go.' He drew a shuddering breath. 'Do you want me?' Although his voice was assured, the question held a stark note of painful vulnerability that touched Mia deeply.

For the first time Alessandro was surrendering his control...and in this, the most important and elemental aspect of their relationship.

She'd been fully anticipating him to sweep her into a masterminded and smoothly thought out seduction, and she'd been willing to go along with it, to be caught up in it and, in a way, relieved of any real and active choice... even though that was what she'd been fighting for all along.

But Alessandro wasn't giving her that option. He was making her choose now, making her fully own the decision she thought she'd already made, back in the ballroom. This could be no silent surrender, defeat by acquiescence, overwhelmed by his sheer force of personality and innate authority that she tried to resent and yet somehow craved. Alessandro wouldn't let it be that. He was making this moment hers, making her choose it to be theirs.

He held her gaze, his eyes burning fiercely, his hands still spread open wide, his stance one of acceptance rather than aggression or authority. For once he was giving her all the power, all the control, all she'd said she wanted... so what was she going to do?

Alessandro waited, his body tense, his heart thudding. Everything in him resisted this moment, the utter, revealing weakness of it. He didn't do this. He didn't let someone else choose his fate, even if just for a night, although this was so much more than a night. He'd always, *always* been the architect of his own ambition.

But over the course of the evening, as he'd reflected on what Mia had shared about her family and her past, he'd realised that in this, of all things, she needed to have the control. He needed to surrender it, even if everything in him still fought against it. And so he waited.

Mia stared at him for a long moment, a thousand emotions chasing across her lovely face, making her eyes sparkle and her lips tremble. 'Do I want you?' she repeated slowly, her voice sliding over the syllables, testing them out, and Alessandro tensed even more, waiting, expectant. *Afraid.*

Then, to his deep disappointment and dread, she shook her head. 'Not like that,' she said, with a nod towards the bedroom waiting upstairs, with its sumptuous king-sized bed and all that it beckoned and promised. The sour taste of rejection flooded his mouth, overwhelmed his senses with the unwelcome acid of it.

*She didn't want him.*

'At least, not *just* that,' Mia clarified, her voice trembling. 'I don't want another night with you, Alessandro, amazing as the last one was, with all of its repercussions.'

She smiled wryly, straightening her shoulders, and Alessandro raised his eyebrows, his stomach clenched hard with anxiety and uncertainty, both which he hated feeling. He'd never felt so vulnerable, so needy, so open to hurt and pain. 'What, then?' he demanded in a raw voice.

'I came up here prepared to be...to be swept away,' she began haltingly. 'I was expecting you to do the sweeping. Then I wouldn't have had to think or wonder or doubt. I could just let myself feel.'

Which sounded pretty good to Alessandro in this moment. Had he made a mistake, in surrendering his own agency? He had been taking a risk, but it was one he had hoped would turn in his favour. Now he wasn't so sure.

'And now?' he made himself ask, although he half dreaded the answer.

'And now I want something else. Something more.'

'More...'

'I don't want a night. I want...' She swallowed, more of a gulp, her eyes huge in her face as she looked at him resolutely, her chin tilted upwards in determination, her slender body trembling with emotion. 'I want for ever.'

Surprise and a far greater relief rippled through him. She wasn't rejecting him. *Them.* 'For ever...'

Her smile trembled on her lips. 'I know you've been hoping or even expecting me to marry you. But I want this to be on my terms, and amazingly you seem to want that, too. So now I'm the one proposing. The one choosing. Will you...will you marry me?'

He laughed, the sound one of shock but also admiration.

He hadn't expected *that.* 'You know I will. In fact…' Fumbling a little, he reached for the small box of black velvet that had nestled in his pocket all evening. 'I was planning to make you a proper proposal tonight, but I didn't want to seem as if I was pressuring you, or arranging things somehow…' He held the box out in the palm of his hand. 'But I can't think of a better moment than this one.'

'Nor can I.' Smiling a little, she reached for it. Alessandro held his breath as she carefully opened the box, her eyes widening at the sight of the simple solitaire diamond nestled amidst its soft velvet folds. 'It's beautiful, Alessandro.'

The ring was stark in its simplicity, a single diamond on a band of white gold. Alessandro had looked at various rings, but they'd all seemed fussy and officious rather than the simple, pure statement of his intent he wanted. *Their* intent, for a life lived together. Mia lifted her face so her eyes, now luminous with the sheen of tears, met his once more. 'Will you put it on me?'

'Of course.' His fingers trembled a little as he took the ring from the box and slid it on her finger, where it winked and sparkled, a promise they were making to each other. He clasped her hand with his own. 'Do you mean this, Mia?'

'Yes.'

'You want this?' he pressed, because somewhere along the way that had become important, too. This wasn't just about winning any more, or getting what he wanted. He needed her to want it, as well. To want *him.*

'Yes.' Her voice quavered. 'I'm scared, Alessandro. I can admit that. I don't know what the future holds, but I also know I don't want to be enslaved to my past. So yes, I want this. For Ella's sake, and perhaps even for…for ours.' Her worried gaze searched his face as she nibbled her lip.

'I know we haven't actually talked about what a marriage between us would look like, besides the obvious…'

No, they hadn't. For a moment Alessandro couldn't speak, as realisation caught up with him and he desperately tried to order his jumbled thoughts. He'd been so focused on Ella, on their being a family, that he hadn't completely considered what their relationship—their *marriage*—would actually look like. What it would mean.

And he was conscious, incredibly so, that in accepting his proposal, or, rather, offering her own, Mia was giving herself to him. Her body, her mind, and yes, perhaps even her heart. Her life. Precious, fragile gifts. And he was even more conscious that in offering them, she'd, inadvertently or not, given him back the power she hated to relinquish, and which he'd always craved.

What if he hurt her?

What if she hurt him?

The second question, he told himself, wasn't a consideration; he would not allow that to happen. He would honour his marriage vows, and give Mia respect and companionship and so much pleasure. Of that he was sure. But as for love? His heart? The ability to reach inside and hurt him?

No. He saw where that led. He'd seen and felt the pain and brokenness all through his childhood. His mother's tears, anger, addictions, helplessness and grief. No. He could not offer Mia that kind of love.

But what he could offer…he'd make sure she'd be happy with. She'd want for nothing. He'd treat her like a queen.

'We'll figure it out as we go along,' Alessandro told her, smiling to soften the prevarication of his words, and what they both knew he wasn't saying. Wasn't promising. He saw it in the cloudy flicker of her eyes, the slight downturn of her mouth before she made herself smile back. 'This is going to work, Mia. I will do my best, my utmost, to give you everything. To never hurt you.' Again he felt the weight of what he wasn't saying.

*To love you.*

She nodded slowly. 'I know you will, Alessandro.'

'When shall we marry?'

'There's no real rush, is there?'

'Why not make it official?'

'We still could use the time to get to know each other,' Mia protested. 'The three months…'

'It's already been nearly three weeks,' Alessandro returned. Why not marry sooner?'

'At least give it a couple of weeks, so we can plan.'

'Very well.' He could wait that long. 'Are there people you want to invite?'

She shook her head. 'No, not really.'

'Then it will be just us, and Ella, exactly as it should be.' He smiled, liking the thought. 'A family from the beginning.'

'Yes.' She smiled back, but he saw a tiny frown puckering the ivory smoothness of her brow, and he drew her towards him for a lingering kiss. 'We will do this properly, and wait for our wedding night,' he said, savouring the thought. 'Trust me, Mia, our marriage will be the beginning of everything.'

# CHAPTER THIRTEEN

SHE WAS A married woman.

Mia gazed down at the two rings now sparkling on her finger, the first the elegant solitaire diamond from the night of her proposal, the second a simple band of white gold that Alessandro had slipped on her finger only moments ago.

They were standing on the terrace at the villa in Tuscany, the gardens and hills spread out before them in all their blossoming glory, the sun shining benevolently down. Alyssa and Paulo had been the witnesses to their wedding, the local priest, a smiling man who spoke no English, the officiant. Ella, clasped in Alyssa's arms and gurgling happily, had been the only guest.

Mia had worn a strapless dress of ivory silk that she'd bought in Rome on an extravagant shopping trip last week; Alessandro had insisted she buy a complete trousseau, including some very sexy lingerie that made her heart race just to look at.

The last three weeks had been a whirlwind, and a wonderful one at that. Mia had let her fears trickle away in the blazing certainty of Alessandro's attention. He doted on Ella and was kind and considerate with her, and the kisses that punctuated each evening had become longer and more lingering, leaving Mia in a welter of unsated desire, wondering why Alessandro insisted they wait, even as she acknowledged she was glad that he had.

He'd given her no reason to doubt the sudden, surprising choice she'd made that night after the ball, when she'd turned down the offer of a night for so much more.

Mia had been shocked by her own audacity and conviction, but in that moment she'd felt the rightness of what she was doing…what *they* were doing.

She could trust Alessandro. That, she realised, was the choice she was making.

With the ceremony finished, Alyssa handed Ella to Paulo, who took the baby with smiling ease, as she went to fetch the refreshments. Alessandro came to stand by Mia, placing a hand on her lower back, warm and sure, as he smiled down at her.

'Happy?' he murmured, and she turned to smile at him, realising that she really was. Over the last few weeks, her fears and doubts had been chipped away until there was very little of them left.

The dread that had taken residence in the pit of her stomach like some fermenting acid no longer pooled there. Yes, she was still afraid, but it was the uncertain nervousness of a new bride rather than the consuming fear of a woman on the brink of some awful abyss.

She *was* on the brink…but perhaps of something wonderful. Mia was trying to stay pragmatic, reminding herself that Alessandro had made no declarations of love, and neither had she. They didn't know each other well enough for that yet, and she still wasn't entirely sure she wanted to give him that much of herself.

And yet, despite her reservations, the possibility remained, in her heart at least, that this could be a marriage not just of convenience and companionship, which Alessandro had already promised, but also of love, something he most certainly had not. Something she'd never let herself consider before, but was now allowing herself to cautiously wonder about, if just a little.

'Yes, I'm happy.' She gazed out at the gardens, burgeoning with blossom and scent. 'It's been a perfect day.'

'You didn't mind not having a big wedding?'

Mia shook her head. 'I never intended on getting married at all, so why would I want a big wedding?' she answered with a little laugh. She glanced again at the rings on her finger, a tremor of excitement rippling through her at the sight of them. There was no going back.

She might have never thought she'd marry, and yet here she was. Here they were...and tonight would be their wedding night. Already nerves sizzled through her at the thought of that.

'Most young girls dream of big, white weddings,' Alessandro remarked.

'Not me. This has been perfect, truly.' She rested one hand on his, curled around the balustrade, the sun warming their skin. 'I couldn't ask for anything more, Alessandro.'

'Nor could I.' He smiled at her, his expression warm and glinting, allaying the last of her fears. This was going to work. It already was working. Then Alessandro nodded towards Alyssa, who was bringing out a magnificent *millefoglie*, the traditional Italian wedding cake of puff pastry, Chantilly cream, icing sugar and strawberries. 'Shall we have cake?'

'I can always have cake.' Mia took Ella from Paulo as Alyssa cut the cake, and Paulo fetched a bottle of champagne. Ella grabbed at her fork as Mia took a bite of the delicious cake, savouring the explosion of sweetness in her mouth. 'Not for you, little one,' she said with a laugh as Ella's chubby fingers latched onto the fork.

'I'll take her.' With relaxed ease born now of experience, Alessandro reached for Ella, cradling her against his shoulder. As it always did, Mia's heart constricted at the sight of father and daughter, husband and child. Her family. A thrill ran through her at the thought, and one that had nothing to do with fear, and all with hope and even joy. This was real now. *They* were.

They ate cake and had champagne in the spring sunshine. Alessandro had planned a dinner for them, and Alyssa insisted on having Ella for the whole night, assuring Mia that the baby could sleep in her cottage.

'Ella is a good *bambina*,' Alyssa said firmly. 'She did not wake up even once. Such a good girl. This is your wedding night, Mia. Enjoy, Signora Costa!'

*Signora Costa.* Another ripple of surprised excitement shivered through her at the realisation of her new status.

The sun was starting to set, sending golden rays slanting through Mia's bedroom, as she exchanged her wedding gown for a cocktail dress in scarlet with a handkerchief hemline and a halter neck. Her wedding ring flashed as she did her make-up and hair, gazing at her face as if to look for changes. She was a married woman. And by tomorrow morning, she would *truly* be a married woman, in the way that mattered most…

Mia's stomach dipped as she considered the wedding night that loomed ahead of her, exciting and yet terrifying. Her one sexual experience had been short and frenzied, mere moments that had been blurred by passion.

Tonight would be in an entirely different category…and that both excited and scared her, with its promises of both pleasure and intense vulnerability. How would Alessandro be as a husband and lover? How would she be? Would she please him? Ella was only a few months old, and her body had changed since the last time he'd seen it, admittedly for only a brief time. What would he think of her gently rounded stomach, her heavier breasts?

A light knock sounded on the door. 'Ready, *cara*?' Alessandro called.

'I think so.' Mia gave her reflection one last tremulous glance before she went to the door and opened it. Alessandro stood there, looking as devastating as ever in a crisp button-down shirt in dove grey and darker grey trousers. He smelled wonderful.

'You look lovely,' he murmured, putting one hand on her waist as he pulled her to him for a prolonged kiss that made Mia's senses spin and reel. She wondered if kissing him would always make her blood fizz and her heart hum, or if it would become natural, even ordinary.

'So where are we going for dinner, exactly?' Mia asked as they headed downstairs. 'The trattoria in town?'

Alessandro chuckled, shaking his head. 'I think not.'

'There aren't any other restaurants...'

'This is our wedding night, Mia. We will celebrate in style.'

They walked out of the villa, and Mia stopped in surprise at the sight of the helicopter resting on the helipad in the distance, obscured by a few plane trees.

'Where...?'

'Come.' Taking her hand, Alessandro led her to the helicopter.

'But Ella...'

'We'll be back home in a few hours, never fear.' He helped her up into the helicopter as Mia's stomach fizzed with excitement. Where on earth was Alessandro taking her?

She found out an hour later, when they arrived in Venice, the city's many canals gleaming under the setting sun, the wedding-cake roof of San Marco Cathedral blazing with gold. Alessandro had hired out an entire restaurant by Piazza San Marco, the dining room flickering with candlelight, the canal mere steps away, the restaurant secluded and romantic as they were served course after course by a discreet waiter.

'This is amazing,' Mia breathed, in awe of the luxury and romance of it all.

The food was delicious, and she allowed herself a glass of champagne to celebrate, losing herself in the warm and unabashed admiration she saw in Alessandro's eyes. Tonight was made for magic.

And the magic continued as they walked hand in hand along the canal, chatting about everything and nothing. Alessandro had a dry sense of humour that made Mia laugh, and a sensitivity she hadn't expected, even though she'd seen it on display with their daughter. As they enjoyed the sights of the city of bridges, she felt as if her heart were a balloon inside her, filling up with hope, buoying higher and higher. Their marriage could work. Their marriage could even be amazing...

Finally, as twilight settled on the city with deep indigo shadows, the placid surface of the Grand Canal nearly black, they took the helicopter back to the villa.

Moonlight streamed through the windows as they walked quietly, still hand in hand, through the villa, up to the master bedroom Mia had been sleeping in alone for the last few weeks but would share with Alessandro tonight.

In the few hours since she'd been gone, it had been transformed: tall white candles flickered and gleamed, and the bed sheets had been exchanged for a silk duvet, folded back to reveal smooth linen sheets beneath. The nightgown of cobwebby lace and nearly transparent white silk that she'd picked out last week was hanging on the wardrobe door. Mia's heart tumbled in her chest at the sight of it.

'Is all this Alyssa's doing?' she asked.

'And mine.'

It thrilled her to think Alessandro had thought of such romantic touches. 'This is all so romantic...'

'And why shouldn't it be? It is our wedding night, after all.' Alessandro stood behind her, his hands warm on her shoulders. 'It will be different this time, *cara*. So much better.'

Nerves fizzed and popped inside her. 'It was pretty good last time,' she admitted shakily. Now that the moment had come, and they were here together in this beautiful room, intending to consummate their marriage, she felt overwhelmed with both excitement and anxiety.

'Even so.' Alessandro nodded towards the nightgown. 'Do you want to change?'

'All right,' Mia whispered, and, taking the beautiful nightgown, she went into the bathroom.

Alessandro paced the bedroom, feeling restless and eager and, he had to admit, nervous. He was never nervous, and yet he couldn't deny the way his stomach clenched and his heart raced. Yes, he was nervous, but he was also excited. *Very* excited. He'd been waiting a long time for this, and more than once he'd questioned his decision to wait until their wedding night.

The evening had been perfect so far—the food and wine, the company, the romance of it all. Alessandro had never seen the point of such gestures before, but tonight they'd been important, and he'd enjoyed them. He'd wanted them. He'd wanted to make this night special for Mia, and special for him, in a way he'd never remotely wanted to before.

*What was happening to him?*

He thrust the question away, determined not to think about it tonight. This was just a bit of romance, that was all. It was a way to show Mia he appreciated her. It didn't have to mean anything more than that.

Besides, tonight he only wanted to think about Mia… and what was going to happen between them.

The door to the bathroom opened and then she stood there, her hair loose and golden about her shoulders, her slender body swathed in ivory silk. Alessandro sucked in a hard breath, dazed with desire at the sight of her. The silk was so thin he could see the lush, shadowy curves of her body beneath it, and they enflamed him. The few rushed minutes they'd shared over a year ago were nothing compared to this.

'You're still dressed,' Mia observed with a shaky laugh.

'Not for long.' His hands moved to the buttons of his shirt before they stilled. 'Why don't you do it, Mia?'

Her eyes widened. 'Me?'

'Yes, you.' His voice turned ragged with the force of his feeling. 'I want you to. I want you to touch me.'

She stared at him wide-eyed for a few seconds before she moved towards him, the silk whispering against her body. As she stood before him he breathed in her citrusy scent, felt her hair brush his jaw as her fingers fumbled with the first button.

'I'm nervous,' she whispered.

'So am I.'

She glanced up at him. 'No...'

'Yes.' He clasped her hand in his own and pressed it against his thudding heart. 'Feel.'

She laid her palm flat against his chest, her fingers spread wide. Even that simple touch enflamed him, made him want more. So much more. 'Why are you nervous?'

'Because this feels important.' The words came of their own accord, heartfelt, honest. He didn't care what they revealed of him.

Mia glanced at him uncertainly, her hand still resting against his heart. 'You've been with plenty of women before...'

'Not like this. Never like this.'

'Truly?'

'Truly.'

She pressed her hand lightly against his chest, absorbing his words, the truth of them, and then she resumed unbuttoning his shirt. This time her fingers didn't fumble, and soon she was parting the material, sliding it over his shoulders so he was bare-chested.

'I never did get a good look at you before,' she remarked, her hands resting lightly on the sculpted muscles of his chest. His heart still thudded.

'You can look all you like now.'

'I am.' She ran her hand lightly down his chest, her fingers tracing the hard ridges of muscle, exploring his body in a way that made him feel dizzy with hunger for her even though her fingers were barely skimming his skin.

'Mia, you have no idea what you do to me.'

She ran her fingers along the waistband of his trousers before flicking open his belt as she gave him a mischievous look from under golden lashes. 'Don't I?'

He let out a choked laugh. 'Maybe you do, you imp.' He couldn't stand still any longer, submitting to her intoxicating touch. 'Now perhaps I need to discover what I do to you.' He put his hands on her arms, sliding them up to her shoulders, enjoying the feel of the silk of her skin, before he hooked one finger underneath the spaghetti strap of her nightgown and tugged it down.

Her breath came in a shudder and she swayed as he pressed a kiss to the pure line of her collarbone before moving lower to the soft swell of her breast.

'Alessandro...'

'It seems we affect each other in a similar way,' he murmured. Already he was blazing with need, on fire with it, and they'd barely touched.

'It does seem that way,' she admitted shakily. Her legs nearly buckled as he drew the other strap down, and then with one gentle twist of her shoulders the beautiful gown pooled at her feet, leaving her naked and beautiful. So very beautiful.

'I didn't wear that for very long,' she remarked with an

attempt at wryness, although he could see the pulse beating wildly in her throat, her pupils dark and huge.

'It was in the way.'

'So are these.' She nodded towards his trousers, and Alessandro spread his hands.

'You may do the honours.'

With a gulp, she reached for the button, her fingers fumbling once more as she undid it and then started to tug down the zip, her slender fingers brushing the pulsing length of him, making him groan.

'Mia…' he began, and then he found he couldn't finish his sentence. He drew her into his arms, and in a tangle of naked limbs, he brought her to the bed and laid her on it like a treasure.

He kissed her deeply, drinking her in, feeling how her mouth and her whole body opened to him, an offering freely given—and utterly accepted.

He stretched out on top of her, relishing the feeling of her pressed against every inch of him, her arms wrapped around his shoulders, her breasts pressed to his chest, all his to explore and savour.

And he did, taking his time, coaxing an unfettered and glorious response out of Mia, his wife.

*His wife.*

The words, the truth of them, reverberated through him as he finally slid inside her welcoming warmth, uniting their bodies in a way they had never been united before, because this was for ever. One flesh, bound by a sacred vow.

*For ever.*

Mia's cry of pleasure was muffled against his shoulder as he began to move and she joined him, finding a rhythm they claimed for their own as it took them higher and higher, united in this, united in everything.

*As one.*

The realisation of it thudded through him in the aftermath of their joined explosion as Alessandro rolled onto his back, taking Mia with him. He never wanted to let her go.

He'd never expected this. All along he'd been planning his strategy, wooing his wife, poised for victory, negotiating the terms. She would be his.

He hadn't realised he would be hers.

But he felt it now in every sated fibre of his being, and this union between them that they had just consummated wasn't just special, it was sacred. It was overwhelming. And he knew, as he held her close, that he was in very grave danger of doing that which Mia herself had been so afraid of—losing himself. Giving everything to the woman he now held in his arms.

The woman who held his heart without even realising it. Without him ever having meant to give it to her.

# CHAPTER FOURTEEN

IT HAD BEEN one month since she'd become Alessandro's wife, one amazing, incredible, pleasure-filled month. The days had been spent with Ella and often with Alessandro, when he could get away from work, spending time together in easy pleasures, exploring the market town and the surrounding countryside, and simply enjoying getting to know one another.

When Alessandro had to work at his office in Florence, Mia had pottered about the villa, taking over some of the duties from Alyssa, as well as learning Italian and attending a local mums and babies group. She'd been surprised how easy and pleasant it was to fill her days in this way, to simply enjoy being.

And as for her nights...those were filled as well, with a pleasure and intimacy she'd never expected or dared to dream of. Every night she and Alessandro explored each other's bodies, learning the maps of their very selves, and offering themselves to each other in a way that felt like the purest form of communication.

Each night left Mia both sated and shaken, as if she'd flown close to the sun, and been engulfed in its brilliance. It warmed her right through, but she also knew it had the danger to burn her right up.

Because, a month on from their marriage, she knew she was falling in love with her husband. She might have fought against it at the start, had worried all along that it would happen, and now she knew it was.

And she had no idea how her husband felt about her. At night she'd swear on her soul that he loved her, and he showed her he did in a thousand ways. But during the day…

Mia hadn't been able to fault him, at least not until recently. He'd been kind, affectionate, humorous, gentle with Ella. Yet all along she had never been able to escape the sense that he was still keeping some private yet essential part of himself from her. Whenever the conversation turned a little too personal, she felt a distance open up between them, a cool remoteness in Alessandro, as if he had picketed off part of himself and it absolutely wasn't up for grabs.

When she was alone, she told herself she must be imagining it. How on earth could she not be satisfied with all Alessandro gave her? It was such a vague notion, after all. Then, when they were together again, she felt it, like a part of her rubbed raw, always chafing. The words he'd never say, the sense that he wasn't hers, not in the way that she knew she was his. The remoteness was real… and it hurt.

And it had grown worse over the last few days, with Alessandro barely spending any time with her at all. He'd worked late, missing dinner as well as Ella's bedtime, coming to bed when Mia had already succumbed to a restless, unhappy sleep.

She hadn't asked him about his withdrawal; she hadn't, she acknowledged unhappily, been brave enough. Maybe he had some important deal at work. Maybe something else was going on.

But then, why couldn't he tell her about it?

*And, more importantly, why couldn't she ask?*

Now, with Ella settled in her bouncy chair as Mia prepared dinner, she could pretend, at least, they were just like any other family, any other loving couple. Alessandro had told her this morning he would be home for dinner, and hopefully they would sit and eat, talk and laugh, and everything so easy and simple…at least on the surface.

And when they went up to bed a little while later, it would be even simpler, because between the sheets Mia felt she had all of Alessandro to herself…body and soul.

There Alessandro never became a tiny bit repressive, a little tight-lipped. In bed, she never saw the flash of something in his eyes that reminded her of the man she'd met back in London, cold and autocratic, ruthless and remote. Not the man she married. Not the man she was beginning, to her own wonder and fear, to love.

Alyssa bustled into the kitchen, chucking Ella under her chin before turning to Mia. 'Something smells *molto delizioso!*'

Mia smiled wryly. 'I hope so. That is…*lo spero.*'

Alyssa beamed her approval. '*Molto buona!* Your lessons are coming on, *si*?'

'*Si.*' She'd been having several hours' tuition every day, and she hoped eventually to be fluent, to help Ella be fluent as well. Alessandro already talked to his daughter in Italian, something that made Mia melt inside. At moments like that, she could let herself believe in the fairy tale. She could be carried away by it.

'Is Signor Costa eating at home tonight?' Alyssa asked, and Mia nodded.

'Yes…that is, I hope so. *Lo spero.*' She smiled wryly again. 'He said he would before he left this morning.' Even though he hadn't for the few nights before, with no real explanation.

She was just setting the table, Ella bathed and gurgling in her bouncy chair, when her phone beeped with a text from Alessandro.

Working late.

Two measly words when she'd already prepared dinner, had everything ready. Mia's stomach swirled with disappointment and a far deeper hurt. This was the fourth night in a row. Feeling a bit reckless, she swiped her phone's screen to dial his number.

'Mia?' His voice was terse. 'Didn't you get my message?'

'Yes, but it's so late, Alessandro. I've already made dinner...'

'It will keep, won't it?'

Mia blinked at his brusque tone. No explanations, no apologies, just that edge of impatience to his voice, as if she was wasting his time.

'That's not the point, Alessandro,' she said, trying to keep her voice even. 'This is the fourth night you've missed dinner—'

'I'm working.' There was no mistaking the edge now. 'Surely you can understand that, Mia. I shouldn't have to justify it to you.'

'I'm not asking you to justify it,' she protested, startled by the definite coolness in his voice. 'Alessandro... what's going on?'

'What do you mean by that? Nothing is going on.'

'You've been so distant...'

'I'm *working.*'

Gone was even the pretence of the gentle, kind and attentive lover Mia had grown to know and love these last few weeks, making her wonder if it had all been a mirage.

'I know that,' she said quietly.

'Then there's no problem,' Alessandro answered, his voice clipped, and before Mia could say another word he disconnected the call.

She stood there for a moment, stunned by what had just

happened, and yet somehow not surprised at all. Hadn't some part of her been waiting for this? For the mask to fall away, the true man to be revealed? All her fears to be realised?

She hadn't had the courage to confront Alessandro, and when she'd tried, he'd put her in her place, brushing off her concerns as if they were of no importance. The same way her father had.

It didn't have to be a big deal, Mia told herself. It was one phone conversation. All couples had arguments. She was overreacting, she *knew* that. And yet…

But she knew it wasn't one conversation; it was everything that had and hadn't happened in the last month. On their wedding day—and night—she'd felt so wonderfully close to him, and the last month had been a sliding away from that, inch by infinitesimal inch.

Alessandro had been becoming more remote, and, worse, she had become more needy. More desperate. She'd heard it in her voice; she felt it in herself.

Drawing in a ragged breath, Mia reached for the pan of sauce simmering on the stove and recklessly she scraped it all into the bin.

She didn't want it to *keep*. Alessandro would most likely come home late tomorrow night as well. And the night after that…the night after that…

*She couldn't live this way.*

The realisation came suddenly, starkly, and was completely overwhelming, every fear she'd ever had rising restlessly to the fore. Here she was, just like her mother, miserable and alone, having just been told off by the man she was coming to love.

In her seat, Ella let out a happy gurgle, startling Mia out of her unhappy thoughts. She picked Ella up, pacing the kitchen, before she decided she couldn't stay in this villa for another moment. It felt like a mausoleum—a mausoleum of her fragile, fledgling hopes and dreams. As melodramatic as she knew that sounded, even in her own head, she also knew she needed some space.

Quickly Mia went upstairs and packed a case for both her and Ella. She needed to get out of here, get some perspective. And, she acknowledged, she wanted to show Alessandro that he wasn't the only one who could change plans.

It didn't take long to pack what she needed and ring a taxi. While waiting for the car to arrive, she'd checked out a family-friendly hotel in nearby Assisi. She'd go there for the night, she decided. Perhaps in the morning, things would feel and look better, and she'd know what to do. How to feel.

As the taxi sped away from the villa, Ella dozing in her car seat by her side, Mia glanced down at her phone. Alessandro hadn't called or texted again, but she knew he deserved at least some explanation as to her absence.

Needed to think, she texted,

And then waited for a reply that never came.

Alessandro glanced moodily at his phone. *Needed to think?* What was that supposed to mean? He hadn't bothered to reply, because he didn't know what to say. In truth, he hadn't known what to say for weeks now, as he fought the feeling that had been growing between them, stronger every day, and more alarming.

After the soul-changing encounter on their wedding night, when he'd realised just how far he'd fallen, he'd found himself inexorably withdrawing, trying to create a safe distance between him and Mia while pretending to her that it wasn't there.

It had been easy at night, when their bodies took over, and yet he knew that those earth-shattering nights were actually drawing them closer together. Making him want even more from Mia—and for her to want more than he was able to give.

Because during the day, when she asked about his family, or looked at him with so much expectation in her eyes, when he felt a welling of need inside him, a need that felt overwhelming and consuming…he started to freeze. To fear.

He was falling in love with Mia; hell, he was already in love with her, and he knew what happened when you loved someone. They rejected you. Eventually, always, they rejected you.

In his mind's eye he could see his mother's haggard face, the weary resignation in her face giving truth to her words.

*'I wish I'd never had you.'*

His own mother had wished him out of existence. His father hadn't wanted to know him at all. How on earth could he expect Mia to love him the way he knew he loved her…especially when she'd said she'd never wanted to love anyone at all? That had suited him admirably…once.

Now the only choice he felt he had was to keep himself safe. Separate. But the result was this restless ache, this impossible anxiety.

*Needed to think?*

He didn't like the sound of that at *all*.

Snatching up his phone and his coat, Alessandro decided he'd confront Mia directly, ask her just what she needed to think about. Even if he didn't like the answer, it was surely better to know.

It took an hour to drive back to the villa, and with each minute Alessandro felt his insides coil tighter and tighter, till everything in him was ready to snap and break. What did Mia need to think about? What was going on?

He'd tell her he loved her, he decided recklessly. He'd admit the truth he'd been trying to hide from himself, even if the thought made his stomach cramp even more. Did he dare be that vulnerable? Open himself up to that much pain?

But what was the alternative? To live in this welter of frustration and fear, walking a tightrope between staying safe and being real? Gaining nothing or risking everything?

He'd always been willing to take a risk in business, and here was the biggest risk of all. He would be man enough to take it.

Filled with determination, powered by adrenalin, he drove up the sweeping lane to the villa, only to find it darkened and empty.

Perhaps she'd gone to bed already, he thought as he hurried upstairs.

'Mia...?' he called softly as he opened the door to their bedroom. It was empty, the bed still made up and untouched. Frowning, Alessandro walked down the hall to Ella's nursery, his blood freezing to ice in his veins at the sight of the empty cot, the open drawers, the missing clothes. Back to the master bedroom, and he saw that a suitcase was gone, along with some of Mia's clothes.

She'd left him, he realised hollowly. She'd actually left him. And she'd taken his daughter with him.

He sank onto the bed, caught between grief and rage. So this was why Mia had needed to *think*? To think about whether she was leaving him—for a night, or perhaps, heaven help him, even for good? He couldn't see any other possibility. Memories of his childhood, of empty apartments, lonely nights and constant uncertainty, tormented him, and made him unable to think clearly, or even at all. All he knew was he was alone, and he hated it.

Alessandro dropped his head into his hands, overcome with emotion. Thank heaven he hadn't told her he loved her.

# CHAPTER FIFTEEN

A NIGHT AWAY hadn't given Mia much rest. The hotel had been small and noisy, and Ella had had an unsettled night. Mia had, as well, missed the strong, solid presence of her husband in her bed. She'd gone away hoping to order her own thoughts, gain a bit of her independence back, but the time apart had only made her realise how much she missed Alessandro—and, yes, loved him.

The truth was stark and real, and she couldn't hide it from herself any longer. As she climbed in the taxi to head home the next morning, she let that realisation rest and then grow inside her, filling up all the empty space.

*She loved him.*

She hadn't meant to, hadn't wanted to, but she'd fallen in love with a man who most likely didn't feel the same way about her.

The realisation thudded dully inside her. This was the exact scenario she'd once feared, the one thing she'd never wanted to come to pass, and yet here she was, knowing it was true and having to deal with it.

*How?*

By telling Alessandro she loved him? The thought filled Mia with frightened panic, and yet she also knew, intrinsically and instinctively, that it was the right thing to do. What kind of love was it if she couldn't even admit to it?

And if he was horrified, if he told her flat out he didn't love her back…well, then at least she'd know.

As the taxi came up the villa's drive, hope warred with icy terror. Could she really do this? What if, improbably, impossibly, Alessandro told her he loved her back? Dared she even dream…?

Mia held on to that hope as she climbed out of the taxi, Ella in her arms. She'd just paid the driver and started towards the steps when the front door was thrown open.

'Where the *hell* have you been?'

Mia froze at the sound of Alessandro's condemning voice, the cold rage she heard in it, as he strode towards her, everything about his taut form and angry voice catapulting her back to her childhood.

'I told you…' she began, faltering at the sight of the thunderous look on her husband's face.

'You told me you needed to *think*! And then I came home to an empty house, no explanation, my daughter *gone*…'

'I went away for a night, that's all…'

'Without telling me so. Without telling me where.' Alessandro shook his head, his eyes dark, his lips compressed. 'How could you, Mia? How could you do such a thing?' He shook his head again before she could form a reply. 'I don't care. No reason is good enough.'

'Then I won't bother giving you one,' Mia snapped, goaded into her own rage by his high-handed manner. To think she'd been about to tell him she loved him! 'It seems you can come and go as you please, but I can't.'

'That's completely different. I was working.'

'While I was playing with the fairies? Never mind.' Anger and hurt choked her voice. 'I don't care. I'm going inside.' She pushed past him, only to have him reach for her arm.

'Mia—'

'Leave me alone.' She shrugged off his hand, her eyes blinded by tears, and hurried inside. It was, she realised as she headed upstairs, the first argument they'd had since they'd been married, and it felt as if it might be the last one as well. How had everything gone so disastrously wrong so quickly? Except it hadn't been quick at all. It had been happening all month. This was just the result.

Ella was fussing, so Mia fed and changed her before putting her down for a nap. Then she had a shower, hoping it might make her feel better, but everything only made her feel worse. She thought of going in search of Alessandro, but couldn't bear the thought of another argument, or, worse, a freezing silence.

How had it got this bad between them? Was there any way to make it better?

'Mia.' Alessandro stood in the doorway of the bedroom as she came out of the bathroom, finger-combing her damp hair. She stilled as she saw him, everything in her poised for flight.

'What is it?' she asked warily.

He shook his head slowly. 'I've been thinking.'

That didn't sound good. 'Thinking? About what?'

'About us.'

Her hands stilled and she turned to face him fully, lowering her hands from her hair. 'Alessandro…?'

'I never gave you a choice, Mia.'

*What…?*

'You did,' she protested, scanning his face for clues to what he was feeling.

'Not really. I as good as sent you to California, and then I took you from there, without you being able to do much about it. I practically forced you to marry me…'

Mia gazed at him, trying to figure out where he was going with this. 'But you asked me to choose, Alessandro. I was the one who proposed, after all—'

'Do you really think that was any choice at all? If you'd said no, I would have seduced you. I would have had my way. I was always determined about that. There was absolutely no way you weren't going to marry me, Mia.' He met her gaze bleakly, and Mia shook her head.

'Why are you telling me this now?'

'Because I realise I can't do this any more. I can't give you what you need, what you deserve.'

'Which is what?' Mia whispered.

'Love.' He spoke the word flatly. 'It's too hard for me, Mia. With my childhood…my parents… I can't do it.'

'Did I ever say I wanted you to love me?' Mia asked in a shaking voice, even though it hurt to say the words, because in her heart and mind she'd been asking him, begging him every day. Had he been able to see that? Had it horrified him?

'A marriage needs love as its foundation,' Alessandro stated. 'Without it, it will always crumble at one point or another. It won't be strong enough to endure. I've realised that now…and I realise that what we have isn't enough.'

'So what are you really saying?' Mia asked, her voice hardening. 'You want a divorce?'

'We could probably arrange an annulment, or otherwise, yes, a quiet divorce.'

'And what about Ella?' Mia demanded, her voice catching on her daughter's name. 'What about her needing a father? You insisted on that—'

'We'll arrange visits. I can still be part of her life. I want to be. That won't change.'

'Visits.' Mia felt faint suddenly, her vision blurring, as the awful import of everything Alessandro was saying slammed into her. Slowly she walked to the bed and sank onto its edge, blinking the world back into focus. 'Why are you telling me this now? Is it because of our argument?

What made you realise all this so suddenly?' Her voice rose and then broke. 'Was none of this real?'

'How could it have been?' Alessandro returned rawly. 'Considering?'

Tears stung her eyes then and she did her best to blink them back. She felt as if her heart was being wrung like a rag inside her, squeezing out its last painful drops of love. 'So all this time, you've just been pretending? Orchestrating a takeover? You are known to be subtle,' she added bitterly. 'Even when it's hostile.'

'Don't think of it like that, Mia…'

'How am I supposed to think of it?' she demanded. 'Either our marriage was real or it wasn't. Either the vows you made were sacred and binding or they weren't.'

'I'm trying to be fair and give you your freedom—'

'Some freedom. What am I supposed to do now?'

He spread his hands. 'Whatever you want. I'll make sure you have a generous settlement. You'll want for nothing—'

'I'll want for everything.' Mia's voice broke. 'Why are you doing this, Alessandro?'

'Because I told you, I realised that a marriage needs more than what we have to grow—'

'And you're so sure you can never, ever love me? Learn to love me, if it's so important?' Her voice broke as the full force of rejection hit her. He stayed silent, and she looked up, and for the first time she saw the torment on his face. 'Or are you worried that I can't love you?' she whispered, barely daring to say the words. 'Is that what this is about, Alessandro? Are you afraid?'

'I'm not afraid.'

'Then say the words,' she demanded. 'Say, "Mia, I don't love you and I never will."' He stayed silent and she rose, her hands balled into fists by her sides, risking everything on this. '*Say* them.'

'Mia...' He stopped and shook his head. 'I don't want to hurt you.'

'Well, you're failing miserably at that, because you already have. Immeasurably. And what I think, Alessandro, is that *you* don't want to be hurt. So tell me now that you don't love me. Make it real.'

He sighed heavily, his gaze averted. 'I'm not sure I know how to love.'

'So...'

A hesitation, endless, awful, as he searched her face, steeling himself. 'No,' Alessandro said finally. 'I don't love you. I... I never will.'

Mia had been bracing herself for it, expecting it, but those two simple, stark words still held the power to fell her. She swayed where she sat and two tears slipped quickly and coldly down her cheeks before she could stop them. She dashed her eyes with the back of her arm and then stood up on wobbly legs.

'Fine. I'll pack in the morning.'

'It's better this way...'

No, it wasn't. It wasn't at all. But at least she knew now. With a leaden heart, Mia walked out of the bedroom—and away from her husband.

He was a coward. Alessandro lay in bed, gritty-eyed as he stared at the ceiling. Mia was sleeping in a guest bedroom, and he missed her presence with a ferocity that undid him...but even more overwhelming and shaming was the truth pounding through him that he hadn't been brave enough to admit.

*I don't love you.*

Except he did. Of course he did. And in the moment she'd asked he'd known what a pathetic coward he was, because he'd been afraid to admit it. The most crucial moment of his life, and he'd blown it out of fear. He'd lied, because it had seemed easier. It had felt safer. Because letting her walk away now was surely better than letting her hurt him later...or, heaven forbid, hurting her.

Except he'd just hurt her unbearably.

I don't love you. The cruellest words he could have said, as terrible as the words his mother had said to him, which had tormented him for decades. How could he have done it? How could he have let himself?

*It would have been worse later*, he told himself for the tenth time. *Surely it would have been worse later.*

Except right now it felt like hell.

He shifted in the bed, knowing sleep would never come. Would she really leave in the morning, with Ella? Had he just fractured his family, and for what purpose? He'd convinced himself he'd been noble, saving her from a loveless marriage. How deluded was he, thinking that was the right choice? Mia had seen through him, of course. She'd known what this was really about.

It wasn't about him not loving her...it was about him loving her too much. It was about how loving someone meant losing yourself, just as they'd both feared, in their own ways. And gaining so much more...if Mia loved him back.

Why was he so scared to risk it? Risk himself? Could this really, possibly, be better?

It had to be.

The next morning, after a sleepless night, Alessandro came downstairs to find Mia already packed, Ella in her arms.

'You're going already...' Even though he'd been expecting it, he could scarcely believe the sight in front of him.

'It seems better.' Mia's voice was flat, her shoulders slumped. She looked as if all the life had drained out of her, as if the very will to live had been sucked from her soul.

He'd done this, Alessandro realised. This was his fault.

This was all going so horribly wrong, simply because he hadn't had the courage to take the biggest risk you could in this life…loving someone else. Giving them your heart. Accepting theirs in return.

And he knew he couldn't let it end this way. He wouldn't. He wouldn't live life as a coward, unwilling to take the biggest risk of all, to let go of control and hand someone his heart. 'Mia, wait.'

She looked at him with lifeless eyes, Ella clutched in her arms. 'Do you love me?' he asked, the words raw, his voice quavering.

She stared at him blankly, her face so weary and sad, tears nearly stung his eyes. 'Why are you asking that now, Alessandro?'

'Because…because it's important. Because I should have asked last night, when you asked me.'

'Why do you care, when you've already told me how you feel?' Mia responded quietly. 'Do you just want to pour salt into my wound? Isn't it enough that you don't love me?'

He hesitated, poised to fly, afraid to fall. Even now, with everything at stake, he held back. And in his silence was his condemnation.

'I've called a taxi,' Mia said. 'It should be here now.'

Alessandro glanced at her one small travel bag. 'Where are your bags?'

'I'm leaving everything here. I… I don't want it. I certainly don't need all those fancy gowns and things.' From outside they heard the crunch of tyres on gravel. Mia hoisted her bag in one hand, Ella in her car seat in the other.

This was it. The end. She was really leaving, because he was going to let her.

*Do you love me?*

She hadn't answered the question, and Alessandro couldn't blame her, considering what his own response had been last night.

He'd said he wasn't capable of love, or even that he knew what it was, and yet…what if he did?

*What if in this moment he really did?*

What if real love wasn't a safe landing, but a dangerous fall? What if it was risking everything, not knowing the result? Letting yourself get hurt, because that was part of the whole, terrifying, incredible deal?

Mia was at the door, one hand reaching for the handle, the seconds sliding past far too fast.

'Mia!' His voice came out in a shout of command that made her stiffen. 'Mia,' he said more softly. 'Please wait.'

'Why? What is there left to say?'

He swallowed hard, his throat impossibly tight. Now. He needed to say it now. She reached for the handle again.

'I love you.'

The words fell into the stillness, and even now part of him wanted to snatch them back. The last time he'd said them had been to his mother, and she'd wearily told him she wished she'd never had him. He'd vowed never to say them again. Never to want or need to say them again.

But Mia had changed him. Loving Mia had changed him.

'Alessandro…' She shook her head slowly. 'Why are you saying this now? You can't mean it…'

'I do. I was too much of a coward to say it before. But the truth is I've been falling in love with you for months now, and fighting it all the way.' His words came faster and more assuredly, and the release of finally being open and honest was strangely wonderful. Freeing in a way he'd never expected. 'I never wanted to love anyone, Mia. My mother didn't love me, and I wanted her to, desperately. She told me she wished she'd never had me…she forgot about and neglected me time and again, and still I wished she'd love me. I loved her.' He swallowed hard, the words coming faster and faster as he tried to explain. 'At a young age I told myself I'd never let someone have that kind of control over me. I'd be the one who was in control, always, and I made that my life's mission. Yet here I am, risking everything because it's too important not to. Because I love you too much, and I don't want to be a coward any more. I love you, Mia. I love you.'

He spread his hands wide, his heart thudding as he waited for her response.

'You…love me?' She sounded incredulous as she turned from the door and put down her bag and Ella's car seat.

'With all my soul. All my heart. I'm terrified, Mia. I'm shaking.' He let out a ragged laugh. 'And yet here I am, giving everything I have to you. You can do with it as you will. You can walk out that door as you were intending to, or you can come over here and slap my face and tell me what an arrogant imbecile I am.' He took a quick, steadying breath. 'Or you can tell me you love me back, or even that you could learn to love me, like you asked me to last night, and you'll give us a chance even though I've been so very stupid and scared. I wasn't giving you your freedom… I was trying to find mine. I'm sorry. I don't want you to go. I love you.'

He was babbling, but he didn't care. He'd say anything to make her stay…even, *especially*, the truth.

'I've been afraid too,' Mia said after a long moment. 'I've been fighting it too, because I was scared of losing myself, like I said. So scared, and yet it happened anyway.'

'Yes.' Alessandro's voice was fervent. 'But I realised last night that loving someone means losing yourself—to another person. Entrusting them with everything that you are. And that's terrifying, but it's also so good and right. I know I'll mess up, Mia, so many times. I'll be angry or thoughtless or bossy or…something. But I'll try. And I hope you'll forgive me. And learn to love—'

'Oh, Alessandro, you idiot,' Mia said with tears in her

voice. 'I already love you. I've loved you for ages. I just thought you'd never love me. You'd never do what you just said, and offer me everything. Ever since our wedding I've felt you've been holding something back…'

'I know. I have been. But it's yours now. All of it— me—is yours. I'll tell you whatever you like. I'll give you the parts of myself I've been trying to hide, the ones that are dark and ugly and needy. And hopefully you won't be put off—'

'Never,' Mia whispered. Tears trickled down her face, and with a jolt Alessandro realised he was crying too.

'So you'll stay?'

'Yes.' Mia walked towards him, her arms held out, so all it took were two steps for Alessandro to catch her up in his, pulling her body closely to his. Home. He was home. 'I'll stay,' Mia whispered as he lowered his head to kiss her. 'I'll stay. For ever.'

# EPILOGUE

*Three years later*

SUN BEAMED DOWN on the terrace as Mia stepped out, baby Milo in her arms. It was her son's christening, three months after his birth. Just like Ella, he had Alessandro's grey eyes and her blonde hair. He gurgled up at her now before catching sight of his father and reaching out chubby arms to him.

'Hello, *caro*,' Alessandro said, scooping up his son easily and planting a kiss on his plump cheek. 'It's your special day.'

'She's been good as gold,' Alyssa said as she joined them on the terrace, holding Ella, now three and a half, by the hand. 'A very proud big sister.'

Mia smiled at Ella, and then shared a loving look with Alessandro. The last three years had been so wonderful, so blessed. Admittedly, it hadn't always been easy. They'd had their battles and struggles, both of them learning day by day to let go of control, of their very selves, as they committed themselves to each other in small yet significant ways.

Now Alessandro brushed a kiss across her lips as he cradled their son. 'Happy?' he asked softly, his eyes full of warmth and tenderness that, even after three years, made Mia melt inside.

She reached for his free hand, lacing her fingers through his. 'Yes,' she told him, thankful for so much, and especially this man by her side who had chosen to share his life, his very self, with her. 'Very, very happy.'

\* \* \* \* \*

# SECRETS OF HIS FORBIDDEN CINDERELLA

## CAITLIN CREWS

# CHAPTER ONE

"His Excellency is not at home, madam." The butler sniffed, visibly appalled.

He did not so much bar the door to the grand and ancient palatial home as inhabit it, because such a glorious door—crafted by the hands of long-dead masters and gifted to the aristocratic occupants likely on bended knee and with the intercession of a heavenly host, because that was how things happened here in this fairy tale of a place that had claimed this part of Spain for many centuries—could not be blocked by a single person, no matter how officious or aghast.

And the butler was both, in spades. "One does not *drop in* on the Nineteenth Duke of Marinceli, Most Excellent Grandee of Spain."

Amelia Ransom, considered excellent by her closest friends instead of an entire nation and with decidedly lowbrow peasant blood to prove it, made herself smile. Very much as if she hadn't, in fact, turned up at the door of a house so imposing that it was unofficially known as *el monstruo*—even by its occupants. "I know for a fact that the Duke is in."

An old acquaintance of hers still lived in one of the nearby villages—"nearby" meaning miles upon miles away because the Marinceli estate was itself so enormous—and had reported that the Duke's plane had been seen flying overhead two days ago. And that the flag with the Marinceli coat of arms had been raised over the house shortly thereafter, meaning the great man was in residence.

"You mistake my meaning," the butler replied, his deep, cavernous face set in lines of affront and indignation that should have made Amelia slink off in shame. And might have, had she been here for any reason at all but the one she'd come to share with Teo de Luz, her former stepbrother and the grandiose Duke in question. "His Excellency is most certainly not at home to you."

It was tempting to take that as the final word on the matter. Amelia would have been just as happy not to have to make this trip in the first place. It had been a gruesome red-eye flight out of San Francisco to Paris, particularly in the unappealing seat that had been all she could get on short notice. The much shorter flight to Madrid had been fine, but then there was the drive out of the city and into the rolling hills where the de Luz family had been rooted deep for what might as well have been forever, at this point.

"I think you'll find he'll see me," Amelia said, with tremendous confidence brought on by fatigue. And possibly by fear of her reception—and not from the butler. She stared back at the man with his ruffled feathers and astonished air, who did not look convinced. "Really. Ask him."

"That is utterly out of the question," the butler retorted, in freezing tones. "I cannot fathom how you made it onto the property in the first place. Much less marched up to pound on the door like some…salesman."

He spat out that last word as if a salesman was akin to syphilis.

Only far more unsavory.

If only he knew the sort of news Amelia had come to impart. She imagined he would cross himself. Possibly spit on the ground. And she could sympathize.

She felt much the same way.

"I expect you go to great lengths to keep the Duke's many would-be suitors from clamoring at the door," she said brightly, as if the butler had been kind and welcoming or open to conversation in any way. "He must be the most eligible man in the world by now."

She'd personally witnessed the commotion Teo caused when enterprising women got the scent of him, long before he'd assumed his title. That was why she hadn't even bothered attempting to get in the main gates, miles away from the front entrance of the stately home that was more properly a palace. The grand entrance and gates were guarded by officious security who could be reliably depended upon to let absolutely no one in. Amelia had therefore driven in on one of the forgotten little medieval lanes that snaked around from the farthest corner of the great estate, there for the use of the gamekeeper and his staff. Then she'd left her hired car near the lake that had been a favorite reading spot of hers back in the day.

That way she could walk to clear her head from the flight and so little sleep, prepare herself for the scene before her with Teo and best of all, actually make it to the soaring front door that would not have looked out of place on a cathedral. Her car would have been stopped. A woman on foot was less noticeable. That was her thinking.

She hadn't really thought past getting to the door, however, and she should have.

The butler was slipping a sleek smartphone from the pocket of his coat, no doubt to summon the security force to bodily remove her. Which would not suit her at all.

"I'm not another of Teo's many groupies," Amelia said, and something flashed in her at that. Because that wasn't *precisely* true, was it? Not after what she'd done. "I'm his stepsister."

The butler did not do anything so unrefined as *sneer* at her for the unpardonable sin of referring to Teo by not only his Christian name, but a nickname. He managed to look down his nose, however, as if the appendage was the highest summit in the Pyrenees.

"The Duke is not in possession of a stepsister, madam."

"Former stepsister," Amelia amended. "Though some bonds far exceed a single marriage, don't they?"

Her smile faded a bit as the butler stared down at her as if she was a talking rat. Or some other bit of vermin that didn't know its place.

"I doubt very much that His Excellency recognizes *bonds* of any description," the butler clipped out. His expression suggested Amelia had offended him, personally, by suggesting otherwise. "His familial connections tend toward the aristocratic if not outright royal and are all rather distant. They are recorded in every detail. And no *stepsisters* appear in any of these official records."

Amelia pressed her advantage, scant though it was. "But you don't know how Teo feels about members of the various blended families his father made while he was still alive and marrying, do you? Do you really dare send me away without finding out?"

And for a long moment, they only stared at each other. Each waiting to call the other's bluff.

Amelia wished that she'd stopped somewhere and freshened up. She'd dressed to impress precisely no one back in San Francisco many, many hours ago, and she was afraid that showed. She didn't particularly care if Teo saw her looking rumpled, but butlers in places like this tended to be far more snobbish than their exalted employers. Her ratty old peacoat was a good barrier against the blustery cold of the January day. The jeans she'd slept in on the long flight from San Francisco were a touch too faded and shoutily American, now that she considered it in the pale Spanish morning. And the boots that hadn't seemed to need a polish back home seemed desperately in need of one now, here on the gleaming marble stair that led inside the palatial house she still dreamed about, sometimes.

Because *el monstruo* was truly a fairy-tale castle, and then some. There were turrets and dramatic spires, wings sprouting off this way and that, with pristine land rolling off on all sides toward the undeveloped horizon. Standing here, it was easy to imagine that the breathlessly blue-blooded family that had lived here for the better part of European history was the only family that had ever existed, anywhere.

The de Luzes would no doubt agree.

Of all her mother's husbands—all the titled gentlemen, the courtiers with hints of royalty, the celebrities and the politicians who had found themselves charmed and captivated and discarded in turn by the notorious Marie French—none had impressed themselves on

Amelia as much as Luis Calvo, the Eighteenth Duke of Marinceli. Teo's father, whom Marie had pursued, caught and then inevitably lost over the course of a few whirlwind years when Amelia was still a teenager.

As formative experiences went, finding herself thrust into the middle of a world like the de Luzes', so excruciatingly exclusive, deeply moneyed and aristocratic that they might as well have lived on another planet altogether—and for all intents and purposes, did—had been as ruinous as it had been exhilarating. Marie had always preferred rich men. But add together every conventionally rich man in the world and it would still barely scratch the surface of the de Luz fortune. And the nineteen generations of power and influence that infused it, expanded it and solidified it.

Amelia had not recovered as quickly from this marriage as she had from the others her mother had subjected her to over the years. Or from this *place*. And most of all, she had never quite gotten over the man who lived here now, his father dead and gone. And when she'd belatedly performed a much-needed exorcism to get rid of the hold those years kept on her, she'd soon discovered that she'd created a far bigger problem.

*You've come here to create a solution,* she reminded herself primly.

Not that it would matter why she'd come if she couldn't get in the door.

Teo de Luz—once her forbidding, stern and usually outright hostile stepbrother, now the latest Duke in a line so long and storied she'd once heard giddy society types braying to each other that the de Luz family was, in fact, *Spain itself*—wasn't the sort of man who could be waylaid. There were no accidental meetings with him in local coffee shops; he owned half the coffee farms in Kenya. He did not frequent public gyms or lower himself to the questionable hospitality of bars or restaurants accessible to the hoi polloi. He had chauffeurs. Private jets. Shops closed to accommodate him, restaurants offered him their private rooms, and he stayed in secluded villas in the few locations where he did not hold property, never public hotels.

The sorts of places he went for fun didn't bother to put names on the doors. You either knew where they were, or you didn't. You were either in the club, or you were out.

If you had to ask, you didn't belong.

Amelia was sure that if she looked closely at the de Luz coat of arms, that's what it would read.

As the daughter of Marie French, Amelia had grown up *close to* a lot of money, but never *of* it. Her mother was famous for her many divorces, and she'd certainly gathered herself a tidy sum from various payouts—alimony, divorce settlements, baubles and properties that had been showered upon her by this lover or that—but the kind of wealth and power that the de Luz family had in spades and demonstrated so decidedly here wasn't the sort that could be amassed by one person. Or within one lifetime.

It would take twenty generations to even make a dent.

If Amelia could turn back the clock and make all of this go away, she would. If she could reach back these few, crucial months and slap some sense into herself long before she'd had her brilliant idea at the end of the summer, she'd swing hard. Her palms itched at the notion.

But wishing didn't change the facts.

"Please tell Teo that it's me," she said sunnily to the dour man towering over her, possibly prepared to stand right where he was for another twenty generations. She smiled as if he'd already agreed. "Amelia. His favorite stepsister."

She was fairly certain she was not Teo's favorite anything, but that wasn't something she planned to share. And for another long, tense moment, there on the front step where she could feel the winter wind bite at her, Amelia thought that the butler would slam the door in her face and let the estate's security detail sort her out.

A part of her hoped he would. Because surely, if she'd gone to all the trouble to fly herself to Spain, turn up on his doorstep and *try* to tell him what she needed to tell him, that was enough. Above and beyond the call of duty, really.

She could only do so much, after all. It wasn't *her* fault the man chose to barricade himself away like this.

*He wasn't barricaded away last fall,* a voice inside her that she was terribly afraid was her conscience chimed in.

It had been late September when she'd found her way here last. She'd come under the cover of darkness, blending in with the extensive crowds who flocked to the estate for the Marinceli Masquerade that took place every fall to commemorate the birthday of the long-dead Tenth Duke. It was a glittering, diamond-edged fantasy that had been going on in one form or another for three hundred years. Amelia had come with such a different purpose then. It had been her one opportunity to enact her exorcism, and she had dedicated herself to the task. She had dressed like a stranger and had even gone so far as to dye her hair and wear colored contacts. Because she had her mother's violet eyes, and people did tend to remember them.

And she'd spent the months since congratulating herself on a job well done. Sometimes immersion therapy was the only way to go. Even when she'd understood what she'd inadvertently done, she hadn't regretted what she'd done—only what the result of it would ask of her.

But today, it was creeping toward midday, and the weather was raw. This part of Spain was covered in a brooding winter storm that had made her drive from Madrid dicey. Particularly when she'd skirted around the mountains—the snow-covered peaks of which she could feel, now, in the frigid wind that gusted at her as she waited for the butler's decision.

She didn't particularly relish repeating that drive, especially without getting what she'd come for here. But she would do it if necessary. And then she would hole up in a hotel somewhere and either try to come up with a new plan to find Teo and speak to him, or she would simply go back home and get on with this new life of hers.

She was giving herself a little pep talk about what that would look like when the butler stepped back, and inclined his head.

Very, very slightly. Grudgingly, even.

"If madam will wait here," he said, beckoning her inside to what she supposed was the foyer. Though it bore no resemblance to any other foyer Amelia had ever seen.

It always seemed to her like its own ballroom, dizzy with chandeliers, mosaic-worked mirrors and statuary clearly meant to intimidate. This was not a stately home built to offer invitations. Quite the opposite. It had been, variously, a fortress, stronghold, the seat of a revolution, a bolt-hole for a deposed king, the birthplace of a queen and a long list of other dramatic accomplishments that Amelia had spent two very long, very lonely winters studying. Right here in the vast library that soared up three floors, commanded its own wing and was more extensive than many university collections.

Amelia smiled at the butler, though she could admit it was mostly saccharine, as he shut the heavy door behind her.

He did not return the favor.

He indicated a stone bench against the wall and waited until Amelia sat.

"This is a private home, madam, not a museum," he intoned. At her. "It is certainly not open to spontaneous visits from the public. Please respect the Duke's wishes and stay right here. Do not move. Do not explore. Do you understand?"

"Of course," Amelia said, frowning slightly, as if wandering off into the house where she'd once lived had never occurred to her.

Then again, the last time she'd actually lived here had been ten years ago and she hadn't felt free to wander gaily about the place then, either. That she was unwelcome here had been made very clear. From Teo, certainly, if not from his distant father, who had been interested only in his scandalous new wife. And certainly from the legion of staff who were possessed of their own opinions about the notorious Marie French as their new mistress. Her teenage daughter had been, at best, a casualty of that war.

Or anyway, that was how Amelia had always felt.

And always stern, usually visibly horrified Teo, with

those simmering black eyes, that blade of an aristocratic nose and that cruelly sensual mouth that haunted her dreams in ways that only made sense later—

Well. That had never helped.

The Amelia who had been so bent on exorcism would have launched herself into action even as the butler's footsteps faded away, echoing off into the maw of the great house that stood proud around her. That version of herself had been deeply committed to reclaiming her life. To making something she wanted out of the things she'd been given and the things that had been pressed upon her, one way or another.

She really had made huge changes in her life last summer. She had settled in San Francisco, for one thing. No longer did she travel about with her mother, forced to act in all kinds of roles that only put strain on their already unconventional relationship.

Her first attempt at setting healthy boundaries with Marie had come when Amelia had insisted on going to college, an enterprise that her mother had found amusing at best and actively baffling at worst.

"There's only one school that matters, silly girl," Marie had said, laughing wildly in that sultry way of hers that Amelia had watched pull men to her from across vast ballrooms. "We call it Hard Knocks University and guess what? Tuition's free."

Unlike many women who, like Marie, married and divorced with the pinpoint accuracy of an expert marksman, Marie had always delighted in the fact that she'd produced a child. But then, that was the thing the dismissive, disparaging tabloids had never understood about her. Was she a gold digger? Almost certainly. But she was also earthy, charming and frequently delightful.

She collected husbands because she fell for them, spent their money because she only fell for wealthy ones and moved on when she was bored. She'd made it her life's work. And yet many of her discarded ex-lovers still chased after her, desperate for another taste.

Amelia never knew if she admired her mother or despaired of her.

"I don't think a life of ease, cushioned by alimony payments from some of the richest men alive, constitutes the school of hard knocks," Amelia had replied drily.

Marie had thrown up her hands. Literally. And Amelia had gotten her first taste of victory.

She had loved college. She had hidden away in Boston for four wonderful years. She'd walked along the Charles. She'd spent lazy, pretty afternoons on the Common. She'd taken trips on the weekend down to the Cape or explored the out-of-the-way harbors that dotted the rocky Maine coast. She'd camped in the Berkshires. She'd hiked through the turning leaves in the New England fall, gotten maple syrup straight from the tap in Vermont and had stayed in stark farmhouses that reminded her of Edith Wharton novels.

She had studied anthropology. Sociology. Poetry. Whatever took her fancy as well as the finance and business courses that gave her a solid foundation to best serve her mother's needs. And for four glorious years, she'd been nothing more and nothing less than another college student in one of the best college towns in existence.

After graduation, she'd gone straight back to the job she'd been preparing for all her life. Her mother's personal assistant, financial manager, moving specialist and far-too-often on-call therapist.

It was that last part that got old, and fast. Last June, Amelia had decided that she was never going to live her own life if she was too busy parsing every detail of Marie's. That was when she'd decided that of all the places she'd been, she could most see herself living in beautiful San Francisco.

"But I almost never go to San Francisco," Marie had protested. And she'd laughed when Amelia only stared back at her blandly. "Fair enough."

Her summer in San Francisco had felt like the life Amelia had always wanted. She was twenty-six years old. The perfect age, or so it seemed to her, to be on her own in a marvelous, magical city. She could handle her mother's affairs from afar, and did, and only rarely had to fly off to sort out whatever disaster her mother had created across the world somewhere.

Amelia had even decided that she might as well start dating. Because that was what normal people did, according to her friends. They did something other than marry in haste, then repent in the presence of swathes of legal teams, the better to iron out advantageous financial settlements.

But a funny thing happened every time Amelia had tried to lose herself in the moment and let passion—or a third glass of wine—sweep her away. Not that there was much *sweeping*. If she let a date kiss her, and even if she enjoyed it, the same thing happened every time.

Sooner or later, instead of getting excited about her date, she would find herself imagining simmering black eyes. That impossible blade of a nose that gave him the haughty look of an ancient coin—ones that were likely made from the piles of gold the de Luz family hoarded.

And that stern, sensual mouth that could only be Teo's.

Damn him.

The terrible truth she'd discovered last summer was that she couldn't seem to get past her once-upon-a-time stepbrother. And she might not have thought of the Masquerade, but she'd been in Europe anyway. Marie had summoned Amelia to attend to her as she'd exited one love affair and started another in Italy. And somehow, while moving Marie's things from one jaw-dropping Amalfi Coast villa to another, Amelia had started thinking about the Marinceli Masquerade at *el monstruo*. Filled with people in the September night, all of them draped in masks and costumes as they danced away the last of summer the way they'd been doing for generations.

Surely it was the perfect opportunity to get that man, her former stepbrother who took up too much space in her head, out of her system. Once and for all. Because Amelia felt certain that in order to have that normal life she wanted, she really might like to do more than kiss a man someday.

That meant she was going to have to *contend with* Teo.

And once the notion had taken hold, Amelia couldn't seem to think about anything else.

But then, the funny thing about life was that there were always so many different and unexpected ways to repent a moment of haste. Her childhood had taught her that. Her mother was the poster girl for repenting over the course of years and through lawsuits, some brought against her by the angry heirs of men who had attempted to win her favor via excessive bequests.

In Amelia's case, it wasn't a single moment she needed to repent. More like a stolen, astonishing hour.

As soon as she could breathe again, she'd crept out one of the many side doors in this monstrosity of a private palace. She had fled under cover of darkness and she had never meant to return.

Therefore, naturally, here she was. A little more than three months later, sitting on a hard stone bench surrounded by grimacing old statues that glared down at her in judgment. As if they knew exactly what she'd done and resented her for her temerity.

"You and me both," she muttered at them.

And regretted it when her voice seemed to roll out before her, tumbling deep into the quiet depths of the house.

Of course, the historic seat of the Marinceli empire wasn't simply *quiet*. It was self-consciously, dramatically *hushed*. Not the sort of sound that came from emptiness or neglect, but was instead one more marker of impossible wealth. Wealth, consequence and a power so deep and so vast it stretched back centuries and more to the point, infused the very stones in the ceilings and the walls.

If a person really listened, they could *hear* all that might and glory in the lush quiet, even sitting still in the foyer, as directed.

Amelia unbuttoned her coat, letting the heavier flaps fall to her sides. She'd learned a long time ago that there was no point competing in places or situations like this. She was always so obviously and irrevocably American, for one thing. That she would therefore be considered gauche and inappropriate by a certain set of Europeans was understood. And no matter what she wore or how she comported herself, or even if she adopted excruciatingly correct manners, she would always be seen through the lens of her mother. So she'd learned long time ago that she might as well stop trying to convince anyone otherwise.

Things that couldn't be changed, Amelia had found, could often be fashioned into weapons.

From far off, she heard the sounds of approaching footsteps, and braced herself. She held her breath—

But it was only the butler again. He appeared before her, gazing at her with suspicion, as if he expected to find her cutting the paintings out of their frames and stuffing them down the back of her jeans. Amelia smiled. Widely.

If anything, that seemed to horrify him more. She could tell by the way his chin seemed to recede into his neck.

"If you will follow me," he said, every syllable dripping with disapproval. "The Duke is a very important man. He is excessively busy. You will do well to bear in mind the compliment it is that he has chosen to carve out a few moments to entertain this untoward and wholly discourteous appearance of yours."

"I'll be sure to thank him," Amelia said, rising to her feet. The butler only stared back at her. "Profusely."

But the added word didn't seem to help. The butler turned on his heel and stalked off. Amelia followed, impressed against her will at the sheer umbrage he managed to carry in his shoulders.

He led her through the great hall, then off into the

long gallery that connected the main part of the house to some of its seemingly haphazard wings. It was thick with portraits of black-eyed, haughty-looking men in a variety of historical outfits. She had been in the same gallery before, as an obsessed sixteen-year-old, tracking the evolution of Teo's features through ages and ancestors.

Today she found it wasn't Teo's features she was thinking of, or not entirely. She was trying to imagine all these fierce old aristocrats combined with her, and coming away with nothing much besides a wholly unwelcome stab of guilt. She did her best to swallow that down as they left the gallery and moved farther into the labyrinth of the grand house.

All the rooms they passed were the same. Everything gleamed, a beacon of understated, exceptional taste. There were no knickknacks. No personal items. No shoes kicked beneath a couch or empty mugs on a table. Each room was arranged around a color scheme, or a view, or some other unifying notion. There were no antiques in the general sense. If she recalled correctly, every item in this house was priceless. Literally without price because any value attached would be too exorbitant. The house was filled with hand-selected, finely wrought pieces of art that had been presented to the family at one point or another by grateful, obsequious artisans and vassals and would-be allies.

The butler stopped, eventually, with the click of his heels and tilt of his head—both of which he managed to make an insult—before a door. Calculating quickly, Amelia figured that this must be the Duke's study. Ten years ago, Teo's father had spent his days here, conducting his business when he was at home. She'd had absolutely no occasion to venture to this part of the house, and after an initial introductory tour, hadn't.

It was only now, as the butler opened the door and ushered her inside, that she acknowledged the flutter in her belly. Not only acknowledged it, but accepted that she couldn't quite tell if it was anticipation, fear or a spicy little mix of both.

The door closed behind her with a quiet click that she felt was as passive-aggressive as the rest. But she had other things to think about.

Because this room, like every other room in this palace, exuded magnificence, wealth and quiet elegance. It was its own little library, and "little" only in comparison with the grand one across the house. There was a fire in the hearth and gleaming bookshelves packed tight with books—and not in matching volumes, with gold-lettered spines, suggesting no one touched them. This was a working library. A personal collection, clearly. There were even photographs in frames on the shelves, almost as if a regular human lived here and collected memories as well as priceless objects. There was a surprising amount of light coming in from the winter day outside, through the glass dome atop the ceiling and more, through the glass doors that opened up over the gardens.

Amelia took all of that in, and then, slowly and carefully—as if it might hurt her, because she was terribly afraid it might—she let her eyes rest on the man who waited there. He leaned against the vast expanse of a very old, very beautiful antique desk that somehow managed to connote brooding masculinity and centuries of power in its lines.

Or maybe that was the man himself.

He was like a song that sang in her, that called the dawn, that changed the world.

Teo de Luz, once upon a time her stepbrother and now a far greater problem in her life, waited there as if he was one of the statues she'd seen in the hallways, crafted by old masters with decidedly famous and inspired hands. And this was not one of the few, very rare photographs of him that a person could find if they deep-dived online. This was not the man she'd found at the Masquerade last September—masked, hidden and diluted in some way, she'd assured herself, even if his touch had not felt *diluted* in any way. This was not even the stepbrother she remembered from ten years ago.

Teo was older now. He was beautiful and he was ferocious, and it was truly awful, how a single man could seem as imposing and great as the ancient house they stood in.

And suddenly, Amelia was all too aware of every choice she'd made that had brought her here to stand before him. She felt as fatigued and threadbare as her jeans.

She ordered herself to speak, but when she lifted her chin to do so, she found herself…caught.

Because even here, in his own private library with the weak winter light pouring in and a fire crackling in a fireplace—all things which should have made this scene domestic and soft—Teo was something *more* than merely a man.

He was always bigger than she remembered. Taller, more solid. His shoulders were wide and the rest of him was long, lean, and she knew, now, that he was made entirely of muscle. Everywhere. His black eyes simmered, like his ancestors' out there in the long gallery, but she had somehow dimmed the effect of them in her mind. In person, he was electric. His hair was still inky black, close cropped, and she saw no hint of gray at his temples. He had those unfair cheekbones that might have seemed pretty were it not for the masculine heft of his nose, and then, below, that sensuous, impossible mouth that made her feel flushed.

Especially because now she knew what he could do with it.

And she hadn't seen him clearly that night in September. That had been the point. She had been bold and daring, and he had responded with that brooding, overwhelming passion that had literally swept her off her feet. Into his arms, against a wall. And then, in a private salon, still dressed in their finery, with fabric pushed aside in haste and need.

Too much haste and need, it turned out.

Even though she had watched him roll on protection.

But now, he wore nothing to cover his face. And he wasn't smiling slightly, the way he had then. Those dark eyes of his weren't lit up with that particular knowing gleam that had turned her molten and soft.

On the contrary, his look was frigid. Stern and disapproving.

It made her remember—too late, always too late—that he wasn't simply a man. He was all the men who had come before him, too. He was the Duke, and the weight of that made him…colossal.

A decade ago, on the very rare occasions that he had looked at her at all, he had looked at her like this.

But it felt a lot worse now.

"This is a surprise," Teo said, with no preamble. "Not a pleasant one."

One of his inky brows rose, a gesture that he must have inherited from the royal branch of his family tree, because it made Amelia want to genuflect. She did not.

"Hi, Teo," she replied.

Foolishly.

"You will have to remind me of your name," he said, and there was a gleam in his eyes now. It made her feel quivery in a completely different way. And she didn't believe for a second that he didn't know who she was. "I'm afraid that I did not retain the particulars of my father's regrettable romantic choices."

"I understand. I had to block out a whole lot of my mother's marriages, too."

A muscle worked in his lean, perfect jaw. "Allow me to offer a warning now, before this goes any further. If you have come here in some misguided attempt to extort money from me based upon an association I forgot before it ended, you will be disappointed. And as I cannot think of any other reason why you should intrude upon my privacy, I will have to ask you to leave."

Amelia considered him. "You could have had the butler say that, surely."

"I will admit to a morbid sense of curiosity." His gaze swept over her. "And it is satisfied." He didn't wave a languid hand like a sulky monarch and still, he dismissed her. "You may go."

Amelia ordered the part of her that wanted to obey him, automatically, to settle down. "You don't want to hear why I've come?"

"I am certain I do not."

"That will make it fast, then."

Amelia could admit she felt…too much. Perhaps a touch of shame for having to come to him like this—

especially after the last time she'd shown up here, uninvited. Her pulse kicked at her, making her feel...*fluttery*. And she was, embarrassingly, as molten and soft as if he'd smiled at her the way he had in September.

When he hadn't ventured anywhere near a smile.

"Never draw out the ugly things," Marie had always told her. "The quicker you get them over with, the more you can think about the good parts instead."

*Just do it, be done with it and go,* she ordered herself.

And who cared if her throat was dry enough to start its own fire?

"I'm pregnant," she announced into the intimidatingly, exultantly blue-blooded room. To a man who was all of that and more. "You're the father. And before you tell me that's impossible, I was at the Masquerade last fall and yes, I dyed my hair red."

She could only describe the look on his face as a storm, so she hurried on.

"And because you asked, I'm Amelia Ransom. You really were my stepbrother way back when. I hope that doesn't make this awkward."

# CHAPTER TWO

HIS EXCELLENCY MATEO ENRIQUE ARMANDO DE LUZ, Nineteenth Duke of Marinceli, Grandee of Spain, and a man without peer—by definition and inclination alike—did not care for American women in general or the loathsome, avaricious Marie French in particular. He had viewed her corruption of his once proud father as a personal betrayal, and had celebrated their inevitable divorce as if it were his own narrow escape from the grasping woman's mercenary clutches.

That his father had fallen for such a creature had been a deep humiliation Teo was terribly afraid stained him, too. They were de Luzes. They were not meant to topple before such crassness, much less *marry* it.

His father's subsequent wives had, at the very least, been from a certain swathe of European aristocracy. Only Marie Force had managed to tempt the Eighteenth Duke into breaking from centuries of tradition. Only her, a coarse and common woman whose gold digging had already been a thing of legend.

Teo was the only heir to dukedom that had never been polluted in living memory—until Marie.

By extension, Teo had never cared for Marie's daughter, either, with those same unearthly purple eyes that had always seemed to him a commentary on her character. Or decided lack thereof.

Even though Amelia had been little more than a child—*sixteen is not precisely a toddler,* came a contrary voice inside him that he chose to ignore—Teo had been certain her sins had been stamped upon her then, every new curve a bit of dark foreshadowing. With such a mother, she had only ever been destined to head in one direction.

"Pregnant," he said, as if tasting the word.

"Coming up on eighteen weeks," she replied, with rather appalling cheer. When he only gazed at her in disbelief, she continued. "If you count backward, you'll find that it matches right up with the Masquerade."

"Thank you, Miss Ransom," Teo replied after a moment, in the frigid tones that usually made those around him quail, scrape and apologize. The woman standing just inside the door of his study looked notably unaffected. "I am capable of performing simple mathematical equations."

All she did was smile. As if she doubted him, but was magnanimously keeping that opinion to herself.

It…irritated him. And Teo was rarely irritated by anything—because his life was arranged to avoid anything and anyone who might dare to annoy him in any way.

Perhaps he should have expected something like this. Pregnancy claims upon him were always and forever naked attempts to grab a chunk of the de Luz fortune and then bask in the glory of the many titles, honors and estates that went along with the name. It wasn't really a surprise that this impertinent, insolent creature of questionable parentage had developed ideas above her station when she'd spent those mercifully brief years thrust into the exalted realm of his family.

Teo understood it, on some level. Who wouldn't wish to be a de Luz?

Amelia Ransom, still cursed with those indecorous purple eyes, stood before him on a rug so old that its actual provenance was still hotly contested by the historians who periodically combed through the de Luz house and grounds and wrote operatic scholarly dissertations on the significance of the family collections. That she should be deeply shamed by her presence here—and the fact that the carpet beneath her feet boasted a pedigree while she did not—seemed not to have occurred to her.

Especially while she was issuing preposterous accusations. Involving fancy dress and dyed hair, of all things.

It was all so preposterous, in fact, that Teo could hardly rouse himself to reply further.

Because he was the current head of one of the most ancient houses in the world, and the favor of his time and good temper was not granted to any bedraggled creature who happened along and turned up at his door.

Not that many creatures, bedraggled or otherwise, usually dared "turn up" in his presence. Or managed to "happen along" in the first place even if they did dare, as he employed what he'd believed until now to be an excellent security service. He made a mental note to replace them. Before the next dawn.

And remembered as he did that Amelia's mother had been notable chiefly for the things she'd dared. All of which she'd gone ahead and executed without the faintest notion of her own gaucheness.

Hadn't he always known that her daughter would turn out just like her?

"I've learned many things since September," said the creature before him. He had recognized her on sight, of course, though he had not intended to gift her with that knowledge. Because she should have assumed that she was entirely unworthy of his notice and his memory alike. Instead, she was talking at him in that same offensively *friendly* voice that made him think of overly bright, manic toothpaste commercials. "One of them—which you would think ought to go without saying—is don't disguise yourself and have relations with your former stepbrother and think there won't be repercussions."

"I have yet to accept that any 'relations' occurred," Teo said in what he thought was a mild voice, all things considered.

"Acceptance, or the lack of it, doesn't change the facts," Amelia replied, and Teo saw a glimpse of something steely in those garish eyes of hers. "And the fact is, I'm pregnant with your baby."

"How convenient for you."

He watched her from his position against his desk, where he felt significantly less at his ease than he had moments before. Amelia, meanwhile, did not seem particularly thrown by his reaction. There were no tears. No wilting or wailing, the way there normally was during outlandish pregnancy claims—if the reports he'd received were to be believed. If anything, she brightened.

"I'm informing you because it's the right thing to do," she told him, with a hint of self-righteous piety about her, then. "Not because I need or want you to do anything. Consider yourself informed."

She turned then, and Teo almost let her go. Purely

to see if she would do what he thought she meant to do, which was march straight off—but only so far, as it was difficult to extort money from a man once ejected from his presence. He assumed she knew it.

He decided he wouldn't play her game. "Surely the point of disguising yourself, as you claim you did, and then deciding to have 'relations' with me under false pretenses, would be to stay. Not to flounce off because I've failed to respond as you would like."

It would have been easy enough to find photos of the Masquerade, he told himself. He had danced with a luscious redhead, then disappeared with her for a time. Anyone might have guessed what they'd been up to.

That certainly didn't mean that *this* woman was that redhead. His mind reeled away from that possibility even as his body readied itself, remembering.

Amelia waved a distinctly impolite hand in the air, and compounded the disrespect when she didn't turn back to face him. "I don't care what you do with the information, Teo. I think we can all agree that it's appropriate to inform a man of his paternal rights. That's all I wanted to do, it's done, the end."

"Surely a letter would have sufficed."

She did turn then. Not all the way. She looked back over her shoulder, and he was struck against his will. Hard.

Teo truly hadn't believed that Amelia Ransom, of all possible people, was the mysterious woman he'd enjoyed so thoroughly at the Masquerade last fall. But he remembered…this. Almost exactly. The hair had been a bright red, the eyes a dramatic shade of green that now, in retrospect, he should have known was false, and she'd worn an intricate mask that took over the better part of her face. The mask had been a steam punk design and so intricate, in fact, that she'd claimed she couldn't remove it—and he hadn't cared, because her mouth had been sweet and hot, her hands had been wicked, and he'd had his fingers deep inside her clenching heat mere steps from his own damned party.

"Right," she said. Drawled, really. And "disrespectful" didn't begin to cover the tone she used. Or that direct stare. "Because you would have opened a letter that I sent."

"Someone would have."

"And believed it right away, I'm sure."

"I don't believe it now, Miss Ransom. I'm not certain what you thought a personal visit would accomplish. All you have done is remind me of the low esteem in which I hold your entire family."

"I'm going to go out on a limb and guess that you don't have a lot of feelings about my poor grandma in Nebraska. I doubt you know about her at all, so lowly is her existence next to this whole...display." And Teo felt the umbrage of nearly twenty generations of de Luzes rise within him as she managed to do something with her face to indicate how little she thought of him, this grand house where history had been made and was still revered, and more or less everything he stood for. "So that low esteem, I'm guessing, is aimed directly at my mother."

"Your mother is little better than a terrorist," he retorted. Icily. "She sets herself a target, then destroys it."

"Yes," Amelia said drily. "This house is virtually rubble at our feet. It was the first thing I noticed."

"Once she got her claws in him, my father was never the same."

Teo discovered, with some consternation, that he was standing straight up from the desk when he hadn't meant to move. More, he was far too tense, with the temper she did not deserve to see kicking through him.

"My condolences." Amelia did not sound the least bit apologetic, much less sympathetic. "I must have misunderstood something. I thought he was Luis Calvo, the Eighteenth Duke of Marinceli, a man possessed of the same great wealth and immeasurable power you now wield. While my mother is…a mere divorcee. Who was the victim?"

"You must be joking. Calling Marie French 'a divorcee' is like calling a Tyrannosaurus rex a salamander."

Amelia's gaze flashed a deeper, darker shade of violet.

"There are very few things that I know to be incontrovertible truths," she said. And though her voice was soft enough, her gaze seemed to slap at him. "But one of them is that wealthy men fend off paternity suits the way a normal person slaps down mosquitoes on a summer night. Since our parents actually were married, no matter what opinions you have about that union, I thought I owed you the courtesy of telling you in person."

"Such courtesy. I am agog."

She turned all the way around to face him then, but if he thought she would lower her gaze meekly, it was his turn for disappointment. Amelia held his gaze steadily, and Teo could admit he found it…surprising.

Not discomfiting. He was the Duke. He was not *discomfited*.

But the truth was that most people did not dare hold

his gaze. Or not for very long. Most people, as a matter of fact, treated Teo with the deference due his title.

A deference he had come to believe was due to him, personally, as the holder of the title, because of course it was no easy thing to quietly command an empire while pretending he did nothing but waft about to charity balls. Thrones were for the powerless in these supposedly egalitarian times, and the de Luzes had always trafficked in influence and strength.

Teo was somehow unsurprised that it would be this bedraggled American, daughter to a woman so coldly mercenary that she was her own cottage industry, who not only dared—but kept staring him down.

As if he was a challenge she could win.

But the fact he was not surprised did not mean he liked it.

"What is it you want, Amelia?" he asked, aware that his tone was cool. The word of a de Luz had once been law. These days it merely sounded like the law, which was close enough.

She blinked at him as if he was…obtuse.

It was not a sensation he often had.

"I've already told you what I want. What you need to hear, at any rate. That's all I wanted. To tell you."

"Out of the goodness of your heart. You wished to inform me of my supposed paternity, and then…what? Blow away like smoke in the wind?"

"Nothing quite so poetic. I thought I'd go back home to San Francisco. Try to enjoy the rest of my pregnancy and prepare for life as a single mother."

And she smiled sweetly at him, though he would have to truly be obtuse not to hear the decided lack of sweetness in her voice.

"I see. You are keeping this miraculous child, then?"

She tilted her head slightly to one side, her gaze quizzical. "I wouldn't trouble myself with coming all this way, then storming your very gate—literally—if I wasn't planning on keeping it. Would I?"

It was Teo's turn to smile. Like one of the swords that hung on his walls, relics of the wars his ancestors had won.

"It is with great pleasure, Miss Ransom, that I tell you I have not the slightest idea what you would or would not do in any given circumstance."

"Now you do."

"I'm taken aback, you see."

He had already straightened from his desk, and he suddenly found himself uncertain what to do with his hands. It was such a strange sensation that he frowned, then thrust his hands in the pockets of his trousers, as he would normally. It was almost as if he wanted to do something else with them.

But no. He might have shared a few explosive moments of pleasure with this woman—a circumstance he had yet to fully take on board—but he was a grown man stitched together with duties and responsibilities. He did not have the option to be led around by his urges.

"That must feel like a revolution," Amelia said. Rather tartly, to his ear. "What's next? Will the serfs rise up? Will they march on their feudal lord?"

"You seem to have mistaken the century."

"Right." Again, that insolent drawl. She made a great show of looking all around her, as if she could cast her glinting eye into every corner of the rambling house that had stood here—in one form or another—for so many centuries. "I'm the one stuck in the wrong century. Got it."

"What astounds me is the altruism of your claim," he said, finding his temper rather thinner than he liked. When normally he prided himself on being the sort of lion who did not concern himself overmuch with the existence of sheep, much less their opinions. "Out of the goodness of your heart, you chose to come here and share this news with me. That would make you the one woman in the world to claim she carries an heir to the Dukedom of Marinceli, yet has no apparent intention of claiming any piece of it."

"I'm hoping it's a girl, actually," the maddening woman responded. In a tone he would have called bland if he couldn't see her face. And that expression that seemed wired directly to the place where his temper beat at him, there beneath his skin. "If I remember my time here—and in truth, I prefer to block it out—there has never been a Duchess of Marinceli. Only Dukes. One after the next, toppling their way through history like loose cannons while pretending they're at the center of it."

His temper kicked harder. And he found he had to unclench his jaw to speak. "If you do not wish to make a bid for the dukedom, and you claim your only motivation is to inform me of this dubious claim of yours, I am again unclear why this required a personal audience."

"I was under the impression that this was the kind of thing that was best addressed in person," she said. Very distinctly. As if she thought he was slow. "Forgive me for daring to imagine that you might be an actual, real, live human being instead of this…caricature."

"I am the Duke of Marinceli. The doings of regular people do not concern me."

She rolled her eyes. At him.

Teo was so astonished at her temerity that he could only stare back at her.

"Noted," she said, in that bored, rude way that he remembered distinctly from her teen years. Though it seemed far more pointed now. "You are now informed. When you receive the legal documents, you can sign them happily and in private, and we can pretend this never happened."

"I beg your pardon? Legal documents?"

Amelia folded her arms, and regarded him steadily, as if he was challenging her in some way. And Teo was beginning to suspect that what beat in him was not strictly temper.

"Of course, legal documents," she chided him. *She* chided *him*. "What did you think? That I would trust you to let this go?"

"Let this go?" he repeated. And then he actually laughed. "Miss Ransom. Do you have any idea how many enterprising women, whether they have enjoyed access to my charms or not, take it upon themselves to claim that I have somehow fathered their child?"

"You're welcome to treat me like one of them. In fact, I'd be perfectly happy if you thought I was lying."

Teo hadn't really made a determination, not yet. He hadn't let himself connect his mysterious redhead to this…disaster. Or he hadn't wanted to let himself. But there was something about the way she said that that kicked at him. As if she really, truly wanted him to dismiss her. And that was so different from the other women who had turned up over the course of his life to make their outlandish claims that it made something deep inside him…slide to the left. A simple, subtle shift.

But it changed everything.

"We will determine if you are lying the same way we determine any other claim," he managed to say despite that…shift.

"What does *that* mean? Ritual sacrifices? Forced marches? The dungeons?"

He lifted a brow. "A simple paternity test, Miss Ransom. The dungeons haven't been functional for at least a hundred years."

"I can take any test you like," she said after a moment. "Though that seems like a waste."

"Funnily enough, to me it doesn't seem like a waste at all. It seems critical."

She shrugged. "We can prove that you're the father if you like, but I'm only going to want you to sign documentation giving up your parental rights."

And something in him stuttered, then slammed down. Like the weight of the whole of this monstrous house he called his home, loved unreservedly and sometimes thought might well be the death of him.

"Miss Ransom," he said, making her name yet another icy weapon. "You cannot possibly believe that if you are indeed carrying my child—the firstborn child of the Nineteenth Duke of Marinceli—that I would abdicate my responsibilities. Perhaps your time here as a child—"

"Hardly a child. I was a teenager."

But Teo did not want to think about the teenager she'd been, too curvy and unconsciously ripe.

Had he noticed her then? He didn't think he had, but

it was all muddled now. The girl he'd tried to ignore and the redheaded witch who had beguiled him into losing his head were tangled around each other and thrust, somehow, into this pale woman who stood before him with her blond hair flowing about her shoulders, not the faintest trace of makeup on her hauntingly pretty face, and eyes the color of bougainvillea.

He was forced to accept that it was not merely his temper that seethed in him.

But he kept speaking, as if she hadn't interrupted him. "Whatever age you were, we clearly failed to impress upon you the simple fact that the members of my family take their bloodlines very seriously indeed."

"I'm well aware." And there was something in her gaze then, and in the twist of her lips. It dawned on him, though he could hardly credit it, that the august lineage of his family was not, in fact, impressive to her. "But if I recall correctly, you're the person who, upon the occasion of our parents' wedding, loudly proclaimed your deep and abiding joy that my mother was too old to—how did you put it?—oh, yes. 'Pollute the blood with her spawn.' I can only assume that any child of mine would be similarly polluted at birth. You should disavow us both now, while you can still remain pristine."

It took Teo a long moment to identify the hot, distinctly uncomfortable sensation that rolled in him then. At twenty-six he'd had a sense of his own importance, but had imagined his own father would be immortal. His recollection of their parents' wedding—evidence that his once irreproachable father had lost it completely, a deep betrayal of everything Teo had ever been taught, and a slap against his mother's memory—was that he had been quietly disapproving. Not that he had actually said the things he'd thought out loud.

"I don't recall making such a toast," he said now. Stiffly. "Not because such sentiments are anathema to me, of course. But because it would be impolite."

"You didn't make a toast. Heaven forbid. But you did make sure I heard you say it to one of the other guests." And he might have thought that it hurt her feelings, but she disabused him of that notion in the next moment by aiming that edgy smile of hers at him. "In any case, I thought it would be *impolite* not to tell you about this pregnancy."

Teo didn't care for the way she emphasized that word.

"But it can end here," Amelia said, merrily. "No legal pollutants to the grand Marinceli line. I'm sure that in time, you'll find an appropriately inbred, blue-blooded heiress to pop out some overly titled and commensurately entitled heirs who will suit your high opinion of yourself much better."

Teo had never heard his duties to his title and his family's history broken down quite so disrespectfully before. It was…bracing, really. Like a blast of cleansing winter air after too long cooped up in an overheated room.

She claimed she was pregnant, and he couldn't dismiss the claim, because it seemed likely—however *impossible* and no matter how he wished it untrue—that she really had been the redheaded woman he had sampled the night of the Marinceli Masquerade.

More than sampled. He had been deep inside her, sunk to the hilt, and had woken the following morning wanting much, much more—another unusual sensation.

But this was not the time to lapse off into that cloud of lust—a cloud he now knew was deeply inappropriate and, if she was telling the truth about her pregnancy and his paternity, might well have already changed the course of his meticulously plotted life. It didn't matter why she'd come here or what game she was playing.

Teo wanted answers.

He prowled away from the desk, moving toward the chairs that sat before the fire. "Come in. Remove your coat. Sit, for a moment, as you deliver these little atom bombs of yours."

He made that sound like an invitation. A request. It was neither.

Amelia did not move. She stood where she was, still just inside the door, and…scowled at him.

Teo was certainly not used to people contorting their face into any but the most obsequious and servile expressions, but that, too, was not the issue here. He reached one of the chairs, and waved his hand at it.

"Sit, please," he said, and this time, it sounded far more like the order it was.

Amelia continued to scowl at him in obvious suspicion. But despite that, she moved closer. With obvious reluctance. In itself another insult.

"Most people consider it an honor to be in my presence," he told her drily.

She sniffed. "They must not know you."

And Teo's memory was returning to him, slowly but surely. He normally preferred to pretend those years hadn't happened. Those embarrassing, American years, when Marie French had draped herself over the priceless furniture, and laughed in that common, coarse way of hers. But now he had the faintest inklings of recollection where the daughter was concerned, and not only about those problematic curves.

Amelia had not faded quietly into the background, as would have been expected of any other girl her age. Not Marie French's daughter. He had the sudden, surprisingly uncomfortable memory of the uppity little chit mouthing off. Not only to him, which was unaccountable, but on occasion to his father, as well.

Which was unacceptable.

He couldn't say he much cared for either the recollection or a repeat of it now.

Amelia took her time moving across the floor, and then even more time shrugging out of her coat. Then, not to be outdone—and not to obey him totally under any circumstances—she then held it to her as if it was a shield as she sat down in the armchair Teo had indicated.

He took his time seating himself opposite her, putting together the pieces. If he squinted, he could see the pieces of the wild redhead who had made the tedious Masquerade that tradition insisted he throw far more entertaining than usual. He wished his body wasn't so delighted at her return. It could only cloud the issue all over again.

Amelia gripped that coat against the front of her, so hard he could see her hands become fists. "Do you need me to tell you how babies are made, Teo?"

"What possessed you to disguise yourself?" he asked coolly, choosing not to rise to her bait. Or choosing not to show her any reaction, anyway. "And not only disguise yourself, but as I recall, taking it upon yourself to make certain you got my attention. I would assume this was all part of an entrapment bid, but you claim you do not want my name, my money or any link to me whatsoever. Explain yourself."

"I don't have to explain myself to you."

"And yet, Miss Ransom, you came to find me in my private home. One assumes to offer explanations, at the very least."

"I came to give you information. That's all. How many times do I have to say the same thing?"

Teo smiled, something raging in him, deep and dark. It wasn't as simple as temper. It was thick with that same lust, and wrapped around it, the possibility that the last person he had ever wished to see again might actually have managed to trap him. *Him.*

A man raised to know better than to ever allow such a fate to befall him.

"Unfortunately for you," he told her, his voice a low lick of fury that rivaled the heat of the fire, "I don't believe a single thing you've said so far. Shall we start testing these claims of yours?"

"Test away," she said, daring to sound bored.

But he could see the heat in her gaze. She likely expected him to summon someone to administer a paternity test—and he'd get there.

First, he wanted to address that heat. And the redheaded woman he'd tried to dismiss from his mind— but hadn't.

"Wonderful," he said silkily. "Why don't we start with a reenactment of that night in September?"

"What?"

And he should likely not have felt triumphant that he'd finally managed to get a reaction from her.

But he did. And he was only getting started.

"Come over here, *cariña,*" Teo said, and it was less

an invitation than a command. "Straddle me the way you did then. Kiss me, this time without your mask. Let us see what truths there are to find without all these words, shall we?"

## CHAPTER THREE

HE DIDN'T THINK she would do it.

Amelia could see the certainty she would not in that dark gaze of his, threaded through with a hint of gold-plated skepticism. It was to be distinguished from his usual expression, which was far too haughty and aristocratic and *above it all* to actually be challenging—no matter how personally challenging she might have found it.

Teo clearly expected her to back off, or maybe he thought she would start flushing and stammering. Perhaps he expected her to start throwing things at him. Or to dissolve into a pool of tears.

She had the urge to do any number of those things, but didn't.

Because it hadn't escaped Amelia's notice that he still hadn't indicated that he believed her. Perhaps it wasn't a matter of belief, as far as he was concerned. It sounded as if she'd convinced him that she had been in disguise the night of the Masquerade. But she should have realized that a man of Teo's stature would never believe a pregnancy claim unless and until he saw it bolstered by cold, hard scientific evidence.

That meant that all of this—letting her into the

house, allowing her into his presence—was all part and parcel of whatever game it was he'd thought he was playing when the butler had given him her name and announced her arrival. He could have had her tossed out with a snap of his fingers. He hadn't.

Whatever else was going on here, including her unfortunate reaction to him that she clearly hadn't exorcized at all, there was no doubt at all that *he* was playing a game. It allowed her to feel all the more ripe with the righteousness of *her* trip here, conducted beneath the mantle of her honesty.

If, that was, Amelia ignored the fact that she was the one who'd played games first. She was the one who had come here, taken what she'd wanted and disappeared. She'd left him none the wiser. The only reason he knew now was because she'd chosen to tell him.

She was the one who had chosen this. She was the one who controlled this.

*The last time you felt that way when Teo was involved, you ended up pregnant,* a voice inside her pointed out.

Amelia ignored that inconvenient fact, too.

She shoved her peacoat off her lap, then stood. Back in September, she'd worn a daringly cut gown that had been all about her cleavage and the glimpses each step offered of her thigh. Almost all of her thigh. She'd worn the highest heels she could walk in without killing herself, and because she wasn't *her*—because, for once, no one would look at her and make all the usual comparisons to her mother—she'd allowed herself to vamp it up.

Amelia had strutted around, welcoming the looks thrown her way when normally she would have gone to great lengths to make sure she blended, and as inoffensively as possible. She'd stood in provocative poses. She'd smiled recklessly and suggestively. She'd tried to channel her favorite screen sirens from way back as if she was trying out for one of those old movies she and her mother had loved to watch together, late at night in the many far-flung cities they'd flitted in and out of over the years.

It had been a delight, if she was honest.

She'd gotten Teo's attention, too. Then a whole lot more than his attention, and that had been...life-altering. Even before she'd learned that she was carrying his child. It had been a heavenly crucible, a stunning test of sensation and need, and she didn't regret a single second of it. She couldn't—not when she'd dreamed about what it would be like to touch him for so long.

But she also had his attention now.

Today she was resoundingly herself. She was wearing nothing but jeans, boots and the so-soft-it-was-basically-a-hug sweater her mother had given her for a birthday one year. She knew that rather than looking vampishly over the top, like an old movie, she looked as if she'd stayed up for far too many hours, packed into the middle seat of an overstuffed airplane.

But that look on Teo's face, for all its challenge and skepticism, was the same. As if he saw the same woman who had made him smile almost four months ago.

*The day you understand that sensuality is strength, sweet girl, is the day you will finally be free,* Marie had always told her.

But Amelia had never understood it. Not until right now.

She shook her hair back from her face, and that, too, was different today. She'd spent hours creating her glossy waterfall of bright red curls for the Masquerade. This morning, all she'd bothered to do was take her hair down from the knot she'd tied it into for the flight. A glance in the rearview mirror of her hired car had suggested that it was a flat, lifeless disaster, and she'd felt unequal to the task of fixing it.

But still, Teo looked at her as if she was edible.

Amelia had the distinct impression that he didn't know it. And the man could make kings and topple governments with a phone call, but she was pretty sure that gave her the power here. Or at least *some* power, and with a man as effortlessly commanding as Teo, that was revolutionary.

She smoothed her hands over her sweater, molding it to her hips, in unconscious imitation of a sly little move she'd seen her mother make about forty thousand times. An unconscious move that became conscious the moment she did it, because she understood it now. Amelia had always liked to roll her eyes at her mother's various shenanigans around men, but it was different, here.

There was something about running her hands over her own curves while he watched. She could feel the heat spark and dance between them.

Amelia told herself that she could use it.

She picked her way across yet another thick, undoubtedly priceless rug. The only sound in the study was the crackle of the fire. The faint hint of winter outside when the windows rattled now and again.

And, of course, the deep kettle drum of her heartbeat—but she was hoping only she could hear that.

It could only have taken a moment to step across the space between their two chairs, but to Amelia, it seemed like one or two forevers, stitched together while the flames danced in the grate. And then she forgot about the fire, because she was standing before him, and Teo's black gaze was no longer simmering. It was a blast of fire.

"What was it you wanted me to do?" she asked, and she wasn't trying to sound sultry. Throaty.

But she did.

"I think you know." His voice was more silk than rough, and still, it seemed to have ridges as it smoothed its way over her.

And worse, she remembered.

First the dance. She'd affected a German accent, spicing up her Spanish. She'd dared him to ask her to dance, he'd acquiesced with that dangerous half smile, and it had really been all over then and there. The dance itself had been decorous enough. His hand had seemed so large splayed there at her lower back. And the way he'd held her fingers in his had made butterflies dance and swirl deep in her belly, as if they were performing their own daring waltz.

They had not spoken while they danced. It had almost seemed a shame, given the work she'd put into her carefully accented Spanish—

But there was too much heat. Dancing with him was like plugging herself in to some kind of generator. She felt the roar of it. The hum. And the longer they danced, the more she burned. Brighter and brighter, until she was certain she must have blinded the whole of the party.

Teo had never looked away.

When the music had stopped, he'd drawn her into one of the side hallways, down past yet another raft of astonishing paintings she recalled from a decade ago, then around the corner. That was where he'd pinned her to a wall and gotten his hands on her.

In her.

And she had come apart once already when he pulled her behind him into a room she wasn't sure she could find again if her life depended on it. That was how shaken she was. How deliriously, spectacularly torn apart.

It was there that he'd fallen back onto one of the sofas, then pulled her down onto his lap. And God help her, but for all her brave talk of exorcisms and getting on with her life, she still dreamed about it.

About the way his hands had cupped her cheeks, then pulled her mouth to his. About the glorious invasion, his tongue and hers, and never once the urge to balk. Never once that sense that she was kissing someone through a thick glass, incapable of feeling anything.

On the contrary, she'd felt too much.

It had all gone too fast. And taken forever, at the same time. He'd pushed her dress and her panties out of his way, handled his own trousers and the condom he'd produced from a pocket, and then had settled her on top of him.

And they'd stared at each other, caught in that electric intensity, as she'd taken the length of him inside her.

Inch by inch, slowly and carefully as if it was a seduction rather than a necessity for her, until they were flush against each other, his gaze was like the night, and she was stretched wide and deep to accommodate him.

She'd been too hot and too red, then, almost limp with the madness of it. That it was finally happening. That he was *inside* her. That she'd managed to handle him without him stopping, frowning and accusing her of being the virgin she was.

Amelia might even have taken a moment to congratulate herself for pulling it off.

But then he'd wrapped his hands around her hips, and taught her about rhythm. Pace. Depth and desire, and how very little she knew about…anything. Everything.

Teo had covered her mouth when she shattered. Then dipped his head to the crook of her neck when he followed.

She remembered all of that, in vivid detail. So vivid she was sure she could feel it still. As if it had just happened. Moments ago, according to her body, which shivered into awareness. She felt the flesh between her legs ready itself for him, molten and soft.

Amelia had been so focused on her pregnancy. More accurately, on the stomach flu she couldn't seem to kick for all those weeks. Then the dawning realization she'd done her best to deny for as long as possible—coupled with a lot of desperate math.

And then, finally, the bitter truth she really hadn't wanted to face.

She had somehow forgotten…this. *Him.*

Teo.

And the reality of the effect he had on her.

If she was honest, it was the same effect he'd had on her when she was a teenager. The difference was, back then, she hadn't known what to call it. And more, he certainly hadn't shared her awareness of it the way he clearly did now.

"Do you need a refresher course?" he asked, and it was a taunt. The expression on his beautiful face was sheer arrogance, then. And yet in no way detracted from his appeal.

Nothing could.

This was where a wise woman would back off. Say something pithy, perhaps. Cutting, certainly. What she certainly should not do was imagine that she could control this thing when she had already proven that she couldn't.

One of Teo's dark, smooth, outrageously haughty brows rose.

*He doesn't think you're going to do this,* she snapped at herself.

And it was bad enough that he was openly contemptuous of her mother. It was insulting that he considered himself so far above her that he could openly disparage her. Amelia thought she really might break into pieces, right here on his fancy ducal rug, if she backed down from this challenge.

She swung her leg wide, then slid herself onto his lap.

And it was a mistake. Obviously.

But it was so *hot*. He was so hard and muscled, lean everywhere, and he caught her around the back, hauling her close to him.

And it was just like September all over again. Their bodies came together like a key in a lock, and she was sure that she heard the dead bolt turn.

But whether it was opening or closing, she couldn't have said.

And she couldn't say she cared, either, because Teo was surrounding her then. He was so much bigger than her, and bigger than he should have been in his rich man's clothes that usually disguised far less impressive forms. His arms were dense with lean muscle and rock hard to the touch, and she had to fight to keep herself from shivering in a way she knew would be much too revealing.

Then again, did it matter? Because there was that gaze of his, dark and demanding, and she was certain that he could see her as clearly as if he'd turned her inside out. Again. Right here with the moody January day kicking around outside.

Amelia reminded herself that she might not be descended from almost twenty generations of near royalty like he was, but what she did have was a direct connection to one of the most desirable women who had ever lived. At least, if the roster of her ex-lovers was to be believed.

She made herself smile and hoped it was sultry instead of scared. "Remember me now?"

Teo took his time, as if he was searching her face for…something. Whatever it was, she didn't think he found it when that sensual mouth of his stayed grim.

"I do indeed." His dark gaze sharpened. "Perhaps you can explain to me why it is you felt the need to crash a party to which you were not invited, conceal your identity and go so far as to have sex with me when you must have known that had you introduced yourself by your actual name, I would have refused you."

Her throat felt dry, suddenly. And no matter how cool his voice was, or how unreadable his expression, she was tight against him. And he wasn't inside her, which meant that she could feel the truth, big and thick and hard between them. She would never know how she kept herself from shuddering.

In desperate, overwhelming need. And something far greedier.

"You are the Duke of Marinceli," she said, wishing she could make herself sound less...throaty. Less obvious. "Surely I can't be the first woman to go to great lengths for the mere taste of you."

He moved a hand, reaching out to run a thick hank of her hair through his fingers. He watched as he did it, so Amelia did, too. And that meant she was completely unprepared when he lifted his intense gaze to hers once more.

"You knew," he said softly. Dangerously. "You could be in no doubt as to my feelings about your mother."

"I know what you felt about my mother ten years ago," Amelia said, her heart kicking and her stomach cramping as if she'd tried to run a mile, or something equally foolish. "I had no idea what you felt about me. If anything."

"So you disguised yourself."

"I wanted to see if there was a connection. A spark."

He looked faintly horrified by the notion and she smiled, because these stuffy Europeans never seemed to understand that Americanness wasn't only unthinking gaucheness and naïveté as they imagined. It could be wielded as a weapon, like anything else.

"You know what it's like," she said, smiling wider. "Every little girl dreams of fairy tales. I realize you're a duke, not a prince, but who's to say there can't be such a thing as Duke Charming?"

She would have said that she'd never seen an expression of offended dignity before, though that probably wasn't completely accurate. But there was certainly no more perfect expression of it than Teo de Luz grappling with the fact that she had just called him... *Duke Charming*.

In all apparent sincerity.

"I had no idea you were so prissy about your title, Teo. And the deference you feel it ought to afford you." She shrugged, letting her smile go bland. "Are you really sure you want to claim a child who will be half Duke Charming the Nineteenth and the other half... me?"

"Miss Ransom." His voice was a sharp rebuke, and somehow, it didn't seem to matter that he was calling her *Miss Ransom* while she was straddling his arousal. While they were pressed together, having a ridiculous conversation, and pretending that nothing was happening between their bodies. No fire. No deep, raging need. "I would like to suggest, in the strongest possible terms, that you never call me such a thing again."

"What should I call you, then? My baby daddy?"

He actually winced. "Certainly not."

She shouldn't have laughed. "You really do make it too easy."

He shifted slightly then, and suddenly she felt that spiraling heat sharpen. And a delicious lassitude swept over her, reminding her of how she'd come apart in his hands.

Again and again.

"I hate to disappoint you," he growled. He actually *growled*. "Allow me to make it hard."

And then he slid a hand around the nape of her neck, angled his face over hers and took her mouth with his.

It was a punishment. It was a prayer.

And even though she was certain that she'd relived *exactly* this a thousand times or more, night after night, Amelia wasn't prepared. She had dimmed it, somehow. Imagined it differently. It was like pain, perhaps. She knew she'd experienced it, she remembered it, but she could never quite *feel* it again.

Because this made a mockery of fire.

This was a supernova.

He took her mouth with certainty. An impossible, consummate skill that made her head spin, and she liked it.

She more than *liked* it.

His other arm wrapped around her, his hand splayed wide as if he was trying to hold as much of her as he could. Her breasts were pressed against the wall of his chest, memory and reality clashing. Tangling. Circling around and around on top of each other until she could hardly distinguish one from the other.

Not that it mattered. Or she cared. He angled his head one way, then the other, tasting her and tempting her, making her surge against him to get more. Deeper. *Yes.*

And she was the one who had taken his bait. He had challenged her, and she'd let him. No one had made her come and sit here on his lap like this. She'd done it, imagining she had control, and now she was paying the price.

It was possible that the Duke of Marinceli wasn't the only arrogant person in the room.

His taste was exquisite. Male and addictive. And she was terribly afraid that those faint noises she could hear in the distance, somewhere, were coming from her own throat. Greedy, needy little sounds.

He kissed her and he kissed her, and then when she could do nothing at all but lose herself in the delirious slide of his tongue against hers, he moved. It took her a baffled, tumbling sort of moment to realize that he was standing up, carrying her with him. So that he supported her bottom on one hand, and her legs found their way to wrap around his waist.

He kept her there another moment, his mouth on hers in distinct possession.

And then he tore his mouth away from hers and set her on the ground before him.

She was afraid he knew exactly how wobbly her legs were beneath her. Her mouth felt swollen. She wasn't entirely sure that there weren't tears in her eyes.

"It is good to know where we stand, is it not?" His voice was silk and slap at once. "What astounds me about you, Miss Ransom, is that I do not think you are quite in control of yourself. Are you?"

"A kiss is just a kiss," she managed to say. "There's a whole song about it."

"Let me tell you what a kiss is today," he said, his voice controlled and even, and Amelia felt a daunting sense of horror as she realized that *he* was certainly not swept away. Or wobbling on his feet. On the contrary, his gaze was sharp and clear, as if he had only been toying with her all along. Her stomach knotted up. "A test, which you have failed."

"Are you sure that I'm the one who failed?" she asked, eyeing the front of his trousers with more bravado than boldness.

But Teo only looked savagely amused.

He moved away, over to his desk, where he swept up his mobile, scrolled for a moment, then typed something out. It took him another moment, then he tossed his mobile back down to the surface of his desk with a clatter.

"You're staring at me," he said, calmly. "And I know it is indelicate to say so, but you seem a bit…spun."

"I'm sure it's the jet lag."

"Here's what will happen." He was all ice and restraint and Amelia wanted to launch herself at him. Slap his face. Claw at his eyes. Behavior she would never condone in a million years, and yet... *Yet.* "I've texted my business manager. I told him another paternity test needs to be administered. I'm sure you will not be surprised to learn that there is protocol in place."

She felt thin and pale straight through, but she smiled. "How lovely to be so prepared for any eventuality."

"My manager will come with at least two members of my legal team, and they will see to the testing. I expect you to allow this test to be taken, but if you do not, never fear. That's why my legal team is involved. They will make certain that paternity is established, positively or negatively."

He didn't say *how* they would make certain, especially if she refused. But she didn't ask for clarification. She thought he wanted her to.

"If I'm not the father of the child you say you carry, or if, as often happens, you are somehow mistaken about your pregnancy in the first place, they will present you with a nondisclosure agreement to sign," Teo said. "Generally speaking, we encourage claimants to sign this agreement. We occasionally even sweeten the pot. My privacy is more important to me than money, which means I'm happy to spend it to make sure false claims against me are never discussed in public."

"Do you have protocol in place for when it turns out you *are* the father?" Amelia asked, impressed with the evenness of her tone when she felt like a giant, deafening scream inside. "Or do you just...wing it?"

His black eyes blazed. "I have every intention of following a very specific protocol if it turns out that you are, in fact, the mother of my child thanks to an act of egregious subterfuge. Believe me."

"I can't say I care what your protocol is, really. What matters is mine."

"You go right ahead and tell yourself that," Teo replied in that same dangerously silken tone. "I think you will find that the de Luz bloodline never, ever releases one of its own. Deny it all you wish. It will not change a thing. I have no intention of allowing any heir of mine to be raised apart from me."

"I don't want your influence. I don't want your money. I want nothing at all from you."

"Then, Miss Ransom—" and there was something in that gaze of his that made her quake, a kind of savagery that made her feel swollen with need "—you had better hope that this test comes back negative."

# CHAPTER FOUR

"YOUR EXCELLENCY." THE deferential voice came from the door.

Teo did not turn, though he inclined his head, knowing that his business manager would read the gesture for what it was: tacit permission to speak.

"The test is positive," the other man said.

For one beat of his heart, then the next, Teo was sure that he'd misheard. Because he must have misheard. "Positive?"

"Yes, sir. The child is yours."

Teo was still in his study, staring out at the winter version of the gardens that, come spring, the public clamored to fawn over on the few holidays he opened the grounds to visitors. But he hardly saw the landscape before him today. And not only because he knew it better than his own features.

His face changed with time, after all. The grounds of the estate did not. Teo employed a battalion of gardeners and groundskeepers to make sure of it.

He cleared his throat.

"Thank you," he managed to say. "You may leave me now."

He waited until he heard the quiet sound of the

door on the latch, and only then did he allow himself to breathe. Or whatever facsimile of breathing he was attempting to perform through the racket inside him.

Because he, Teo de Luz, who had watched his father wreak havoc with his reputation thanks to the terrible women he'd allowed near him—he, who had vowed that he would never, ever bring so much as the faintest stain to the august dukedom that was his to usher into the future, as bright and shining as possible—

*He* had fathered a child. Out of wedlock.

With Marie French's daughter.

Teo felt nearly light-headed with the potent combination of fury, despair and shame.

His life had always been plotted down to its smallest details. He had done the plotting himself. When he had come of age and understood both his place in the world and the importance of his bloodline, the debt he owed not only to his ancestors but to the long line of the descendants who must follow him, he had sat down and determined exactly what it was that he needed to do to accomplish those things. And how best to make certain that he did so with dignity.

He would become the Duke after his father. That was ensured.

But he had eighteen examples of the kind of Duke of Marinceli he could choose to become, with portraits to match that hung even now in his gallery. Teo had taken the various lessons of his ancestors' lives very seriously indeed.

It was all very well to have one child, the way his father had, and hope that the son he raised would be worthy of the gifts his birth accorded him. Teo had never been a gambler. He had no interest in risk. He planned to marry, produce an heir, and several spares besides. He did not wish to risk the possibility that the dukedom could fall to some far-flung cousin who had not been raised as he had been. Not if it was in his power to make it otherwise.

And not only because he liked the idea of continuing the bloodline through his direct descendants. For while he was avowedly arrogant, he was not quite *that* arrogant. What he truly wished was to make certain that he would have the opportunity to teach his own children what it meant to be members of the de Luz family. He would teach them what it meant to him, and in so doing, connect them with that long sweep of history and myth that was a part of who they were.

He wanted to fill them with as much gratitude as greatness.

He'd seen his future so clearly, always.

Even when his father had started his downward spiral into unsuitable women, it hadn't changed Teo's plans. How could it? He had never planned to look around for a wife until he was older, more settled and more capable of making certain that any wife he took would obey him as required. Because while Teo was fond of a spirited discussion when appropriate, there was only one true expert on the Marinceli legacy, and it was him. He'd accordingly spent a lot of time fashioning the perfect wife in his head, and she was not at all like the sensual redhead he'd indulged in last fall.

Certainly not.

His Duchess would be refined. Elegant in blood and action. Blameless, spotless and without a whisper of scandal attached to her name. Educated, dedicated and capable of assuming the duties that came with overseeing the Marinceli holdings and estates. He'd been thinking of a certain kind of heiress, bred for a life that looked like leisure—and certainly had its charms and compensations—but was often far more complicated than outsiders imagined.

He had always planned to marry a woman like his own mother.

His mother, who had given him softness where his father had given him duties. His mother, who had taught him the beauty of nature and how to find peace there no matter what. His mother, whom he had loved as fiercely as he loved the land and whom he had lost anyway.

And then lost again when his father had chosen to wash away her memory with a woman who was little better than a common streetwalker.

He had vowed he, by God, would honor his station and his mother's memory alike.

And now this. This...tragedy.

Because it didn't matter what Amelia Ransom said. Or what plans he might have made. The die was cast. She was carrying his child and that made her—*her*— the next Duchess of Marinceli.

Losing the appropriate heiress he'd planned to install here, to reclaim his mother's quiet glory in some small way, felt like losing her all over again.

Teo would marry Amelia, because it could go no other way. There was no alternative. The Dukes of Marinceli might divorce—or arrange timely accidents, in some centuries—but only after the line was secured.

And even then, rarely.

He glared out at his grounds, stretching on as far as the eye could see in every direction. But if he was looking for an escape, it was futile.

Teo had no choices here.

And in truth, he supposed it didn't matter. If he stepped back from his own reactions, there was something to be said for infusing an ancient family line with some literal new blood. Whatever else could be said about Americans, there was no denying that their brand of peasantry was…enterprising. The child would be hale and hardy and Teo would be on hand to guide him into his role as successor to the dukedom.

The question was, what was he to do with this woman whom he was going to be forced to wed?

He turned, his gaze falling on the crackling fire. Something popped, and a log collapsed into ash and soot. And she'd spoken of fairy tales, had she not? Called him *Duke Charming*, perhaps the most nauseating thing he'd ever heard.

But as nauseated as the name made him, it did give him an idea.

Amelia liked fairy tales. He could give her one. After all, she was playing a deep game here that she'd started last fall, dressed as someone else—and in his experience, no one came after him who wasn't, ultimately, after his title. His wealth. His consequence, the very least.

She'd lived here when she was younger and he couldn't remember all the conversations that must have been had in her presence. About the dukedom, about Teo's role, about all the expectations and history heaped upon him. But he knew they must have taken place.

That made it hard to imagine that she didn't already know how this would go.

He would insist upon marrying her. He would insist on claiming his heir in the time-honored fashion, be-

cause outside the dukedom, it was the modern age—
but here, always and forever, it was medieval. And the
same rules applied now as had then.

Teo was sure Amelia knew all this. That he would
do what was necessary to secure his bloodline, always.

But that didn't mean he had to make it pleasant for
her.

If she wanted to play Cinderella games, he would be
more than happy to oblige her.

Amelia had been taken off to one of the guest suites,
carefully tucked away in the main part of the house,
where a visitor could feel as if she was a part of things
without ever straying into anything private.

First she had seen Teo's business manager, and a pair
of lawyers, who had come in with perfunctory smiles
and a sheaf of legal documents. Reading through those
documents had taken more time than the actual physical
she had also subjected herself to with the quietly competent doctor who'd accompanied them, and whom she
recognized from her years here before.

*She* wasn't in any suspense. Amelia already knew
who the father of her baby was.

Still, she'd had to sit there and look suitably grave
as a pack of disapproving men had given her news that
wasn't in any way news to *her*, but likely meant all kinds
of things to *them*. Bless.

Then they'd all taken themselves off to handle the actual purpose of their visit—telling tales to Teo—though
none of them said that directly.

"If you could wait here, madam," Teo's business
manager murmured.

And when the door shut behind him, Amelia was faced with a decision.

The events of the morning were already a tumultuous jumble in her head. From the plane ride to that long drive to everything that had happened when she'd arrived here. She wanted to tell herself it all felt as if it had happened to someone else—

But she could still feel *him*. Vividly.

His taste was in her mouth again. She could feel that thick ridge of his need where their bodies had met. And she felt herself get soft and hot—even at the memory.

It made a mockery of her attempts to tell herself that she was immune to him. That she had somehow vaccinated herself against all things Teo de Luz.

And she was acutely aware, as she sat there in the elegantly appointed living room of the suite where they'd left her, that nothing was holding her here. All those legal documents that she'd signed had been about protecting Teo in the event that she was not carrying his child. Very few had addressed the possibility that she might be, because, of course, no one had imagined that could be a possibility.

She'd known. And she'd told him. Now he had the additional proof he needed.

Amelia had absolutely no reason to sit here waiting for him to make good on the vague threats he'd already made.

But no matter how many times she thought the same thing, or told herself it was time to rise and go for the door, she didn't.

She waited.

She waited, and she waited, her eyelids getting heavier by the moment. And she couldn't have said when she fell asleep, exactly. One moment she was sitting there, fretting about when and how she should leave this place—and for good this time—and the next she was waking up in a rush, confused and faintly irritable.

The light in the room had changed, the shadows gone long and deep, and Teo stood over her. He stared down at her with a look on his face that she was tempted to call murderous.

Amelia told herself it was nothing more than the dreams she'd been having, one more intense than the last. She sat up, rubbing at her face, and looked around as if she expected to find someone else in the room with them. But no one else was there and she realized that whatever noise there was, it must all be in her head.

"What's happening?" she asked hearing the sleep in her voice.

The part of her that had been a notably awkward teenager in this same awe-inspiring house cringed at that, because if that was how she *sounded*, how must she *look*—but she had to shove that aside as best she could.

"We're having a baby," Teo said, and this time, that aristocratic voice of his was grim. It instantly put her on alert. "Allow me to extend my felicitations, Miss Ransom."

She was already frowning, so it was easy enough to sit up straight and slip on into a full-on scowl. "I think it might be time to stop calling me Miss Ransom, don't you? We didn't only have sex, Teo. We actually made another human life. I think the intimacy barrier has been well and truly broken."

He smiled, but it was a mirthless thing. "I took the liberty of having my security detail locate the vehicle you used to sneak onto my property."

"I didn't sneak. Just because no one regularly uses those old lanes doesn't mean driving on them is an act of subterfuge, does it?"

He ignored her. "I took the liberty of collecting your case."

She assumed he meant that he'd had a servant do it, as she couldn't imagine the Duke of Marinceli toting luggage about the place, and normally she would have pointed that out. Made a joke out of it—or a weapon. But the shadows in the room seemed darker than they should have been, her head was still full of jagged anxiety dreams, and she stayed quiet.

Teo studied her a moment, and it took all the self-control Amelia possessed to keep her hands from her face, to check for something embarrassing. "If you will follow me, we have a trip to take and it is already getting late."

He started for the door. Amelia stood automatically, then glanced out the windows. Sure enough, she'd slept most of the day away if the creeping dusk was any guide. And even though it was winter and sunset came early, it still seemed remarkably lazy on her part. She didn't normally succumb to jet leg, really. She'd discovered that no matter where she went on the planet, come three thirty in the afternoon of whatever time zone she found herself in, she was ravenously hungry. Other than that, she normally acclimated fine.

But everything was different in a pregnant body, she was discovering. She chose to be happy that the only symptom she was experiencing at the moment was some fatigue, here and there. It was better—anything was better—than the weeks upon weeks of nausea.

She was hurrying after Teo, out in the hallway and

trying to catch up to his long strides, before she bothered to ask herself why. She didn't need to run around after him like a harried member of his vast staff. She didn't have to do anything with him at all, for that matter.

"Wait," she said, throwing the word at his back. "Why did you collect my bag?" Teo didn't stop walking. He didn't even look back over his shoulder. And it was as if, now that she was moving, Amelia couldn't quite bring herself to stop. "And what do you mean, we're going on a trip?"

"All will be revealed in good time," Teo said, and there was something about the easy authority in his voice when he said it.

It was comforting, almost. As if he had the answers, when Amelia had spent the whole of her life in the presence of adults who never had answers, even when she was a child. She'd always been the one sent off to do her level best to find whatever answers were required. Even the great and powerful men her mother married turned to her when the relationship went bad, as it always did. Amelia always knew it was coming when the stepfathers or lovers suddenly showed a marked interest in taking her out to dinner, or to coffee, or invited her on a long walk out of the blue. These things always led to uncomfortable questions about her mother's favorite things. How best to talk to her. And as she got older, Amelia's own take on the situation—that situation being her mother's love life.

Having never experienced the opportunity to show anyone blind obedience, because she'd never trusted anyone with even wide-eyed, considered obedience, Amelia really hadn't understood how nice it was. Not to have to come up with the answers. Or a plan.

To trust that he had everything under control. Including her.

*You probably shouldn't find that liberating,* she chastised herself.

She followed Teo for miles and miles through the sprawling house. Then outside, briefly, to note the frigid slap of the January evening before climbing into a waiting car. Only then did it occur to her to ask herself—again—why this man made it seem perfectly reasonable to follow him off into the gathering night without the slightest idea where they were headed. Why she trusted him when she shouldn't.

But even as she asked herself the question, she knew the answer. The car pulled away, heading not toward the long drive that would lead them down to the gates and toward the village, but deeper into the property. And behind her, the magnificent house stood, lights blazing, *el monstruo* in all its glory.

And she understood that no matter how unimpressed she pretended to be with the Nineteenth Duke of Marinceli, the fact remained that he was safe, relatively speaking. He had kept this house wholly itself, and inarguably beautiful, when it could so easily have been turned into a tourist attraction. A hotel or event space. Or any of the other things aristocrats fallen on hard times liked to do with the old, stately homes that had once been the seat of their families' power.

She couldn't say she knew Teo well, only that she knew him in a variety of interesting ways. What she did know—what she'd known even as a teenager—was that he took his responsibilities very, very seriously.

If he was driving her off into the night alone, she might have worried. But she was carrying his child.

And Amelia had to think that made her precious cargo to a man like him. Whatever he had planned, it couldn't be *too* bad.

Or anyway, it certainly wouldn't risk the child.

So she was very sedate, really, as the car pulled up to the private jet that waited for them on the estate's airfield. And it was the easiest thing in the world to climb aboard and settle herself inside, not at all surprised to find that Teo—unlike some of her mother's past lovers, tacky unto their very souls—preferred a quiet elegance even here. Nothing garish or over the top. Simply the height of comfort augmented by his tremendous wealth.

Because the more money a person had, the simpler the things they surrounded themselves with could be. If a person used it well, money was magic in reverse.

It was a short flight, but then, this was Europe. Everything could be reached quickly enough, and she had no idea how to even begin to figure out where they were as the plane landed. It seemed remote, if the few, scattered lights out her window were any indication on the way down.

Teo, who had disappeared into one of the staterooms for the flight, emerged. And she blinked, because unless she was hallucinating, the too-aristocratic-to-breathe Nineteenth Duke of Marinceli was...wearing jeans. And a T-shirt that she could only gape at before he tugged on the sort of wool sweater that looked better suited to northern fishermen than pampered Spanish dukes. He was even wearing winter boots, she realized in shock as she looked down at his feet.

But he was gazing at her, his dark eyes simmering and steady at once, and she refused to give him the satisfaction of asking.

Even if that meant she had to bite down hard on her own tongue.

Amelia expected the usual pomp and circumstance when they climbed down the stairs from the plane to the ground, but she found herself instead on a remote, abandoned strip of land that barely qualified as an airfield. It was dark, but she still had the sense of mountains looming all around. And it was *cold*. Bitter and harsh, not simply raw.

"Are we in the mountains?" she asked, as the cold cut into her. "Which mountains?"

"Welcome to the Pyrenees," Teo responded and he waited, there at the bottom of the jet's steps, as Amelia buttoned up her heavy peacoat and shuddered deeper into it.

And she didn't feel quite as comfortable or trusting or safe as she had before. But she followed him as he strode off into what seemed like nothing but darkness, her heart walloping her ribs from the inside, because what other choice did she have?

Luckily, all he was doing was walking over to an SUV that waited a little too far into the shadows for Amelia's peace of mind. There were no people. There wasn't even anything resembling an airport building. When she looked over her shoulder toward the plane, the jet was already pulling up its staircase, clearly readying itself to take off again.

With a sudden, prickling sense of foreboding, Amelia wanted to turn and run back for that plane. It was in her like a scream, the need to do it, to escape, to do anything but subject herself—

But she did nothing. And when Teo opened the passenger door of the SUV for her, with a mocking flourish, she even smiled.

She didn't smile again for some time.

Because Teo took to what passed for a road and all Amelia could do was grip the handle set in the door of the car and pray for deliverance.

The road wound around and around, barely wide enough for the car they were in at some points. The headlights picked up looming rock walls and catastrophic cliffs that tumbled down to God only knew where.

Teo didn't consult any directions. He simply drove, and she couldn't tell if he knew exactly where they were going, or if he was on some kind of a suicide mission. But no. She was revising her opinion on whether or not he was a murderer, but she still didn't think that he was likely to do away with... How had he put it? The heir to his dukedom. The Twentieth Duke of Marinceli, as a matter of fact.

Since the physician had let drop the fact that yes, it was a boy.

Amelia had vehemently not wanted to know—but now that she did know, it was as if she had always known that she was having a son. And she could hardly wait to meet him.

If she survived this car trip, that was.

Eventually, it ended. And not because Teo turned off somewhere or slowed down, but because the road simply...ended. And delivered them to what she thought was a gatekeeper's cottage, perhaps. It was a small sort of hut, hewn from wood and topped with layers of snow, and looked dark and unfriendly in the SUV's headlights.

Amelia expected one of Teo's staff to come out then and lead them somewhere else. But Teo turned off the engine, leaving the headlights bright. He sent a swift, shuttered look in her direction, then climbed out of the car.

And it turned out that she no longer felt any particular urge to follow him around. She stayed where she was, one hand creeping over that thickness in her belly that she knew, now, would be a little boy one day. She watched the father of that little boy—the *father*, which might be the correct thing to call him, but still felt a little too much, too intimate—march over to the front door of the little shack. He pulled something from his pocket that she understood was a key when he used it to open the front door. He disappeared, and for moment, there was nothing but darkness inside the hut, the headlights and Amelia's own too-fast breath.

Then, slowly she saw light inside. Moments later, Teo came back out. He switched off the headlights and pocketed the car keys, then went to the back of the SUV and she heard him removing things. And when he trudged past her, carrying not only her bag but several others, she finally stirred, and made herself get out of the SUV, too. Even if everything in her was telling her that was a mistake.

He'd left the front door open, so she pushed inside, not sure what she expected to see. And also not sure why the whole thing filled her with the greatest unease.

Inside, there was a fireplace that looked nothing short of medieval. It was large, a sort of grate stuck in the middle, and some kind of iron apparatus that held a pot over the flames. She was so struck by how archaic it was that it took her a moment to take in the rest.

It was a hut. A hunting cabin, maybe, if the decor was anything to go by. The fireplace was in what she supposed was the kitchen part of the great room. It boasted a small table, a counter next to the sink, and little else. The rest of the room was taken up with two very old leather couches, and a door behind them that led into the bedroom. She could see it was a bedroom because Teo was standing in there next to a large bed, doing something that didn't make sense. Until he straightened and she saw that he had lit a lantern.

A *lantern*. An actual *lantern*.

Her heart understood before she did, kicking wildly. She looked around again. The fire. A few lanterns here and there.

Unless she was mistaken, they were on top of a mountain with no electricity.

"Teo," she said when he came out of the bedroom, that enigmatic look on his beautiful face. "What are we doing here? Time traveling?"

And her pulse picked up when the Nineteenth Duke of Marinceli…smiled.

Like the spider to the fly.

# CHAPTER FIVE

*HE IS A DUKE, not a spider,* Amelia told herself crossly. *And you are certainly not a fly.*

But Teo's smile still made the back of her neck prickle.

"I come here at least once a year to escape the many pressures of modern life," he told her, his voice cool and unbothered in a way that she found very nearly offensive. Especially as he prowled back into the great room and settled himself on the couch facing the door. In a decidedly leisurely fashion. "I hunt for my food or make my own meals from what's on hand, I marinate in the silence of nature, and I often learn a great many things about myself. I can't recommend it highly enough."

Amelia lived in California. She could talk about *communing with nature* around the clock without batting an eye…but not with Teo.

"You thought that it was time for us to go on a rustic retreat?" she asked, her voice much too high-pitched. Because she wasn't really taking this the way she was sure she was supposed to. Then again, how was someone supposed to take this?

"I don't know how you will enjoy the accommodations," Teo continued. He looked almost smug, she thought. Entirely too self-satisfied, and something cold trickled down the length of her spine. "*If* you will enjoy the remoteness. But I can't say I particularly care. You are carrying the heir to the Marinceli dukedom."

"Yes, Teo. I was already aware of this when we were still standing in your other antique property. You know. The one with electricity."

"The trouble with all my other properties is that they're too connected to modernity," he said, almost as if he was musing his way through this conversation. When the look in his dark eyes suggested otherwise. "Up here, there is nothing between a person and her God. Ample time and space to reflect."

"I have nothing to reflect on, but thank you."

And she could hear that higher pitch in her voice with her own ears. Again. She refused to call it hysteria, but it sure was close.

Teo moved farther into the room, and tossed himself down on one of the couches. "We will do our reflecting together, I think."

"What?"

He smiled at her, but again, it wasn't any kind of nice smile. It reminded her that he was directly related to warlords. To men who stood in the shadows behind kings, dark puppet masters who never minded that the light shone elsewhere.

"All my life I have done my best to avoid this moment, Miss—" But he stopped. That smile of his deepened, and that definitely wasn't good. "Excuse me, *Amelia*. And yet here I am. Well and truly trapped into something you knew perfectly well I would never have wanted if I'd had any choice."

"We both saw you use a condom," she gritted out. "If

you're trying to say I tricked you by deliberately getting pregnant, you'll have to explain to me how I managed to do that when you're the one who had the condom, put it on and supposedly knew how to use it."

She was perilously close to telling him that she'd been a virgin that night—and Amelia didn't want to go *there*. It felt like a weapon, but one that could be used against her. She swallowed it down.

Teo was watching her in that same cold, considering way that she was beginning to understand was where he hid his temper. "We would not be having this discussion if I had known who you were last September."

"That doesn't—"

"Stop, please."

He didn't raise his voice. He didn't need to. Her tongue seemed to stop of its own accord, freezing there in her own mouth.

And it occurred to Amelia that she'd thought she'd seen all the power this man carried with such offhanded grace. That she'd made a study of it. Of him.

When the truth was, she'd had absolutely no idea.

Until now.

Here, in a bare-bones shack stuck on the top of a mountain in the middle of Europe. Without the slightest possibility that she could get help. There wasn't only no electricity, there appeared to be no phone lines. A quick glance told her there was no cell phone signal.

There was nothing but him.

It turned out that panic tasted metallic.

"I am not going to argue with you about what happened," Teo said in that same soft yet thunderous voice. "I do not wish to hear evasions or excuses, and it wouldn't matter what you said in any case. We both know what you did."

She found her hands on her belly again, and his gaze dropped to track the movement.

It felt shocking. Like a touch.

"And now here you are, Amelia." He sounded as dark as the cold night that had fallen hard outside, and her name in his mouth made something deep inside her quiver. "Pregnant with my child."

Amelia took a breath, aware that she was standing inside the door of a place this man owned, again. Just as she had earlier, she felt very much as if she'd been summoned to see the headmaster. It was probably a good moment to remind herself that she hadn't been. There was no headmaster here.

Teo might be the Duke of Everything and Then Some, but he wasn't the boss of her.

She looked back over her shoulder, through the door that still stood open. But she knew he hadn't left the keys in the SUV, so she didn't bother to race for it. She slammed the heavy front door shut, which had an instant result, both positive and negative.

In the positive column, it was significantly warmer. Instantly and happily.

But the downside of that was that she was now standing sealed in a room with Teo.

She shrugged out of her coat and tossed it on one of the kitchen chairs, then took her sweet time sauntering over to sit on the couch opposite him, stretching out her feet just as he was doing.

As if neither one of them had a single care in the world.

"Forgive me, Your Excellency," she murmured, smiling edgily right back at him. "But this is starting to feel an awful lot like a kidnapping."

Teo did something with a single finger that might as well have been a shrug. "You can call it what you like. I brought you here because it is such an excellent place for…contemplation."

He wanted her to react to the emphasis he put on that last word, obviously. So, clearly, she refused to give him the satisfaction.

Amelia gazed back at him steadily. "I live in San Francisco. I enjoy contemplation as much as the next girl. But somehow, I'm getting the feeling that this is rather more of a guided meditation than an opportunity to pursue my own thoughts."

"This is the situation before us, *cariña*," he said, and the endearment was like a scrape. Because he wasn't above infusing it with all that sharp, acid mockery. Amelia hated that it got to her. "The Marinceli heir cannot be born out of wedlock."

"I'm not marrying you."

"This has nothing to do with preference or inclination. It is a simple statement of fact. My child—my son—will be the next Duke. The Twentieth Duke. Not only must he be born with my name, he must be raised to uphold the traditions that come with it. And he must learn a great, bone-deep awe for the responsibilities inherent in his position."

"I'm not marrying you, and you're certainly not raising my baby."

She only realized she sounded a shade too shrill when Teo's eyes gleamed with what she was terribly afraid was satisfaction. Especially when he relaxed back against the leather.

"It will perhaps not surprise you to learn that you are not the first reluctant Marinceli bride," he said after a moment, his voice...more caressing, somehow. "Some say a reluctant bride is what spurred the first Duke to build what would later become the family home... *El monstruo* was as fine a prison as he could make her."

Amelia lectured herself against the odd sensation in her jaw—and throughout her body—that made her teeth want to chatter. And then shake her, everywhere.

"You're not listening to me, Teo," she made herself say, in repressive tones. "There will be no wedding. I made a vow a long time ago that I would never get married."

"I vowed I would never touch Marie French or anyone associated with her." He really did shrug, then. "Vows are made to be broken, apparently."

"I should probably tell you now, but I have a very strict rule about dating only normal men," Amelia continued as if she hadn't heard him. "Regular, down-to-earth men who think a typical first date is meeting for coffee. In an actual coffeehouse, where you have to pay entirely too much money to drink burnt coffee and eat insipid pastries. That's a *good* first date, Teo. It doesn't involve security details. Or stately homes. Or more titles than sense."

"Or, to pick an example at random, disguising oneself and seducing the unwary."

She laughed. "I would never call a man with your investment portfolio *unwary*."

"Is that the appeal of the date you described? Because I prefer dating women who require more from me than an insipid croissant."

That frozen, almost affronted look on his face suggested she was lacking, somehow, in not being one of those women.

"The thing about being around very wealthy people for a lifetime is that it ruins the mystique of it all." Amelia lifted a shoulder, then dropped it, in a delicate sort of shrug that she'd seen her mother perform a thousand times. "I want credit card debt, pizza takeaways and a real, decent man who wants me for me. No trophies, no talk of bloodlines, just…a normal life."

His lip didn't *actually* curl. "That sounds like a remarkably squalid fantasy."

"You don't have to fantasize about it, then."

"Whereas you can fantasize about it all you wish," Teo replied silkily. "But it won't change a thing. You will marry me. You will become the Duchess of Marinceli, and if you think it gives me any pleasure to say this, you are gravely mistaken."

She would not pay attention to the teenager inside her, who shriveled into the fetal position at that. The teenager who had wanted nothing so much as Teo's approval and affection, no matter how unlikely it was she might ever witness either. Much less receive it.

Not being that teenager any longer came with a great many benefits. And one of them was not letting that hurt her.

Much.

"It must be some kind of pleasure," she said, pleased when she sounded as unbothered as he did, "or you would not have abducted me, marooned me on the top of a mountain, and then think it made perfect sense to sit around making pronouncements."

"You have a mouth on you." And something flickered in Teo's dark eyes that made her catch her breath.

And wonder if she would ever let it go again. "You had it when you were a child. I see time and maturity have done absolutely nothing to temper it."

She sniffed. "All the more reason you shouldn't marry this untempered mess, then."

And she almost believed what she was saying. She could almost convince herself that she was as blasé about this whole situation as she should have been. *Almost.*

"You are beneath me in every possible way," Teo said, so lightly that it took her a moment to register what he'd said. And that bright fury in his gaze. "It is a humiliation almost beyond bearing that I should be forced to sully my name, my station and the whole of the Marinceli bloodline with the daughter of a known mercenary."

That, too, he said so politely, so quietly, that it was tempting to imagine she'd misheard him.

"Not just any mercenary, out to dig for whatever gold she might find, but *Marie French*," he said, and there was nothing soft about the way he said her mother's name then. His eyes flashed. "But there is nothing to be done. You chose to do what you did, it is done, and now we both must pay the price for the rest of our lives."

His conversational tone made insult into injury. As if this was hardly worth discussing. As if it was simple fact.

As if she was a bit dim and very foolish indeed not to have acquiesced already.

"You're not such a prize yourself," she retorted.

But all Teo did was laugh.

"I am far more than a mere *prize*, Amelia. And well

you know it." He laughed again, though there was more offended astonishment than amusement in the sound. "The price you have to pay for the actions you took is an almost inconceivable elevation in status you in no way deserve. An unfathomable reward. I can't think of a single member of any royal family in Europe who would not consider it a privilege to become a Marinceli, and instead *el monstruo* may well crumble to dust in protest after all."

Amelia was shaking again, but this time she knew full well it was temper, not temptation.

"I'm not sure I'm getting your point," Amelia said, not bothering to conceal the edge in her voice. "It *almost* seems as if you're suggesting that I'm beneath you in some way? I can't really tell. Maybe you could give me more insulting examples."

"It is what it is," Teo said, with another aristocratic shrug. "The bloodline will no doubt be improved by the application of all this unexpected…"

"Peasantry?"

His eyes gleamed again, and Amelia really, really wished she couldn't *feel* that the way she did. Inside and out.

"None of this matters," Teo said, back to silken menace. "We have months yet before you will bring my heir into the world. Ample time, in my opinion, to concentrate on what is truly at stake."

"My child is the only thing at stake, obviously," she threw back at him. "Or I would be safe at home in my apartment in San Francisco, happily continuing to forget you exist."

He watched her as if she was an exhibit in a rather distressing zoo. "Can you categorically state that you did not deliberately go out of your way to create this situation?"

"I didn't set out to have your baby, if that's what you mean." She'd set out to do something else entirely, but she couldn't quite bring herself to say that. Not here, when they were the only people around for miles, and he had that knowing look about him that made her think he already knew everything already. "This pregnancy was a complete shock. Whether you believe it or not, it was an accident. But let's you and I be really clear about something, Teo. The child—*my* child—will not be."

But Teo was sitting forward, that black-gold gaze tight on her. "You didn't deliberately entrap me into this in a bid to enrich yourself. Is that what you're saying?"

"Yes, you've found me out. What I wanted most in this world was to link myself to a man who hates me but will force me to marry him anyway. A man who cares more about his bloodline than is at all healthy and proves that by a spot of kidnapping to liven up a January evening."

"It is a pity, Amelia, that I am not convinced."

"I would rather die than spend the rest of the night with you, much less the rest of my life," she hurled at him.

With, she could admit, a lot more of that poor, brokenhearted teenager inside her than she wanted to admit.

But His Excellency didn't erupt into arrogance.

"No need to fling yourself off the side of the mountain," he said drily instead. "Especially not as now, I'll be forced to save you." He waved a languid ducal hand, taking in the whole of the cabin around them. The jagged peaks outside. The snow and the dark. "Consider this your chance to prove yourself to me. There is nothing for miles in any direction but you and me. No hint of wealth or consequence to be found. I would expect a typical gold digger, like—"

"If you say like my mother, I won't be held responsible for my actions."

Teo nodded, though it wasn't any kind of surrender. More like noblesse oblige.

"You may have forced us into this," he said instead. "But that doesn't mean you get what you want."

"Clearly."

"We'll stay here as long as it takes," he said quietly. "If you didn't plan this to extort me, it's your opportunity to show it."

She shook her head. "And if I feel no particular need to prove myself to anyone, thank you, because I'm a grown woman who doesn't actually require your approval to take her next breath?"

Teo considered her, all black-gold flame and that stern mouth of his. "Then, *cariña*, I fear you are in for a very hard winter."

# CHAPTER SIX

AT FIRST SHE clearly thought he was kidding.

"We're not staying here all winter," she said.

"Are we not? That is entirely up to you, Amelia."

And Teo watched impassively as she stared back at him, obviously waiting for the other shoe to drop. For the punch line to roll out and break the tension.

Instead, he gazed back at her and let the moment stretch out.

He had no intention of making things easier on her.

Especially because the more he looked at her, the less he understood how he had failed to recognize her last fall. She'd worn very bright lipstick, it was true, but there was no disguising that lush, sensual mouth.

There never had been.

And it settled on him, with a weight he wouldn't call *heavy*, exactly, that this was the first time he could indulge himself when he looked at her. She was no longer too young. She wasn't his stepsister. And she wasn't wearing a theatrical mask to hide behind.

Teo had already resigned himself to the fact that she was carrying his son. He knew all the implications. He had always known precisely who and what he was.

And the longer she stared back at him, trying to read

his intentions, the more he became aware of something else in him that he suspected had been there a good, long while. A heat that seemed to grow into a kind of roar—

But he was not a man who succumbed to his passions. The only time he could remember doing so, in fact, was last fall at the Masquerade.

The Duke of Marinceli was expected to play host at the Masquerade, not nip off into a private room with a strange woman. Teo had never allowed himself such spontaneity. His entire life was a monument to plotting, planning and premeditation.

He had not said anything in that quiet drawing room when the passion between them had been spent. He had hardly known himself. He'd watched his masked redhead as she smiled at him. Had he recognized that mouth of hers even then? Was that the reason her smile had settled so heavily on him, like a reprimand?

She had slipped from the room. And Teo had not been sorry to discover that when he rejoined the ball, she had disappeared. He'd been less sanguine when he'd woken the following morning as hungry for her as if none of that had happened.

Teo had spent the months since assuring himself that one small indiscretion could not possibly count against the backdrop of a lifetime of responsibility. He had been *certain*.

And now he was here. With her.

Worse, it was more difficult by the moment to convince himself that his body wasn't having the same enthusiastic response to her that had gotten him into this mess in the first place. Something he would have been happy to blame on a spectacular woman dressed to cause a riot, the way she had been at the Masquerade.

But Amelia wasn't dressed to do much of anything today, unless it was to highlight her general unsuitability for the role her pregnancy had thrust upon the both of them. Teo had not imagined his wife—his Duchess—in the sort of clothing a regular person could obtain at one of the strange shopping malls they apparently favored. He had certainly never entertained the notion that she might be an American.

And if he allowed himself to think about Marie French again, he didn't know what he might do—

He stopped.

He let the silence between them drag on, and thought about the situation he'd created for the two of them instead.

This cabin had been a favorite retreat of his grandfather, the Seventeenth Duke. He'd kept it stocked with essentials, including the whiskey he preferred in the evenings—and that Teo only permitted himself to sample here.

He stood, enjoying the way Amelia stiffened as if she was bracing herself for an attack, and went to help himself. Then he selected a book from the broad, sprawling collection generations of his ancestors had left here for nights like this, and then settled himself in by the fire to enjoy a peaceful evening.

Or to appear to enjoy a peaceful evening, as if he didn't care what she did—when the truth was he was aware of every breath she took.

Entirely too aware.

"You're…just going to sit there and read?" she asked at one point, sounding strangled.

He'd taken his time looking at her. "What else do you suggest I do?"

And he'd enjoyed the way she flushed far too much.

When he was ready to take himself to bed, he did so without further comment, leaving her to her own devices. He heard her start to say something, then bite it back.

Uncertainty could only make the seriousness of their situation more clear to her, he told himself, feeling very nearly self-congratulatory as he climbed into the bed. And if this gambit of his had more to do with revenge? He was fine with that, too.

He kept telling himself that as he lay there in bed, glaring at the ceiling, everything inside him tense and too hot. He decided it was fury, because it should have been.

Because she was going to marry him, sooner or later, and he didn't know if he was more insulted at the prospect of marrying so below himself—or at the fact *she* seemed more insulted than he was.

Because his life had taken a drastic left turn when it was meant to proceed as a gentle, straight line—when he'd gone to great lengths to make sure it did—and it was all her fault. It was that damned dress she'd worn. It was her bright red lips and the molten heat of her.

He played and replayed that night last fall in his head, which was not helpful. And he tried to make himself forget that she was just there, in the next room…

Also not helpful. Or successful.

And Teo was not at all surprised, come the dawn when he finally gave up on his restless sleep, to find her curled up in a ball on the sofa where he'd left her. There were empty wrappers of nutrition bars on the table, telling him what she'd had as her dinner. She'd piled a selection of throws on top of her to keep her warm, which tugged at him in ways he planned to ignore, and had let the fire go out.

It struck him as an excellent opportunity to educate her in how this little retreat of theirs was going to go.

And maybe he took a little too much pleasure in waking her up, keeping his voice and expression stern as he asked her what she thought she was doing.

"It's winter in the mountains," Teo continued, staring down at her as she blinked sleepily, then looked around in confusion. "You cannot allow the fire to go out, Amelia. Surely a woman who plans to give birth to a child—and presumably care for it and keep it alive and well—should have better survival skills."

She was still wearing her clothes from the day before. Her long blond hair was in a glorious snarl, and she only shoved it out of her way as she pushed herself up to sitting position. Then she frowned at him. Blearily.

And there wasn't a single part of that he should have found attractive. Or appealing. She was common. Unrefined. A pageant of inelegant, indecorous vulgarity.

But tell that to the hardest part of him.

"I wasn't planning on raising my child in a shack on the top of the mountain, actually," she said, adding that knee-jerk defiance of hers to the list of her sins. That she was not impressed with him or his position and consequence was clear.

He found her...confounding.

"Is it that you don't know how to build a fire?" he asked, folding his arms and making his voice into granite. "I find this difficult to believe. Surely you must have *some* use."

"I have never built a fire, no," she said, "because I prefer to gaze at nature from afar rather than fling myself into the midst of it and hope for the best."

He only stared at her, fascinated against his will by

that stubborn jaw of hers. And the echo of that mulishness in her sleepy gaze, a thick purple at this hour.

"I don't camp," she said. "My skills run more to finance and asset allocation, not to mention good old-fashioned companionship. Fire starting never seems to be on the menu."

"Of course not. Because why would Marie French teach her daughter anything useful?"

"Your obsession with my mother is not a good look," Amelia said mildly. It was only that brighter gleam in her eyes that told him the truth about her temper. "Though it's humanizing, certainly. In the sense that it makes you just as boring and run-of-the-mill as any other man I've ever met."

She was trying to get under his skin, and what irritated Teo was that it was successful. More successful than he wanted to admit, in fact. But that didn't mean he had to show *her* that it was working.

The trouble with Marie French wasn't only that she'd married his father, both usurping and staining his mother's memory. Because there were a number of women who had done the same thing after she had whom he disliked, but not with this same fervor. And it wasn't only that Marie's station was so decidedly below the de Luzes, though that had certainly always confounded him. His problem was that his father had been besotted with her in a way that the old Duke had never been with anyone else. Including Teo's mother.

That wasn't something he intended to forgive.

No matter that he was now bound to the daughter, with chains he knew he'd never break.

Even if they choked him.

"Let me explain to you how this will work," he said,

looking down at her, and he was sure that he could see her fight to stay where she was. That jaw of hers tensed farther, and he flattered himself that she was struggling with her urge to leap to her feet and face him on more equal footing. "You have two choices."

"Choices? What choices? I thought you relieved me of such things when you abducted me yesterday."

He didn't smile, exactly. "There are always choices, *cariña*. They may not be good choices, but they always exist."

"This is pointless." Amelia rubbed at her face. Then scowled at him, as if she'd been hoping that he was a bad dream and if she rubbed her eyes, he'd go away. "You must know that I don't want to marry you. I certainly don't want to coparent with you."

"I beg your pardon? *Coparent?*" He pronounced the word as if it offended him. It did. "I am unaware of any such designation, thank you. I plan to parent my child, personally and completely. It does not require a prefix."

"Funny, I remember your father talking about the fleet of nannies who raised *you*," she replied. "And if memory serves, you felt you had been raised beautifully. So did he."

"I am not my father."

And it was not until his words hung there between them that Teo understood how profoundly he meant that.

But that wasn't something he planned to excavate at dawn. With the daughter of the woman who had single-handedly ruined the old man.

"You can lock me away for the rest of my life and I won't change my mind," Amelia was saying, her voice ringing as if she was making her own vows.

Teo only smiled. Darkly. "Then I fear we will stay here a very long time indeed."

She regarded him steadily, though certainly not politely. "I thought you were offering me choices. Not a prison sentence."

"A prison is a prison, Amelia, and you chose these bars when you decided to sneak into my party and deceive me last fall." He dared her to look away, but she didn't. And that only made him want to reach out and get his hands on her again—the very opposite of what he should have wanted. "It is up to you how you would like to serve your time, that is all."

"How appealing." Her voice was crisp, her violet gaze sharp. "It's becoming less and less of a mystery how the most eligible bachelor in the world has remained single and unattached all this time."

Teo did not spend a great deal of time questioning himself. There was no need—he was the Duke. That was the beginning and the end of it and there was no one in his life who dared question him.

Much less mock him.

To his face.

He could not say he enjoyed the experience, not least because it forced him to face the fact that he was perhaps more precious than he'd always imagined he was. Because for a hot, wild moment, all he could focus on was his need to make her pay for her temerity—and surely a man of his stature should have been secure enough in his place to laugh off rudeness and slights alike.

Then again, the method of payment he had in mind had nothing to do with laughter.

He reminded himself that he had not brought her

here, to the very top of a mountain his family had owned since the Crown of Aragon ruled the area in the twelfth century, to concern himself with her rudeness. It was her defiance he intended to conquer.

And would. Because his firstborn son would have his name. There was no other option.

"We have a certain chemistry," he said now, which struck him as a vast understatement. The mouth he had so enjoyed last fall, so luscious and red, should not have called to him as it did now. Bare and unsmiling. Her hair a disaster. Her gaze insolent at best. "Some marriages start with far less than that."

"Marriages that took place in the first century, perhaps." Amelia pushed to her feet then, bringing the soft throw with her and clutching it to her chest as if she was preserving her modesty. When she was still wearing all her clothes. "I understand that the Marinceli family is stuck in the past. But that doesn't mean you have to stay there, Teo. Or that you have to drag me down with you."

He'd been standing there over the sofa, looking down at her. And a gentleman would have stepped back as she rose, to give her space.

Teo had been raised a gentleman, but that didn't seem to apply here. He couldn't seem to access the manners that had been imprinted on him so long ago they were usually second nature to him. He didn't move—and was instantly rewarded for that with the simple pleasure of watching her tilt her chin up. Then tip her head even farther back so she could raise her gaze to his—all the way up to where he towered above her.

He liked the way her cheeks flushed. And the way that curiously magnetic temper of hers lit the violet of her eyes, making them gleam all the brighter.

"The Marinceli family is timeless," Teo said, almost amused. "It doesn't matter what century it is, we endure."

"Is that one of my choices? Because I'll go ahead and pass on *enduring* right now. That sounds like a joyless march to a grim death. No, thank you."

Teo blinked. *No, thank you* was not the typical response to any offer he made. It certainly wasn't the expected reaction to an invitation to join the family. This woman was maddening.

He wanted to believe she was simply ignorant, but she had spent those years in Spain. With his father, and with him, too. There was no question that she might not know precisely who and what the Marincelis were.

Teo was perilously close to losing his self-control. "When you are ready to stop this foolishness, accept reality and take your place at my side, you are welcome to sleep with me in the bed."

He watched the pulse in the base of her neck go wild. He felt an answering beat in his own neck. And far lower, where he was too hard, too ready.

Amelia took her time swallowing, delicate and deliberate at once. "You're saying you want me to have sex with you."

"Oh, yes," he said, his voice low. Dark and rich. "A great deal of sex, one can only hope. Have we not already demonstrated that that is what we do best?"

"We've demonstrated that we *can* do it," she shot back. "But whether or not the one time makes it *the best*, I couldn't possibly say."

"I can think of a way to find out."

Amelia sniffed as if the notion revolted her, but he was still too close to her. He could see the truth in her flushed skin, her dilated eyes.

"I get to sleep in the bed only if we're having sex. Am I getting the terms of your little blackmail attempt right?"

Teo shrugged as if he didn't care either way. He felt that he really shouldn't have cared either way, but that did not appear to be in the cards.

"It's not a blackmail attempt, *cariña*. It's a choice. If you wish to share the bed, you must consider it the marital bed. That hardly seems unfair."

"I have no intention of marrying you," she said, with insulting directness. "Or sharing a bed with you. Under any circumstances whatsoever, Teo."

"That is a pity," he said coolly. "If you share the marital bed, I will treat you as my Duchess. And we will enjoy a rustic retreat together ahead of our wedding. If you do not—"

"I won't. Ever."

"If you say so."

"I would stake my life on it," she threw at him.

He nodded. Sagely. "Then you may sleep on this couch, and I will treat you like a servant."

"Is this a good time to talk about what's wrong with you? And how women can actually be more than your Duchess or your maid?"

"*Women* can be anything they like," Teo retorted, his tone harsh. "You have fewer choices because you stole mine."

It was a grim victory, certainly, but a victory nonetheless when she paled. And didn't throw something back at him, for once.

He chose not to point out that she'd already differentiated herself from her mother. Since Marie French was shameless, through and through, as Teo had personally witnessed in the dark days of her marriage to his father.

"I expect the fire to remain lit, if banked, at all times, as I do not wish to freeze to death. I expect three meals a day, and you may rejoice in my benevolence, as I expect very little in the way of haute cuisine here."

"Oh, happy day," she muttered. No longer quite so pale.

"And this might be the most difficult for you, Amelia," he continued. "But I expect deference."

"I expect you to go to hell," she shot back.

"I'm afraid I insist on courtesy," he said, almost sadly. "And if I were you, I'd figure out how to obey. Before I lose my good humor altogether."

# CHAPTER SEVEN

"I THINK YOU'VE forgotten that there's also a third option," Amelia managed to say, somehow *not* commenting on Teo's supposed "good humor." Though it was hard to get the words out through gritted teeth. And a jaw so tight she was worried it might shatter at any moment. "I could also do neither of those things. I could sit back down on this couch, ignore you and wait for you to tire of whatever game this is."

"You could," he agreed, but there was something far too dangerous in the way he said it. It shivered through her, far more intense than a mere dare. "But I'm a simple man, particularly here. If you are not functioning as a servant, I will only be able to recognize you as the woman who is to be my wife." This time, he didn't shrug. He stared at her in a kind of steady demand that made her…restless. "And I will act accordingly, of course."

Amelia felt as if she'd cinched herself into something horribly tight. For a moment she wasn't sure she could force a breath, and that restlessness made her itch. But she made herself stand still.

And she kept her voice cool. "I want to make sure we're both really clear about the fact that you're threatening me. With sex."

She thought that might slap at him. Offend him, at the very least.

But instead, Teo smiled in that edgy way that had been making her pulse jagged since she'd jolted awake to find him standing over her, taking over her field of vision. For a wild moment she hadn't been able to tell if she was asleep or awake.

There was no mistaking the fact she was awake now. He reached over and slid his hand over her hard, clenched jaw.

And then slowly, almost lazily, dragged his thumb over her lips.

Amelia felt as if she was the fire behind them, then. As if he'd stoked the flames—her—that easily, shaming her.

Or maybe she only *wanted* to be shamed. Because what she felt was a storm of sensation, galloping through her. Her nipples felt bright, hard. Her breasts were heavy. She felt something like chills running down her limbs, then sinking deep inside her until they formed a kind of tangle, too hot and too greedy down low in her belly.

"Do you feel threatened?" Teo asked her. Goading her. "Or do you feel something else entirely?"

"Everything you do is a threat," she managed to say. What she didn't do was pull away from him. "That's a natural consequence of kidnapping and abducting someone, I think you'll find."

But his hand was still on her face, and she could feel herself shaking, deep inside. Like the tectonic plates that kept her upright—that made her who she was—were shifting whether she liked it or not.

"I think you are trembling, *cariña*. I think you are

terribly, surpassingly hungry." And somehow she couldn't pretend, even to herself, that he was talking about food. "Hot and wet, are you not?"

"Of course not." Her voice was barely more than a whisper.

"Here's another choice," he said, all that edge and quiet insinuation. "I'll make it easy for you. No need to declare yourself too openly, in a way you will not be able to take back. No need to remind us both too closely of that night back in September. All you have to do is stay exactly where you are."

He didn't elaborate on what would happen if she did that. He didn't have to.

"...or?"

"Or you can go into the kitchen and find a different way to please me." One arrogant brow lifted. "I prefer to start my days with a hot fire and a small *desayuno*, which I keep far simpler than you Americans are wont to do. No platters of dessert masquerading as breakfast foods." That brow seemed to arch even more intensely. "A *café con leche*, please."

He said *please*. Amelia heard him. But she wasn't foolish enough—yet—to imagine that was anything but an order.

And there was only one choice, obviously. No matter what he seemed to think. There was only one possible choice—and yet, for a terrifying moment that seemed to stretch on into eternity, she wavered.

Amelia stood there, gazing up at him, wondering if she could truly read that austere face of his or if she only wished she could.

Wondering what would happen if she let herself melt the way she wanted to do.

Wondering too many things that she should have known better than to allow into her head in the light of day, when wondering what it would be like to indulge herself with this man was what had gotten her into this position in the first place.

*Pull yourself together,* she snapped at herself. *Now.*

She didn't only step back, then. She jolted away from him and around him, wrenching herself out of the way of too much temptation.

Because worse by far than the molten heat between her legs was the ache in her chest.

Amelia blinked back the unexpected moisture in her eyes as she tried to find her way around the small kitchen. The deep sink basin boasted a pump in place of a faucet, and the water that poured out was clear and fresh. And even as her body shuddered through leftover reactions—to Teo, to this situation she found herself in, to her own body's betrayal of her—she tried to focus on the task at hand.

Outside the window a pretty winter sun peeked over the frozen slopes of the surrounding peaks. They were clearly very high up—and Amelia clung to the altitude as an explanation for why she felt so dizzy. It was the height, not the man. Clearly.

And it was almost helpful, really, to have something odd and a little overwhelming to do, like become a rustic barista in an ancient cabin, on command. But then, that was the part of her unconventional life with her mother that she liked best. Amelia had always done well thinking on her feet, and making herself into whoever and whatever the moment required.

The pumped-in water was ice cold, and she filled a

small bucket and then brought it to the open pot over the fire. Then she set about building up the fire below.

She'd assumed that this was the kind of absurd task that featured in the kinds of reality shows she liked to watch to relax, and so was pleasantly surprised when she found ground espresso in the stocked cupboards, and better still, a classic silver stovetop espresso maker to put it in. She ladled water out of the pot, then put the espresso maker on the grate.

And when she turned to see if Teo was watching her come to grips with his medieval kitchen, she found that simmering black gaze steady on her in a way that made her chest ache. Again.

She reminded herself it was the altitude.

"Is this what hereditary dukes do for fun?" she asked. Perhaps more archly than the average servant might. "Take themselves off into the mountains and pretend to be one with the common folk? I'm assuming it didn't occur to you that us common folk like electricity and gas mains these days, just like you people in your big houses?"

"I prefer my servants to express their deference in silence," he said, sounding deep and mysterious, like a brick wall of privilege and that damnable sensuality she wished—oh, how she wished—didn't get into her veins like that.

"Then you should have kidnapped a better class of personal maid," she shot back.

But she was the one who turned away again, unable somehow to hold that stare of his.

When the espresso was finally bubbling, she poured it into a cup, added milk and delivered it. And then felt that itchy restlessness sweep over her again. More acutely this time.

"Now what?" And, yes, her voice was belligerent. Her body language matched it. "I've waited on you. Is that really what you want?"

Teo took his time lifting his cup. He took his time tasting the *café con leche* he'd asked for, until Amelia started fidgeting with the need to slap it out of his hand—

"Ordinarily I would say that you should go directly into cleaning, as this floor is appallingly dirty." Teo's gaze raked over her in a way she might have thought was dispassionate had she not been standing so close to him. Close enough to see the gleam in those black eyes. "But I am ever mindful that no matter the choices you made, and no matter my feelings about them, you are carrying my heir. I will therefore allow you an hour to yourself. I suggest you clean yourself up. Eat something. And then reapply yourself to the task at hand—and with a pleasant demeanor more suited to your role, please."

"I have no intention of getting naked in a tiny, remote cabin with a man who feels justified in holding me prisoner and making me his own, personal Cinderella, thank you."

Of course, the moment she said the word *naked*, all she could picture was Teo naked. It made her head spin all the more.

"If you do not do as I ask, I will take it as an invitation to do as I wish," Teo replied, his attention on the coffee she'd made him as if he was making offhanded remarks instead of threats.

Threats she fully believed he would carry out.

And for once in her life, Amelia decided that the

smart move was to keep her mouth shut. Discretion was the better part of valor, or so she'd read once in school.

Maybe being trapped on the top of the mountain with a brooding, uncompromising duke who had it in for her—and who might very well take what he wanted, with her body's enthusiastic consent, a possibility that horrified her even as it made her belly quiver with longing—was an excellent place to discover if that were true.

The days took on their own, unique shape.

Amelia slept on the couch by the fire, and though she didn't strip down to the T-shirt she normally preferred to sleep in, she found that it wasn't necessary to keep herself fully dressed, either. Teo made no further attempts to put his hands on her.

She told herself that made her riotously glad.

The cold, careful light woke her in the early mornings. She built the fire back up, then started the water boiling. In the first few days there, she'd wondered how far he was going to take it. Would he send her out into the wilderness in some attempt to rustle up food from the snow and ice? Would he make her scrub the floors with a toothbrush, like some kind of Catholic school nun?

But she should have known that even Teo at his most rustic was far too sophisticated—or pampered— to leave himself victim to the vagaries of either nature or Amelia's hesitant servitude. The cabin was well stocked. The cupboards were filled with dry goods and she quickly discovered that there was also a cold chest that had been conveniently filled.

Amelia got to indulge her self-righteous indignation

at his high-handedness and arrogance every time she served him, as ordered. And better still, she secretly got to indulge every last domestic urge she'd ever had, but had never had the occasion to entertain. Because Marie French did not lower herself to domestic chores. She had raised Amelia to disdain anything that smacked of what she called *chambermaiding*.

*A smart girl aspires to run the house, not clean it,* she always said.

But Amelia quite enjoyed a good clean. It was satisfying. It was a clear, indisputable accomplishment. And maybe it also felt a bit like penance, for deceiving Teo in the first place—something she would die before she admitted out loud.

While the water warmed in the mornings, she liked to go outside—wrapped up tight against the cold—and breathe in the frigid air. There was nothing in any direction save snow-covered inclines, the winter sky and, not long after she rose each morning on clear days, the full, glorious sunrise.

"Looking for your escape route?" Teo asked on one of those mornings, coming out to stand behind her there in the small clearing that she liked to think of as their yard. "It's a long walk down."

And she'd only looked over her shoulder at him, hoping she looked enigmatic, because she hadn't been thinking about walking down at all. She'd been thinking about staying here forever, happily cut off—cut free—from the noise and hustle of her life.

Winter days were short, and sometimes the sun never rose at all. It was all snow and storm, howling winds, and the days bled one into the next, dark outside and bright within.

As the days passed, Amelia found her shoulders seemed to drop from their usual place up at her ears. She found herself holding her breath less as she bustled around, oddly delighted that the tasks before her were simple and easily executed. Cleaning a floor was a far more appealing prospect than untangling her mother's money issues. Sweeping or dusting felt like a holiday compared with the usual long, torturous phone calls in which her mother would tell her things no daughter wanted to know, usually involving sex. Amelia had never been much of a cook, but it was only possible to produce simple things here, so that was what she did. She didn't have to worry about whether or not her culinary attempts were good, only that they were edible.

And that, too, was infinitely preferable to presenting herself as her mother's escort of an evening, subject to Marie's cheerful critique of her clothes, her hair, even the expression she wore on her face. Not to mention the running commentary on how Amelia ought to have been living her life.

Teo, meanwhile, was remarkably...easygoing. In comparison.

Well. Perhaps that wasn't the right word.

He didn't critique her, but he watched her. She would look up from some menial task or other to find him studying her, that stern mouth of his unsmiling and whole worlds in his eyes that she couldn't quite read.

Teo made her heart stutter in her chest, and she found herself in a constant state of awareness. She always knew exactly where he was, and when he went off on his hikes the cabin felt strange and almost too large without him.

One night, after they'd eaten the simple dinner she'd

made—that he insisted she serve, then eat with him—she went to rise and clear the plates as usual, but he stopped her.

"It has been ten days," he said, and it occurred to her with a jolt that she'd stopped counting. What did that say about her? "I expected far more complaints."

"Are you asking for a list of complaints? Or bemoaning the fact that I haven't offered any?"

"If you think you can wait me out, you should know that you can't." His voice was blunt, that gaze direct. "I told you already. I come from a timeless bloodline. Ten days, ten months. It is all the same to me."

"I'm afraid it won't be the same, actually," she said drily. "Because unless you plan to hand deliver this child yourself, there's a very specific time limit to how long you can keep me here."

He made a soft noise that was not quite a laugh. "Do you imagine me incapable of flying in a medical team?"

"Threat, threat, threat," she said lightly, mocking him. "You gave me a choice, Teo. I took it. It's not my fault if you're rethinking that now."

To her surprise, his mouth curved. "*Cariña*, I am not the one who wakes in the night, gasping for air."

He couldn't possibly know what she dreamed about. Amelia told herself that, fiercely and repeatedly. *He couldn't know.* He could have no idea that she woke up flushed so hot she had to toss off her blankets though the room was always cold. That her thighs ached, her breasts hurt, and between her legs, she burned.

Oh, how she burned.

He couldn't know any of those things. He thought she was gasping for air, not gasping his name.

But as she gazed at him, and the way he lounged

there like the Duke of impeccable lineage he was, the faintest trickle of what she told herself was horror snuck down her spine. It had to be horror, and not any of the other things that swirled around inside her, daring her to look at them straight.

"What do you get out of this?" she asked him.

Or, really, threw out there into all that "horror" that danced between them as surely as the snowstorm howled about outside.

"You will have to be more specific," Teo replied.

"I can see the appeal of this place," Amelia said, more sternly than necessary. Because she was desperate, suddenly, and just as desperate not to show it. "It's so easy to forget that there's a whole world that doesn't live inside a mobile phone. There's something rewarding in stepping away from it all. Learning how to listen to the thoughts inside, for a change, instead of all that external noise."

All of that was true. But there was also him.

Teo, whom she had never managed to get over. Or past. Even the exorcism she'd thought she'd performed so brilliantly hadn't worked—even before she'd learned she was pregnant. She'd still woken up in the night, longing for him so hard she worried it might have physical repercussions. She'd wondered if her "stomach bug" was actually an extended reaction to having him and walking away from him.

She'd begun to think that she'd imprinted on him at too young of an age. That he'd stamped his mark on her, even though he hadn't liked her at all, and she was stuck with it.

Amelia certainly wouldn't want a lifetime of performing menial tasks and acting like a servant. But this felt…different. Like a gift, somehow. And she knew it wasn't the scrubbing. The polishing of this or that, however mindlessly meditative the task.

It was *him*.

It was breathing his air. It was looking up to find that gaze of his on her, because these days, he didn't look at her the way he had when she was a teenager. As if he couldn't fathom what such a lowly creature was doing in his life, invading his family. That was gone now. In this cabin, he looked at her the way a man looked at a woman.

That look heated her. Beguiled her. It made her head go funny and her legs feel wobbly, and she tried to pretend none of that was happening even as she tucked it away like a bit of treasure to hoard. Because there had been many years where all she'd ever wanted was Teo to see her. Really, truly *see* her, as a woman. And here, now, *finally*, he did.

And it only occurred to her while the question she'd asked him hung in the air that perhaps she was a little too invested in what Teo was getting out of this arrangement.

Amelia was old enough to know that a wise woman didn't go asking questions when she already knew that the answers could very well break her heart.

Or at least bruise it, significantly.

For the first time in almost ten full days, she found herself holding her breath.

"I enjoy my solitude," he said, and she got the impression that he chose those words carefully. Too carefully.

There was something in the way he sat there that was different, suddenly. Too tight, maybe. Coiled.

"How can it be solitude?" She tried to sound light and airy and wasn't at all sure she hit the mark. "You're not alone."

"Downgrading from a staff of hundreds to one is the next best thing," Teo said drily.

Amelia found herself studying her hands, but not looking at him didn't exactly help her. She could see him perfectly no matter if she was looking at him or not. He was like a brand on the inside of her eyelids. She felt like those kittens she'd read about in college, who spent their early lives behind bars, then saw bars forever whether they were caged or not.

And surely, if she was normal in any regard, she wouldn't find the notion of being caged by this man forever to be so…comforting.

He hated her. He might have been playing a waiting game here, but it was just another game. Why couldn't she remember that the way she should? He wanted to marry her and claim his child, but she would be very foolish indeed if she imagined that had anything to do with *her*. She knew better.

There was no reason at all that Teo de Luz should make her feel safe.

Especially not when he'd kidnapped her for the express purpose of bending her to his will—and she knew it. He'd been open about it.

"I'm delighted I make you feel like you're alone," she said, making her voice wry. Amused.

"On the contrary," he murmured, an edge she didn't quite understand in his voice. "I find it difficult to remember a time when you were not here."

"Did you come here often with your father?"

She blurted that out. Because there was that gleam in

his gaze and a shuddering in response, deep inside her. And she could tell herself any number of truths, or try. But that was very different from telling them to him.

Teo's sensual lips twitched. "My father and I were not friends, Amelia. He did not encourage intimacies of that kind."

She nodded, too eagerly. "My mother always said that the tragedy of your father was that he wanted to feel, but couldn't."

Teo's gaze cooled dramatically, and Amelia froze, in direct response.

"Did she indeed? What other insights did your mother have to share about her blessedly brief time as the Duchess of Marinceli, pray tell?"

And frozen or not, there would never be a better opportunity for her to say things to him that she had never dared speak aloud when she was younger. Things she hadn't even said when she'd come to find him in that palace of his.

Things she knew he had no interest in hearing. Ever.

"You've never understood my mother," she said, briskly. "All you see is the surface. Too blonde. Too comfortable showing off her body. All flash, no substance. Though I'm certain you use different words."

"I prefer not to discuss your mother at all."

"It's easier to talk about her than it is to understand her," Amelia said, staunchly. "She'd be the first person to say that it's just as easy to fall in love with a rich man as a poor one, but the key point is, she actually does fall in love."

For a moment it was as if the storm outside had breached the walls, the howling was so intense. But in the next moment she realized that was nothing more than the noise inside her.

Teo looked about as approachable as a slab of granite. "If you are about to launch into some kind of poetic rhapsody about the depths of your mother's heart, Amelia, I would beg you to rethink."

"It doesn't last, perhaps, but when she commits, she means it. She loved your father."

"She conned him," Teo said, his words distinct and a kick of menace beneath them. "He made a fool of himself over that woman."

"She has that effect," Amelia said softly. "But that doesn't mean it wasn't real. It was. I understand that all you can see is what it meant to your bloodline. Your title. Your—"

"My *family*, Amelia," he belted at her. "My bloody *family*."

That sliced through Amelia like the vicious winter wind outside. She lost her breath, staring across at him while an expression she'd never before seen on his face twisted him up.

His eyes blazed. But this time with a kind of torment.

"My parents used to tell me stories about their great luck," Teo bit out, still lounging there, though there wasn't a single part of him that wasn't tense and coiled to spring. She could see it with her own eyes. "Because their marriage, while not technically arranged, might as well have been. Their parents chose them for one another when they were small. But they were lucky, they said, because they liked each other. Loved each other, even. And in a family like mine, that is never a prerequisite for a long marriage."

Suddenly, this cage of hers seemed tighter all around her. But Teo was still talking.

"When she died, I expected my father to mourn. Instead, he dated." And the way he said that word was like a slap. "I understand a man has needs, even if I would prefer not to think of my father's. And I resigned myself to these things because it was his personal business. Not mine. Who cared how many women he squired about? He had been married for a long time. The line of succession was secured. Why shouldn't he sow some oats, if he was so inclined?"

Amelia didn't really think that was a question. Certainly not one that required an answer from her. Especially not when his expression was so harsh.

"But then he met your mother," Teo said darkly. "And he was not content with sowing, or squiring. He fell in love."

"A fate worse than death," Amelia murmured.

His gaze seemed to blaze even hotter when that should not have been possible. "He loved her. And she left him. And he grieved your mother, not mine. He engaged on a downward spiral of inappropriate lovers, drink and despair. I believe that led to his death five years ago. And no, I do not forgive her."

Amelia told herself to bite her tongue. She meant to. But she couldn't.

"I think you mean you couldn't forgive *him*," she said softly.

And she watched Teo…implode.

He didn't move. He didn't shake or roll his eyes in the back of his head, or anything so dramatic. But still, she could see it. The bomb, the burn.

His eyes blazed. And then he seemed nothing so much as haunted.

And she felt her heart lurch painfully in her chest.

For a long, endless sort of moment that could have been years, ages, millennia, she stayed where she was. Suspended in Teo's gaze, where ghosts lurked, and beneath it, she saw a different version of the ruthless, uncompromising Duke.

A son who had lost a mother, then a father—the latter some time before his death.

Amelia had wanted so badly for Teo to see her all these years. Why hadn't she realized how little *she* saw *him*?

The wind howled outside. A log collapsed in the fire.

"I suggest you clean up," he said, his voice too quiet. It rang in her like condemnation, making her fight to restrain a sob. "And you should know that you have ash on your face. Soot, perhaps."

And at another time, maybe, that would have embarrassed her. How long had it been there? Had he ever planned to tell her? But tonight those questions hardly seemed to matter. Amelia lifted her hand and rubbed at her cheek, not surprised when her fingers came away smudged black.

"Better soot than sorrow," she replied.

And she didn't see him move. It was a kind of blur of ferocity and grief, a new take on that same old hunger they'd been dancing around for too long now.

One moment he was sitting opposite her. The next, he was hauling her up to her feet and then holding her there, his big hands wrapped around her shoulders.

"My servants do not talk to me of sorrow," he gritted out at her. "And they do not presume to mention my esteemed, late and much lamented father. Do you understand me? Either know your place or change it, Amelia. Those are your only choices."

His hands clenched tighter, digging into her skin—but in a way that made her whole body ignite. The fire in the grate paled next to the flames that danced between them, brighter and hotter by the second.

And she was sure that he would pull her close, then take her mouth—

But he didn't.

Teo let her go. Then he turned on his heel and strode from the room.

Leaving her there alone as the winter wind battered at the walls.

Amelia told herself she'd won. She was the victor. But she looked down at her hand, and wondered why she felt as if all of her was ash, instead.

# CHAPTER EIGHT

AMELIA STOOD WHERE he'd left her for a long while.

Slowly, she sank back down onto the sofa behind her, not sure whether she chose to sit or was forced to because her knees no longer functioned properly.

She kept staring at her hand and without entirely meaning to, found herself rubbing her fingers together, transferring the dark soot from one finger to the next. From one hand to the next.

And no matter how long she sat there, no matter how still she held herself, she couldn't seem to catch her breath.

She felt all the usual things she always did when she was in the presence of Teo. Frustrated desire, as ever. The driving need to impress him, somehow. That greedy, voracious thing in her that *wanted*—wanted anything he would give her and hundreds of things he never had. Not entirely.

But underneath it all, she felt a funny, new knot in her gut that she was terribly afraid was shame.

Because through all of this, since she was a teenager and on into her adulthood, she'd thought about Teo far too much. She'd thought about him. Dreamed about him. Found him unaccountably stuck between her and any attempt she made to transfer this hunger to someone else. She'd raged about him. Cried about him. Made vows to stop fixating on him and then, finally, she'd come up with a plan to exorcise him.

But had she ever really thought of him as a man? A whole person?

She knew she hadn't. He was her stepbrother. The Duke's son. Then the Duke himself. He was a hundred titles and had a thousand names, many she'd made up purely to entertain herself, especially when she'd been sixteen.

But she'd never thought of him as just a man back then. Or since. As a complicated, layered person.

In her fantasies, whether he'd been good or evil or something altogether else, she had never thought of him like that.

Like her.

The reason she'd concealed her appearance at the Masquerade wasn't because she'd worried that sleeping with her would cause him to have any kind of feelings. It had never occurred to her that Teo had any feelings. Not really. Not unless they were acrid and accusatory, or tangled up somehow in his title.

She'd told herself it was because he wouldn't let her close to him if he knew who she was. And that was a part of it, certainly.

But she'd always imagined that if anyone *could* see her, truly, it would be Teo. And when it came down to it, she'd wanted to make sure he didn't.

Just as he hadn't wished her to see the real part of him tonight.

Almost as if they were similar, after all.

And it was a strange and comprehensive sort of shattering, then, that took her over. That broke her apart into shards of guilt and shame alike, and something else. Something that she couldn't quite name, but knew had to do with the things they had in common.

Far more than the enormous gulf between a commoner and a duke.

Because the notion that Teo might be no more than flesh and blood, perfectly capable of feeling every last thing that she did made her...hurt.

More than simply *hurt*.

It pounded in her temples and turned her stomach like too much wine. It tangled around itself, like a thick and braided thing.

And still, that scalding heat seemed to lick her, head to toe.

She rose again, and she didn't bother to wash the ash and soot from her hands. She'd crossed this room a thousand times since they'd arrived, but tonight it seemed to take on marathon proportions. Miles upon miles, she was sure, and then she was at the door to the bedroom.

She pushed it open, her hand flat against the door, dimly aware that she was leaving her handprint behind—one more thing it would fall to her to clean in the morning. Her throat was so dry she was surprised it didn't turn into its own kindling, and her eyes were glassy, almost foggy.

But that didn't in any way prevent her gaze from cutting straight to Teo.

And staying there while her heart leaped.

The bedroom was deceptively simple because it was dominated by the bed at the far wall that offered a stunning view out over the Pyrenees. She had cleaned in here defiantly, certain that he expected her to balk, and she'd been unable to avoid thinking about what it would look like from the bed. A person could wake up of a morning and watch that very sunrise that she stepped outside to look at every day.

Or a person could concentrate on what was in the bed, instead.

Teo was sprawled there as if he'd seen all those dreams she kept having after all, and was trying to re-enact them in the soft light from the lanterns. His dark gaze was unreadable, and stormier than usual. And it was something, wasn't it, to know that she was responsible for introducing all that thunder to his gaze tonight.

She wanted to feel that as a victory, but she didn't. She couldn't.

And Amelia couldn't keep her eyes on his face. Not when he had bared the whole of his chest to her view, which should have made him seem smaller, like any naked thing.

But Teo looked...bigger. An immensity in human form, as if the trappings of his title and general magnificence were mere props to distract the unwary from the truth of him. He was golden and beautiful, like the sort of sculpture he would collect to display in his gallery and scholars would flock to, to fawn over.

She felt a bit like fawning herself, and all he was doing was sitting up against the headboard, a book at his side that he'd clearly tossed aside when the door had opened.

And even at the Masquerade, she had only seen him clothed. She had never gotten to look at all his smooth, toned flesh stretched across muscle and bone.

It was like staring into the sun.

She was afraid that if she kept it up, she would go blind.

And yet she couldn't seem to make herself stop.

"Let me guess what I've done to merit a personal visit," Teo said, and his voice held all that thunder, all the storms she could see with her own eyes. "Have you had an attack of conscience, Amelia?"

"Of course not," she said, trying to sound certain as she stood there, half in and half out of the bedroom. "The truth might be uncomfortable, but it doesn't require the intervention of conscience…depending on your truth, I suppose."

"Are we telling truths tonight?" And there was a warning in that voice of his. Something dangerous wrapped up in silk and heat. A wise woman would walk away. Amelia stayed where she was. "Perhaps you can explain to me why you've taken so easily to a life of drudgery."

She swallowed, because that cut a bit. It stung. "Not a life. Just a little while. You can do anything if it's temporary."

An odd look moved over his beautiful face. "I wouldn't know."

And he wouldn't. Of course he wouldn't. There wasn't a single thing about the life of a member of the de Luz family that was *temporary*. Everything was stone and consequence, handed down throughout time and stretching far off into the future.

*A prison is a prison,* he'd told her. *It is up to you how you would like to serve your time.*

Why had she never stopped to think how those words applied to him, too?

"I do not think it is the temporary aspect that you

like," he continued, in that same dangerous way. "I think it is quite the contrary. You imagine yourself in a place like this. It is a small cabin, but sturdy, and has stood right here in one form or another for centuries. You are thirsty for that kind of connection, are you not?"

Her throat hurt, it was so dry. "I'm not thirsty for anything."

"I am not the only one who grieves," Teo said, as inevitable as thunder. As terrible as the storm outside. And in here, too. "But you lost something rather different, did you not? The whole of your childhood."

She had wanted to be seen. By him, specifically. And now she wanted to hide.

But there was ash on her hands and that aching thing where her heart should have been. And she was the one who had hidden herself last fall. She was the one who had made all of this happen. She owed him the penance she'd been paying.

And that likely meant it wasn't up to her to dictate the terms of that penance. Even if this was the price she had to pay.

"I had a marvelous childhood," Amelia retorted, a knee-jerk response that seemed to roll up and out of her whether she liked it or not. Because it was one thing to think about penance and scrub a not very dirty floor. It was something else entirely to pry herself open and expose herself to him. To anyone, but especially to him. "My mother took me everywhere with her."

"Like a pet."

"Like a *friend*."

"Parents are not meant to be friends," Teo said with soft menace. "One cannot parent one's friend. And children are by definition in want of a parent. I think you will find that it is all right there in the titles. Parent. Child. Friend. Not the same, is it?"

Amelia made herself laugh, trying for airy and bright—but what came out made his dark brow lift.

"Not everyone was raised up into a glorious blood-line, filled with tedious history and mausoleums with their names chiseled into the stone at birth," she said. "Some people prefer a more carefree existence."

Her childhood had been many things, none of them *carefree*. And Amelia couldn't understand why she felt one thing and then opened her mouth to find something else entirely coming out. As if her tongue was more afraid of vulnerability than she was.

And meanwhile, Teo lounged in that bed half-na-ked, like some kind of god. Or satyr. And whatever he was, he made her dizzy. She wanted to fall down all over him, and burn herself on all that smooth, hard male perfection.

The way she had last fall, but with all of her, this time. All of him.

But she couldn't seem to make her body move. Her legs were planted into the floor, as if her feet had taken root.

Because if she went to him like this, without the mask or the dress, the lipstick or the red hair, she would be wide open. Exposed.

He would know how much she wanted him.

How much she always had.

"You might convince me that your mother loved my father, in time," Teo said darkly, that gaze of his too hot. "You might even convince me that your mother is not the gold digger she seems, but a woman who cannot help but fall in love. Repeatedly. And only upward on the social ladder. But you will never convince me that Marie French loves anything so much as she loves herself. Not even you, Amelia."

It wasn't as if Amelia hadn't heard such things before. Or some variation thereof. But she had never heard it quite like this.

Quietly.

With that devastating certainty that rolled through her like truth.

The truth she had never wanted to look at face-on.

Something walloped her, and she wanted to tip back her head and let it out. Sob through it. Scream about it. Just get it out—

But almost before she could process the hit of it, something else smacked her down.

Because she didn't think that Teo was being cruel for the sake of it.

He was lying there, naked to the waist—and for all she knew, naked beneath that sheet—and he was looking at her as if he could see deep inside her. To the place where that great sob remained trapped. To the place where she'd hidden from everything and everyone for as long as she could remember.

Even him, last fall.

But here, in this cabin on top of a remote mountain in the Pyrenees, he saw her.

Just as she'd wanted. Just as she'd feared.

*He saw her.*

Amelia had a brief thought for that sixteen-year-old version of herself, who would have done anything to gain his notice. Anything at all. No matter what it took, no matter the cost. And now she understood things she couldn't have, then. That some prices hurt to pay almost beyond bearing, because the way he looked at her was ruthless. Pitiless. Merciless, even.

It wasn't in any way the kind of longing looks she'd imagined in her youth.

But it was perfect.

Scathing, serious, beautiful and perfect.

And Amelia still couldn't look away.

"Much as I enjoy watching you squirm in my doorway, with soot on your face and ash prints on my walls," Teo said, "this is not what I would consider an ideal way to end a trying evening."

He lifted that brow of his, an arrogant query that on a face like his was more properly a demand. And some part of her was amazed that he could seem just as untouchable, just as remote and powerful, lying down half-naked in a bed as he did when he was standing—likely surrounded by portraiture and statuary, all of them bearing features that looked like his and taken together, told the story of Spain.

"What is it you want?" he asked, holding her gaze hostage.

For once in her life, Amelia didn't dare look away. She didn't dare hide.

She felt torn asunder, though she knew she stood in one piece. She had spent the whole of her life trying her best to pretend a great number of things. That her mother loved her the way a mother should. That her life was a madcap adventure.

That this man did not matter to her. Because he shouldn't have.

Amelia had tried to forget him. And when that didn't work, she'd tried a spot of immersion therapy.

And here she was again, and it was worse this time. She carried his child. His son. The heir to that absurd monster of a house.

Amelia knew that he would never allow her to take their son away from him. That he would not have allowed it if the only thing he planned to leave his heir was debt. Perhaps she'd known that before she'd gotten on that plane in San Francisco. Perhaps she'd always known it.

She could pretend all she liked that if she was stubborn enough, dedicated enough to this penitent game she was playing, he would give in—but she knew better, didn't she?

The Duke did not give. He did not bend. There was not one part of his life that required compromise or quarter, and accordingly, he offered neither. He never would.

And suddenly Amelia felt as exhausted as if she'd crawled up that winding mountain road on her own hands and knees. She felt as if he'd clawed away a crucial veil she kept between her and the reality of her life, of her, of what she'd done to both of them, and it hurt.

It all hurt.

Maybe it had always hurt, and she was only now admitting it.

Her hands crept over her belly, and she thought about longevity. About centuries upon centuries of one family, one house, one enduring vision that united them all.

And how, in comparison, the ragtag itinerant lifestyle she'd lived with her mother seemed so shoddy.

If she could choose a life for her baby—and she could, by God, and would—she would not choose hers.

All she had to do was surrender.

And risk that he would see the real truth about her stamped all over her face, her body. That without her various masks, he would know the real her.

And scarier still, her heart.

"I will ask again," he said, his voice more stern, if such a thing was possible. All ice and disapproval, and she was a twisted creature, wasn't she, that she craved that from him. It made her restless, hot. "What do you want? Why did you come in here?"

"I'm ready," she said, and had the sense that she'd run to the edge of one of the mountain cliffs all around and instead of stopping, had catapulted herself out into the great abyss.

Now came the fall.

And if she was very, very lucky, a little bit of something like flight on the way down.

"Are you indeed." He considered her while her heart hurt and between her legs, she was bright and needy. "Ready for what, *cariña*?"

"I'm ready…"

And she couldn't bring herself to say it all. He wanted a wife. A duchess. It didn't mean he wanted her. Though at the same time, she knew the ways he did want her. She could feel them all, a molten thing inside her.

She wanted those things, too.

She wanted everything.

And she had to imagine that if she gave him what he wanted, someday—some way, as she marched along this road that had been carved out for her by Marinceli brides for hundreds and hundreds of years, because love was not a prerequisite for a duke of his magnificence—she would convince him to give her what she wanted, too.

All the things she wanted.

She cleared her throat, because it was still so dry she was surprised it didn't catch flame. But the rest of her was taking care of that. She was surprised she wasn't burnt straight down to a cinder.

"I'm ready," she said. And found herself smiling, almost despite herself, because a Pyrrhic victory was still better than a total loss. It had to be. "Are you going to share that bed?"

# CHAPTER NINE

TEO TRIED TO tell himself that passion was not the point here, that this had been an exercise in obedience only, but his body was paying him no mind. He was hard and ready, on the verge of desperate—the way he'd been since she'd strolled back into his life.

Amelia stayed in the doorway for another moment, as if she was hesitating. Waiting, he realized. For him to answer her question.

It was hard for him to imagine she couldn't see his answer, stamped all over him.

The past ten days had been torture. Sheer and utter torture, that he'd had to pretend didn't affect him at all. Amelia had bustled about playing house, which hadn't been why he'd brought her here. Quite the opposite, in fact. He'd assumed that a woman like her—a woman like her mother, more properly—would be unable to last twenty-four hours pretending to be a servant. He been certain they'd be back home and planning their wedding, and their future, within two days' time at the most.

Amelia was nothing like he'd expected.

He had actually spoken to her about his father's besottedness with Marie, something he had never really discussed with anyone—because it was too easy, from there, to delve into his own sense of loss over his mother. And how his father's obvious obsession with another woman had seemed to Teo like he was making a mockery of not only Teo's grief, but of his first marriage altogether.

How had he even started down this road with Amelia?

He didn't understand how he could have been so wrong about her. Assuming he was actually wrong, that was. Assuming this wasn't simply some game she was playing.

But he thought not. Not when her remarkable eyes were so big and bright. Not when her lips parted as if her breath was its own kind of torture—a sensation he knew too well just then. And not when she'd left a perfect handprint of ash on his door.

"By all means," he said, fighting to sound appropriately unaffected when really, he wanted to leap from the bed and charge her like an untried boy. "Join me."

He waited.

And still, she hesitated, there on the threshold with something too raw to be hope in her gaze and soot on her cheek.

"Let us be clear about what it means if you climb into this bed with me," he found himself saying, every muscle in his body clenched tight in anticipation. Need. And a driving force he wanted to call rage. Though he knew better. "What it means if you take this step."

He was afraid he knew exactly what it was, and it wasn't rage.

"I know," Amelia said softly. "Believe me, Teo. I know."

For a moment that he was certain lasted a thousand years or more, their gazes clashed. Held. And he could see something in the violet depths that made him shake.

It threw him. It humbled him. It made him feel as if he was soaring.

All at once.

But before he could catalog it, process it, compartmentalize it and move to counter it, somehow, she began to move.

She wore her usual uniform, which would never have passed muster if she was an actual servant in a grand house. She liked stretchy pants that clung lovingly to her thighs, her calves, and layered-on distractingly soft T-shirts and that finely woven sweater that she'd worn the first day. And since.

There wasn't a single part of her that was appropriate. From the ash on her face to her bare feet, where her toenail polish was bright red and chipped.

Teo had been used to the best of everything, all of his life. He had never understood until these past ten days how limiting that was. And all the glorious, mesmerizing things it left out of the equation.

Like the way Amelia frowned so fiercely as she slept, and how flushed her cheeks were when she first woke in the mornings. The soft little noises she made, of delight or frustration, as she found her way through the various chores he'd set for her. How her blond hair looked when she knotted it carelessly on the top of her head, and the little curls that sprang up at her nape when she worked over the fire.

Ten days ago he would have sworn up and down that his baser urges aside, he could only ever view a woman like this is as a convenience, or temporary fix. His tastes were too refined, too deeply aristocratic, to seek permanence with so little effort toward outward perfection.

But that was before he'd spent ten days battling his own intense urges when it came to this woman.

There was nothing perfect about her. And yet somehow, every imperfection he found made him want her more.

Her face without makeup. That crooked smile she wore when he lapsed off into some history lesson she hadn't requested. The look of wonder and hope on her face when he caught her with her hands on her belly.

More and more and more. Teo was full up on *more*, but it didn't stop. It only got worse.

Amelia came to the side of the bed, then lifted one knee to slide it onto the mattress, slowly. As if she still wasn't certain about what she was doing.

Meanwhile, Teo was so greedy for her he thought he might burst into flame. Or perhaps he already had.

"There's no going back," he warned her, his voice gruff. "If you choose this, it is done. We will marry. And soon. The legitimacy of the Marinceli heir can never be in question."

"Must you threaten me even now?" she asked, and though her violet gaze was intense, he thought her smile was real. And that shook him, too. "Is this a duke thing? Or just a you thing?"

"I want to make sure this is an informed decision on your part," he said, dark and low because it was all he could manage. "Because once the decision is made it is permanent."

"Why are you acting as if I have a choice now?"

She pulled her other leg onto the bed with her, so she

was kneeling there at his side. And her bougainvillea eyes were alive with heat and laughter. And he, who had been surrounded by interchangeably lovely things for the whole of his life, had never glimpsed anything as beautiful as this.

Amelia beside him, her eyes bright and laughter like a new flush on her face.

*Like hope,* he thought, and that made something in him lurch.

"I am prepared to wait here as long as it takes," he said, even darker and more gruff, to cover that lurch inside him where he should have felt nothing at all. "Once it is done, it is done."

"Your Excellency," she said, and he could hear the laughter then, too, "do you ever shut up?"

And there was no time to take umbrage at that impertinence, because she simply…toppled forward, flinging herself across his chest with a thud.

Teo had never thought of himself as a man of extremes, because there weren't any in his life. Marincelis endured. The centuries passed. Extremes came and went, like little pops of color and moments of theater, but there was always the dukedom. Unchangeable and eternal.

But Amelia was a tangle of too much color to wave away. A snarled, hopeless knot. There was something profoundly silly in the way she flung herself against him, and he was not a silly man. She made him wish he was.

Amelia was touching him, then. He could feel the sweet weight of her breasts and felt it as her nipples turned to hard points against his chest.

And Teo had never felt this strange mixture of heat and laughter, silliness and that punch of sensuality that was all Amelia. Only Amelia. He felt almost breathless. Altered.

She lifted her head and grinned. When he frowned, she grinned more. So he frowned all the harder.

Only after he did so did he realize he *wanted* to see her grin as she did then. Big. Bright. Fearless and beautiful.

"A good duchess does not tell her Duke to shut up, *cariña*," he said frostily. Though he couldn't maintain the tone. Not with her soft weight in his arms.

"You didn't say I had to be a good duchess," she said, laughing at him in that way only she dared. "Only that I had to become one. If you're expecting me to excel in the position, you should resign yourself to disappointment here and now."

But all Teo could think about then, like a flash of heat, was that he could no longer imagine anyone else in the role. Only her. Only Amelia, with soot on her face like an urchin, too loud and too inappropriate, and as of this moment, his.

Entirely his.

And with that, he was done waiting. Or playing Cinderella games.

He wrapped a palm around the nape of her neck, then drew her mouth to his.

And finally, the Nineteenth Duke of Marinceli claimed his Duchess.

His mouth was all demand, delirious and divine in turn.

Any power Amelia might have imagined she was claiming by throwing herself on top of him—something she probably wouldn't have done if she thought it through—shifted in an instant. She still lay there on top of him, but he was the one in delicious control.

He held her head where he wanted it and he took her mouth with a lazy certainty that rolled into her, then through her, like a wildfire.

Every time he angled his head, every time he took the kiss deeper, the fire burned hotter.

And she felt delicate, and sacred, and something far earthier than either as he pulled her more tightly into his arms. The shift made her legs spread as she sprawled over him, and his hard thigh was *right there* where she was so soft and so hot.

It made her head spin.

Then again, it was hard to say which particular sensation was making her head spin.

And then her head was the least of her concerns, because he shifted again. She'd been paying attention to his hand at the nape of her neck, but it was the other one that got her attention then. His fingers splayed out over her bottom, and found their way beneath the hem of her shirt and sweater to find her bare skin.

Amelia had enjoyed two previous encounters with this man. At the Masquerade there had been the wild pleasure in that hallway, followed by what had happened in that salon after. And then there had been the morning she'd come to Spain to tell him about her pregnancy.

Both times she'd been fully dressed throughout.

She was dressed now, too. But the way his palm moved over the small of her back, then upward, she understood that she would not remain clothed for long. And the notion made her shudder.

In the next moment, he jackknifed up in the bed, taking her with him. He kept kissing her. Long, drugging kisses, so hot and intense, and in between each one he methodically rid her of her clothing with a certain skill that made her heart do cartwheels inside her. The sweater and the shirt he pulled off her in one go, and he easily removed the soft bra she wore. His big hands of his wrapped around her waist, then he tore his mouth from hers.

Amelia was dazed. Her lips felt swollen. She felt *glorious*, and she was half-naked, right there where he could see her.

The look in his dark gaze slammed through her, thick like greed.

Teo lifted her toward him, then took one hard, proud nipple in his mouth. And sucked.

And it was as if her head…*flatlined*. Except Amelia was fully aware of the sensation storming through her. Washing over her. Tossing her from one hot burst of flame into the next, brighter blaze.

There was so much…*skin*. He was hard in all the places she was soft, and the slide of her body against his elated her. *Tempted* her. She wanted to taste every inch of him. She wanted to rub herself against him, and see what happened. She didn't know what to do with her hands, so she put them everywhere. Anywhere.

He made a low noise that she remembered from before. It was so *male*. So deep and rumbly, and she could feel it like a new heat between her legs.

Then he slid one of those wicked hands around, slipping beneath the waistband of the stretchy trousers she wore, and again, it was as if her head blanked out.

Leaving her nothing but a mass of sensation and need, so intense it ate at her.

Then the whole world spun as he rolled them over. And this time, he found his way into her pants yet again, but from the front.

She remembered so vividly, there in the hall where he'd taken her that night last fall. The music and noise from the Masquerade had filled the hallway where they stood, his mouth on hers, and his clever, determined fingers tracing the slit in the side of her dress before making his way beneath it. And finding the center of her need. So easily.

Amelia almost shattered from the memory.

But reality was far better than any memory, because this time, instead of stroking her heat, he helped her strip the pants from her body. One leg then the next. She had the vague impression of his flat, ridged abdomen and his strong, hair-roughened thighs.

And the fact that he had been naked under that sheet, all this time, was like another bright flame.

Then they were naked. Together.

It felt like a storm.

She was in the storm, and he *was* the storm, and together, skin on skin, they were like thunder.

Teo plundered her mouth and Amelia died, again and again, but lived again to keep tasting him. Learning him. Losing herself in him, over and over again.

But then he was between her legs, the hardest part of him flush against her. Teo tipped his head back to meet her gaze, and she was keenly aware that she wore no mask this time. And neither did he.

Amelia was open and vulnerable and *herself* as he

pressed against her, then into her. He was thick and big, and it was different, lying on her back on a bed.

She felt possessed. *Taken.* And it was so much better. So much hotter.

It took her a confused jumble of a moment to understand why.

"You're not…" But she had to stop and shudder when she felt him, lodged deep inside her body, filling her completely. "You're not wearing…"

He was propped up above her, his weight on his elbows and a fierce, intent look on his face. "No."

Her own breathing seemed too loud to her then, too wild. Too revealing.

And something clawed at her, some great sob or scream, or possibly it was panic. His chest was like a wall, and he surrounded her. He was *inside* her and he could *see* her, and the look on that austere face of his was pitiless.

But as she stared up at him, trying to catch her breath, trying to adjust to the size of him, he moved his hands to cup her face.

And Teo leaned his head down and pressed a soft kiss on her mouth.

It was a peck, really. But to Amelia, it felt like a poem.

The simplicity of it, the sweetness, pried open that tight little noose that had tightened around her. His thumbs moved against her jaw, she found air to breathe, and inside, she felt her body accept him.

And when this was over—when she felt like herself again—she would take the world to task for failing to mention that sex wasn't magically more comfortable when a person had only had it once before.

But here, now, Teo's gaze was black and intense. He was a hard length of steel deep inside her, almost too hot to bear. With no condom to dull the potency of his possession this time.

And her body had rolled straight from that would-be sob, that almost scream, into a delirious sort of desire. So intense she felt herself clamp down, and heard another growl from him as a reward.

So she did it again.

His mouth curved. "Okay?"

"Okay," she agreed, in a voice that sounded far too breathy and needy to be hers.

It felt like a chain between them. A set of vows like iron.

And that was when he began to move.

She remembered this part. That slick pull and thrust, that impossible rhythm. It was more than simply hot. He was so hard.

And it was different like this, with his weight and so much skin and his mouth against her neck.

She shattered at once, and then again. On and on he went, until she couldn't tell if she was shattering or recovering, climbing or falling.

It was all fire. Calamity and crisis, glory and need.

And this time, there was no one to hear them.

So he taught her how to scream. How to sob. How to cry out his name as she fell apart.

And when he took his own pleasure at last, he added his voice to the chorus and carried them both over that edge one more time.

She slept, hard and deep. And when she woke, it was still night. Teo was sprawled out beside her, one heavy arm anchoring her to his side.

The room was cool, but he was hot at her back.

It stunned her how safe that made her feel. How protected. When she had never slept in a bed with another person and had always imagined it would be strange, cluttered and uncomfortable.

The lantern still flickered beside the bed and when she turned beneath his arm, she watched it dance over his golden skin.

And she was somehow unsurprised when his eyes opened.

"You're awake," she said quietly. Foolishly.

The lantern light spun between them, all around them, and Amelia felt caught in it. Glued to him and lost in that dark gaze of his.

And she couldn't say she minded.

"We'll leave at first light," Teo said, but she didn't want to talk about that.

She didn't want to talk at all. She put her hand out and slid it over those sculpted, serious lips. And she smiled as his arrogant brows rose.

This time, she understood that the feeling expanding behind her ribs was as much a longing as it was lust. It was hope and fear entwined. But she didn't tell him that. She didn't intend to tell him any of that, ever.

Amelia crawled on top of him, smiled wickedly at him and then did exactly as she pleased. She tasted him. Everywhere.

By the time he flipped her over again, and rocketed them both toward that same bright finish, Amelia had convinced herself that she'd made the right choice. Because surely two people could not burn like this unless what fueled those flames was real.

*It had to be real.*

That was what she told herself the next morning, when Teo did exactly as promised and took her back to the historic seat of the Marinceli dukedom.

And set about making her his Duchess.

# CHAPTER TEN

"FAIRY TALES ARE for little girls," Marie said in that way of hers, half a throaty laugh and half an accusation. "Silly girls. Not grown women, Amelia."

If Amelia made it through her wedding without killing her mother, she thought it would be a miracle.

Teo had taken her back down from his mountain and put the rest of his plan into motion. Exactly as he told her he would.

"We will get married on the grounds of the estate," he told her as they flew out of the Pyrenees. He had boarded, disappeared into a stateroom and reappeared in a crisp suit. He had looked devastatingly attractive, of course, but Amelia had found herself mourning Teo in his jeans and a fisherman's sweater. "There's an ancient chapel that dates back to the Third Duke, which will suit our purposes."

By which he meant, his purposes. But Teo's purposes suited Amelia well enough.

Because this time, when she had her things sent from San Francisco and moved back into that same sprawling monstrosity of a house, it felt a whole lot more like a home. Because she got to share the ducal suite with Teo.

And while Teo was the remote, demanding Duke

outside the doors to the bedroom suite, within them, he was hers.

There was not a single surface they did not explore. Not a single possibility they did not exploit for the greatest possible pleasure.

And she was so dizzy with the wonder of it in those first days after they came down from the mountain that she would have agreed to anything he asked. She was giddy, made of lust and delight, and it all seemed like a blur to her, looking back.

But reality had a way of intruding, even in the hushed halls of *el monstruo*. Teo gifted her a wardrobe she would have said she didn't want, particularly as he called it her "appropriate clothes," but he made it his business to compliment her so much when she wore what he'd chosen that she found herself reaching for his significantly more upscale selections. And when she was dressed in the sleek, quietly elegant clothes he liked, she found herself doing more with her hair. Wearing jewelry.

Becoming a duchess by default.

Teo also had his people confer with the appropriate authorities, produce the necessary documents—hers as well as his—and set a date for their wedding a week out. He further decreed it would be a simple affair.

"Just the two of us and the priest," he told her.

"You must be joking," she'd replied, sprawled out in cheerful abandon in his bed. Because that was where they always seemed to end up, on his side of the vast master suite that took up the better part of its own wing. "I can't get married without my mother."

"Whatever for?"

"She may be complicated," Amelia had admitted.

"But she's my mother even so. She may love herself more than she does me—" And it should have bothered her, the way her voice cracked then. But his gaze was on her and she let her poor voice do as it would. "That is likely true. But that doesn't mean she doesn't love me deeply, you know."

"Your mother has already attended the wedding of one Duke of Marinceli," Teo had replied after a moment, sounding resigned. "Surely that is more than enough."

And if she wasn't hoarse from the way he'd just made her scream, and still a bit dizzy with it—not to mention the emotional wallop of considering Marie's selfishness all over again—Amelia might have taken offense at that.

"I promised that I would marry you," she'd reminded him instead. "I did not promise to marry you in secret, which would break my mother's heart forever."

Or dent it, anyway. Which to Amelia's mind was the same thing.

She thought that perhaps he was more affected by these things that went on between them, skin to skin, than he let on. Perhaps even as rocked as she was. Because all he did was sigh.

Amelia had taken that as assent.

But then she'd had to...tell her mother. Not only that she was pregnant, but that the father of her baby was, of all people, Teo de Luz. And more, that she was going to marry him and become the newest Duchess of Marinceli.

Soon.

The initial conversation had not gone well.

But now the wedding was in two days. Marie had arrived in all her state the night before, dripping in conciliatory smiles to celebrate with her only child. And her former stepson, who had looked as if he was suffering through elective dental surgery rather than a happy family dinner to celebrate Marie's arrival.

"I could very easily not have invited you," Amelia said now. Pointedly. She sat on the settee in the dressing room of the guest suite where her mother had been installed, literal miles away from where she and Teo were. "If I thought you would come here and say snide things about fairy tales, I wouldn't have."

"You would have invited me no matter what," Marie said, with that laugh of hers, and that she was right only made Amelia scowl. "I'm your mother. We're stuck with each other no matter what."

"You're reminding me why I prefer to be stuck with you from a distance."

Marie had been attending to her toilette, but she turned around then, meeting Amelia's gaze straight on instead of through the mirror. And Amelia knew it wasn't what she'd just said, because such things rolled right off her deceptively steely mother.

"Are you sure you know what you're doing?" Marie asked instead.

"I'm getting married in two days," Amelia replied lightly. "It seems pretty straightforward. White dress, aisle, husband."

Her mother's smile was sad. "And then you're a duchess."

"There have been a great many duchesses. *Most* of them lived long enough to die of old age. Or what passed for old age in their time." She shrugged. "Again, perfectly straightforward."

"There's nothing straightforward about the de Luz

family." Marie rolled her eyes, seeming to take in the whole of this impossible house, from all the treasures it held to the pedigree that seemed to ooze from its very walls. "You cannot simply marry the Duke. You must marry the dukedom, too. And everything that goes with it."

Amelia didn't like the way Marie was looking at her. "I thought you enjoyed endless wealth, social standing, cachet, whatever you want to call it."

"I do indeed." Her mother's gaze was kind, then, Amelia realized, but no less sad. Something inside her seemed to clutch at her heart, then hold it with too-tight claws. "But you do not care one way or another for any of those things. And if I found the Marinceli name too heavy a burden to bear, I wonder, what will it do to you?"

Her throat was dry, indicating a panic Amelia refused to entertain. "That hardly matters. I'm carrying his baby."

Marie made a small sighing sound. "Yes, yes. I'm sure he thundered on impressively about bloodlines that predate Spain, but so what? You can raise a child on your own, love. Whether Teo de Luz gives you permission or not."

"I don't know that I have it in me to deny my child a father when he's on offer, actually."

"You didn't miss having a father around," Marie said dismissively. "In fact, I think you thrived without one."

"That's a lovely story, Mom," Amelia said. Maybe with a little more heat than she'd intended, because that was bypassing all kinds of hurtful things that they pretended they'd settled years ago. Like the fact that Marie hadn't encouraged Amelia's relationship with her father while he was alive. And hadn't thought to save any keepsakes, either, since Amelia could barely remember a man she'd barely seen who'd died when she was five. It was one more reason she'd been determined to tell Teo about his child, so that part of history need not repeat itself. Not by her hand. "But it's your story. Not mine. I didn't have *my* father, but that didn't mean there weren't all kinds of father figures around. Most of them terrible."

"Most men are terrible. That's the tragedy of loving them." And if Amelia had thought that she could shame her mother, she was disappointed. Marie smiled, as merrily as ever. "And that's what I'm trying to tell you. You've had a thing about Teo forever."

"What? I haven't had a *thing*—"

"What I thought would save you is that he really, truly hates me and everything I touch," Marie continued as if Amelia hadn't protested. Or gone a shocking shade of red. "On the other hand, look at you."

Amelia didn't want to look at her reflection, because she didn't want to see herself turning into her mother. Right here in real time. Or maybe she wasn't turning into Marie fast enough. "I know what I look like."

"Fair enough," Marie said airily. But then her expression grew solemn again. "But Amelia, marrying the Duke of Marinceli is something that sounds good on paper. When really, it's a cage. I couldn't see myself in that cage. Are you sure you can?"

Amelia changed the subject, and Marie let her, but she couldn't get her mother's words out of her head as easily.

Later that afternoon, as the winter sun brooded its way into a gloomy evening, she made her way back to that study where she'd found Teo on her first day here. There was something about walking down that same hallway that got to her. She almost wanted to go fetch the butler and have him march with her, so she could fully reexperience it.

Then again, she already knew how it ended.

Amelia pushed open the door silently, and stood there a moment, watching Teo at work.

And she knew him now, in a way she never would have imagined was possible back when all she'd had of him was that *thing* her mother had clearly known about all the while. She knew what his close-cropped black hair felt like beneath her palms. She knew that his jaw would feel rough at this time of day, an erotic abrasion against her skin. She knew how he slept, which seemed an improbable miracle. What his face looked like in repose. She'd tasted him, everywhere. She'd felt those beautiful, aristocratic hands on every part of her body.

And yet as she looked at him, sitting at his desk going through stacks of documents his business manager would have left him earlier in the day, Amelia thought that she had never in her life seen a man so alone.

That wasn't something that seemed to change, no matter how well they seemed to know each other in bed. No matter how they talked, late at night, when the dark held him close and it seemed so much easier to share things that might make her blush in the light of day.

He told her secrets, there in the dark. His big hand on the back of her head she lay against his chest, his voice a rumble she could hear as well as feel beneath her. He told her what it was like to grow up knowing all of this would be his one day. She couldn't really remember her father, so he'd told her about his mother. She made him laugh. He made her heart swell.

It was those nights, laced together, that gave her hope. Or the mornings he would wake her, his hands spread over her growing belly, and that curve in the corner of his stern mouth as he talked in a low voice to their baby.

She thought they were getting somewhere. She really did. But her mother's words pounded her head tonight. They felt like a prophecy. Like a curse.

"I want more than a marriage of convenience," she blurted out.

And when Teo raised that simmering black gaze of his to hers, she understood that he'd known she was there all along. Had known it from the moment she'd turned down this particular hallway, if she had to guess.

"What do you propose instead?" he asked, and he still sounded austere. As affronted as he had the day she'd come here to tell him she was pregnant, but she could hear the laziness beneath it tonight. That casual hint of a drawl that she was sure was only hers.

"I want everything."

The ducal brow rose. "If there is more to everything than a lifetime as a Marinceli Duchess, I must confess I do not know what it is." He sat back in his chair, regarding her with that steadiness of his that was in itself reproving. "Is there something you want that you feel you cannot have? I find that hard to believe, Amelia. Look around. I am fairly certain I have everything. This means you do, too."

And she understood, as little as she wanted to, what her mother was trying to tell her.

It was easy to roll around in a bed. To let sex cloud

her head and make her think it was the same as love. When it was only a part of it. An expression of it, certainly, but not the whole.

She slipped her hands over her belly and held them there, taking strength from the child she carried. Their child. The Twentieth Duke of this magical, monstrous place, and it was up to her to see to it that he was more than just a collection of musty old titles. That he was vivid and vulnerable, able to love and live. She didn't want for him the kind of life that her mother had given her, that Marie would call a madcap adventure and Amelia considered far more of a collection of catastrophes.

But Teo was a result of his childhood, too. And a father who had made certain Teo knew his duty, then left him to it.

There had to be a place between the two. *There had to be.*

And Amelia could think of only one way to achieve it.

"You have everything that money can buy," she said softly. "Ancient money. Modern money. And everything in between. If it can be claimed by might or money, you have it. I know that."

His brow rose even higher. "You are welcome, *cariña*."

"I want more," she said simply. Terribly. "I want love."

And she expected the very walls to crumble, perhaps. Or Teo to burst into flame. Something suitably dramatic for a man she was fairly certain had never experienced much love at all. Not in so many words.

"Love," he repeated, looking as if she'd suggested he fly naked over the whole of Spain. "I beg your pardon.

Is it the wedding that is addling your senses, Amelia? What has love to do with anything?"

"Love has to do with everything," she said, and if it wasn't so important she might have been embarrassed by her own earnestness. "My mother gave me none of the security you take for granted, but she loved me. And you can argue *how much* all you like. You can claim she loves herself more. I know she does. I don't want to know it, but I do. And I may have spent too much of my life trying to get her to love me that much, too, but in the end, she still loves me just as much as she's able. What else is there?"

"This feels like a very Californian conversation," Teo said, distinct acid in his voice and his gaze dark. "Does it require my participation?"

There was nothing in that that should have emboldened her, but Amelia moved farther into the room, walking over to that massive desk of his and slapping her palms down on the surface—mostly to keep herself from reaching out to him.

"You can make fun all you like. But we're bringing a child into this world, and life is hard enough—even as a de Luz—without whatever version of tough love it is that your father gave you."

The ice Teo wore like armor cracked a little, then. She could see it in his eyes. And the tightness of his jaw. "My father raised me to step confidently into my position as Duke. A man is not a man unless he teaches his son how to take his place, and do better than he ever could."

"Then do better," Amelia challenged him. "What would happen if you not only trained your son to take your place, but taught him how to love? Openly. Fully.

Not hidden behind talk of duties and bloodlines. What would happen then, Teo?"

"I don't understand any part of this conversation. We already made a deal. The wedding is in two days. Or is this some kind of a threat?"

Amelia made herself take a breath. She straightened from the desk, but still stood there, staring across at him. And he looked like some kind of a god. Haughty, untouchable. But it occurred to her for the first time that that thread of arrogance she saw in his expression was as much of a mask as the one she'd worn to the Masquerade.

*The Duke* was a costume.

The truth about this man was the dark. The weight of his hand on the nape of her neck. The stark need on his face as he drove inside her.

This urbane performance, this role, was the character he played.

She knew this as surely as she knew how much she already loved the son inside her. It was a simple fact made entirely of complexities and *what-ifs* and ferocity.

"I was a virgin," she said, suddenly flooded with a sense of calm. A purpose, even.

Teo laughed. "Do you mean, you were once a virgin? So were we all, Amelia."

"The night of the Masquerade," she said, and watched as he reacted to that. Badly. "That was the trouble, you see. I could never get past a kiss with another man. You were always in my head. It was as if I locked myself away when I left here as a teenager. And you were the only key."

"This is absurd."

"I thought so, too," she agreed. "That's why I went

to such lengths last fall. I didn't want you to know who I was because I didn't want to explain this to you. I just wanted to do it, if it could be done."

"How could you have been a virgin?" he demanded, and he sounded almost…anguished.

And suddenly he was on his feet, separated from her only by the wide expanse of his desk.

"I think the usual way is by not having sex."

"That is not what I mean." To her astonishment, she saw Teo's hands curl into fists at his sides. "I mean you. How could *you* have been a virgin then?"

Understanding dawned, a bit like a kick to the solar plexus. It was possible she wheezed.

"Because, of course, you think my mother is a whore." She shook her head, but it didn't help. "And it must be catching. Is that it?"

"I don't know what game this is you're trying to play," Teo threw at her, his voice low and hard in a way she'd never heard before. "And I don't know what you want out of this. Of me. Is it not enough that I am making you my wife? My Duchess? That because of that night, you have everything any reasonable person could possibly want or need? I don't understand the point of twisting it all around."

"It's not twisted," Amelia managed to say, though her lips were numb. "It's the truth. No more and no less."

"Enough of this, Amelia. It helps no one."

"Why does my innocence that night upset you?" she asked, but for all that odd calm inside her, there was a sadness, too.

Because she knew.

Teo said nothing. He only stared at her, and the stark expression on his face made her want to weep.

"It's so much easier if I'm simply the villain, isn't it?" she asked softly. "It makes so much more sense if I'm the Mata Hari in this story, who had my wicked way with you. You already know how to play the role of the victim, don't you?"

"How dare you call *me* the one playing victim."

But she ignored him. "What we know about you, Teo, is that you dearly love a role to play. Your father loved my mother too much and foisted her upon you. How could you do anything but hate her? And then there's me. My mother's daughter. Wouldn't it make everything perfect if I was a whore just like her?"

"Stop calling yourself a whore," he gritted out. "I have never used that word."

"You don't have to when it's written all over you."

"Amelia—" he started, but she didn't let him finish.

Not now. Not when she was this close to being fully and madly and foolishly honest with him. About everything, at last.

Because she didn't know any other way forward.

"Do you know why I did it?" she asked him, one hand on her belly. And not caring at all if he could see her emotions right there on her face. "Why I went to such lengths to give my virginity to a man who I knew wouldn't take it if it was offered? A man who I had to hide it from, hide my face from, hide *me* from?"

"I shudder to think."

She shook her head, sadly. And for a moment, she wondered if she really did dare to push this as far as it could go.

But she could feel the swell of her son beneath her palm. And she didn't know if it was possible to truly have everything. All of the Marinceli wealth and power *and* love? Could anyone really have all of that?

*If anyone can, it will be you,* she promised their baby. Fiercely.

And it had to start here. With her.

And with Teo.

"I think you already know," she said, letting out a sound that was like a laugh, but far too hollow. But she pushed away the fear, pressed her hand against her belly and held Teo's gaze with hers. Unflinchingly, so there could be no mistake. "I love you."

# CHAPTER ELEVEN

TEO WAS FROZEN SOLID, yet ash straight through. Charred, somehow, and the longer Amelia stood here dropping these bombs of hers, the less likely it seemed that he would ever recover.

"You do not love me," he told her, hardly recognizing his own voice. "Love is no part of this."

"Then how do you plan to be a father?" she replied.

Far too calmly, to his way of thinking.

"My father—"

"Your father, as far as anyone can tell, loved one person, Teo. You told me so yourself." And her hands were on her belly, making it impossible for him to look away. Making it impossible for him to think. "Is that what you want for this child?"

He had the sense that the walls around him were crumbling, when he could see full well that was not the case. Because it was never the case. This house, this dukedom, endured. As he would endure, whether he liked it or not.

He tried again. "The Dukes of Marinceli—"

"I care about the dukedom," Amelia said quietly, cutting him off as surely as if she'd wielded a machete. "Don't get me wrong, I do. Because you care so very much. Because it is so important to you, and you have dedicated your whole life to it. I care about it, Teo. But I care a great deal more about the man. About you."

"I did not ask for any of this." He heard the words come out of his mouth, and the strangest part was, he couldn't even bring himself to pull them back. To temper them. "I did not ask for your disguise. Your virginity. Or this child. But I'm fully prepared to do what must be done. That does not mean—"

"I don't believe you."

Something in him stuttered, then stopped. He was terribly afraid it was his heart. He waited for the storied shooting pains in his arm. To drop to the floor and be done with this conversation, at the very least.

But Amelia's gaze was steady. Not without pain, it hurt him to note, but she didn't waver. And he didn't understand how on the one hand, he wanted to do something utterly out of character, like make a run for it. While on the other, he wanted to give thanks that this fierce creature would be the mother to his son. To the next Duke.

His own mother had been elegant. Soft and sweet. He had missed her when she was gone. He missed her still. He sometimes thought he would go to his own grave never ready to forgive his father for moving on, so fast and so shamelessly. But he had never considered her *protective* in any way. She had not had that kind of fierceness in her. Rather, she was one more thing he needed to defend.

He had done his best, hadn't he? He had hated Marie French in and out of his father's life, and still. He had done what he could in the face of his father's betrayal of her.

"You don't believe me?" He heard the harshness of his voice, yet did nothing to fix it. "I'm not the one who has made a habit of lying, Amelia. By omission or otherwise."

"I'm not even sure I believe that." When he stared at her, she shrugged. "Did you really not recognize me, Teo? Are you truly that unobservant? A different hair color and a mask, and suddenly a person you've known for half your life is a stranger? Why do I find that difficult to imagine?"

How ash could turn into more ash, and grow colder, he could not fathom. "I don't know what you're suggesting."

"And then, I turn up here out of the blue, and you let me in." Her head tilted slightly to one side, though that steady gaze didn't waver. "Which makes more sense, do you think? That you admitted the daughter of a woman you profess to hate without question and even claimed at first you couldn't remember her? Or that you admitted a lover who you'd seen quite intimately only a few months before?"

Teo was moving before he knew it. But not toward her. He rounded the desk and headed for his door before these things she was saying took root in him. And grew.

"These conspiracy theories are fascinating, I grant you that," he said gruffly as he went. "But they only make me question what goes on in your head. And whether or not I will need to limit your influence on the child you carry."

"Threats, threats, threats," she murmured, as he remembered she had before. "You say you don't want me. That I'm beneath you in every way. But it seems to me, Your Excellency, that the only way you're really interested in seeing me beneath you is in bed. And getting me there was the entire crux of your argument in that cabin. It wasn't that you need me to marry you. It was that you insisted on the marital bed."

Teo had stopped, there on the carpet where she had once stood and he'd imagined that she might know her place. But did he know his? Because the walls of this house might not have been crumbling. But he was.

He was already ash. He was quickly becoming little more than dirt, fit for little but a return to the earth. The land outside these walls that his ancestors had fought and died for.

What would he fight for? And if he didn't know the answer to that, how could he know what he would die for?

"I don't believe you," she said again.

And some other, terrible fury rose in him then. Suddenly, instead of making for the door, he advanced on her instead. But this was Amelia, so she did not shrink away. Her hands found her hips, her chin tilted up and she paid him exactly none of the deference that he was due. That he was given by every other person on this earth.

It was like a panic in him. Instead of finding it the greatest insult of all time, all Teo wanted was to get his hands on her.

Again. More. Always.

He did.

He gripped her shoulders in his palms, and he didn't know which one of them he was punishing when he didn't pull her close to get his mouth on her.

"I do not know what this is," he said as sternly as he could, as if he could hide the way he was crumbling inside. "But it's too late. Nothing you say to me, nothing you use to goad me with, will change the course of events. You will marry me."

"You're damn right I'm going to marry you," she shot back. "Here's a newsflash for you, Teo. I'm not my mother. I've loved one man, ever. And I have every intention of loving you for the rest of my life."

"I cannot help you in such a futile endeavor."

"And you will love me back," she told him, again with that steady, demanding gaze. "Believe me. You will. I won't accept anything else."

"You will accept what you are given," he told her, furiously. "Which in your case, is a great deal indeed."

"The truth is," she said softly, "I'm halfway to believing you already love me."

His hands tightened on her shoulders, and her lips parted, and he could feel that awareness that was always between them sizzle. He knew what it meant. It would be so easy to follow it. To shift this conversation onto ground he understood.

Instead, he released her.

Though it cost him.

"I cannot love you," he told her, stiff and formal, every inch of him the Duke of Marinceli he'd been trained to become. Handing down his word as law. "I'm not capable of it, don't you understand? Nor do I wish to become capable of it. That is not who I am."

Her eyes were still too wide, that impossible violet, and he had the terrible sensation that she could see everything. As if he was transparent.

"It is exactly who you are," she said, fervently. "I'll show you."

"Like hell you will," he threw at her. "I am the Duke

of Marinceli, Amelia. This is not a coffee date with credit card debt to look forward to. This is an ancient dukedom and *that* is the prize. *That* is what you get. I would strongly suggest you work on gratitude, but if you do not, there is no need to worry. There is a reason the estate is as big as it is." When she stared back at him without comprehension, his lips twisted. "There are ample alternative residences on the property to stash a duchess who has given herself over to bitterness. You should have paid more attention to the history books while you were here as a teenager."

And then, before he lost control of himself completely and did something he couldn't take back—like surrender to the emotions racking him that he wasn't sure he even believed were real—Teo made himself walk away.

That night, for the first time since she'd come into his bedroom in the cabin, Teo did not share a bed with Amelia. Or touch her at all. He avoided the dinner he knew she was having with her mother, and lost himself instead in estate matters he could easily have put off if he'd wished.

He did not wish.

And another cold winter's morning was dawning when he found himself wandering the halls of this place he knew too well, as if all the history his ancestors had lived out here had sunk into the floorboards. As if it could infuse him with the lessons they'd learned. Or not learned.

Teo found himself in the gallery, staring at portraits of the nineteen men who had come before him. Some who had fought wars to keep this land and this house in the family. Others who had fought their own inclinations, grasping kings and queens, and their own baser instincts.

He stood for a long time in front of the portrait of his own father.

Until yesterday, he would have said he knew his father at least as well as he knew this house, these lands. Strengths and weaknesses alike.

Now he felt he didn't know anything at all. Least of all himself.

He braced himself when he heard a soft sound behind him, a footfall, expecting it to be Amelia.

But it was worse. It was her mother.

"Jet lag," she said, smiling at him with too much familiarity. "I've been up since three o'clock."

"My condolences, madam," Teo said in as frosty a tone as he could manage.

"Only you can make that word sound like an insult. *Madam.*" She let out that bawdy, problematic laugh of hers that had bothered Teo for over a decade. "Marie will do just fine, thank you."

Teo had no intention of spending enough time talking to this woman that it would matter what he called her. He inclined his head stiffly, then made to go.

"I know you think I broke his heart," Marie said, shocking Teo into standing still. "It was the other way around."

Teo decided he'd had enough of up being down. Inside being out.

Then and there.

"Is that what you call it?" he asked tightly, glaring at her. "Heartbreak? I've heard other terms used to describe what you do, *Marie.*"

If his tone ruffled her feathers, she didn't show it. "Your father was exciting. Inventive in a variety of ways, though I don't expect that's something you'd like to hear any more about."

It took Teo a moment to understand her meaning. Then he was appalled. "I cannot think of anything I would like to know less."

"But he didn't love me," Marie said, very simply and distinctly. And there was something about the way she was looking at him. That clever face of hers that he saw too much of Amelia in, washed with something he was very much afraid was sadness. Real sadness. "Your father loved one thing and one thing only."

"It wasn't my mother," Teo retorted. "If you mean the dukedom, that was his duty."

Marie smiled, but that didn't wipe away the sadness. "He cared for your mother, in his way. And he took the dukedom very seriously. But what your father truly loved was getting his way. That wasn't a broken heart you saw when we were done. It was a temper tantrum."

Teo shook his head, refusing to take her words on board. "You ruined him. He lost himself in a bender of scandalous women and—"

Marie reached over and tapped her finger against the ornate frame that held Luis Calvo's portrait in place.

"Come now, Teo," she said quietly. "When do you recall your father truly losing it? Ever?" She actually laughed at Teo's expression, then. "It was his way or the highway. Always. I chose the highway. And here's my advice to you, jet-lagged though it might be at this hour. You need to choose, Teo. Because a little-known truth in this world is that you usually have to choose between being right, or being happy."

His heart was pounding again, but still he didn't fall. "I don't know what that means."

"I have faith in you. You'll figure it out. And if you break my little girl's heart the way I think you will?" This time, Marie French's famous gaze was as steady as her daughter's, and far colder. "I'll actually do to you what you think I did to your father. Public shame is a game I play entirely too well."

Then she sauntered off and left him there, staring at the portrait of a man he could no longer recognize at all.

And if he didn't know his own father... If he didn't know the blood in his own veins when he had spent his life immersed in his own bloodline and what it meant and what it made him, then... Who was he?

Teo couldn't seem to move, as if he'd already been committed to stone, made a statue and had been left here in this gallery to take his place with all the other ciphers who gazed back at him from the walls.

If he didn't know who he was, how could he know who they had been? He'd studied their stories, taking notes on how best to be the Duke—but what kind of men were they? Had they loved anyone at all? Or were they all the same as his father? Powerful men who wanted their way above all things?

He couldn't dispute what Marie had said, though he'd wanted to. His father had liked his own way. And had always gotten it, running roughshod over anyone who came near him, including over Teo's mother—until he'd met Marie.

How had Teo managed to forget that?

Teo thought of his own behavior since Amelia had turned up here, pregnant with his child. Something he'd acted as if she had done herself when he could remember what had happened between them in vivid detail all these months later.

He had abducted her, taken her away and kept her there—treating her like a servant, which she had taken to alarmingly well but certainly didn't excuse him—until she'd agreed to come to his bed. He might as well be that warlord Duke from the early centuries, who had sacked whole cities in his zest to preserve his title.

Teo did not doubt that he could handle the dukedom. He'd been training for it his entire life.

But what kind of husband was he going to be? What kind of father? He wanted Amelia the way he'd had her in the cabin. The way he'd had her here, when they were alone. All that heat, intimate and raw.

And he wanted to be a better father than his own had been. He wanted to actually *be* a father—something more than a distant figure handing down pronouncements. Teo had no idea what that would look like, or what it would take, but he thought of that bump he liked to whisper to in the mornings and he wanted it. He wanted everything.

What was he willing to give it in return?

Amelia had offered him honesty. She had taken everything he'd thrown at her and handled it with an easy grace that humbled him. She'd come to him with soot on her face, thrown herself into his arms and dared him not to love her.

And that, right there, threatened to unman him entirely.

*Love.*

That was not what he would have called it, that night last fall. When he'd had his hands in her soft heat. When he'd taken her with such stark ferocity in that salon.

She'd braced herself above him, and he'd held her there as she'd slowly impaled herself on him.

And he'd known her.

He'd denied it later, he'd called it a trick of the drink, but he'd known her.

Something on her face had changed as he'd lodged himself deep inside her, and a mask and red lipstick couldn't hide it.

Her name had scraped through his mind like a whisper. Like a curse.

After she'd left, he'd told himself that it hadn't happened. That he'd been mistaken.

And when she'd reappeared at his door, he'd told himself it was a coincidence. Even when she'd told him her news and confirmed what he'd already known, it had been easier to lose himself in the fury of her deception than it was to face the facts.

That he'd known. He'd suspected he knew who she was and he'd gone right ahead and done it anyway. As he'd sworn he wouldn't do.

And far more stunning than his own self-deception was the fact that she knew it. She knew all of it. The lies he told himself, the lies he told her. And still she said she loved him.

Teo felt those walls inside him crumble all the more.

He stood here in this gallery, surrounded by the stern faces of the men who made up this bloodline he was sworn to protect. And would, to his dying day.

But God help him, he wanted to be a better man while he did it.

He wanted to be the man Amelia loved.

*All her life.* That's what she had said.

And this house couldn't help him. This glorious mausoleum to a highly curated past. He looked around this gallery at all those dark eyes so much like his and knew they couldn't help him. These men knew how to hold things in tight fists, not how to open themselves up.

Nothing here could help him.

But Teo thought he knew what would.

## CHAPTER TWELVE

THE NIGHT BEFORE the wedding was scheduled to take place, Amelia was giving herself a stern talking-to in the master suite that Teo had not entered since their confrontation in his study.

She wanted to rage about and throw things, the way her mother often did. But she wasn't her mother. And much as she imagined it must be satisfying to shatter something, the truth was... She just missed Teo.

That was the problem. And this time, she doubted very much that red hair dye and a mask would do the trick.

She was contemplating an heirloom vase, thick with flowers, that would make a lovely mess when tossed against the ancient wall when she heard the clearing of a throat from behind her.

Amelia turned to find the butler there, staring back at her in that way of his that managed to be both condescending and obsequious at once. Now that she was going to be the Duchess of Marinceli in the morning, there was significantly more of the latter than the former. She was sorry that in her current state, she couldn't even enjoy it.

Because it was one thing to throw in Teo's face that she loved him, and would marry him as planned and continue to love him, and that she didn't much care what his take on that was.

It was something else again to…do it. To psych herself up for that walk down an aisle in an old chapel toward a man who claimed he could not love her. For the life that came after that walk, locked away in the timeless splendor of this place, like one more pretty object cluttering up the vast house.

For the family she would create with him, one way or another, and would have to do whether he loved her—or their son—or not.

It was the *or not* part that was sloshing around inside her tonight, making her feel as nauseated as she had throughout her first trimester.

"Your presence is requested, madam," the butler intoned, with excruciating courtesy.

Amelia didn't really want to go anywhere. Or do anything but sit where she was, and perhaps break some crockery. The wedding in the morning was private, mostly so that Teo could manipulate the timeline later to suit his purposes. A quiet announcement in five months' time to cover both the wedding and the birth of his heir, Teo had said.

Because the Duke of Marinceli did not explain himself to anyone. Much less perform for the masses. He was a de Luz, not a Windsor.

But, of course, a private wedding meant that her friends wouldn't be there. The people she loved, who loved her, unreservedly. In theory, she understood why it had to be this way. In her heart, she knew her friends would understand, *because* they loved her unreservedly. And she knew with every part of her, heart and soul and body, that she loved Teo enough that it would all be worth it.

There was tonight to get through, that was all. A little dark night of the soul before a lovely morning after. Teo thought he couldn't love anyone, least of all her, and she might have decided to ignore that—but that didn't mean it didn't hurt.

Amelia, by God, would be a little blue if she felt like it.

But she got up and followed the butler anyway, because there was a point at which *a little blue* became full-on wallowing, and she was pretty sure she'd already passed it some ways back. And besides, she preferred her crockery intact.

The butler led her out through the house, processing in all his state down one meandering hallway to another. He took her out the grand front entry and handed her into a waiting car, then presented her with her coat with theatrical flourish.

Amelia shrugged into her coat as the car slid away from the front of the house. When the driver turned deeper into the property instead of down the drive, Amelia felt a little prickle of foreboding. Or premonition, anyway. Sure enough, the car delivered her to the waiting private jet out on the estate's airfield.

And there seemed to be nothing to do but board it. Amelia climbed up the steps as the winter wind picked up around her, playing with her hair and sending icy fingers creeping down beneath the collar of her trusty peacoat.

Inside, she expected to find Teo lounging about, looking like royalty. But the jet was empty, save for the staff.

She even checked the staterooms, but no. She had the sleek aircraft to herself.

And when the plane landed sometime later in that same remote airfield high in the Pyrenees that she knew all too well, Amelia had worked herself into a full-on temper.

"The Duke is waiting for you, madam," the captain told her when he emerged from the cockpit. He gestured deferentially toward the door.

Amelia considered refusing to leave the plane. But she had the feeling that wouldn't go quite as she wanted it to. She imagined Teo would have no problem whatsoever storming onto the plane and collecting her, if he had a mind to. And she was in a righteous temper, thank you, and didn't want him *collecting* her like a recalcitrant child.

She made herself get up. She stepped outside, gasping involuntarily at the slap of the cold, complete with dancing snow flurries. Something she found markedly prettier when she was indoors, preferably next to a crackling fire with something warm to drink. But the weather wasn't the only thing that stole her breath.

At the bottom of the jetway steps, Teo waited.

Seemingly impervious to the weather.

Amelia forced herself to take a breath. She thought uncharitable things about the humanity of the average duke. And then she stormed down the metal stairs until she reached him.

"You must have truly lost your mind if you think that I'm going to play this Cinderella game with you again," she threw at him, not caring if the captain was watching them. Not caring if he heard every word she said. "Cinderella only works when you know how it ends. The point isn't the toiling away at all that menial labor. It's when the charming prince rescues her and sweeps her away from all that. Prince Charming, Teo. Not…you."

That muscle moved in his cheek, broadcasting his own temper. But he didn't say a word. He only beckoned her to the SUV parked to the side of the runway with its engine running. He opened the door for her to get in, then waited. Watching her.

Daring her.

"I'm not kidding, Teo," Amelia said crossly. "I will not—"

"Do you wish to argue with me here?" he asked in that silky, dangerous way of his that still did things to her she would've preferred not to acknowledge. "I am personally not interested in hypothermia in such a remote place, *cariña*. I cannot imagine it will suit our son. But for you, I will risk it."

Wordlessly, furiously, she climbed into his SUV.

And even though she was prepared for it this time, the winding road still got to her. Around and around and around, lurching this way and that as he headed for the top of the mountain and the cabin that waited for them there.

Finally, they reached the summit, and Teo drove straight to the cabin door as he had the last time. The memories Amelia had of this cabin were fond, so it made something in her ache to see it again now, when she was so much less certain about where they were headed than she had been when they'd left here.

She added that to the fire inside her that was keeping her temper humming along nicely.

It was much snowier and much windier this high

up. Amelia hunched her shoulders deeper into her coat as she got out, picking her way across the snowy yard to the heavy front door. She wasn't dressed for this weather. The shoes she wore were better suited to a San Francisco winter, which was often wet and cold, but was certainly not a mountaintop blizzard, for God's sake.

She was already simmering with fury about the fire he would make her build. The orders he would bark at her and the demands he would make. But this time, she had no intention of doing a thing. Not one thing. He could—

But what he did was swing open the door, and her breath—and temper—went out of her in a rush.

Because the fire was already built and crackling along nicely, heating up the cabin. The lanterns were lit. It was homey, bright.

It made her throat feel thick. Tight.

Amelia moved inside on legs that felt suddenly jerky and strange, and felt the jolt of it when he closed the door behind them.

"Did you bring your own maid this time?" she asked, and much as she might have wanted to pretend that she kept the bitterness from her voice, she could hear it herself.

"Only if you consider me a maid," came Teo's cool, amused voice. "And I must tell you, *cariña*, I do not."

He moved past her, farther into the room. Toward those couches that loomed large in her head. She'd slept on one of those couches, in what she could see, now, had been an extended act of defiance. Because, against her will—and though she'd been so sure she'd exorcised him from her life, no matter that she carried his child—she had fallen in love with him. When she was sixteen. Again last fall.

And most certainly—permanently and irrevocably— here.

"I don't understand why you brought me back here," she managed to say, miserably. "Especially with all that snow out there. What if we're trapped here? Have you forgotten that we're to be married in the morning?"

"Are you afraid of being stuck here, Amelia?"

She was. She scowled at him. "It's more accurate to say I would prefer not to be stuck anywhere."

"It is our wedding, *cariña*," he replied, and though his voice was soft, his expression was all stone and strength. "If we're not there, they will simply have to wait until we are."

He was over by the couches now, standing there as if he expected her to come and join him. But Amelia didn't want to move from the door. She felt the same mess of things she always felt when it came to Teo. All tangled around each other, snarled and knotted and bent back on themselves. And it all grew inside her chest as she looked at him, and in her gut, like a terrible sob.

She understood that she would love him forever. She had accepted that. But she had wanted tonight—just tonight—to mourn what couldn't be. To prepare herself for a wedding to a man who had vowed he would never love her. She might not believe he was right about that, but her belief didn't make the reality any easier to bear.

But this was worse.

"I had hoped you might sit and talk to me awhile," Teo said when all she did was glare at him. "But you don't look as if you wish to step another foot inside this cabin."

"I don't know what you want from me." That sob was inside her, growing all the while, but she fought valiantly to keep it there. "If it's for me to act like a domestic servant the way I did before, you should know that I only ever took to that because it was temporary. And my choice. You can't really think you're going to haul me up here every time you need a floor mopped or a—"

"Amelia."

It was the way he said it. His voice seemed to ring in her, loud and long. As if her name was a song all its own and he alone knew how to sing it.

And then he was prowling back across the floor toward her, never shifting that black-gold gaze from her face.

"I do not want you to clean my floor," he said as he came closer. "I do not want you to do anything, unless you wish to do it."

She pulled in a breath, but when she went to speak… She couldn't.

Teo was before her. And then, while she watched—her heart in her throat and that sob so much of her that maybe it *was* her—he sank to his knees. Right there on the floor she'd once scrubbed on her hands and knees.

"What are you doing?" she whispered.

"I have already ordered you to marry me," Teo said, still holding her gaze, seeming unaware that if he was another man this might have been a humbling moment. But he looked proud. Certain. And he gazed only at her. "And you have graciously indicated that you would obey. Tonight I rather thought I would ask."

It was as if the world stood still. Or turned too fast. Amelia couldn't quite tell.

All she knew was that everything was different, impossible. And Teo, the Nineteenth Duke of Marinceli, was on his knees.

Gazing up at her as if she was the world, still or spinning or both.

And, while she watched—stunned—he reached into his pocket and pulled out a ring.

There were no fancy boxes, no ribbons. But this was the sort of ring that needed no extra ornamentation.

It looked like the kind of ring that wars were fought over. And given who was holding it, Amelia assumed that was a distinct possibility.

"This belonged to the Twelfth Duchess," Teo told her, holding the ring so the lantern light caught it and made it shine like a promise. "She had an eye for the finer things. But, more importantly, she is chiefly known for refusing the Twelfth Duke. Three times, or so the story goes. It was not until he took the time and trouble to abduct her, convince her and get her with child, that she condescended to accept his suit. Such as it was."

"She sounds like my kind of girl," Amelia managed to say, though her throat ached. And that sob she'd been trying to keep at bay had transferred too much heat to the back of her eyes. She was afraid that at any moment tears might tip over and betray her completely.

"The Twelfth Duke and his Duchess lived a very long time," Teo replied in that same steady, certain way. "Together. And if the stories are true, they loved each other very much."

He reached over then and took her hand in his, and Amelia stopped pretending that she could breathe through this.

"Amelia." And again, her name was like a song in his mouth. "I've spent my whole life training how to become not just any duke, but the Duke of Marinceli. To live up to all these stories, all these august men in this world they built and left to me to protect. There is nothing I do not know about my land, my house, my history. But I neglected to make certain that I was also becoming a decent man."

"Teo…" she tried to say.

"And I don't know if I can be anything approaching decent," he said as if she hadn't spoke, his voice rougher now. "I don't know if that's possible, after all these years spent ignoring that part of me. But I will tell you this. I want to be him, for you. A better man, whatever that looks like. Whatever it takes. Because you deserve nothing less."

And the tears fell then, but Amelia did nothing to wipe them away. She let them fall.

As if this was a kind of baptism, hers and his alone.

"I knew it was you," he told her then, his gaze so intense it almost burned. But she didn't look away. She couldn't bear to look away. "At the Masquerade. Your name was in my head, and I dismissed it. I told myself I was mistaken. But it was there."

Amelia pulled one of her hands from his, and slid her palm along the hard line of his jaw. And then she held him there, this beautiful, powerful man, who seemed in no way diminished because he knelt before her.

On the contrary. He seemed raw. Sincere.

More powerful than ever before.

And he made her heart thump hard and wild inside her.

"I don't know that my father truly loved anything but his own position," Teo said in that same quiet way that rang in her, through her, until her bones seemed

a part of that same ringing. "I had to go back generations to find the Twelfth Duke and Duchess, because
as I told you, de Luzes do not marry for love. Not usually. But Amelia, I want nothing more. I want to marry
you. I want to have this baby and raise him with you,
with love. And I say this as a man who has no idea if
I'm even capable of these things."

"Of course you are," she said then, fiercely. "You
are the Duke of Marinceli, aren't you? You're capable
of anything. By definition."

"This is what I believe, with all that I am, Duke and
man alike," Teo said then, his face in her hand and that
glorious, ancient ring between them. "If you believe in
me, if you have this faith in me, I can be and do anything at all."

And he held up the ring then, so it caught the dancing light from the lanterns. It was an impossibly large
sapphire, ringed with perfect diamonds and scattered
here and there with rubies. It didn't look like a ring so
much as it looked like a coronation.

And yet when Teo slipped it on her finger, it slid into
place. And fit so perfectly it made a different sort of
sob well up in Amelia's chest.

"Amelia," he said with that same intensity. "Will you
marry me? Will you become my Duchess in every possible way? Will you teach me how to be a better man,
point out when I stray too far into my title and remind
me I am a husband and a father first?"

And she couldn't believe this was happening. But
there was the weight of that ring on her finger, and the
shine of it, which paled into insignificance next to that
brilliant gleam in his beautiful dark eyes.

"It would be my honor to love you forever," Amelia said solemnly. "I already have, Teo. I always will."

"I love you, Amelia," Teo said, and that raw look on his face almost brought her to her knees, too. "I am not sure I have ever loved anyone or anything else. I know I never will."

Then he smiled, and it was not that stern quirk of his austere lips.

Tonight, he smiled wide. Open.

And Amelia knew that this Teo was the better man he thought he needed help to become, not the Duke he already was and ever would be. And both of them were hers.

Forever.

"And I love you, too," Teo murmured, spreading his hands over the thick swell of her belly and leaning close to press his mouth there, too, as if to speak directly to the baby. *"Te adoro, hijo mío."*

And that time, Amelia really did sink down to her knees, so she could get close to him.

This man who had cast his shadow over the whole of her life, and only now, only here, had they turned that shadow into dancing light. The two of them, together.

"I love you, Teo," she whispered, his face between her hands and all that bright light gleaming like hope around them.

And it was right there, on the floor that she had scrubbed on her hands and knees, that they stripped each other of their last remaining inhibitions—along with all their inconvenient clothes—and pledged themselves to their future.

As long as it was together.

# CHAPTER THIRTEEN

IT SNOWED FOR DAYS, stranding them at the cabin and pushing back their wedding a full week.

Neither the bride nor the groom appeared to care.

Teo stood at the head of the small aisle in the medieval chapel tucked away in the Marinceli estate near one of its private lakes, and felt his heart crack wide open as Amelia walked toward him with that gorgeous smile on her face. And nothing but love and happiness in her violet eyes.

She promised to be his forever.

He made the same promise.

And intended to keep it, if he had to dismantle every last stone of *el monstruo* to do it.

He would use his own two hands. Cheerfully.

The months passed, and Amelia grew big. Then bigger still. Then so truly enormous that she began to joke that she might need a golf cart to get around the sprawling house.

"It is beneath the dignity of the Duchess of Marinceli to zoom about the ancestral seat of the dukedom in a mechanized conveyance, *cariña*," Teo told her in that cool, stuffy voice he liked to use. Because it always made her laugh.

And he loved to make her laugh.

"As you wish, Your Excellency," she replied when her laughter faded, grinning at him. "I hope it is not beneath the dignity of the Duke of Marinceli, then, to cart me about from place to place upon command."

"It is a very height of dignity, in fact. It is also a privilege."

And then he showed her exactly how dignified he could be as he swept her into his arms, then carried her to their bed.

The much-anticipated, already beloved Twentieth Duke of Marinceli was born at home, in the guest suite that had been made over into a neonatal clinic for precisely this purpose. And the Twentieth Duke was not concerned with dignity. He was big, healthy and very, very loud.

"He's suitably arrogant already," Amelia declared as they lay on the bed together with their perfect, beautiful son between them. She was smiling down at the baby, and Teo couldn't imagine how he'd gotten this lucky. "Can world domination be far behind?"

Teo laughed, overcome at the miraculous thing his wife had done. And at the tiny, shrunken, perfect creature with red fists and an unholy temper that was now his, too.

And he did not plan to raise another robot of a duke. He would raise a good man, first. And see to the dukedom afterward.

He swore it, there and then, on the bed where he and Amelia had brought a new life into the world—and this ancient house—and had become a family.

Over the years, he and Amelia did not always get along. They did not always see eye to eye. But they fought behind closed doors, so as not to inflict their turmoil on their children. And they made up behind those same closed doors, because whatever else they felt, and no matter how furious they were with each other, they always had that flame.

That beautiful need that had drawn them together, and kept them together.

And as the years passed, Teo and Amelia added considerably to the bloodline. But they called it their family. Three sons, two daughters, and Amelia always said she would stop when she grew tired.

So far, neither one of them was tired.

And when one or the other of them felt that tiredness coming on, or felt that things had gotten too distant between them, whether through intent or accident, they removed themselves from the dukedom. A weekend here, another ten days there, they went back to the cabin and reminded themselves who they were.

"I love you," he said on one such morning, stripped out before the fire with his violet-eyed love. "It seems impossible, but it grows and grows. I love you more now than I did before. I keep waiting for it to diminish, but it keeps expanding."

"That's the magic of fairy tales," she said, propping herself up on his chest and smiling down at him, the way she had in this very cabin so many years before. The way he hoped she always would, with precisely that smile, and that dancing light in her pretty eyes.

"I thought Cinderella was all toil, a spell and then a lot of carrying on with mice and a pumpkin."

"Yes, but that's not the most important part," Amelia said. Sternly, even.

And Teo looked over her smooth, naked shoulder to

that door she had pushed open all those years before her, and opened herself up to him. That was the second gift he'd given her the night he proposed, like a man. Instead of the orders he'd given her as the Duke. Her sooty handprint had remained, so he had carved it into the door. Then blackened it. So it would always be there, reminding him that whole lives could change in an instant. All one had to do was reach out a hand.

"I thought the most important part was you," he said. "It is certainly the most important part to me."

"I love you, too," she said. Her smile widened. "You know how fairy tales end. It's happily ever after. Ever after, not, you know, a few years here and there, in a nasty divorce, and happy forever means that you have to keep falling in love. It's right there in the rules. It has to grow, or doesn't count."

"Funny, I've never heard this law before."

"Stick with me," she told him, her violet eyes sparkling. "I'm the Duchess of Marinceli. My word is law."

Her word was certainly his law, but as besotted as Teo might have been, he wasn't quite so foolish as to say so.

Instead, he rolled her over, and smiled down at her.

And then, together, they got to work on that ever-after.

* * * * *

# DOUBLE THE ROMANCE WITH MODERN 2-IN-1S

From January 2020, all Modern stories will be published in a 2-in-1 format.

## MILLS & BOON
### MODERN
## Power and Passion

Eight Modern stories in four 2-in-1 books, published every month. Find them all at:

## millsandboon.co.uk

# MILLS & BOON

## Coming next month

### CINDERELLA'S ROYAL SEDUCTION
Dani Collins

"You're genuinely asking me to marry you. And if I do, you'll give me this hotel and spa, all the property and rights to the aquifer. Everything," she clarified.

"If you'll live in Verina with me and do what must be done to have my children, yes," he said with a dark smile.

She was still shaking her head at the outrageous proposition but found herself pressing her free hand to her middle, trying to still the flutters of wicked anticipation that teased her with imaginings of how those babies would get made.

She veered her mind from such thoughts.

"Why? I mean, why me?" She lifted her gaze to his, catching a flash of sensual memories reflected in the hot blue of his irises.

"I've already told you. I want you in my bed."

"And that's it? Your fly has spoken? That's the sum total of your motivation?"

His eyes narrowed, becoming flinty and enigmatic. "There are other reasons. I'll share them with you, but they can't leave this room."

That took her aback. "What if I don't want to carry your secrets?"

"You're going to carry my name and my children. Of course you'll keep my secrets. Would you like to tell me yours?" He regarded her over the rim of his glass as he sipped, as though waiting for her to tip her hand in some way.

She shrugged her confusion. "I'm not exactly mysterious," she dismissed. "The most interesting thing that's ever happened to me is happening right now. You realize how eccentric this sounds?"

"Eccentric or not, it's a good offer. You should accept it before I change my mind."

She snorted. "You're quite ruthless, aren't you?" She spoke conversationally but knew it as truth in her bones.

"I do what has to be done to get the results I want. You understand that sort of pragmatism, even if you've pointed your own efforts in dead-end directions. I look forward to seeing what you accomplish when you go after genuinely important goals."

"This is my home. It's important to me."

"Then claim it."

A choke of laughter came out of her. "Just like that? Accept your proposal and—" She glanced at the paperwork. "I'm not going to agree to anything before I've actually reviewed that offer."

"Due diligence is always a sensible action," he said with an ironic curl of his lip. He waved his glass toward the table, inviting her to sit and read.

Gingerly she lowered onto the sofa and set aside her whiskey.

Rhys kept his back to her, gaze fixed across the valley as he continued to sip his drink, saying nothing as she flipped pages.

His behavior was the sort of thing a dominant wolf would do to indicate how little the antics of the lesser pack affected him, but she was glad not to have his unsettling attention aimed directly at her as she compared the two contracts. Aside from the exchange of money on Maude's—and the fact that hers finalized on her wedding day—they were essentially the same.

"I want possession on our engagement. If I decide to accept your proposal," she bluffed, fully expecting him to tell her to go to hell.

"Done. On the condition we begin the making of our children on the day our engagement is announced." He turned, and his eyes were lit with the knowledge his agreement had taken her aback. "We'll keep the conception part as a handshake agreement. No need to write that down in black-and-white."

He brought her a pen. His hand was steady as he offered it. Hers trembled as she hesitantly took it.

"Are you completely serious?" she asked.

"Make the change. Sign it. I'll explain why I want you to marry me. You'll accept my proposal, and Cassiopeia's will be yours."

*Continue reading*
CINDERELLA'S ROYAL SEDUCTION
Dani Collins

*Available next month*
www.millsandboon.co.uk

Copyright ©2020 by Dani Collins

# COMING SOON!

We really hope you enjoyed reading this book. If you're looking for more romance, be sure to head to the shops when new books are available on

# Thursday 9th January

To see which titles are coming soon, please visit

**millsandboon.co.uk/nextmonth**

MILLS & BOON

# MILLS & BOON
# DARE

## *Sexy. Passionate. Bold.*

Sensual love stories featuring smart, sassy heroines you'd want as a best friend, and compelling intense heroes who are worthy of them.

Four DARE stories published every month, find them all at:

## millsandboon.co.uk/DARE

# JOIN US ON SOCIAL MEDIA!

Stay up to date with our latest releases, author
news and gossip, special offers and discounts, and
all the behind-the-scenes action
from Mills & Boon...

 millsandboon

 millsandboonuk

 millsandboon

*It might just be true love...*

**GET YOUR ROMANCE FIX!**

# MILLS & BOON
*— blog —*

Get the latest romance news, exclusive author interviews, story extracts and much more!

**blog.millsandboon.co.uk**

# MILLS & BOON

## THE HEART OF ROMANCE

## A ROMANCE FOR EVERY KIND OF READER

**MODERN**
Prepare to be swept off your feet by sophisticated, sexy and seductive heroes, in some of the world's most glamourous and romantic locations, where power and passion collide.
**8 stories per month.**

**HISTORICAL**
Escape with historical heroes from time gone by. Whether your passion is for wicked Regency Rakes, muscled Vikings or rugged Highlanders, awaken the romance of the past.
**6 stories per month.**

**MEDICAL**
Set your pulse racing with dedicated, delectable doctors in the high-pressure world of medicine, where emotions run high and passion, comfort and love are the best medicine.
**6 stories per month.**

**True Love**
Celebrate true love with tender stories of heartfelt romance, from the rush of falling in love to the joy a new baby can bring, and a focus on the emotional heart of a relationship.
**8 stories per month.**

**Desire**
Indulge in secrets and scandal, intense drama and plenty of sizzling hot action with powerful and passionate heroes who have it all: wealth, status, good looks…everything but the right woman.
**6 stories per month.**

**HEROES**
Experience all the excitement of a gripping thriller, with an intense romance at its heart. Resourceful, true-to-life women and strong, fearless men face danger and desire - a killer combination!
**8 stories per month.**

**DARE**
Sensual love stories featuring smart, sassy heroines you'd want as best friend, and compelling intense heroes who are worthy of them.
**4 stories per month.**

To see which titles are coming soon, please visit

**millsandboon.co.uk/nextmonth**